WINTER IS NOT FOREVER

Dedicated
to the memory of Amanda Janette,
our third grandchild,
daughter of Terry and Barbara, and baby sister of Ashley,
who came to join our family on June 25, 1987,
and completed her brief mission on September 10, 1987,
taken from us suddenly by crib death.

She was such a healthy, happy responsive little
sweetheart!
We loved her dearly and miss her greatly.

And to Amanda's grandparents
Koert and Carol Dieterman
and all readers who have suffered through like pain.
Our loving and faithful God wipes our tears,
mends our broken hearts, and heaven becomes a dearer
place.

"For where the treasure is, there will the heart be also."

JANETTE OKE was born in Champion, Alberta, during the depression years, to a Canadian prairie farmer and his wife. She is a graduate of Mountain View Bible College in Didsbury, Alberta, where she met her husband, Edward. They were married in May of 1957, and went on to pastor churches in Indiana as well as Calgary and Edmonton, Canada.

Janette's husband is president of Mountain View Bible College, Didsbury, Alberta. The Okes have three sons and one daughter and are enjoying the addition to the family of grandchildren.

Edward and Janette have both been active in their local church, serving in various capacities as Sunday-school teachers and board members.

Two books in one special volume

Janette Oke's

WINTER IS NOT FOREVER

SPRING'S GENTLE PROMISE

Bethany House Publishers
Minneapolis, Minnesota
A Division of Bethany Fellowship, Inc.

Published by Bethany House Publishers
A Division of Bethany Fellowship, Inc.
6820 Auto Club Road, Minneapolis, Minnesota 55438

Printed in the United States of America

First Combined edition for Christian Herald Family Bookshelf: 1990

Library of Congress Cataloging-in-Publication Data

Oke, Janette, 1935-
  Winter is not forever.

  (Seasons of the heart series ; bk. 3)
  Sequel to: Winds of autumn.
  I. Title. II. Series: Oke, Janette, 1935-
Seasons of the heart series ; bk. 3.
PR9199.3.038W56   1988   813'.54   88-2882
ISBN 1-55661-002-5 (pbk.)

Contents

Characters

Joshua Chadwick Jones — Josh was raised by his grand-father, great uncle and young aunt after his own parents were killed in an accident when he was only a baby. Once Josh reached his late teens, he lived with his Aunt Lou and her preacher husband, Nat Crawford, and went to school in town. On the weekends he returned to the farm to spend time with the men-folk.

Lou Jones Crawford — Though she was his aunt, Lou was only a few years older than Josh. Now Lou is a parson's wife and anxious to be a mother after losing her first child at birth.

Grandpa — The owner of the farm where Josh grew up and the only father Josh has known.

Uncle Charlie — The quiet yet supportive brother of Grandpa. For many years they have run the farm and the household together.

Willie — Josh's boyhood friend. They shared many adventures and a strong, personal commitment to their faith.

Camellia — Josh's first love, though he soon realized that his faith and her faithlessness were not compatible.

Mr. and Mrs. Foggelson — Camellia's mother and father. He was the local schoolmaster and raised concerns with his teaching of evolution. She had been a Christian until her marriage.

Chapter 1

Decisions

"Have you decided yet?"

Willie's insistent voice demanded my attention. I swiveled around to get a look at him, for the words didn't make any sense to me at all.

"What do you plan to do—after graduation?" he prodded. "Are you gonna be a minister—or what?"

Or what? my mind echoed in frustration. *What?*

I had been asking myself the same question over and over, just as Willie was asking me now. And I still didn't have an answer. Graduation was only a month away, and it seemed that I was the only one in our small town school who didn't know exactly what to do with life after the big day. It wasn't that I hadn't given it a thought. In fact, I thought about it most of the time. I prayed about it, too, and my family members kept assuring me that they were praying as well. But I still didn't have an answer to Willie's question, except to say honestly, "No—I don't know yet." And I'd been saying that for a long, long time.

I must have been frowning, and I guess Willie understood my dilemma. He didn't wait for my answer—not in words, anyway; instead he went right on talking.

"God has different timing for different people, and with a reason," he mused. "That doesn't mean that He hasn't got your future planned out. When it's time—"

I quit listening for a minute, and my mind jumped to other things. Willie already had his future clearly mapped out. God had called him to be a missionary; Willie would leave for a Bible school in the Eastern United States at the end of the summer. I envied Willie, I guess. "It must be a real relief to know what God wants you to do," I muttered under my breath.

"I still can't believe it," Willie was saying when I tuned back in. "I mean, most of my life—at least what I can remember of it—I've been goin' to school, day after day. And here we are about to graduate. I just can't believe it! It doesn't seem real to me yet."

I twitched my fishing pole as if I were trying to stir up some fish. Actually I was just thinking about Willie's words. It did seem strange. We had done a great deal of talking over the years about how glad we would be to graduate and leave the old school behind, and here we were on the brink of graduation and I didn't really feel glad about it at all. In fact, I felt rather scared. I never would have dared to tell any of the fellas how I was feeling—we always crowed about the day that we'd be freed from "prison." We'd run and holler and toss our caps in the air. I knew we'd have to do it to carry on the tradition. A fella was supposed to loathe school and be more than glad to be rid of it, but at the same time I got a funny feeling down in the pit of my stomach whenever I thought about graduation.

I mulled over Willie's words and squirmed on the creek bank, pretending to have a kink in my back from sitting in one spot for so long waiting on a fish to decide he was hungry. I wiggled my pole again and noticed that I'd lost the bait off the hook. I hoped Willie didn't notice. I didn't feel much like fishing anymore and I didn't want to be bothered with baiting my hook again. Still, I wasn't ready to head for the house yet, either.

I couldn't remember much about life without school, just like Willie had said. When I was honest with myself, I knew

I'd miss the daily lessons, the recesses, the access to books. Maybe I'd miss it a whole lot, but I wasn't about to share my thoughts with anyone—not even Willie.

'Course, Willie needn't worry, I reminded myself, almost enviously. Come fall, he'll be off to a new school, new books, and new friends. I squirmed again.

"Here," said Willie, "lean against this stump for a while."

"Naw," I responded slowly, casting a glance at the sky. "It's almost time for chores anyway. And the fish sure aren't bitin' today."

Willie's eyes twinkled the way they did when he was trying to hold back something that made him want to laugh. I had seen the same look on his face when our teacher held his book upside down when lecturing to the class, and when Agatha Marshall took a bite of her sandwich and ate the ant that had been crawling on it, and when we tied Avery's shoelaces together as he lounged on the school grass waiting for the bell to ring.

I looked at Willie suspiciously now.

"Never seen fish bite without bait, Josh," he said, the twinkle openly showing in a grin now. "You haven't had bait on that hook for the last half hour," Willie informed me with a chuckle.

"So why didn't you tell me?" I threw at him, trying to sound miffed.

Willie sobered. "Didn't think you cared about fishin'. Your thoughts have been off someplace else all day."

I jerked up my empty hook and set about wiping it carefully on the grass and removing it from the line. Willie let me work in silence until I had finished with my fishing gear.

"You still bothered about Camellia?" he finally ventured as we picked up our gear and started down the trail to the farm.

"Camellia?" My head swung up at her name.

Willie held my eyes with a steady gaze. The question was still there, unanswered. I couldn't hide much from him, and

I sure did need someone to talk to. I decided to stop playing games.

"I guess so—a little. I mean, here we are, almost finished with school—and I've been praying and praying, and trying an' trying to show Camellia that the Bible is right, no matter what her pa says, an' she still won't even listen to a thing I have to say. She'll be done with school, too, Willie, and then she plans to move off somewhere and take some training to be a decorator—"

"Interior designer," Willie corrected.

"Interior designer," I amended with a shrug. "Who knows who she'll meet or what she'll get herself into in some god-forsaken city somewhere—"

"New York," said Willie. "Her pa says New York. If you wanta learn from the best, then you need to go to New York."

"New York? That's even worse than I thought!" I raged. "That's about as wicked a city as there is."

Willie just nodded his head solemnly.

We trudged on in silence, me wrestling with the idea of Camellia alone in a city like New York. Then Willie cut into my thoughts again.

"You still care about her, Josh?"

For some reason the question caught me wrong. Of course I cared about Camellia! She was a friend, wasn't she? And we were commanded to care about—or love—everyone, weren't we? Willie knew the Bible as well as I did. He knew I was supposed to care about Camellia.

"That's a dumb question!" I threw at Willie. "We're *supposed* to care. I've been praying for Camellia for years now—Nat and Lou have been praying, too. We all—"

"That's not what I mean, Josh, an' you know it," Willie cut in. "Do you still like Camellia?"

I wasn't prepared to answer that. In the first place I didn't see that it was any of Willie's business, even if he was my friend. In the second place, though I didn't want to think about it at the moment, I wasn't sure of the answer myself. Did I still care for Camellia—as a girl, not as just a human?

I had given up any special friendship with Camellia because she and I did not have the same spiritual values. In fact, Camellia declared that anything to do with religion was silly and superstitious. She didn't even believe that God existed, she said. Religion was a crutch for insecure people. But I believed with all my heart that God not only existed but had sent His Son to die for *me*, for my wrongdoings, and that He had a special plan for my life. How could I even consider a special relationship with Camellia? I couldn't, I knew, but I kept hoping and praying that Camellia would become a believer and then—then— Now, here we were at school's end, and still Camellia would not even listen to my side of the argument. There was more than one reason why graduation bothered me.

Willie did not pursue the question.

"Are you coming to town for the social tomorrow night?" he asked.

It was a church social—one of the few activities meant just for our age group, and they were always fun. Aunt Lou and Uncle Nat saw to that. Several teenagers from town had started coming to church as a result of the socials that Uncle Nat organized. Most of the young people eagerly anticipated the monthly social, and I enjoyed them, too. At any other time I would have answered Willie with an enthusiastic, "Sure, I'll be there," but instead I mumbled, "I'll see."

"Well, sure hope you can make it." Willie shifted his pole and the one fish he had caught into his left hand so he'd have his right one free to untie his horse from the hitching rail.

I hadn't been very good company, and suddenly I felt ashamed because of it. It wasn't Willie's fault that Camellia still wasn't a believer, and it wasn't Willie's fault that I still didn't know what God wanted me to do with my life, and it wasn't Willie's fault that graduation was quickly approaching with its unsettled questions. Willie had no more control of the ticking clock than I did. I had no right to be owly and disagreeable with Willie.

I tried hard to shift my troubled thoughts to the back of

my mind and bid my friend the kind of goodbye he deserved.

"Thanks, Willie," I said, and then didn't quite know how to finish. "Thanks for coming out."

I saw the twinkle in Willie's eye again.

"Sorry the fish weren't biting."

"Next time I might even try using a little bait," I teased back. "Though at least now I don't have fish to clean and can loaf a bit before chorin'."

Willie looked down at the one fish that dangled beside his saddle. A mock frown crossed his face.

"I think I might just stop off and present a fish to Mary Turley," he said, "and invite her to the social tomorrow night." I wasn't sure if Willie was serious or not.

We both laughed and Willie moved his horse off down the lane.

"See you tomorrow night, Josh," he called back to me.

I answered as he knew I would. "I'll be there."

Chapter 2

The Social

That next night I hurried through my chores and ran for my bedroom to bathe and change. After adjusting my tie and slicking down my hair, I picked up my jacket and started down the stairs, avoiding the step with the worst creak.

"Big night tonight, Boy?"

The question came from Grandpa. He and Uncle Charlie were sitting at the kitchen table going over some farm bills together.

I grinned. I guess the night was no bigger than any other social night, but it still was pretty special to me. I nodded.

"Nat says the Youth Group is really growin'," continued Grandpa.

I nodded again, then added, " 'Bout twenty of us now."

"That's good," said Grandpa. "Any of the new ones comin' to church too?"

"Yeah, three of 'em are."

"Good!" said Grandpa again.

Uncle Charlie took a gulp of coffee and let the legs of his chair hit the worn kitchen linoleum with a dull thud. He looked me over carefully, from the crease in my best pants to the straight part of my hair. Then he nodded, as though I passed inspection.

"Enjoy youth, Joshua," Grandpa said. "The cares of adulthood will be upon ya soon enough."

I couldn't help but smile. Grandpa knew little about *youth*. If he thought that I wouldn't have any worries or concerns until I stepped out into the adult world, he was all wrong. Or he had forgotten. He had no idea about the things I had been grappling with lately. But I let it pass as though the only thought in my mind was a night of games and singing, followed by some of Lou's punch and cake. But at Grandpa's words I could feel my mood change somewhat. I wasn't in quite the same hurry that I had been a few minutes before.

Uncle Charlie's sharp eyes were on me again. He was searching for something, I knew. I mustered a grin and moved out of his range. I didn't want to be answering any questions. Not that Uncle Charlie would ask—not outright, anyway—but I felt the probing and had always squirmed some under it.

"I shouldn't be too late," I said as a parting remark of some kind. They knew I'd come straight home as soon as the social was over, and that it would be well chaperoned by Uncle Nat and Aunt Lou.

"Take yer time. Have fun," Grandpa responded.

The thought of Aunt Lou filled me with a bit of concern. Her baby was due in a couple of weeks, and after what had happened with her first baby I was uneasy about her. Over and over she assured me that there was no need to worry. She had lost little Amanda because she had had the measles during the pregnancy. Aunt Lou had been the picture of health all through this one. Doc had told her over and over that the baby seemed healthy and energetic. He was predicting a strong baby boy, but Aunt Lou still had her heart set on another daughter, and I guess I secretly hoped for a girl, too.

In the barn I was greeted by Chester, the beautiful bay that Grandpa and Uncle Charlie had surprised me with on my last birthday. I still couldn't believe that such a horse was really mine. I patted his shining round rump and reached for the saddle. He nickered at me and rubbed his nose against my chest looking for a treat from my pocket.

"Cut that out," I scolded him. "You'll mess my Sunday clothes!" But he didn't care about that; he went right on sniffing and blowing. I moved so he couldn't reach me and smoothed the blanket for the saddle.

I walked Chester out of the barn, closed the door securely, and mounted. Chester was eager to be on the road, even if I had forgotten to bring him his sugar lump or bit of apple. I had to rein him in to keep him from leaving the farmyard on a dead run. Grandpa didn't take too kindly to running animals, but it sure was tempting when I was up on Chester. He loved to run, and his strong legs and smooth body fairly trembled with excitement whenever he was turned toward the road.

It was a warm spring night. The sun was still lighting my way, but I knew that by the time I returned home it would be dark. Chester could find his way back to his stall in total darkness if need be, but it would be nicer traveling by moonlight. Only a few carelessly drifting clouds crossed the sky; the moon should give some light later on.

My thoughts turned back to the social, and I wondered if there would be any new young people there. Wouldn't it be something if Camellia decided to come! *Maybe if more of the girls her age* . . . I thought. But there were several girls Camellia's age who attended, and that had never influenced her before. Nothing, in fact, seemed to influence Camellia in favor of coming to church.

As I began going over the list of who might be in attendance, my eagerness to get there increased. Chester must have sensed my feelings, for before I knew it we were racing down the dusty road at a reckless pace. I reined Chester in, and he snorted in disgust. He tossed his head and pranced along the roadway, fighting against the bit while I busied myself trying to brush the dust from my dress clothes.

In spite of my intentions to be there early, young people were already milling about when I entered the churchyard. I tied Chester securely and called out hellos as I hurried to the parsonage to see if I could help Aunt Lou with any last-minute preparations.

"Josh!" she called out excitedly. "Good to see you! How are things at the farm?"

Aunt Lou always greeted me as though we hadn't seen one another for months, when the fact was that I had left town to stay at the farm only the day before.

"Fine," I responded. "Just fine. How are you?"

Aunt Lou looked down at her expanding front. She placed a hand tenderly on the growing baby and smiled at me.

"We are both just fine, aren't we, honey?" she said to her unborn child.

I smiled. Aunt Lou talked to her baby all the time. I was used to it by now. And she did look fine—her eyes shone and her cheeks glowed.

"Is there anything I can do to help?" I asked.

"Everything is already done. Nat is over at the church and we carried all of the refreshments over earlier."

"I'm sorry I was so late—" I began, but Aunt Lou stopped me.

"You're not late. Everyone else is just early. Impatient to get started, I guess. My, how this group has grown! I hardly know how much food to fix anymore."

I could tell by the smile on Aunt Lou's face that she was pleased to have such a problem.

We walked the short distance across the churchyard together. Other young people were arriving, calling excitedly back and forth.

I was lounging on the outside steps talking to some of the fellas when a rig rounded the corner and headed our way. At first I thought it must be someone new, and then I recognized Willie. Willie never drove; he always rode horseback, same as me. It *was* Willie, all right—and he wasn't alone, either.

For a moment none of us spoke. We just stood there gawking as Willie climbed down and tied the horse, and then reached a hand up to help a girl step down. She was wearing a full-skirted pink dress and she had her hair piled up on her head with little curls spilling down here and there. She looked familiar, yet I couldn't place her. Willie had tied his horse some distance away from the steps where we waited. We all stood there, straining to figure out who Willie was with.

"By jingo!" hissed Tom Newton, "it's Mary Turley—an' all dolled up, too."

It can't be, I thought. *Surely he wasn't serious!* But, sure enough, there was ol' Willie leading Mary Turley up the walkway to the church.

I wanted to laugh, to howl at Willie. My first impulse was to slap him on the back and tease him some, but I didn't. I stood there quietly and watched.

Mary had certainly changed! And so had Willie—he was so spiffed up and shining I scarcely knew him. And he seemed so gentlemanly and grown-up too. All of us were put to silence by it all, and I bet other fellas besides me were wondering why we hadn't thought of inviting Mary ourselves.

Mary smiled shyly at us as she brushed by, and Willie gave me just the slightest wink. I was sure no one else had seen it, but I caught it, just as I caught that twinkle in his eye.

Avery gave me a hard jab in the ribs that made me gasp for air, and then we all shuffled and moved on the steps and made an about-face as we followed Willie and Mary into the church.

We found some places to sit. As usual, the girls sorta lined up in the seats on the south side of the building and the fellas took the seats on the north. All except Willie, that is. He seated Mary alongside Martha Ingrim, but instead of coming over to the boys, he sat down right beside her!

Uncle Nat took charge of the meeting, calling it to order by welcoming everyone and having first-timers introduced. There was another new girl from town too, but she had come with Thelma and Virginia Brown, so none of us paid much attention.

Then Willie introduced Mary. He spoke clearly and without embarrassment. I couldn't help but marvel at the way he handled it.

"This is Mary Turley," he said. "Mary lives out our way. We—Josh and I, and several others here—went to school with Mary for a number of years."

As we played some games, there was some mixing up of the seating, and Willie and Mary got separated. But Mary seemed to be having a good time. I was glad to see that she felt at home among us.

I had always thought of Mary as a plain girl, and maybe she really was, but tonight she was pretty in her own way. She had a smile that drew smiles in return, and her eyes were deep and intense. Her manner kept my eyes wandering back to her. She seemed so grown-up and self-assured compared to most of the girls I knew.

And then I remembered why I hadn't seen much of Mary for the last several years. Her ma had been sick, and Mary had needed to take over the running of the household and the cooking of the meals. She hadn't been able to go on to school in town like she had wanted to. I hadn't given it much thought when I heard about it. But now, looking at Mary, I realized she had likely done more growing up than the rest of us who hadn't borne similar responsibilities.

Not at all somber or morose, she laughed and enjoyed the games as much as anyone at the social, but she did carry the air of one who had learned a good measure of self-assurance.

After the games were over, Uncle Nat brought out his guitar and we gathered in a circle and sang every hymn we knew by heart. Mary didn't seem to know many of the words, but she listened in appreciation and once or twice I noticed her small foot tapping in time with the music. Though I wasn't sitting close enough to her to be sure, I had the feeling that she was humming right along.

When Aunt Lou served refreshments, Mary volunteered her help. I was busy pouring the punch, so we exchanged a few pleasantries. I asked about her ma, feeling apologetic that I hadn't taken more of an interest sooner. Mary smiled when she told me that her ma was much better—even able to be back in her own kitchen again.

I thought of Mrs. Turley and that big kitchen. I well remembered the day that Willie, Avery, and I stopped by on the way back from our hike along the creek. We were half-starved, and Mrs. Turley's well-stocked kitchen had about saved our lives. I remembered Mary too, a rather gangly, freckle-faced girl at the time. I never would have dreamed that she would become the well-poised young lady that I saw before me now.

"I'm glad about your ma," I assured her.

"Me, too," said Mary. "It was hard to see her so sick."

There was no mention about the hard years that she had put in being housekeeper and nursemaid. She just seemed to have a sincere appreciation that her ma was feeling better.

"Maybe you can come to our next social," I dared venture.

"I'd love to," responded Mary and I could tell by her shining eyes that she really meant it. I wanted Mary to be a part of our Youth Group. I wanted her to feel welcome. Yet she really wasn't a believer, and I couldn't help but question Willie's actions. Here he was courting a girl who was not a Christian, and I—I had to give up my relationship with Camellia for that very reason. It didn't seem fair somehow, and yet I had no doubts about Willie and his commitment to his faith. Still—was Willie taking chances going out with a non-Christian girl? My line of reasoning directed my thoughts to Camellia and they lingered there, remembering her sparkling eyes, her long, burnished tresses. She was the prettiest girl I had ever seen. *If only*—but my thoughts were interrupted by Aunt Lou's call for me to refill the punch glasses.

Chapter 3

Great News

All the next week we had glorious spring weather, and folks began talking about spring fever. I don't know exactly what kind of fever hit me, but I had an awful time concentrating on my studies.

Final exams were just a few weeks away, and our grades on those finals could have a great deal to do with our being accepted into college. Maybe that was why I was having such a difficult time. Most of the others already had a college picked and a vocation to pursue as well. Daily, it seemed, someone asked me, "What are your plans, Josh?" and I would mumble, red-faced, that I still hadn't decided for sure.

For sure? That made it sound like I had several considerations. The truth was, I was about as far from knowing what the future held for me as I had been on the first day I climbed the steps of the schoolhouse.

I avoided folks as much as I could. I didn't want to answer any questions when I still didn't really have an answer.

As a result, I hung around home a lot. I pretended to be studying, and Aunt Lou and Uncle Nat certainly approved of that. I was trying, but my mind just didn't seem to want to stay with the books.

On one particularly lovely spring evening, when the fragrant smell of early spring blossoms wafted in my open window, making it even more difficult to concentrate, I sat at my small desk trying hard to think through the math computations before me, but my mind refused to deal with the equations.

My thoughts insisted on flitting about. Graduation was getting nearer with each passing day. I thought of my future still unplanned, as far as I could see. I thought of Camellia and her intention to leave for distant New York and her training in Interior Design. How would she ever manage in such a big, indifferent city? How could her father sanction such a venture?

The soft spring breeze brought a fresh whisper of fragrance to my nose and reminded me of the roses along the creek bank every springtime. I could picture the young blades of greenery poking their slim heads through the soil. I could almost smell the freshness of the gently flowing water and hear the splash of a fish breaking the surface to snatch at a fly, then slip back into the coolness of the stream again.

The call of the creek turned my thoughts to Gramps. I still hadn't gotten used to his being gone. Each time that I went home to the farm I found myself searching for signs of him. The empty chair at the table looked too forlorn, the place where his worn farm sweater had hung looked bare and dejected, the padded chair by the well-lit kitchen window where he sat to read his Bible and work his crossword puzzles looked far too lonely.

I wouldn't have wished him back; I knew that. He had gone to a far better place than his dwelling here had been. But even that thought did not erase the ache I carried around with me.

Even though I stayed here in town during the week with Aunt Lou and Uncle Nat, I loved the farm. I loved the soil. I treasured the spot that held my roots buried so deeply. I loved the springtime and the planting of the seeds. I loved the summer as we watched the green begin to appear and then mature as the weeks passed by. I loved the autumn, when it was so evident that God was good and was again supplying the needs of His people.

Even the winter months were enjoyable. I loved the frosty mornings when the steam rose from the pail of warm milk I carried from the barn to the house. I loved the smell of the warm straw I spread out to bed down Bossie or one of her stallmates. I loved the soft mewing of the barn cats as they coaxed for their morning breakfast of warm, fresh milk.

The farm was a good place to be. I guess I loved most everything about it.

And then I thought again of Grandpa and Uncle Charlie, and suddenly a new thought occurred to me. What would happen to the farm when they were no longer able to care for it? I had never thought about it before; I just assumed that they would always be there, farming, just like they had been doing ever since I could recollect. But of course they wouldn't. Couldn't. The quickly passing years were taking their toll on Grandpa and Uncle Charlie. They didn't walk as erectly or as quickly as they used to. Even I could see that. And Uncle Charlie seemed to be faring a bit worse than Grandpa. I had noticed it the last time we had chored together. He was getting much slower in movement than he used to be, even a bit clumsy with his hands. I'd had to undo the knot that tied the gunny sack of grain. He had tried but couldn't manage it.

The thought of Uncle Charlie and Grandpa no longer able to carry on the farming made me restless and uneasy. I couldn't imagine life without the farm. It didn't matter if God called me to be a preacher in some far-off city or even a missionary, like Willie, to some distant land, I still wanted to think of the farm as home. I still wanted to be able to visit it when I had opportunity, to bring my family, if I ever had one, to feel the kinship with the soil and to watch things grow. I felt that my roots would always be there in that land that Grandpa had tilled ever since I could remember. To sever those roots would in some way be losing a part of me.

My reverie was interrupted by a soft whine under my feet.

"Pixie!" I said. "I didn't know you were here. I haven't been paying much attention to you, have I, girl?" The little dog wagged her tail happily and jumped into my lap. I snapped shut my math book and pushed it aside. I couldn't study now. I needed a break. Pixie jumped down as I stood and stretched. "Maybe I'll go to the kitchen for some of Aunt Lou's cookies and a glass of milk." I was about to leave the room when I sensed more than I actually heard a strange commotion in the kitchen.

It wasn't loud and it wasn't hasty. It was just different somehow. I listened more carefully; for a time I heard nothing. Pixie ran to the door and barked softly; then I heard the quick, quiet step of Uncle Nat approaching my door. I stood motionless, my hand going up to push back the hair that flopped over my forehead.

Uncle Nat didn't even knock. He opened the door gently and poked in his head. He was wearing his hat, something that Uncle Nat didn't usually do in the house.

"Lou says it's time, Josh," he said in almost a whisper. "I'm going for Doc."

My mouth went dry and my breath seemed to catch in my chest. *It was time.* The very thought sent a shiver of fear running all through me. I had known all along that we would face this eventually, yet I still wasn't prepared.

For some reason the little unknown somebody that Aunt Lou had been carrying had seemed so safe and protected as long as her body enclosed it. But now it was time for this baby to enter the world—a world where sickness and dangers abounded. Would the little one make it? To face the loss of another baby would be too much for any of us to bear.

I wanted to run to Aunt Lou to assure myself that she was all right, but my feet refused to move. I tried swallowing, but my mouth was too dry. I felt like urging Uncle Nat to hurry, but I realized we had things rather backward.

"I'll run for Doc," I managed to say. "You stay with Aunt Lou."

Uncle Nat didn't argue. He stepped wordlessly aside so I could leave the room.

I was almost to the kitchen door before he called softly after me, "No need to run, Josh. Lou says there is lots of time."

I heard him, but I was already running by the time I had reached the back door. By the time I left the parsonage yard I was in full stride.

All the way to Doc's house I prayed urgently for Aunt Lou. I prayed for the new baby. I prayed that Doc wouldn't be out in the country somewhere on a house call.

By the time I reached Doc's front door I was breathing hard. I rapped loudly and stepped back to wait. I could hear movement inside, and that was encouraging. Doc answered the door himself and didn't even make a comment when he saw me standing there, my sides heaving from running. He just reached to the hat tree by the door to retrieve his hat and picked up his black bag from the small table, all in one motion, and called out to his wife that he would be at the parsonage, and we were gone.

We didn't run. Doc's slower pace frustrated me, and I found it hard to match his methodical stride, but I did try. We walked in silence until Doc seemed to feel I had enough breath to talk.

"When did the contractions start?" he asked me.

"I dunno," I admitted dumbly. "Uncle Nat just came to my room and said it's time."

"Did Lou have supper with you?" Doc asked further.

"She—she—" I thought back. "She was at table with us, but she didn't eat much. Just sorta pushed her food around on her plate."

I hadn't paid much attention to it at the time.

"She didn't say anything," I added.

"She wouldn't," commented Doc, and he picked up speed, for which I was thankful.

When we reached the house Uncle Nat was not there to greet us. Doc knew the way to the bedroom, so after letting him in, I knew there was little else that I could do—except keep praying.

The time dragged on forever..Or so it seemed. In reality I guess that things happened in good time and order. But for me, it seemed an eternity. I paced back and forth in the kitchen, and I paced back and forth on the porch, and I paced back and forth on the front board walk that led up to the small parsonage.

At last I heard the small, funny, squeaky cry of a new-born, and I knew it was finally over. I strained with my whole body to catch any further sounds. I guess I was listening for a cry from Aunt Lou. None came. And then I heard laughter and the voice of Uncle Nat raised in prayerful thanksgiving. I breathed again and ran toward the back entrance.

Uncle Nat met me in the kitchen, his face beaming. We didn't even speak to one another, just stopped long enough for a quick embrace and then hurried on to the bedroom. I suppose there were tears on both our cheeks, tears of relief and joy.

Doc was talking when I entered the room. I wasn't sure if he was talking to Aunt Lou or the tiny bundle he held in his big hands.

"Sure surprised me," he was saying. "I was looking for a big, bouncing boy, but just look at this young'un. Healthy and hearty as you please."

Lou was smiling a contented, love-filled smile. She still looked pale to me—but, oh, did she look happy!

Doc continued speaking to Aunt Lou. "You did a fine job, little lady—and just look at your reward. Beautiful baby. Just beautiful. Reminds me of her mamma when I delivered her some twenty-odd years ago."

The word *her* caught my attention. It was a girl! Aunt Lou's dream had come true and Doc's "big boy" had been a girl instead. I grinned and suddenly felt shy and awkward. I hung back a bit, not really knowing what to do or say. Aunt Lou sensed it immediately. She raised slightly from her pillows and held out her hand to me.

"Come see her, Josh," she encouraged. "Like Doc says, she's beautiful."

I moved slowly forward just as Doc reached down and laid the precious bundle in Aunt Lou's arms. The little face was red and wrinkled and her eyes were almost squinted shut. She had a thatch of dark hair that for the moment was plastered tightly to the well-shaped little head. She really wasn't all that beautiful, as Doc and Aunt Lou were insisting, but even I knew she was very special.

And then she waved a small fist frantically in the air and went searching for it with a puckered-up mouth. Miraculously, she managed to connect the two and began sucking noisily. We all laughed and Aunt Lou held her even closer and Uncle Nat's eyes filled with tears again. She *was* beautiful.

When Aunt Lou could speak again she looked down at her baby and then up at me. "Sarah Jane," she said, "meet your cousin, Joshua Jones. He's about the finest cousin a little girl could ever have. You're a lucky little girl, Sarah Jane— No, not lucky—blessed." Aunt Lou gave me one of her special smiles. I could feel the firm arm of Uncle Nat about my shoulders, and it gave me a warm, family feeling.

I looked down again at the tiny bundle in Aunt Lou's arms. Since my own folks had died, Aunt Lou had been like a mother and aunt all rolled up in one. Now I had little Sarah Jane too. I might not be all that Aunt Lou had generously boasted me to be, but I knew one thing. I loved that little bundle with all of my being, and I knew instinctively that no harm would ever come to her that I had the power to stop.

Chapter 4

Sharing the News

"Somebody's gotta go to the farm!" I burst out excitedly, tearing my eyes from the baby and Aunt Lou to implore Uncle Nat.

"I guess that can wait 'til morning," Uncle Nat said, and I could see he wasn't too anxious to leave his wife and new daughter.

"Morning? This news will never keep until morning. And Grandpa and Uncle Charlie would never forgive us!"

"It's pretty late," Uncle Nat continued. He reached down to lift his pocket watch. "It's almost midnight." Then he spoke to brand-new little Sarah Jane. "You missed being born on your grandmother's birthday by about ten minutes, little one."

Uncle Nat didn't talk about his ma too often, but I could tell by his tone that he would have been real pleased if Sarah had prolonged her coming just a bit.

I wasn't put off by Uncle Nat's diversion.

"Midnight or not," I went on, "someone should go out to the farm. I can go. Chester could find his way even if it was pitch dark—and it's not. Looks really light out yet. Moon must be shining—"

"Well, Lou?" Uncle Nat asked. Lou just smiled and nodded. "Bring me a pen and the writing tablet," she said, and

I knew it was decided that I could go.

Aunt Lou had to have her hands free to write, so Uncle Nat lifted the small bundle of baby from her arms and began pacing the floor with her, talking softly to her all the while. I didn't listen to what he said, but now and then I caught a word. He was already telling her about God. Imagine! A tiny tyke like that, and Uncle Nat was already preaching the little one her first sermon.

Aunt Lou found it a bit difficult to write, propped up on her pillows like she was. I guess she wanted to tell Grandpa and Uncle Charlie about the new baby herself, because she seemed to write on and on. I wondered how she could find so much to say about someone she had just met, so to speak.

At last she was done and folded that paper and handed it to me and laid the tablet and the pen on the small night table by her bed. She smiled again—that contented, happy smile—but I could see she was really tired.

A movement caused us all to look at the doorway. It was Doc. I had quite forgotten about him. Guess he had been in the kitchen having himself a cup of tea while we all got acquainted with Sarah Jane, and now he was back again to check everything one more time and tuck Aunt Lou and the baby in for the night. I kissed Aunt Lou on the cheek, took one more look at Sarah Jane to see if she had grown or changed any yet. I was always hearing ladies exclaim how quickly babies did that. But she looked just the same to me, only she had fallen asleep—right in the middle of Uncle Nat's sermon.

Chester seemed to sense my mood, and once we were on the road he was ready to run. I guess he thought that this time he might be able to get away with it. I didn't let him though, for even though there was a bit of a moon and even though his night-eyes were better than mine, I still knew it was unwise to let a horse travel at full gallop in the dark.

It seemed to take an especially long time to cover the distance to the farm. Normally I would let my mind wander to many things, but tonight I could only think of the new baby. Whole and well and brand new and Doc said that she was fine, just fine.

At last I reached the farm and was a bit surprised to see the house all dark. But I should have known it would be. Grandpa and Uncle Charlie went to bed somewhere around ten each night, and this night being no different than any other as far as they were concerned, they would have followed their usual pattern.

I argued briefly with myself as to whether to flip Chester's rein over the gate post and run in with the news or to take Chester to the barn—as would need to be done eventually anyway—and then go to the house. I decided to go ahead and bed Chester down. It was hard to make myself go to the barn first but I knew I would hate to come back out to care for Chester after I had delivered the good news.

Chester was glad to see his own stall. I didn't figure him to be too hungry, knowing that he had already been well fed, but I hurriedly forked him a bit of hay just in case he had a notion to eat. He started in on it right away.

I scarcely took the time to secure the barn door before I was off to the house on the run. It was a fair distance between the house and the barn—a fact I had never particularly noted before. I was puffing by the time I hit the back porch. The back door, as usual, was not locked. I wasn't sure my Grandpa could lock it even if he wanted to. I pushed it open and it squeaked just a bit.

I wanted to holler out my news, but my good sense held me in check. If I came in shouting I'd scare Grandpa and Uncle Charlie half to death.

I climbed the steps quickly, trying not to make too much noise. I never even thought about the squeaky one until I heard it protest beneath my foot.

"Who is it?" Grandpa called out.

"Me," I answered in a whispery voice.

I heard Uncle Charlie stirring, but the noise didn't come from his bed. He was sitting near his window in the old chair. I knew then that he had watched me ride into the yard, take

Chester to the barn and run for the house.

For a moment I forgot about Grandpa, about Aunt Lou, even about the new baby.

"What are you doing up?" I quizzed Uncle Charlie.

"Nothin' much," he answered evasively. "Just can't git along with my bed sometimes."

Grandpa called out again, "Be right there." I could hear the bed springs groaning as he lifted himself from the bed and began to pull on his pants.

"I take it you have some news," Grandpa said as he came out of the bedroom, a lighted lamp in his hand.

"Sure do," I beamed, my thoughts jumping immediately back to Sarah Jane.

"Well?" prompted Uncle Charlie.

"Another girl," I fairly cheered. "And she is just fine."

"And Lou?" asked Grandpa. In his heart he knew very well that I wouldn't be grinning from ear to ear unless Aunt Lou was just fine, too. But Lou was his little girl, and Grandpa wouldn't be at ease until he heard it said.

"Fine!" I said. "Just fine—an' happy."

"Thank you, Father!" Grandpa said softly and I understood his little prayer of gratitude. Then he began to grin. I could see his face by the light of the lamp he held in his hand. He was beaming.

Uncle Charlie had moved to join us in the hallway. He was grinning too—a wide, infectious smile. He looked about the happiest I had ever seen him. But I was surprised at how slowly he moved. Grandpa turned to him with concern in his eyes and voice.

"Another bad night?" he asked, and Uncle Charlie nodded. I didn't understand the question—or the answer. Why was Uncle Charlie having bad nights? Why was he moving toward the stairs like an old man? Why did he reach out a hand to assist himself as he descended? I hadn't known about any of this. Why hadn't someone informed me?

"Was Doc there?" Uncle Charlie asked. He knew that

sometimes Doc was out on one call when he was needed elsewhere.

"Got him myself," I explained. "He was right at home when I went for him."

"Was Nat there?" asked Grandpa, and I knew that Grandpa was thinking of the last time.

"All the time," I answered.

"Good!" said Grandpa, and he beamed some more as he set the lamp on the kitchen table.

Uncle Charlie shuffled to the stove, shook it up, and put in a few more sticks of wood. The stove had been banked for the night; before long the wood caught and I could hear the blaze grow. Uncle Charlie pushed forward the coffeepot.

"Tell us about her," Grandpa was saying, excitement filling his voice.

Uncle Charlie eased a chair toward the table and lowered himself slowly onto it. He leaned forward eagerly, not wanting to miss a word.

"She's not very big," I started, indicating with my hands, much as I often did when I told a fish story.

" 'Course not," cut in Grandpa.

"An' she—she—" How could I say that she was red and wrinkled and sort of puffy? Would they understand?

"Has she any hair?"

"Lots of it—dark."

"Just like Lou," cut in Grandpa.

"What color are her eyes?" Uncle Charlie asked.

"I—I—don't really know. She didn't open them much, but they are sorta dark, I guess."

"Did Doc say how much she weighs?"

I hadn't heard him say anything about her weight. I just shook my head.

"Tell us about Lou," Grandpa was prompting.

"Well—"

"Was it a long—?" began Grandpa again.

It had seemed half of forever to me, but I shrugged and said honestly, "Doc said it was real good. Real good. I went for him about quarter-to-nine and Sarah was born just before midnight."

Grandpa and Uncle Charlie exchanged grins and nods and I understood that they were well satisfied with that.

"But Aunt Lou says that she was having some—some—"

"Contractions."

"Yeah, from about one o'clock on. But they didn't get strong until about suppertime." I didn't want them to get the idea that it had been too easy.

"But she's fine now?" This was from Grandpa again.

"Just fine," I reassured him.

Uncle Charlie eased himself off his chair and went for the coffeepot. I wasn't sure that the coffee would be hot enough yet, but perhaps Uncle Charlie needed something to occupy his hands.

He poured three cups and brought two of them, a bit of steam rising from each, to the table. He passed one cup to Grandpa and put one down in front of me. It was the first time I noticed that his fingers looked funny. I was about to ask if he had hurt his hand when I noticed that the other hand looked the same way. I shut my mouth quickly on the unasked question and looked at Grandpa, but he didn't seem to read the question in my eyes. I guess he was still too busy celebrating his new granddaughter.

"Her name," he said suddenly. "You haven't told us her name."

"It's Sarah," I told him. "Sarah Jane."

"That's nice," said Grandpa, and Uncle Charlie, who was just returning to the table with his own cup of coffee, repeated the name after me. "Sarah Jane," he said, "Sarah Jane. That's nice."

I suddenly remembered Aunt Lou's letter. I fished it from my pocket and handed it to Grandpa. He opened it eagerly and began to read it aloud to Uncle Charlie. There wasn't much more for me to say about little Sarah Jane. Aunt Lou was saying it all.

We sat and drank our coffee and chatted some more about

the new baby and Aunt Lou and Uncle Nat. But watching Uncle Charlie's clumsy fingers try to lift the coffee cup to his mouth took some of the joy out of the event for me. He spilled a bit as he tried to drink. I noticed the dark liquid dribble over his fingers more than once as he raised the cup to his mouth. Maybe this was why Uncle Charlie didn't let the coffee get as steaming hot as he used to.

I thought of all the times I had watched Uncle Charlie lift the cup to his lips and take a full gulp of steaming hot coffee and somehow manage to swallow it with no harm done. But he had steady hands then. Not gnarled fingers that couldn't grip things tightly.

"I'm pretty tired I guess," I finally excused myself. "Think I'll go on up to bed."

Grandpa was still grinning but he stifled a yawn. "Me, too," he said and reached for the lamp.

"You two go ahead," Uncle Charlie waved us on. "I think I'll just sit here for a bit longer. Maybe have another cup."

I looked at Grandpa.

"Did you take one of the pills?" he asked.

Uncle Charlie nodded.

"Still no relief?"

"Some." Both Grandpa and I knew that Uncle Charlie wasn't admitting to much.

Grandpa left the lamp on the table and we climbed the stairs without it.

When we got up to the hallway I reached out a hand to Grandpa.

"What is it?" I asked in a whisper.

Grandpa didn't seem to understand my question.

"What's the matter with Uncle Charlie?" I asked then.

"What do you mean?"

"His hands—all—all twisted, and his walk so slow and—"

"Oh, that," responded Grandpa matter-of-factly. "That's just his arthritis. It's gettin' worse."

Arthritis! Worse! How come I'd never noticed it before?

"How long—how long has he been this way?" I found myself asking.

"He's had arthritis some for years," Grandpa responded. "But he has his good days and his bad days. Folks say the weather. It's steadily getting worse, though. It's really into his hands bad now. Used to just be in his knees and his back."

There wasn't much that I could say, so I let Grandpa go. "See you in the morning," I muttered and turned to my bedroom.

I lay awake a long time that night—thinking of more than our new Sarah Jane. I thought a great deal about Uncle Charlie. It scared me, this arthritis. Already it had made him into an old man. It had happened so gradually that I had missed it.

But not now. Now it was very obvious. Uncle Charlie was not a complainer, but it was easy to see that even small tasks were hard for him to accomplish. And how could he ever farm?

I fought for sleep, both to escape my uneasy thoughts and because I knew I would need it. Grandpa had said that we would leave for town just as soon as we could finish up the chores the next morning, and I knew without asking that Grandpa would start those chores a little earlier than usual.

Even so, it was a long time until I could lay aside my excitement—and my worry—and let sleep claim me.

Chapter 5

Graduation

It took several days for things to fall back into a normal routine. Grandpa and Uncle Charlie visited the parsonage with far more frequency than usual. I think they were a little afraid that young Sarah Jane might grow up when they weren't looking. Anyway, they came in often to check on her.

Sarah Jane greatly changed the procedures of the household. Aunt Lou didn't seem to get as much baking done as she used to, and both Uncle Nat and I found ourselves helping around the house more. That baby was either hungry or wet every five minutes.

She was a good little tyke, though. Lou kept telling Uncle Nat and me over and over what a good baby she was, and I was quite willing to take Aunt Lou's word for it. She certainly did a great deal of sleeping. Whenever I brought one of my friends in for a peek at her she was either sleeping or eating, it seemed to me, and neither one worked too well for showing her off.

She very quickly lost her redness and her wrinkles, and soon she had a soft, pinkish look and a little round head capped with dark downy hair. She opened her eyes more, too; often she would lie in my arms and look at my face as if she knew just who I was and how I fit into her life. I loved it when she looked at me that way; if no one was close enough to hear, I'd talk to her and tell her things about myself so that she really would know me. We all adored her—after all, we all loved Lou, and had waited for this special baby for a long time.

I expected that now it would be even harder to study, and in some ways it was. But suddenly it became very important for me to get good grades as I left the school system and went out into the world. I wouldn't have admitted it to a soul, but I didn't want Sarah to ever have reason to be ashamed of me. So I pitched into those textbooks like I'd never done in my whole life—and it worked, too. I ended up with the best set of marks I had ever gotten.

Willie dropped by now and then. Sometimes we studied together, and we played with Sarah, but mostly we just took a break from our books and talked. One Thursday afternoon he tapped on my window, and I could tell just by looking that he was really excited about something. I pushed back my Advanced Speller and opened the window.

"Is Sarah sleepin'?" Willie asked.

I nodded.

"Then come out." Willie didn't want to take any chances on his excitement waking the baby.

I eased the window back down quietly and headed for the back door.

"What is it?" I asked as soon as I was clear of the kitchen.

"Mary," beamed Willie. "She became a Christian."

Now I knew why Willie was excited. I was excited, too. We gave each other a big hug, pounding one another on the back. Mary had been coming to church every Sunday since she had been to the Youth Group with Willie.

"When?" I asked when I could speak.

"Just this afternoon. I came to tell you just as soon as I could."

I slapped Willie on the back again. I couldn't help but think how happy I would feel if I had the same good news about Camellia.

"That's great!" I said. "Just great."

Afraid that my tears might show, I pulled away and headed for the backyard swing that Uncle Charlie had built for Lou. Willie followed me without a word; I guess he knew I was feeling rather emotional.

Avoiding Willie's eyes, I gave a little push with one foot to start the swing in gentle motion and looked at it carefully like I had never done in the past. Uncle Charlie was skilled with simple tools. Each board was carefully fashioned and properly joined. The arm where my hand rested was polished smooth and shaped for comfort. I ran my hand idly over it, wondering if Uncle Charlie would ever be able to hold a hammer or a plane again. Then my thoughts jerked back to the present.

"What do her folks think?" I asked Willie.

"I don't know about her pa. He hasn't said much. But her ma says that it's Mary's decision and that she'll support her in her new faith. I think she wishes that she had the courage to make the commitment herself. She must have done a great deal of thinking when she was so ill."

"I suppose," I agreed.

"Mary is already praying for her ma. She says it's just a matter of time, she knows, until her ma will become a Christian too. She says she thinks that her ma has been searching for God for a long time, just hasn't known where or how to find Him. An' now that Mary knows, she can help her ma."

The excitement had grown in Willie's voice again. His eyes were shining.

"Josh," he said, "this is the first person that I have talked to about my faith, the first one to become a Christian because of it. It's—it's—well, it is the most exciting thing that has ever happened to me."

I had never had the experience myself, although I had tried—with Camellia, with her ma, even with Jack Berry in prison by letter after I finally forgave him. None of those had worked. I still prayed for all of them, though.

"Does Mary feel called to the mission field too?" I asked.

Willie looked just a bit puzzled.

"I dunno," he answered.

"Isn't that—isn't that pretty important?"

"Well, she needs to learn a bit more about being a Christian before she thinks about where God wants her, don't you think?"

"But you already know where God wants you," I pressed.

"So?" said Willie with a shrug.

"So it just might be important where He wants your girl."

"My girl?" Willie really seemed confused now.

"Mary!" I said impatiently to jog his failing memory. "The girl you just brought to the faith. Mary! If you are going to train to be a missionary, then perhaps it would be a bit handy if your girl would be one, too."

Willie looked dumbfounded.

"Mary isn't *my* girl," he said at last.

"What?"

"Where'd you ever get that idea?"

"From you," I said. "You brought her to Youth Group and you've been bringing her to church an' you—"

"But she's not my *girl*."

"Does Mary know that?" I threw back at Willie.

"Of course! We're just friends. Mary's understood that all along. We talked it over the first night I asked her to Youth Group."

"And you came together as *friends*?" It seemed preposterous to me. "You mean you brought her and talked to her and shared your faith, just as a friend? Not because you *liked* her?"

Willie shook his head as though he couldn't believe just how stupid I was.

"Josh, you don't just share your faith with girls you want to go out with." Willie couldn't hide his grin, even though he was a bit impatient with me. "I brought Mary to the Youth Group because she is a great girl, a good friend—one who has never really had a chance. She never attended church. Never got to spend time with those of us from the church. How else was she going to hear?"

"I just thought—" I interrupted. "Well, everyone thought that you liked Mary—special like."

"I couldn't court a non-Christian girl, and you know it, Josh. You know that God wants me to be a missionary. How could I be a missionary if I went and got sweet on a girl and married her and she didn't even share my faith? Why—"

"I had thought of it," I admitted. "It didn't make much sense to me either."

We sat in silence for a few minutes and then I dared to say, "Well, she's a Christian now, so if you decide you do like her—no problem."

Willie stepped from the swing, making it stop with a jarring movement. His hand reached up to smooth back his hair. I recognized the movement as one of exasperation.

"Okay, okay," I said quickly before Willie had a chance to speak. "So she stays a friend."

I got off the swing too and started back to the house.

"I guess I'd better get back to the books," I said defensively. "Only two more exams left."

Willie grinned. "I know. You want to get a 99 again."

I blushed.

"Where's it taking you, Josh?" asked Willie.

"What?" I stopped and eyed Willie.

"I shouldn't have asked it like that," continued Willie. "I didn't mean it to sound that way. I was just wondering if you knew something that you were holding back. Thought maybe you were trying for admittance in some super college where you needed great marks or somethin'."

I shook my head. I hadn't even applied to any colleges.

"You still don't know?"

I shook my head again.

"I'll keep praying for you, Josh," Willie said, slapping my shoulder.

"Thanks." I headed back to my bedroom and the open textbook.

I envied Willie. He already knew exactly what God wanted for him. He had no problem figuring out what to do in order to prepare himself. He could just plunge right on, getting himself ready for the task.

When graduation finally did arrive, I felt all strange. On the one hand I was excited about having completed high school. There were some awfully nice and embarrassing things said about me at the ceremony, too. I noticed Aunt Lou straighten in her chair and slightly lift little Sarah Jane so that she wouldn't miss any of the compliments. I could see the grins on the faces of Grandpa and Uncle Charlie, too. Grandpa was fairly busting his buttons. So I felt a measure of honest pride myself.

On the other hand, I felt all empty inside. Here I was, finishing up my schooling without the faintest notion of what I was to do next with my life. As I already said, Willie was going off to train as a missionary; Camellia was going to New York; Janie and Charlotte were both setting out to be teachers; Avery was going to work with his pa; Polly was getting married—the list could go on and on. But Joshua Jones, head of the class, didn't have any idea of what he would do with all this education.

I still felt all mixed up when we got back to Aunt Lou's and she served punch and cake in my honor to a number of friends and our family. She bustled around, chatting about me as she served, and Grandpa boasted some and Uncle Charlie just sat in the corner, quietly rubbing his knotted hands together as he grinned my way now and then. I could see, even then, that Uncle Charlie's hands were giving him pain again, but he, as was his way, didn't make any mention of the fact.

Over and over the question of my plans came up. I brushed them aside with comments such as, I was still "sorting it through" or "looking at possibilities" or "waiting to make a decision." Grandpa and Aunt Lou strengthened my position—"Lots of time," they'd say, or, "Josh has too much at stake to decide hurriedly." It made it sound like I had all kinds of choices.

In our private conversations they had already informed me that I shouldn't rush into deciding, should take my time and consider carefully the field that I wanted to pursue or the job that I would consider of interest, as God directed me. I knew that they were all still praying. I knew that they were all behind me, but I was quite sure that none of them knew just how much the question of the future weighed on my mind.

"You can stay right here and find a job in town until you decide what God wants you to do," Aunt Lou assured me. "We won't need the bedroom for Sarah Jane for a long time yet."

And I guess that was what everyone expected me to do. I had already had offers to work in the hardware store and the print shop. I was deeply thankful for the opportunity of choice but neither job really appealed to me.

So this was *my* reception—*my* time of honor. People came and went, giving well-wishes and enjoying Aunt Lou's refreshments and the friendly conversation. There was talking and laughter and a great deal of commendation. I tried to be a part of it, but my eyes kept straying back to Uncle Charlie and his bent shoulders and gnarled hands.

Suddenly something became very clear to me. As soon as I could, I excused myself and went to my room. I began to pack my few belongings into my duffle bag. It was spring. Planting time. I could see by Uncle Charlie's hands that he was in no shape to hold the reins. Grandpa would never be able to do all the planting alone. They needed me at the farm. The sorting out of my future could wait for now. I inwardly thanked God for putting it off for a while. We could work it out later, the two of us; but for right now I had a job to do.

I hurried faster as I packed, the emptiness within me filling up with anticipation. I loved the farm. I'd plant this one crop before I moved on. There wasn't time now to get any other help for Grandpa, and he needed his crop. If I didn't help him, who would? Scripture did say, after all, that we are to honor our parents. Grandpa wasn't really my parent, but he was the only father I had ever known. I figured that was what God meant when He spoke the words.

I sure would miss Aunt Lou and Uncle Nat, and I would dearly miss little Sarah, but I'd be nearby and able to see them often. God could have asked me to go to some far-off college or to a job in some distant town. Then I wouldn't get to see them at all. This was better—much better, for now. The decision felt right to me; and I had the impression that God approved of it. I was glad that I would have this extra time with family.

It was quiet again when I came back out to the kitchen. Grandpa and Uncle Charlie were just getting ready to head for home. They looked a bit surprised to see me out of my Sunday suit and into my everyday clothes. They were even more surprised to see my duffle bag.

"Mind if I throw my things in the wagon?" I asked. "I'll ride Chester."

"Sure," said Grandpa agreeably. "You plannin' on doin' some of yer sortin' out at the farm, eh?"

"No sortin' to be done," I answered him evenly. "At least not for the time being. Right now we got a crop to plant, and I aim to help."

"But what about a job—the further education?" Grandpa puzzled.

"We'll handle all of that when the time comes," I answered confidently. And the funny thing was, I felt confident. Uncle Nat had continually been trying to tell me that God would lead me. He would show me what I needed to know in plenty of time to do it. For me, right now, it was to help Grandpa and Uncle Charlie. That was all that I needed to know.

There were expressions of surprise on the faces before me, but gradually, one by one, heads began to nod assent.

"We're going to miss you," Aunt Lou whispered as she moved close to me and let her hand linger on my arm.

"That's the joy of it," I said. "I'll be nearby. I'll need to

come to town often. Got to check up on Sarah, you know."
We all laughed a bit and the tension in the room relaxed.

Grandpa and Uncle Nat helped me to load my things in
Grandpa's wagon. I left nothing behind; I wanted no excuses
for turning back. I went in to where Sarah was sleeping and
gave her a little pat as I whispered a goodbye. Then I hugged
Aunt Lou and Uncle Nat and scooped up Pixie.

"You ride with Grandpa and Uncle Charlie," I told her,
and handed her to Uncle Charlie.

"I'll be along shortly," I promised them. "I'm just going
to drop around and thank Mr. Lewis and Mr. Trent for their
job offers and tell them that I'm needed on the farm—for
now."

I don't know if I imagined it or not, but Grandpa seemed
to walk with a lighter step and Uncle Charlie with a bit more
straightness to his back as the two of them went toward the
wagon.

Chapter 6

Farming

Thoughts about my future sometimes tugged at me as I prepared the ground for seed and planted the crop that spring, but for the most part I enjoyed what I was doing.

I had never had much to do with the planting before. Grandpa and Uncle Charlie had been in charge of that and I had been the chore-boy, but now the roles were reversed. Grandpa and I worked the fields and Uncle Charlie, in his own slow way, did the chores—at least most of them. I still did the milking, because Uncle Charlie found the job too difficult with his crippled hands.

Uncle Charlie took care of the household duties, too. Cooking and cleaning didn't seem to bother him too much, but scrubbing the weekly laundry sure did. I sometimes winced as I watched him trying to wring out a garment. That night, to get Grandpa alone I asked him to come with me to the barn to check old Mac's hoof. "What seems to be the trouble?" Grandpa asked, bending over to lift Mac's right front foot.

"Oh, no trouble," I quickly assured him. "I was just wondering if it should be trimmed just a bit more."

Grandpa looked disgusted for a moment, but he quickly caught himself.

"Boy, you are taking your farmin' serious, aren't you?"

he commented. "Never seen anyone with so many questions."

It was true. I had been asking a lot of questions. There were so many things that I didn't know about farming and planting, and I had to learn somehow. Grandpa and Uncle Charlie seemed to be my only source of knowledge.

"That's not—not really what I wanted," I began. "I wanted to talk to you, and I didn't know how to do it without Uncle Charlie—"

"Anything you got to say to me you can say in front of Charlie," Grandpa said firmly; I could tell by the tone of his voice that he wanted that straight right to begin with.

"But it's *about* Uncle Charlie," I protested. "Doesn't seem right to talk about him right out."

"What about Charlie?" asked Grandpa cautiously. "Seems to me he does the best he can."

"That's it exactly," I quickly pointed out. "He tries so hard, but some things are so—so difficult for him."

"Like?" asked Grandpa.

"Like wringing out those clothes."

Grandpa thought on that. He too had seen Uncle Charlie struggling with the clothes.

"Don't know what can be done about it," he said slowly and moved away from old Mac, slapping him playfully on his full rump as he did so. "Neither you nor I can take time to do the laundry when we're planting," he went on.

"I know, but—" I crossed to a wooden bucket and upended it to make myself a stool. "I've been thinking, and it seems that it might be the right time to get us some more modern equipment."

"Modern equipment?" Grandpa had always scorned anything that was too mechanized.

"One of those new machines for washing clothes," I hurried on. "They have a wringer thing that you just put the clothes through and turn the handle and they squeeze all of the water out from the cloth."

Grandpa knew all about washing machines. They had

been around for a number of years. He had just felt that they were unnecessary—up 'til now.

I waited. I had more sense than to press the issue. Grandpa stood there chewing on a straw and thinking.

"Lou has one," I finally mentioned.

"Lou needs one," said Grandpa. "She's got all those white shirts and fancy dresses and dozens of diapers."

"Lou had a machine long before she had diapers to wash."

"It work good?" Grandpa surprised me by asking.

"Real good," I answered. "I've used it myself. You just stand there—or even sit, and work the handle back and forth, and the agitator does the washin' of the clothes. Then when you've washed them long enough, you put them through the wringer and rinse them in the rinse tubs, wring them out again and you're done."

Grandpa took the straw from his mouth and teased one of the barn cats with it. It batted and swatted, enjoying the fun but never able to hit that straw. Grandpa always moved it just a bit too soon.

"I'll think about it, Boy," said Grandpa. "Might bear some looking into."

That was as close to consent as I expected Grandpa to come to right off.

There were other changes I felt needed to be made on the farm, but I reminded myself that it would be smarter to take them one at a time. For now the most important one seemed to be to get Uncle Charlie some help with that washing.

We headed back to the house then, both of us studying the evening sky to see if we could read what kind of a day we would have on the morrow.

"How's that east field coming?" Grandpa asked.

"Should finish tomorrow," I answered, "if the weather holds."

"Looks good," said Grandpa, his eyes back to the sky. "We're getting the sowin' done in time. Should have a fair crop."

When we reached the house Uncle Charlie was still puttering with the supper dishes.

"How's Mac?" he asked.

"Nothin' wrong with Mac," Grandpa answered easily. "Josh here did ask if his hoof needed a bit more trimmin'. But it was really just a ruse."

When Uncle Charlie looked up, I avoided his eyes and washed my hands so that I could wipe the dishes.

"He was really worried about other things," went on Grandpa. "Hates to see you wringing out those clothes on washday. Thinks you need one of those fancy machines."

I cringed. The way Grandpa was putting it, it sounded like I was making Uncle Charlie out to be some kind of sissy. I hadn't meant it that way at all, and if Uncle Charlie took it that way, he'd buck the whole idea.

"I've thought about that myself," said Uncle Charlie slowly. "Watched Lou use hers. Seems like a sensible gadget."

Grandpa just nodded like he wasn't surprised at all.

"Josh says that it is," he informed Uncle Charlie. "Guess we should look into gettin' one. We got the money for it?"

Now Grandpa had never concerned himself much with the day-to-day expenses of the farm and house. That was Uncle Charlie's job. You couldn't really say that he kept the books. There were no books involved, but Uncle Charlie always knew to the penny just where the financial matters of the household stood.

"Guess we've got the money if we decide we want one," he answered honestly. "Happen to have a bit extra right now. We had talked about adding some new hogs to the pen—"

"That can wait," said Grandpa.

"Suppose we'd have enough to do both," went on Uncle Charlie, "but hate to get too low just in case somethin' should happen to this year's crop. We get hail or anythin', and it might make it tight."

Uncle Charlie went on washing dishes and I began to dry them and place them back in the cupboard.

"We don't want to be short," Grandpa said emphatically. "No sense doin' that. We can wait on those new hogs."

In all my years of living at the farm I had never heard Grandpa and Uncle Charlie discussing finances as openly as they were now.

"We've got what we laid aside for Josh," went on Uncle Charlie. "Now that he's not heading right off to college—"

But Grandpa interrupted him. "He still might go this fall, and we sure don't want to be short of funds. We'll just leave that right where it is for now."

"We've got our savings—"

"We're not touching a penny of that," Grandpa said adamantly. "We worked hard to earn it and we sure aren't gonna go spend it."

Uncle Charlie nodded in agreement. It was the first I had heard of savings, or of the money for my further schooling.

"How much does one of those there machines cost?" asked Grandpa.

"Dunno," said Uncle Charlie. "I'll check next time I'm in town."

They seemed to have forgotten all about me. I dried the dishes and rattled them a bit as I put them back on the shelf. That didn't seem to work so I cleared my throat. They still ignored me.

"If you find out that it's what you want, just go ahead and order one," Grandpa was telling Uncle Charlie. Uncle Charlie nodded.

"How long do you think it'll take to come?" Grandpa pulled back a kitchen chair and sat down, removing his work boots and pushing his feet into his slippers.

"Dunno," said Uncle Charlie again.

I cleared my throat again. I had been there when Uncle Nat had ordered the machine for Aunt Lou. I knew what he had paid and how long it had taken to come, too. But I wasn't being asked and I hated just to butt in.

"Throat botherin' you, Boy?" asked Grandpa.

I shook my head, feeling a bit annoyed and embarrassed.

Uncle Charlie turned to me then.

"Do you recollect what Nat paid for Lou's machine and how he went about choosin' it an' all?" he asked me.

By the time I finished telling what I knew, Grandpa and Uncle Charlie had picked the make they wanted and decided that Uncle Charlie would head for town come morning and order himself a washing machine. I felt good about it as I headed up to bed. I had initiated one small change for improvement on the farm.

Chapter 7

More Decisions

I was so busy that spring and summer I scarcely even got to town. If it hadn't been for Sundays, little Sarah Jane would have grown up without me even seeing her. As it was, she seemed bigger and stronger and a little more attentive each time I saw her.

She soon learned to smile when she was talked to and to coo soft little bubbly noises. Soon she was content to lie there and talk. Her dark hair got lost somewhere, and when her new hair thickened and lengthened, it was a soft golden brown. Her eyes changed, too; they weren't as dark now and were showing definite blue.

As Sarah was growing physically, Mary was developing spiritually. Willie still picked her up for church, but now he was bringing her ma along, too. Mary was really excited about that, and Mrs. Turley seemed to enjoy the church services.

Willie was all excited about leaving in the fall for school. He kept getting letters telling him about the courses and what he was to bring, and every time he got one he'd rush right over and show it to me. He'd usually bring it out to the field where I was planting or cultivating or cutting hay.

We kept talking about fishing but we never did get around to going. There was just so much to do that we never had time. When I finished one job I was already behind in taking on the next one. I hadn't realized that farming kept a man so busy.

Grandpa said I should slow down a bit, but I kept seeing things that needed to be done. I hadn't been around long before I realized that some areas had been rather neglected in the last few years. I guess the farm had become too big a job for Grandpa and Uncle Charlie. I could remember a time when neither of them would have let such things go unattended.

Aunt Lou and Uncle Nat were pretty busy with church affairs and didn't get out to the farm too often. One Friday night they joined us for supper, and Aunt Lou did the cooking. Boy, was it good, too. Uncle Charlie did his best, but his meals were mostly boiled potatoes and meat.

"How's the work coming, Josh?" Uncle Nat asked after I had finished off a second piece of lemon pie.

"Good," I said, feeling kind of grown up and important. "We're haying now."

"How's it look?" Uncle Nat had been in a farming community long enough to know how important a good hay crop was.

I sobered a bit then. "Not as good as I had hoped," I said honestly. "Don't really understand. We got lots of rain, but it still looks a bit skimpy."

Grandpa entered the conversation then. "Soil's getting a bit tired," he offered. "It's been planted for a lot of years now. That hay field has been givin' us a crop for nigh unto forty years, I guess. Deserves to be tired."

"Could you use some help tomorrow?" Uncle Nat asked. "I could spare the day."

"Sure," I grinned at him. "I sure could use someone on the stack."

"I'll be here," he promised.

"I'll send the lunch," promised Aunt Lou. "I'll need to get rid of the rest of this chicken somehow."

I looked forward to the next day as I climbed the stairs to my room that night. It would be good to have Uncle Nat's help. But more than that, it would be good to have his company.

The day was a hot one; both Nat and I sweated in the midmorning sun.

When it was time to take a break for lunch, we decided to slip into the shade of the trees on the creekbank to have our meal. We gave the horses a drink from the stream, then tied and fed them and lowered ourselves to the cool grass in the shade of a large poplar.

After Uncle Nat asked the blessing on the leftover chicken and Aunt Lou's other good things, we chatted small talk for several minutes. At length Uncle Nat looked directly at me and asked candidly, "How's it going, Josh? You liking being a summer farmer?"

"Sure," I answered. "Like it fine."

"Are you any nearer an answer?"

I hesitated. "You mean, about what I should do?"

Uncle Nat nodded and I shook my head.

"Still bother you?"

"I guess it does," I answered honestly. "If I let myself think on it, it does."

"You planning to go to school somewhere this fall?"

"That's the problem," I said quickly. "I'd thought that I'd just come on out and help Grandpa get the crop in and then I'd stay long enough to help with the hay. But as soon as haying's over it'll be time to cut the green feed, and then harvest—and on and on it goes. There doesn't seem to be a good time to leave."

Uncle Nat nodded.

"Another thing," I said confidentially. "Things need a lot of fixing up around here. I hadn't realized it before, but I guess farming is getting too hard for Grandpa and Uncle Charlie." I hoped with all of my heart that Uncle Nat would understand my meaning and not think I was being critical of the two men. After all, I was still smart enough to know that they knew far more about farming than I did.

"I'd noticed," said Uncle Nat simply.

I took heart at that and dared to go on. "This hay crop,

for example. I think Grandpa is right; the land is tired. But it's gotta do us for years and years yet. There isn't any more land than what we've already got, Nat. We've gotta make this do for all the years God gives us. What do we do about it? Do we just wear it out?"

It was a hard question, one I had been thinking on a good deal lately.

"There are ways to give it a boost," said Uncle Nat, reaching for another sandwich.

I perked up immediately.

"Like what?"

"Well, not being a farmer I don't know much about it," Uncle Nat went on, "but I know someone who does."

"Who?"

"There's a fella by the name of Randall Thomas who lives about seven miles the other side of town," went on Uncle Nat. "I was called out there to see his dying mother. She wanted to talk to a preacher. Don't know why. She had things to teach *me*. A real saint if ever I met one."

I wasn't too interested in the saintly woman who probably had gone Home to glory by now. I wanted to hear about the farmer.

"Well, this farmer has been busy studying all about the soil and how to —what did he call it?—'rotate' crops to benefit it. Real interesting to talk to."

I was all ears. So there *was* a smarter way to farm the land!

"You think he'd talk to me?" I asked, very aware of the fact that I was still only a boy in some folks' thinking.

"I'm sure he would. Said if there was ever anything that he could do for me in return for calling on his mother, just to let him know."

I took a deep breath.

"So when do you want to see him?" asked Uncle Nat.

"Well, I don't know. Hafta get the hay off, and then the green feed—"

"And then the harvest," put in Uncle Nat.

"But I would like to talk to him," I continued. "I'd like to get the crops planted right next spring an'—"

Uncle Nat was looking at me.

"So you plan to farm again next year?"

I shrugged. "I guess so. I mean, I still don't know what else I'm supposed to do, and Grandpa still needs me an' . . ." It tapered off. There was silence for a few minutes and then I found my voice again.

"Do you think I'm wrong? Do you think that I should be tryin' harder to find out what God wants me to do with my life? It's not that I don't want to know, or don't want to obey Him."

"Are you happy here?" Uncle Nat asked me again.

"Yeah, I guess I am."

"You don't feel uneasy or guilty or anything?"

"No." I could answer that honestly. I was still puzzled, still questioning but I didn't feel guilty.

"Then, Josh, I would take that as God's endorsement on what you are doing," said Uncle Nat. "For now, I think you can just go ahead and keep right on farming. If God wants to change your direction, then He'll show you. I'm confident of that."

It sure was good to hear Uncle Nat put it like that.

We tucked away the empty lunch bucket and moved to the creek for a drink of cold water.

"And, Josh," said Uncle Nat just as we turned to go for the horses, "while you are here, you be the best farmer that you can be, you hear? Find out all you can about the soil, about livestock, about production. Keep your fences mended and your buildings in good repair. Make your machines give you as many years of service as they can. Learn to be the best farmer that you can be, because, Josh, in farming, in preaching, in any area of life, God doesn't take pleasure in second-rate work."

I nodded solemnly. I wasn't sure how much time God would give me to shape up Grandpa's tired farm before He moved me on to something else, but I knew one thing. I would give it my full time and attention until I got His next signal.

Chapter 8

Sunday

Willie came over to say goodbye before boarding the train that would take him away from our small community to the far-off town where he would continue his education. He was so excited that he fairly babbled, and for a moment I envied him and his calling. I would sure miss him, I knew that. It wouldn't be quite the same without Willie.

"You'll write?" Willie asked.

" 'Course I will."

"I'll send you my address just as soon as I'm settled," he promised.

"Let me know all about your school."

"I will. Everything," said Willie.

"What happens now—with Mary?" I asked suddenly, feeling concern for Mary and her mother.

"What happens? What do you mean?"

"For church? How will they get to church?"

"Mary is going to drive. I suggested that you might not mind picking them up, but Mary insisted that she'd drive them."

"Good," I said, and then hastily added, "but I sure wouldn't have minded taking them."

"I was sure you wouldn't, but Mary is quite independent."

We were quiet for a few moments; then Willie broke the

silence. "Take care of her, Josh. She's a pretty special person."

I looked at Willie, my eyes saying, "I told you so," but Willie didn't seem to catch the look.

"She's my first convert, you know," he went on, and then added quietly, "She often surprises me. She knows some things about being a Christian that I still haven't learned in all my years of trying to live my faith."

I nodded. Mary certainly was putting many of us to shame.

"I saw Camellia off yesterday," Willie said, and my head jerked up. I had hoped to learn of Camellia's parting date so that I could see her off myself, but I had been so busy with the farm. A funny little stab of sadness pricked at me somewhere deep inside. I couldn't even answer Willie.

"She sure was excited," Willie went on.

Yes, Camellia would be excited.

"Her pa seemed excited too, or proud or something, but her ma didn't seem to be too sure that they were doing the right thing."

I wanted to ask Willie how Camellia looked, how she was wearing her hair, what her traveling dress was like, all sorts of things so that I could sort of picture Camellia in my mind, but I didn't.

"She had more trunks and baggage than would be necessary for ten people," Willie was laughing. "I think her ma even packed her a lunch."

I still said nothing, and Willie thought that I'd missed his point. "They feed you on the train, you know."

I hadn't known. I had never traveled by train in my life, but I didn't admit my ignorance to Willie.

"She hasn't decided if she will get home for Christmas," Willie went on, answering the question that was burning in my mind.

"Will you?" I asked, making it sound like that was the most important thing in the world to me at the moment.

Willie shook his head slowly. There was concern in his

eyes. "I wish I could, but it's far too expensive to travel that distance. I'm sure I will be ready for some familiar faces by then. Four months away is about long enough for the first time from home, don't you think?"

I nodded.

"Well, I'd best get going." Willie reached to shake my hand. I extended mine, and then we both forgot that we were grown men saying goodbye to each other. We remembered instead that we were lifetime buddies, and the months ahead would be very long. Before I knew it we were soon giving each other an affectionate goodbye hug.

After Willie left I tried to get back to work in the field, but it was hard. Seeing my best friend riding off down the road, knowing that he would soon be on his way to Bible school, gave me an empty feeling in the pit of my stomach. Besides, Willie's news that Camellia had already left on the train for New York without my having the chance to tell her goodbye didn't do much to cheer me up. I had never felt so lonesome in all my life.

It wasn't long until Willie's first letter arrived. He was so full of excitement that he wrote pages and pages. I read it over and over, trying to get the feel of how it would be to be away from home.

I wasn't expecting any letter from Camellia, though I would have welcomed one. I did take a bit of a walk one Sunday while the rest of the family lingered over another cup of coffee after Aunt Lou's dinner. I went by the Foggelsons', hoping that I might accidentally meet Camellia's mother. It took quite a while and quite a few trips past their place, but eventually I did see her. She was watering her marigolds and I tipped my hat and greeted her like a mannerly boy was supposed to do. Then I casually asked her about Camellia.

Tears came to her eyes and she fought to control them. It frightened me. For a moment I was afraid that something dreadful had happened to Camellia, but when she spoke I realized that it was just the loneliness of a mother for her child.

She tried to smile.

"She is very excited about—about being on her own and the city and her classes and new friends." Then she added thoughtfully, "She—she hasn't said so, but even though she sounds cheerful, I think she has been just a bit lonesome."

The tears came again and Mrs. Foggelson attempted to smile in spite of them.

"I hope she is," she said wistfully, as though to herself. "I am."

I waited for a minute and then asked the question that I had really come to ask.

"Will she be home for Christmas?"

"No. Her father decided that she needs to make the adjustment to being on her own, away from family. It's much too far to travel, he says. I suppose he is right, but— Oh, my! How I dread the thought of Christmas without her!"

I was surprised somewhat that Mr. Foggelson, who doted on his only daughter, could consider Christmas without Camellia.

Mrs. Foggelson continued. "Mr. Foggelson needs to make a business trip east the last week of November. He will travel on to New York and take Camellia's gifts, and check to see how she is doing. He says that's quite enough."

My feelings for Mr. Foggelson hit an all time low. He had always felt that Camellia was his individual possession, but how could he do this to the girl's mother? And her friends? And how could he do it to Camellia? If she was really homesick, did he think that the sight of "dear old dad" was all she needed?

I couldn't even speak for a few moments. The angry thoughts were churning around inside of me. I looked away from the tears in Mrs. Foggelson's eyes and studied the distant maple tree, its bare arms empty as they reached upward against the gray autumn sky.

At last I found my voice. I even managed a smile. I guess

I felt more compassion for Mrs. Foggelson at that moment than I had ever felt before. This man, her husband, had robbed her of so much—her faith, her self-esteem, and now her only child. I wondered just what kind of account he would give before God on the Judgment Day.

I smiled and touched my hat again. "I'll keep in touch," I promised, and then stammered, "If that's all right."

"I'd love to see you, Josh. I need someone to talk to, and one of Camellia's friends would—"

She didn't finish, but I thought I understood. And her words, "one of Camellia's friends," echoed in my mind as I tipped my hat again and started back down the sidewalk toward home.

"Josh," Mrs. Foggelson's soft voice called after me.

I turned to look back at her.

"Keep praying—please," she almost pleaded.

I nodded solemnly and swallowed hard. I wasn't sure if she meant to pray for Camellia, or for herself, or that she would soon see Camellia again—or all three, but I'd pray. I'd pray lots and often. Living with a man like Mr. Foggelson, I felt that she really needed prayer.

I still hadn't controlled my anger toward Mr. Foggelson by the time I reached Aunt Lou's. I thought of walking right on by and spending some more time alone with my thoughts, but the realization that I didn't have too long until I'd need to go home for choring prompted me to turn into the yard.

Baby Sarah had just been fed when I reentered the house. She was in a happy mood, and Aunt Lou passed her to me, knowing that I would soon be asking for her if she didn't. She gurgled and cooed and even tried to giggle. Then she did the unforgivable. She spit up all over my Sunday shirt.

Aunt Lou jumped to run for a wet cloth, and Uncle Nat reached out to quickly rescue Sarah. I loved Sarah, but I sure did hate the feel and the smell of being spit up on. I guess I made some faces to show my disgust, and they laughed at me and ribbed me a lot.

Aunt Lou cleaned me up the best that she could, apologizing for the mess. She offered to wash my shirt, but I didn't have anything else along to wear and I figured I ought to be man enough to put up with a little bit of baby spit-up.

The need for laundering brought our thoughts back to Uncle Charlie and his washing machine.

Uncle Nat agreed to order the machine, and Grandpa and I both felt good about that. Now laundry wouldn't be quite so hard for Uncle Charlie—especially after my Sundays with little Sarah!

After a while I unobtrusively left the dining room and wandered down to the room that had been mine for so many years. The door was open, and it sure looked different. Aunt Lou had everything so neat and tidy, with new curtains on the window—white and frilly, not the kind of curtains a boy would have enjoyed. I had preferred my old tan ones, but these did look real nice. Little throw cushions were propped up against the pillows, too. I would have found them to be a nuisance.

I stood there for a few minutes looking around me and thinking back over the years; then I reached out with a toe and pushed the door shut. I knelt by the bed. "Father," I began, "you know how I feel about Camellia, and how sorry I am for Mrs. Foggelson. Well, I'm too angry right now to pray for Mr. Foggelson, but I do want to ask you to take care of Camellia and bring her into a relationship with Jesus . . ."

As I prayed for Camellia and her mother, my anger began to subside, and I began to realize how wrong my own attitude had been.

"Lord, Mr. Foggelson is a possessive and selfish man, and he's done some terrible things to his family. But I guess he needs you about as much as anyone I know. Help him find you too, Lord—and help me forgive him."

By the time I finished praying, I could think of the Foggelsons without feeling that turmoil of anger inside.

I rose and left the room, peeking into Aunt Lou and Uncle Nat's bedroom, where little Sarah now slept peacefully in her crib. She looked sweet, one little hand clutching the edge of her blanket and the other curled up into a tiny fist by her cheek. Her soft lashes against the pinkness of her skin looked so long and thick. Her hair, a little damp, curled closely to her tiny round head. It was getting lighter in color all the time; eventually it might be the same color as Aunt Lou's.

I reached down and smoothed out her blankets, then stroked the top of her head. She didn't even move. When Sarah slept, she really slept. Aunt Lou was thankful for that. There were many interruptions in the parsonage, and if the child had been a light sleeper, she might have never gotten a decent rest.

I heard stirring in the kitchen then and I knew that Grandpa and Uncle Charlie were preparing to leave for home. I whispered a few words to the sleeping baby and went out to get the team while they said their goodbyes.

Chapter 9

Winter

I was kept so busy that fall that I scarcely had time to miss Willie and Camellia. It seemed that I should have been in about three places at one time. There was so much to do, and only Grandpa and I to do the farming.

Grandpa had slowed down a lot, too. I hadn't realized until I was working with him just how difficult it was for him to put in a full day's work at the farm. I should have never left them alone while I went to school in town; I should have been there sharing in the responsibility. Maybe then things wouldn't have gotten so far behind.

But inwardly I knew that they never would have agreed to my staying at home. Even now, comments were made about my "calling" and I was reminded that I was not to hesitate when I felt God was prodding me on to what I "really should be doing" with my life.

I asked myself fairly frequently if I felt Him prodding, but I also found myself bargaining with Him.

"Can I wait, Lord, until I get the pasture fence mended?" I'd pray. "God, would you give me enough time to get in the crop?" And each time I asked His permission, I felt like I got His nod of approval.

Uncle Charlie's washing machine arrived in mid-October. I hadn't realized how much it meant to him until I watched him grinning as he uncrated it. He stroked the wringer lovingly, then gave it a few cranks and grinned some more. It was going to be a good investment.

The weather didn't cooperate that fall. The fields would dry just enough for us to get back at the harvest; we'd work a few hours, and then another storm would pass through, delaying us again. In my frustration I would go to fence-mending or repairing the barn or cutting wood for our winter supply.

I went to bed worn out every night and slept soundly until morning. Then I got up, checking the sky for the day's weather before I even had my clothes on, and started in on another full day.

It was late November before the district threshing crew moved in for the last time and we got the final crop off. Because of the rain, it wasn't as good a quality as we had hoped it would be, but at least it was in. Our hay crop of the year had been scant and poor, also.

Grandpa relaxed a bit then. The lines seemed to soften on his brow. Grandpa had too much faith for worry, but he was a little less concerned than he had been with the crop still in the field.

Uncle Charlie seemed to feel the lessening of tension too. For one thing, I knew that he was relieved to have his kitchen back to himself. We'd had a neighbor woman and her daughter in helping to cook for the threshing crew. Uncle Charlie needed the help, we all knew that, but he sure was glad when the last dish was washed and put away and the women went home.

I turned my attention to other things—cutting wood, fixing door hinges and banking the root cellar. And I talked to God some more.

I had thought I might be ready for His call at the first of the year, but now I realized that I would never be caught up enough to turn the farm back over to Grandpa and Uncle Charlie that soon. I needed more time to get things back into shape. God seemed to agree. I did not feel Him nudging me to hurry on to other things. Instead, He seemed to give me assurance that my job on the farm wasn't finished yet.

And so I worked feverishly, trying to get as much as I could done before the snow came. When it did come, it came with fury. The thermometer dropped thirty degrees over-night, and the wind blew from the north with such intensity that it blew down several trees. The snow swirled in blinding eddies. I was thankful that I had repaired the chicken coop and lined the floor with fresh warm straw. I was glad, too, that the barn was ready for winter. But I still hadn't gotten the pigpens ready. I worried about the pigs, especially the sow that had just given birth to eight little piglets. I strug-gled against the wind with a load of straw for bedding.

It was useless even to try. The wind whipped the straw from my pitchfork as soon as I stepped from the barn. After trying several times, I tossed my fork aside and gathered the straw in my arms. Even that didn't work well. As I fought my way toward the pigpen the wind pushed and pulled, pull-ing the straw from me. By the time I had reached the pigpen I had very little left.

I tried again, over and over, and each time I arrived at the shed with only a scant armful of straw.

At last I gave up. I was winded and freezing as I bucked the strong gale. I hoped that the bit of straw I had managed to get to the pigs would help to protect them against the bitter storm.

I spent most of the day fighting against the wind, trying to ease the discomfort of the animals. Several times Grandpa and Uncle Charlie came out to assure me that I had done all I could, that the animals would make it through on their own. But I wasn't so sure, so I kept right on fighting.

When the day was over and I headed for the house with a full pail of milk, I was exhausted.

The kitchen had never looked or smelled more inviting. The warmth from the cookstove spilled out to greet me, mak-ing my face sting with the sudden heat after the cold. The odor of Uncle Charlie's hot stew and fresh biscuits reminded me of just how hungry I was.

Grandpa took the pail from me and went to strain the milk and run it through the separator. I didn't argue, even though it was normally my job.

Pixie pushed herself up against me as I fought with cold-numbed fingers to get off my heavy choring boots. She licked at my hands, at my face, anywhere that she could get a lick in. I guess it seemed to her that I had been gone for a very long time.

When I went to wash for supper, Uncle Charlie spoke softly from the stove where he dished up the food.

"Your face looks a bit chilled, Josh. Don't make the water too warm. You might have a bit of a frostbite there."

I felt my nose and my cheeks. They seemed awfully hard and cold. I heeded Uncle Charlie's advice and pressed a cloth soaked in cool water up against them. Even the cold made them burn.

Over the meal we discussed the storm and all I had done to try to prepare for it. I noticed that the woodbox was stacked high. Grandpa had been busy, too.

"Looks like it could be with us for a while," commented Grandpa. "Sky is awful heavy."

I didn't know much about reading storms, and I hoped that Grandpa was wrong. One day of this was enough.

We listened to the news on our sputtering radio while we warmed ourselves with coffee. The forecast wasn't good. According to the man with the crackling voice, the storm could get even worse during the night and wasn't expected to blow itself out for at least three days.

I could sense even before I awoke the next morning that the radio had been right. The storm was even worse than the day before.

When I went out to face the wind and the cold, the range cows were pushing tightly around the barn, bawling their protest against the storm. I knew that they needed shelter; I also knew that they could not all fit inside. The barn was reserved for the milk cows and the horses. I felt sorry for those poor animals. We really needed some kind of a shed to protect them against such storms. *That's one thing I'll do first thing next summer,* I vowed to myself.

The next day was a repeat of the two that went before it. All day the wind howled. Then, near the end of the day the wind abated and the snow slackened. The temperature dipped another five degrees.

Even in the farmhouse we were hard put to keep warm. Uncle Charlie lit a lamp and put it down in the cellar to keep Aunt Lou's canned goods from freezing. We added blankets to our beds and set an alarm so we could get up in the night to check the fire.

The next morning arrived clear and deathly cold. The water in the hand basin in the kitchen was skimmed with ice. I lit the lantern and started for the barn, hating the thought of going out to face the intense cold. My breath preceded me in frosty puffs of glistening white. Even the moon that still hung in the west looked frozen into position.

Now that the wind had died down, I really had work to do. The animals outside hadn't really eaten properly since the storm had begun. It had been just too hard to fight the wind. Now they stood, humped and bawling, hungry and thirsty, and nearly frozen to death.

By the time the storm had passed and the temperature was back to normal again, we had lost three of the piglets, two of the older cows, and half a dozen chickens. Three cows had lost the lower portions of their tails to frostbite, and our winter supply of feed had already been seriously depleted. If the winter continued this way, we would find it difficult to continue feeding all of the stock. Even so, we fared much better than some of our neighbors. The storm had killed a number of the animals in some herds.

As Christmas approached, I was eager to spend time with Aunt Lou and Uncle Nat. Little Sarah was sitting by herself and even attempting to pull herself up. And the opening of the Christmas gifts was, of course, even more fun with a baby in the house. We all had a gift for Sarah, and we took her on our laps and pretended that she was taking part in the opening of the present. We also pretended that she was excited about each new rattle or bib. She wasn't; in fact, she liked the rustle of the wrapping paper better than anything else.

I even brought Pixie with us. In the colder weather I usually left her at home when we went to town, but today I tucked her inside my heavy coat and she managed just fine. Sarah loved her, and I put Pixie through all of her tricks just to make Sarah squeal and giggle. She seemed to like it best when Pixie "spoke" for a little taste of turkey. Then Sarah would wave her chubby arms and squeal at the top of her voice. We all had a good laugh over it.

In the afternoon I slipped out and hurried over to the Foggelsons'. I wanted Mrs. Foggelson to know that I was thinking about her—still praying for her, too. Besides, I was a little anxious to hear any news about Camellia.

Before I went up their walk, I could see that there was no one home. The heavy curtains were pulled shut and no one had cleaned the snow from the walk for several days. The shovel was leaning up against the back porch, so before I headed home again I decided to clear the snow from the walk. I didn't know when the Foggelsons would be back again or if it would even be evident to them that someone had been there, but I did it anyway.

I wondered if there was some chance that Mr. Foggelson had changed his mind and they had gone together to see Camellia. I hoped so. It would be a lonely Christmas for both Mrs. Foggelson and Camellia if they were to spend it apart.

I thought of Willie, too. I had received a letter from him just a few days before Christmas. "I really miss the family and friends," he wrote. "As exciting as my studies are, I'm lonesome, even weary. But I've been invited home with one of the guys from the college who lives nearby." I was glad that Willie had somewhere to go.

When I was younger, I had always thought that as soon

as Christmas had come and gone, we should be working our way toward spring. I hoped that it would be true this year. I had loved winter as a boy, but then I hadn't had the responsibilities of seeing that everything and everybody made it through without mishap or suffering. Winter had simply been a time of sport—sleigh rides, tobogganing, ice skating, snowfalls and snowmen. I had loved it. Now winter was a time of struggle against the intense cold, the biting wind, the deep snow, the shortened days. The weather made it harder to chore, and the supply of winter feed and cut wood seemed to evaporate before my eyes.

Thinking of all this as I walked back to Aunt Lou's, I began to feel rather dejected. Then, it began to snow again—huge, soft, gently falling flakes. I looked up toward the sky to see the snow drift toward my face and marveled anew at the beauty of it. It might not be easy to live with winter, but it certainly was beautiful when I just took the time to look closely at it.

Chapter 10

Making It Through

I may have been ready for spring as soon as Christmas was over, but I guess no one thought to tell Mother Nature. She stormed and fretted and gave us a hard time all through the month of January. I looked forward to February—surely things would improve!

But they didn't. When we couldn't get to church a couple of Sundays, I missed the church service, the good dinner, and the brief visit with little Sarah.

And the bad weather didn't help Uncle Charlie improve, either. His arthritis seemed to twist his fingers off to the side more and more each day. I inwardly ached for him when I watched him trying to accomplish some simple task. But he was independent and needed to feel that he was carrying a full share of the workload.

About mid-February Grandpa came down with a bad cold. He struggled along trying to treat himself for several days but got no better.

"Grandpa!" I insisted. "You're just getting worse. I'm gonna fetch Doc to take a look at you."

"Bah!" he sputtered. "Doctors can't do nothin' I'm not already doing."

When it got worse and he had a hard time breathing, I

saddled Chester and headed for town—over Grandpa's protests.

"Sure enough," Doc murmured. "Pneumonia. You get that girl of yours out here to take care of you 'til you get back on your feet."

So Aunt Lou and Sarah moved out to the farm to nurse Grandpa back to health. Doc had sent him to bed with orders that he was to follow; Aunt Lou and I both knew he wouldn't obey if she wasn't there to insist.

I was sorry that Grandpa was sick, but it sure was a treat to have Aunt Lou and Sarah. Uncle Nat came out as often as he could. He missed his "two girls," as he called them, but he was awfully good about it.

It took Grandpa a couple of weeks before he was out of bed, and even then he had to lie down often because he was too weak to do much. In that time Sarah, crawling incessantly, had learned how to stand by herself. One morning I came into the kitchen, and she deserted her toy to crawl to me and pull herself up by my pantleg.

"Hey! You'll be running footraces soon!" She laughed, bouncing up and down on pudgy baby-legs.

I was really sorry to see Aunt Lou and Sarah leave for town again. The house would seem strange and empty with them gone.

By March winter had still not given up, and we were short of feed for the livestock. I worried about it each time that I doled out the hay and oats.

Grandpa must have sensed it, mentally measuring the feed each time I went out to chore. I didn't say anything to him about it but one morning at breakfast he surprised me.

"About enough for two more weeks, eh, Josh?"

I nodded silently.

"Can you cut back any?"

"I think I've already cut back about as much as I dare."

"Any chance of buying some feed off a neighbor?" Uncle Charlie asked.

"I've asked around some," I admitted. "Nobody seems to have any extra."

"We'll go out an' take inventory and see—" Grandpa started to say, but Uncle Charlie cut him short.

"You'll do nothin' of the sort!" he snorted. "Doc says yer to stay in out of the cold fer at least another two weeks."

"But Josh needs—" Grandpa began and Uncle Charlie waved his hand, sloshing coffee from his coffee cup.

"I'll help Josh," he said. "Nothin' in here that needs doin' today anyway."

Grandpa didn't argue any further, and after Uncle Charlie had washed up the dishes and I had dried them and set them back on the cupboard shelf, we bundled up and set off to take inventory.

It didn't take much figuring to know that we'd be short of feed. Uncle Charlie said what we were both thinking.

"If spring comes tomorrow it won't be in time."

By noon we had completed our calculations and headed back to the warmth of the kitchen. Grandpa had fried some eggs and sliced some bread. That, with cold slices of ham and hot tea, was our noon meal. I inwardly longed for Lou's full dinner meals again.

While we ate, Grandpa and Uncle Charlie juggled numbers and shuffled papers until I felt a bit sick inside. I wasn't sure where this all was leading us. I had never remembered a time when Grandpa and Uncle Charlie had had a tough time making it through the winter—but maybe it had happened and I just hadn't known.

In the end I was dispatched on Chester to take a survey among the neighborhood farmers. If there was any feed for sale, our dilemma would be solved.

But it wasn't that easy. Everywhere I stopped I found that the other farmers were in the same fix as we were. There just wasn't going to be enough feed to make it through this extra-hard winter.

With a sinking heart I headed for home. I decided to stop at the Turleys' on my way, more to see how Mary and her

mother were doing than to check for feed. Mr. Turley fed
several head of cattle and he didn't raise much more feed
than we did.

When Mary opened the door, she looked genuinely glad
to see me. I was even a bit glad to see her.

Mrs. Turley was busy darning some socks, and she sat
there near the fire rocking back and forth as she mended.
She seemed quite content and peaceful, even though she
must have known that her husband, too, was facing a tough
time.

"God will see us through, I feel confident about that," she
assured me. "He always has—even when we didn't have
enough sense to turn to Him—and I'm sure that He won't
desert us now that we are His children."

My mouth must have gaped open at her words, for she
looked at me and laughed softly.

"Don't look so surprised, young man. You young folks
aren't the only ones who need converting, you know."

"Mother has become a believer, too," Mary whispered, a
sense of awe filling her voice.

"Yes, praise God, thanks to the changes I saw in my Mary
here, after she took up with your friend Willie—and his
friend, Jesus."

"That's wonderful, Mrs. Turley," I stammered, still
amazed at her words. "And you're right—we do need to trust
Him."

Mary fixed some hot chocolate and cut some cake and we
sat at the kitchen table and shared bits of news from the
church and community. It seemed that she had chafed as
much as I had over the snowed-in Sundays.

"Did you hear the Foggelsons are moving?" she surprised
me by asking.

"They are? Where?"

"Mr. Foggelson has found a teaching position in a small
college somewhere near New York. He went there to see
about it in November and then he went back again over
Christmas."

"Did Mrs. Foggelson go with him?" I cut in.

"No, he went alone."

"But she was gone—" I started to say, thinking back to the empty house and unshoveled walk.

"She went to her sister's. She didn't want to be alone."

"I don't blame her," I muttered, annoyed again with Mr. Foggelson.

"Camellia said her ma enjoyed her visit even if—" started Mary, but I cut in again.

"Do you hear from Camellia?"

"Oh, goodness no," she answered, shaking her head as though the thought were preposterous. "I hardly know her. I've just seen her on the street, and she would never have anything in common with the likes of me."

Then Mary blushed as though she were afraid that her words had somehow put Camellia down.

"I mean, well—we are—she's educated and all, and I—"

I rescued Mary from her embarrassment.

"Where did you hear about her?"

"From Willie. He wrote all about it. He keeps in touch with Camellia."

"Oh-h," I said. But it was rather an empty sound. I heard from Willie—often—but he had never informed me of all of Camellia's plans.

"Does Camellia like school?" I asked, because I was sure that Mary was expecting me to say something.

"Hadn't you heard?" asked Mary, taken aback. "She quit."

"Quit?" Now I was really surprised.

"She was only there for a couple of months when she quit."

"Then what is she doing? Why didn't she come home?"

"At first she was afraid to tell her pa. And then she left New York and managed to get some kind of job. A telephone operator, I think, out East. So she stayed."

What a disappointment that must have been for Mr. Foggelson. And then I thought of Mrs. Foggelson. She would have been disappointed too, but not that Camellia had dropped out of Interior Design. Her disappointment would have been that Camellia didn't come back home.

"Well, Willie says that she likes her job just fine."

"So she writes to Willie?" For some reason, the news was both encouraging and threatening at the same time. I wished with all of my heart that Camellia felt free to write to me, but at the same time I was glad that Willie was keeping in touch. He had led Mary to become a Christian. Now it seemed he was working on Camellia. Inwardly I prayed for Willie's success.

But Mary was speaking again, with a bit of a laugh. "Oh, she doesn't need to write. Her job is right there in town."

"Right where in town?" I asked stupidly.

"Where Willie goes to college. She is right there, working on the town switchboard. Willie found the job for her."

Well, that was news to me. *Why hadn't Willie mentioned it to me in one of his letters?* And then I smiled to myself. Willie knew that I was already praying for Camellia. But he didn't want me to get my hopes up too soon. Her father had influenced her so strongly that it might take many weeks, even months, before she would see the light after so many years of antagonism toward Christianity, and I wouldn't ask any questions of Willie. He'd share with me when he felt that the time was right.

I suddenly realized that I had been sitting at Mary's table for longer than I had intended. It was already getting dark and there were chores to do. Besides, Grandpa and Uncle Charlie would be anxious for my report—even if I wasn't returning with good news.

"I've gotta get," I said to Mary and rose from the chair, reaching for my coat and cap all in one motion.

Then I thanked her for the refreshments, told her mother goodbye, and was on my way.

Mary saw me to the door.

"I'm sorry, Josh," she said quietly.

"About what?" I asked, startled.

"About the winter being so hard and all," she went on. "It's been a tough year for your first year farmin'—it was such a long, hard fall, and then—and then this," she finished lamely.

I was relieved at her words. I had been afraid that she had been going to say something about the Foggelsons. I had counted the days until Camellia would be done with her schooling and come back to our little town, and now with her folks moving, it didn't look like there was much chance of that happening. But I was relieved that Mary couldn't read my mind.

"Like your ma says," I returned, trying to sound brave and full of faith, "it'll turn out all right. God won't forsake us."

Mary gave me a big smile. She really had a very pretty smile, with white, even teeth and a dimple in each cheek.

I found myself smiling back. Maybe it was just that Mary's smile was contagious, or maybe I hoped she'd smile again. But for whatever reason, I did feel better as I mounted Chester and headed through the chilling weather for home.

Chapter 11

A Visit

We had to sell several head of cattle and all but two good sows. It would be a long time until we would get the herd and the pigpens built back up again, and I wondered if Grandpa and Uncle Charlie's decision was the right one. What if spring was just around the corner, and the new grass would soon be available? Maybe we would have been able, with careful rationing, to make it through.

It turned out that they had done the right thing. Another and then another storm struck, making it difficult to feed the few head of stock that remained. Neighbors who were trying to ration feed and make it through without selling off livestock lost most of their herd, and they didn't have cash from a sale to help them in rebuilding.

Our own stock diminished, and we lost one of our best milk cows when she got weak after giving birth to a fine calf. Grandpa and I sat all night with her, trying to keep her warm and pouring warm mash down her throat, but we lost her. I was sure we would lose the beautiful little heifer too, but Grandpa told me to carry her up to the kitchen, and Uncle Charlie took over from there. I don't know how he did it, but he pulled that little calf through. We all knew that she would be important in building up the herd again.

It seemed that all our days and nights were taken up with

fighting to save what Grandpa and Uncle Charlie had worked so many years to build. It just didn't seem right.

As soon as the weather began to warm some and I had a bit more time, I went off to town to see Uncle Nat.

"You know that fella you told me about who changes his crops around and such?"

He nodded. "Crop rotation."

"Yeah, rotation. Well, I was wondering if I might go and see him," I went on. "I've been wondering how he made it through the winter."

"Haven't heard," said Uncle Nat. "They mostly shop in Gainerville. Don't come here too often."

"Could you tell me how to get to his farm?"

Uncle Nat gave me directions. They sounded simple enough, and I headed Chester out of town. The day was bright, and the warmth of the sun shone down on the snow-banks. Chester was tired of winter and being shut up; he wanted to run, but I held him in check. I didn't want him to get all lathered up and then catch pneumonia. We had enough problems without losing Chester.

I found the farm without any trouble, though it took longer to get there than I'd thought it would. No wonder the family shopped in Gainerville—they were quite a ways from our small town.

Mrs. Thomas welcomed me cordially enough and informed me that her husband was down at the barn, so I declined her invitation into the kitchen and told her that I'd just go on down there to see him.

The Thomases were a big family. I saw three girls of varying sizes through the open kitchen door, and when I got to the barn there were four boys working along with their pa.

Randall Thomas was a big man, about forty, with a firm handshake and a kind twinkle to his eyes.

"Pastor Crawford's nephew, you say? Well, right glad to know ya, son," he said. "Sure did appreciate the trip yer uncle made out here to see Ma."

We chatted for a few minutes, my eyes traveling over the

barn and feed shed all the time I was talking or listening. It didn't look to me like there had been a feed shortage at this farm.

At last we got around to talking about the winter that we hopefully had just passed through.

"Sure a tough one," the big man said. "Worst I remember seein'."

I agreed, though it was evident that I hadn't seen quite as many winters as Mr. Thomas had.

"Looks like your stock made it through just fine," I said, nodding my head toward a corral holding some healthy looking cattle.

"Sold some of 'em way last fall," he surprised me by saying.

"You did?"

"Didn't want to wait until they only made soup bones," he went on. "A farmer has to think long-range. You figure about the worst that a winter can do to you and then plan accordingly. I figured out the feed I'd need to git each critter through to the end of May. By then the new grass should be helpin' us out some, even in the worst of years."

"We didn't have near enough feed to take us that far," I commented. "We had to sell several head."

"Too bad," he said sympathetically, shaking his head at our misfortune. "Heard some folks lost a lot of stock before they could even sell 'em."

"Grandpa sold early, before things got too bad," I informed him.

"That was smart thinkin'," went on the man. "The way I see it, a few real good, healthy head of stock are better'n a whole herd of weak, half-starved ones."

I could see his point.

"A herd can get themselves into pretty bad shape if you don't keep upgradin' 'em," he went on. "Then they can't take much cold an' poor feed."

I looked at his sleek cattle. They didn't look like they had just been through a tough winter.

A bird overhead drew my attention to the sky. The sun had already moved far to the west, losing much of the warmth of the day. It was a long ride back home, and I knew I should soon be making it.

"I really came to see you about your crops," I told Mr. Thomas. "I've a feeling that we would have fared much better this winter if our land were producing like it should be. Seems to me the hay that we took off was only about half as high or heavy as it could have been."

His eyes glinted with interest as they met mine.

"You just startin' to farm?" he asked.

I nodded, then corrected myself. "Well, I was raised on that farm but until this year I've been doin' the chorin', not the farmin'. Grandpa and Uncle Charlie have been farmin' the land. They aren't able to do it all now so—"

He cut in. "So you are farmin', and you wanta start out right?"

I nodded again.

"Well, yer a smart boy." His hand fell to my shoulder and he gave it a squeeze.

"A man can farm his land right out iffen he plants the same crop year after year. Only stands to reason. Why, even way back in the time of the Israelites, God gave a command that the land was to get a rest ever' now an' then. Same thing now. The land needs to rest—to build up its reserves agin." And then he began an enthusiastic explanation of how that was to be done.

I listened attentively. But the sun was moving on, and there was so much to learn. I felt frustrated and tense, and I guess that the man sensed it.

He stopped and his eyes followed mine to the sky. "There's too much to learn in one afternoon," he told me. "You come on back—as often as you like—and we'll pick it up from here."

I was glad he understood my need to be on the road and for the invitation to come to see him again.

"Tell ya what," he continued as we walked toward Chester. "You draw up a plan of yer fields. Mark what's been growing in each for the last seven, eight years, and then come see me agin. We'll see what ya should be plantin' come spring."

I could only stammer my thanks. I hadn't expected that kind of help.

"It's important to get good seed, too," the man continued. "Some farmers try to skimp on the cost of seed. But that costs 'em more than it saves 'em. Just like it is with livestock. The Bible says, 'Ya reap what ya sow.' Now I know that wasn't talkin' 'bout the grain and the stock as much as it was what ya sow in life, but the same holds true."

I hadn't thought of it that way before, but it made sense. It was a totally different approach to farming than I had been used to, but I promised myself that I would learn all I could about it. I thanked the man for his kindness and mounted Chester.

"Now that," he said appreciatively, running a hand over Chester's thick neck, "is good breedin'. Where'd ya get a horse like this, son?"

I explained that Chester had been a gift and reached down to rub his neck myself.

"First-rate horse!" the man exclaimed, making me beam with his praise.

On the way home I let Chester do a bit of running, though pacing him so that he wouldn't get too heated. But, like the man had said, Chester's good breeding showed. He could run a lot without getting winded or sweated up.

I had so much to think about that my head was swimming. Good seed, good blood lines, crop rotation—those were things that spelled out productive farming. And if a man was going to farm—even if it was just until God called him into his real life's work—then he ought to try to do a good job of it. I determined that I would find out all I could about doing the job right. Maybe the next time we had a bad winter we wouldn't need to suffer such serious setbacks.

Chapter 12

Looking for Spring

As my interest in farming techniques increased, I found some farm magazines with articles about crop rotation and pored over them. I sent away to the Department of Agriculture for free information that was mentioned in one of the magazines. I also asked them for information about building up the herd with proper blood lines. Soon pamphlets and sheets of information were coming back through the mail. I hadn't realized that there was so much to farming—or that the government had information available to help farmers. There were even agricultural courses that a fella could take at home. I had always thought that a man became a farmer because he had been born and raised on the farm and his pa needed help.

"You been gettin' an awful pile of mail lately," Grandpa remarked, glancing at the three brown envelopes and a magazine on the kitchen table.

"There's a lot more to this farming than I ever knew from just growing up on one," I commented. "You and Uncle Charlie made it seem so easy—"

"Oh, we did the best we knew how, and it worked pretty good most of the time," Grandpa interrupted, "but it looks to me like yer findin' some real important things 'bout farmin' in those magazines and booklets of yers. Charlie an' I've been readin' some of them, too," he said to my questioning look. "We're real glad yer learnin' some new ways to do things." From the shine in his eyes, I knew he meant it.

All through the chill of spring I worked with the stock, trying to keep them comfortably warm so their energy could be reserved for putting fat on their bodies. I still couldn't feed them the way I would have liked, but I made a warm mash for them on the cooler days, and kept the animals in the barns all I could. It meant more barn cleaning, but if the stock benefited, then it would be worth it.

On the sunnier days I let them out to pasture. The snow-drifts were slowly melting down and the horses led the way for the cattle, pawing back the snow in order to get to the left-over grasses from last fall. They even began to discover some fresh new blades of grass and that increased their desire to forage. The cows followed along behind, eating from the open spots the horses had left.

Every day I watched the sky, the snow patches, the weather, mentally measuring the feed I had left with the number of animals.

At night I read the magazines and information booklets, and I began to see what Mr. Thomas had been trying to tell me—there was a *system* to good farming.

I drew out a map of the fields, and Grandpa and Uncle Charlie and I went over them one by one. It was hard to remember every field back for seven or eight years. Sometimes Grandpa and Uncle Charlie disagreed about the crop that had been planted in a particular field and then they would have to sort through their thinking, trying to figure out which one was right. I decided then and there that an accurate account of each field would be kept year by year, along with the yield and any other information I might come up with.

Daily I checked my feed rations; I was still anxious that we wouldn't make it to the end of May. Finally we held a consultation and decided to sell off two more young heifers.

They looked small-boned, and we wanted to build up our herd with larger animals.

Instead of going to see Mr. Thomas alone, I suggested to Grandpa and Uncle Charlie that they come with me. I wanted them to hear firsthand what the man had to say, and to catch some of the excitement that he generated.

Thus on a mild day that held a promise of spring, we hitched the team to the wagon. The road was rutted and messy with dirty puddles of half-melted snow. The ground had not yet yielded up its frost, but still it was hard pulling for the team, and we didn't travel very fast. I drove and Uncle Charlie and Grandpa just sat there and soaked in the warmth of the sun. It had been a long time since they had been able to feel the sunshine.

It was just as I had hoped that it would be. We were welcomed with a handshake that made my hand tingle. I thought of Uncle Charlie and his arthritis and almost said something, but Mr. Thomas must have noticed the crippled hands, for he took my uncle's hand very carefully and didn't squeeze at all.

This farmer's enthusiasm was contagious. He talked about the importance of good seed, of planting in weed-free fields, of rotating the crops so that the soil wouldn't become depleted, and of fertilizing properly each year.

With the livestock kept in so much of the winter, at least we wouldn't be short of fertilizer. But I winced as I thought of the unpleasant task of scattering it over the fields.

With the help of Mr. Thomas, we analyzed our field situation and determined what crops should be planted where and which field should go fallow. The next step was to find a source of good seed grain. We were in the favored position of being able to afford a bit of good seed. Before we left, Mr. Thomas promised to come out and take a look at our livestock. He would help us sort out the best that we had and then figure out how to start developing better stock.

My head was whirling by the time we put down our coffee cups and headed home. We had so much to think about and so much to get done—even before planting time.

All the way home I was planning the days ahead. Even if spring was slow in coming, I still didn't think we'd be ready for it. There was so much to do to prepare the ground for the coming crop year.

Because I knew I would be more than busy once we could drive the wagon out to the fields, I decided to call on Mrs. Foggelson before I got too rushed. I was sorry to hear she would be leaving us. I guess I was even a little sorry to hear that he would be going. I wished with all my heart that he could realize that there was a God—a God who was in charge of the universe. How could someone with such a brilliant mind be so wrong about something so important?

With the move, I wouldn't be seeing Camellia again. I had hoped the day would come when both she and her mother would become believers. Mr. Foggelson, I knew, would be hard to convince after so many years of resisting the truth.

When I got to the Foggelsons' the snowbanks had almost disappeared off their front lawn. Little shoots of spring plants pointed up through the final snow covering the flower beds. I knew that Mrs. Foggelson dearly loved her flowers, and I wondered who would be caring for them after she had moved away.

In answer to my knock, Mrs. Foggelson came hesitantly to the door. When she saw me, her face lighted up and she flung the door open with a welcoming smile.

"Josh! So good to see you," she said, sounding glad that I had come. I sat twisting my cap in my hands in her parlor while she rushed to the kitchen for tea. Once we were settled with our cups, Mrs. Foggelson chatted about spring, about her garden, about the hard winter, and finally about Camellia.

"Did you know that Camellia quit studying Interior Design?" she asked. I had to admit that I did.

"Did you know that she is working as a telephone operator?"

I nodded again.

"I am so glad," went on Mrs. Foggelson. "I was so worried about her in New York. She got in with the wrong choice of friends almost immediately, and I was so worried."

I hadn't known about that.

"Does she like her work?" I asked.

"Not really. But it is good clean work with good people. That's the most important thing. Camellia might be smart, and she might be independent, but she has had no experience dealing with people. Especially the kind of people who would lead her into—into wrong living."

I hardly knew what to say. I just nodded my head in understanding, trying to balance the light flakes of pastry that didn't want to stay on my fork.

"I'm glad she's no longer in New York." Mrs. Foggelson sighed with relief.

I nodded again, then ventured, "But you must be sorry that she won't be close by when you move."

Her eyes dropped and she was silent for a few minutes. When she looked up again, her voice was very soft and low.

"I won't be moving," she said.

"There's been a change of plans?" I asked hopefully.

She just shook her head.

"But—but I was told that Mr. Foggelson got a teaching position in a small college—somewhere near New York City."

She let her eyes look evenly into mine.

"Yes," she said, "he did."

Silence.

"Well," I prompted, "then he has changed his mind after all."

"Oh no. He'll be going as planned."

"But—" I felt that we were talking in riddles. I stopped and waited for her to enlighten me.

"Mr. Foggelson will be going as he has planned," she said carefully, "but I will remain here."

I must have looked as shocked as I felt. I lowered my fork, scattering the last of my flaky pastry onto the white damask cloth. My face flushed hot with embarrassment.

Mrs. Foggelson reached over to pour me some more tea. I didn't have a voice to refuse it, even though I didn't think that I could drink another drop.

"Did you notice that the early tulips are already showing some?" Mrs. Foggelson asked, as though flowers were all we had been discussing since I had come in.

I nodded and cleared my throat again.

"I do so hope that we have a nice spring," said Mrs. Foggelson. "We can't have an early one—it's already too late for that, but I do hope it's a nice one. I am so tired of the dreary winter."

My eyes drifted to a picture of Camellia on the corner table. Mrs. Foggelson had lots of pictures of Camellia. Or were they Mr. Foggelson's? I looked about the room, my mind busy with embarrassing thoughts. Who would get the pictures? Who would get the brocade sofa? Who the silver tea service or the china cups?

What did folks do when they separated company, anyway? How did they ever go about portioning out a house? A home? I knew absolutely nothing about such things. But surely some rough days lay ahead for the Foggelsons.

Then another thought quickly came to my mind. With Mrs. Foggelson staying, maybe— "Does Camellia plan to stay on in the little town where she is, or—or might she come back home again?"

For the first time I saw the tears threaten to form. Mrs. Foggelson shook her head slowly, and suddenly her lovely, gentle face looked old.

"I don't expect so," she said candidly. "Camellia does not approve of my staying here. She has always been her daddy's girl, you know. If she goes to anyone, it will be to him."

I pushed back my chair and got to my feet. I felt so sorry for Mrs. Foggelson, but there was really no way I had of telling her. What could a young fella like me know about the way she hurt? How could I understand her reason for doing what she was doing? And yet, from the expression in her eyes I knew that her decision to remain behind was not made lightly.

"I'd best be going," I said hoarsely. "I still have things to do before I head for home."

She nodded in understanding and smiled. "You drop in anytime you can, Joshua."

I worried about her as I left. The tulips were appearing. Mrs. Foggelson would do just fine tending her beloved spring flowers. But who would be responsible for the many other things that needed tending?

The school year was almost over, and Mr. Foggelson would undoubtedly leave as soon as he was finished with his teaching obligation. That would leave Mrs. Foggelson totally on her own. She hadn't made many friends in town, either. She would need someone.

I had been brought up to not take kindly to neighborhood gossip, but I knew I had to talk to Aunt Lou. I knew she was busy with all her housework, the church, and baby Sarah, but Mrs. Foggelson would need some lady to talk to, and I figured that Aunt Lou would be just the one. I would help Camellia's mother all I could. I wouldn't be able to do much, but I'd pray. And I'd get Aunt Lou.

Chapter 13

Building

Days passed into weeks, weeks to months, and months to years. During those two years I worked hard, occasionally wondering if God would suddenly make up His mind about what He wanted me to do and move me on before I had things under control at the farm. If I had thought it through at the time, I would have realized that our heavenly Father doesn't do things that way.

With the help of Mr. Thomas, we got the quality seed that we needed and began our crop rotation. But there were no miracles. The land did not turn more productive overnight. By the end of the second year of our new program, Grandpa and I both hoped we were seeing some improvement in the yield—but maybe it was just that we had a wonderful summer for growing.

The herd, too, was slow to increase. We were able to purchase a few good animals from Mr. Thomas, and with the best from our own herd, we began to build for the future. But there were no quick profits on our investment, and we had to watch the farm budget carefully so we wouldn't overextend ourselves. The calves of that spring were the first real return we saw on our experiment; even Uncle Charlie had to come out to the barnyard to have a look as each one arrived. One of the cows had twins—both little heifers that would one day greatly strengthen our herd.

Aunt Lou's family was increasing, too. Jonathan Joshua joined Sarah at the parsonage. Sarah, at two years, was so excited that she could hardly contain herself. She called him "my brudder," and squeezed him each time she came near him. She wanted to share everything with him, from her fuzzy teddy to her breakfast toast. Aunt Lou had to watch her closely.

Willie came home the first summer, excited about how God was helping him with his studies and also his finances. He was just bursting with it all. But he ended up getting a summer job at Gainerville, so I didn't get to see him nearly as much as I would have liked.

He did talk with me about Camellia, however. She was still angry about her ma staying on in town. Willie said that Camellia had, at one point, become quite open and willing to listen to him as he tried to explain his faith. Then when she got the word about her folks, she completely turned it all off again. Willie said he didn't dare raise the subject after that. Everytime he attempted to say anything about Christianity, Camellia would remind him that her ma had at one time professed faith, and look what she had done to her pa. It wasn't fair of Camellia, we both knew, but people can reason in strange ways sometimes. Willie urged me to keep on praying, and I promised I would.

Mrs. Foggelson didn't stay on at the big house after Mr. Foggelson left town. She moved the few things that she still called her own into a single room at the boardinghouse in town and started to take in sewing. There were no silver tea services, no sets of fine china, no flower beds of tulips and roses—nothing but a sewing machine and the bare necessities of life.

But Aunt Lou did befriend her, and she responded. She often walked over to the parsonage for a cup of tea. Aunt Lou was even able to get her to start reading her Bible again—but she still wouldn't agree to come to church.

Willie didn't even come home the next summer. He had a job there near the school. I missed him, but I was really too busy to think much about it.

The harvest weather was better and the crops were in on time. The next winter was milder, too, and our few animals fared much better.

When spring returned, we planted again—this time with some of our own seed. We had chosen the best, spending many of our winter evenings gathered around the kitchen table carefully sorting out seed for planting. For Uncle Charlie it was difficult; his twisted hands found it almost impossible to handle small things.

That third year on the farm, the crop that we planted gave us the best yield we had seen for some time. The hay did especially well, and the pruned-back fruit trees began to bear again like they hadn't in years. We'd have several pigs ready for fall market, and the cattle, though slow to make a comeback, showed good quality in the small herd we were developing.

We were even able to put out money for paint, and in between the haying and the harvesting I was able to paint the buildings, including the house. It sure did make the whole farm look better.

I even began to think about a tractor, though I didn't mention it to Grandpa and Uncle Charlie. I knew they would be likely to think I was moving a bit too fast.

The crop was all in, and I had just celebrated my twenty-first birthday when I got a letter from Willie. We hadn't been writing quite as often as we once had, and I was pretty excited when I saw his handwriting. Willie was now in his final year at the college and would soon be a mission candidate. I knew he was excited about finding which foreign field God had in mind for him. I would have been excited too, but the thought of Willie graduating was a reminder to me that I was already four years behind in my preparation time. It would take a good deal of extra hard work once God showed me what He wanted me to do with my life.

I just had to write, Willie said, *and share with you the most exciting news. Camellia has become a Christian. I won't tell you any more about it than that, as she wants to tell you all about it herself when we come home for Christmas. Yes, you read that right. She is going to come home to see her mother. She knows that they must get some things straightened out between them.*

I couldn't believe it! It was just too good to be true. And yet I didn't know why I found it so hard to believe. I had been praying daily for several years for that very thing to happen. The tears began to fill my eyes, and I brushed them away with the back of my hand.

Camellia was a Christian! Camellia would be coming home at Christmas! It all seemed like a miracle. Praise God! Bless Willie!

I read on, the pages blurred now from the tears in my eyes.

We'll be there on Monday's train, Willie went on. *It arrives at 11:35 a.m.—or is supposed to. Remember how we used to go down to the station to watch for the train—not to see the train as much as to watch the people? Remember how some of them would get so irate because the train was always so late? Well, if it's that late on Monday, the 21st of December, I might understand for the first time why they acted as they did.*

My eyes slid to the calendar. The twenty-first was twelve days away. How would I ever be able to stand the wait?

Then I let out a whoop and raced the stairs two at a time to tell Grandpa and Uncle Charlie the good news.

Chapter 14

Sharing the News

I daydreamed my way through the rest of the day and tossed my way through the night. After such a long time, I would see Willie and Camellia again! Camellia had become a Christian!

The next morning I saddled Chester and headed for town. I couldn't wait to tell the good news to Uncle Nat and Aunt Lou.

Sarah saw me coming and met me at the door. "Hi, Unca Dosh!" she shouted before I even had time to dismount. She was still having trouble with her *j's*. And I was still waiting for the day when she could properly say uncle, though I must admit that I secretly thought "Unca" sounded pretty cute.

I picked her up and gave her a kiss on the cheek. "Hi, sweets."

"Have you been to da store?" she asked coyly.

"No, I came straight here to see you." I kissed her cheek again. Sarah knew that only shopping brought us to town midweek.

She squirmed to get down and I set her on her feet.

"Can I go wif you?" she asked, her big blue eyes pleading.

"I don't need to go to the store this time," I replied, feeling quite flattered that she wanted to be with me every moment that I was in town. "See?" I continued, pointing to Chester,

"I didn't even bring the wagon—just Chester."

Sarah's lower lip came out, and I thought for a moment that she would cry.

"I'm not going to the store," I repeated quickly, crouching down to her level.

The tears came to her eyes then, and she looked at me as she tried to blink them away. "Then how can you get candy?"

For a minute I didn't quite understand. Then it dawned on me. We came to visit *after* shopping, and we always had a small bag of treats for Sarah.

I couldn't help but laugh. The little beggar hadn't done a great deal for my ego, but at least she was honest and forthright.

"No candy this time," I said, tousling her curly hair. "Too many sweets aren't good for you. Where's your mamma?"

"She's wif brudder." The tears were already disappearing.

"Where?"

"In the kitchen."

"Is she feeding him?"

"No," said Sarah, shaking her head, "baffin' him." Then she suddenly seemed to remember that she was missing one of her favorite parts of the day. She turned from me and ran back through the porch into the kitchen, calling as she ran, "Mamma! Unca Dosh is here."

"Good," Aunt Lou answered, "Come right on in, Dosh." I could hear the chuckle in her voice.

I wasn't really uncle to Sarah and Jonathan, of course— I was cousin. But Aunt Lou was training the children to call me uncle since our relationship fit with that title better.

Sarah ran ahead of me and climbed up on a kitchen chair beside the table before I got there.

"See!" she pointed excitedly. "Brudder can sit now."

I couldn't believe how much he had grown just since the last time I'd seen him.

Aunt Lou smiled at me. "I'll be done here in a second; then I'll fix you some—whatever you want. Coffee, tea, milk, lemonade."

I nodded, reaching to chuck Jon under the chin. "How ya doin', big fella?" I asked him. He rewarded me with a grin.

"He's got a tooth already!"

"Two," corrected Sarah. "Mamma say two."

"Two is right," informed Aunt Lou. "Another one is just coming through."

Aunt Lou finished dressing Jon and handed him to me.

"Will he spit?" I would have taken him even if she had assured me that I was bound to get spit up on.

"He's good about that," she said instead. "Hardly ever spits up. And I haven't fed him yet, so you're safe."

Sarah and I played with the baby while Aunt Lou made hot chocolate and cut some slices of lemon loaf. "So, how is everyone?" she asked.

"Fine."

With her question and my reply, my good news again came foremost in my thinking.

"Uncle Nat here?" I asked. I had hoped to tell both of them together.

"No, he went out to the Lewises'. Mr. Lewis is the new Church Board Chairman and they have some things to discuss."

I was disappointed, and it showed.

"Did you need him?" asked Aunt Lou.

"Oh no. I—I just got some great news, and I wanted to tell both of you."

Aunt Lou's head came up from the stirring of the hot chocolate. Her eyes searched mine. "Well, you aren't going to make me wait just because Nat isn't here, are you?"

I grinned. "Naw," I said. "I wouldn't be able to stand it."

"Good!" she said emphatically and set the two cups of hot chocolate on the table. Then she reached for a glass partly filled with milk for Sarah.

"So?" she asked, passing me the lemon loaf.

"Just got a letter from Willie," I began.

"Did he get his assignment?"

"Nope. Even better than that."

"He's coming home?" said Aunt Lou, knowing I would be pretty excited about that.

"Yeah, for Christmas—but there's more."

I was really enjoying this little game. We had played it many times over the years, savouring some bit of exciting news and making it stretch out just as much as possible.

"And?" prompted Aunt Lou.

"Camellia is coming, too."

"Camellia?" Aunt Lou sounded almost as excited as I had been.

I nodded, my face flushed with the wonder of it all.

"Here?"

"Here! To see her ma."

Aunt Lou surprised me then. She started to cry. I think she started to pray too. She was talking softly to someone, and I knew it wasn't me.

I sat there hardly knowing how to respond; then I got up from my chair and gently laid Jonathan in the small bed that stood in the corner of the kitchen. I had the feeling that Aunt Lou might need me, but I still didn't know just what move I should make. Sarah brought me back to attention. She reached for Aunt Lou's hand, concern in her eyes.

"Mamma," she said. "Mamma, why you cry?"

Aunt Lou's face changed immediately and reached out to gather Sarah to her. She began to laugh softly. "It's all right, sweetheart," she assured Sarah. "Mamma is crying for joy. I'm fine. Really. It's all right."

Then Aunt Lou turned to me. "Mrs. Foggelson will be so happy. I told her I'd pray that Camellia would forgive her for what she had to do."

Had to do? The words echoed and reechoed in my mind. But I didn't ask questions—at least not then.

Then Aunt Lou put a hand on my arm and, looking at me with tears starting again, pleaded, "Oh, Josh! We've got to pray like we have never prayed before. We've got to pray that this time together might be a time when Camellia and Mrs.

Foggelson will realize how much they need God in their
lives."

"Well," I began, then abandoned all caution and rushed
on, "that's the rest of the good news. Camellia has already
realized that."

Aunt Lou's eyes got big and she searched my face to see
if I had really said what she understood me to say.

"You mean—?" she began. I nodded and then I gave a
whoop and reached out for Aunt Lou and we laughed and
cried and praised together.

"I've gotta go," I said to Aunt Lou finally. "I really didn't
have time for a trip to town today, but I just couldn't wait to
tell you."

"Oh, Josh," she said, "I'm so glad you came. That is the
most exciting thing that has happened since—since Jonathan," she ended with emphasis, and turned to her little son.

Jonathan sucked his fist noisily, reminding his mother
that he was still unfed. Aunt Lou kissed his forehead and
murmured something to him.

I heard a deep sigh from the chair beside me and looked
down into the forlorn face of little Sarah. She sighed again,
gave her little shoulders a shrug and turned her small palms
up.

"Nonny sweets," she said. "Nonny" was Sarah's own
word. As far as we could figure out, she meant "not any" or
"none" when she used it.

Both Aunt Lou and I laughed.

"Here," I said, fishing in my pocket. "Here's a penny for
your piggy bank."

Her face immediately lit up and she took the penny from
me, scooted down from her chair and called as she ran toward
her room, "T'anks you, Unca Dosh."

We heard the penny clink as it joined the others in her
bank. I grinned as I shook my head.

"That's an awful little beggar you're raising there, Lou,"
I said.

"Me?" responded Lou. "*Me?* Seems to me her begging has something to do with three men in her life."

I shrugged my shoulders, turned my palms upward, "Nonny sweets." I grinned and left.

Chapter 15

Homecoming

I suffered terribly waiting for the twenty-first. I kept trying to imagine what it was going to be like to see Camellia again. I wondered what the *new* Camellia would be like. She was a believer now. She would undoubtedly have a new softness, a new understanding, a new gentleness to her.

On the other hand, I hoped she hadn't changed *too* much. I would have been terribly disappointed if she had put her beautiful coppery hair into some kind of a tight bun or something. And I couldn't imagine her in strict, plain dresses either. Somehow they just wouldn't suit Camellia.

And Willie—it seemed like such a long time since I had seen him. He was bound to have changed. I thought I had grown away from Willie; that after my first awful months of missing him so, I had finally learned how to get along without him. But now that he was due home, all the old memories of our friendship returned, and I missed him more than I ever had.

A glance in my mirror told me that I had changed over the years, too. I tried to think back to how I had looked at eighteen and I couldn't really remember. I knew I had filled out since then. The clothes I had worn as a teenager just hung in my closet, waiting for someone to sort through them and discard them. But somehow it felt comfortable to have them still hanging there day after day, month after month, even though I knew I would never be able to wear them again.

I looked at my muscular arms. Shoveling the grain on the wagon and shoveling the fertilizer off had made me quite well developed, not the skinny teen I had been.

I rubbed the outline of my jaw. At seventeen I had shaved a few times, but not really because I had needed to. It made me feel rather grown-up to pull the razor over my face. But now I had to shave, and to my surprise it hadn't turned out to be nearly as much fun as I had dreamed it to be.

But apart from growing up and filling out and needing to shave rather than just wanting to, it seemed that there really hadn't been that much change in me. I was still the same farm boy that I had always been. And now Willie would be cityfied and book-learned.

I thought of other changes. We had all been a lot younger in more than years when we had last seen one another—kids, still thinking that life had only good things in store for us, I guess. Willie had his dream of being a missionary, and looked like he was about to realize that dream. Camellia had high hopes of becoming someone important in the field of Interior Design; for some reason I had never been told, her dream had gone sour. She had quit and taken a somewhat mundane job.

And I was still "treading water" as far as what I was to do with my life. After I finished straightening out the farm and getting Grandpa and Uncle Charlie cared for, that is. It was taking much longer than I had first thought, but things around the farm were slowly improving.

The only problem was, Grandpa and Uncle Charlie weren't improving. Grandpa was no longer a young man. Slightly stooped, he grumbled some when he went to climb anything and he grunted when he leaned over. I knew Grandpa had neither the strength nor the desire to run the farm again.

And Uncle Charlie really worried me. Week by week it was more difficult for him to handle the household chores, things like the hot pots and peeling the vegetables. More and more Grandpa was needed to help him in the house. For now I could handle the chores and most of the farm duties myself, but what would happen after God had directed me into my life work?

It weighed heavily on my mind. But Uncle Nat had told me time and again that God would make things clear to me one step at a time. When it was time for me to pursue my life's calling, God would have someone else to care for Grandpa and Uncle Charlie.

Still, I couldn't help but speculate just how God might do that. He could arrange for hired help. But that was so costly. Unless the farm really did *much* better on the new program, I didn't see how that plan would work. He could have one of the neighbors sharecrop the farm. The Turleys were our closest neighbors, and they were really struggling after the setback of the hard winter when they lost most of their stock. They wouldn't likely be able to afford it.

Or He could direct Grandpa to sell the farm. That thought really bothered me. I knew that after having put so much time and energy into making the farm more productive, I would have a tough time watching someone else take over—especially if that someone let it go back to the way I had found it! I'd have to do a lot of praying to be able to accept the sale of the farm.

But as much as I pondered the questions about the farm, even that failed to occupy my thoughts in the days prior to December twenty-first. Most of my thinking was of my two school friends and how we would feel about each other after so many years and so many changes.

I couldn't, of course, expect Camellia to come back home and consider me her beau. I mean, I had called it all off when she didn't believe as I did. Now it would take some time and some getting reacquainted to get things back to where they had been.

I was prepared for that. In my mind I began to list all of the things that young fellas do when they court. Flowers were hard to come by this time of year, but candy was readily available. A fancy necklace or a bracelet might be nice. I might even be able to find one that would match the ring I planned to buy later on.

One thing troubled me. I didn't know how long Camellia expected the courting to take. Would she expect me to come calling for a number of months, or could we take a shortcut since we had once been sorta sweethearts? I decided that I would just have to play that part by ear.

But the wait seemed forever.

I checked out the time of that train. Three times, in fact, I had checked just to be sure. I shaved especially carefully that morning and shined my Sunday shoes and pressed my shirt. Uncle Charlie had already ironed it, but he couldn't do the job that he used to do.

After getting myself dressed I fussed and polished and smoothed and patted and all the time I kept an eye on the clock. I caught Grandpa and Uncle Charlie exchanging grins and winks now and then, but I paid no mind to them.

I had intended to ride Chester; then I thought that maybe Camellia would be anxious for a chat. We could go for a little drive if I had the sleigh, so I harnessed up the team instead. I threw in a warm blanket so Camellia could bundle up and keep warm, then finally headed off for town.

I was still early, but I couldn't bear to wait another minute. Besides, I had to stop at the store to pick out a box of candy. I had looked a couple of times before but hadn't been able to make up my mind.

When I reached the store I tied the team and went back to the candy counter. The girl behind the glassed-in goodies looked at me with a friendly smile on her face. She was new in the store, but I recognized her as one of the Tilley girls. We had gone to school in town together but she was younger, so I hadn't paid much attention to her. I didn't know if she expected me to greet her now or not. I said "Howdy," but I kept it very impersonal.

I still didn't know which candy to buy, and after trying

to sort it out in my thinking for some time I finally blurted out, "If a fella brought you candy, what would you like best?"

She smiled rather coyly and picked out a large box of assorted flavors.

"That one?"

She nodded.

"I'll take it," I said and started to count out the money.

"Could you wrap it nicely for me please?" I asked, and she nodded and went into a back room. When she returned and handed me the package, I could see she had done a good job with the wrapping. I smiled and thanked her, took the package, and left.

It wasn't far enough from the store to the station to justify driving the team. Besides, some horses spooked at the train as it whistled and chugged its way into town. I didn't want to have my mind worried with skittery horses.

I kept checking the watch that Aunt Lou and Uncle Nat had given me for my twenty-first birthday. At one point I was sure it must have stopped, but when I put it to my ear it was still ticking.

"I'll just explode if it's late," I said to myself, kicking a small pile of frozen snow near the walk. I was immediately sorry. The snow splattered all over the toe of my boot, and I had to get down and wipe it off with my handkerchief. I hoped that the handkerchief wouldn't be needed any further. It sure wouldn't do to pull it out in public all smeared up like it was now.

My impatience reminded me of the childhood game Willie had referred to in his letter, and I smiled at the memory. We loved to watch the reaction of people in trying circumstances; only we had never realized that waiting for a late train was so trying.

I had been vaguely aware that the platform was crowded, but I hadn't really looked to see if I knew anyone. In fact, I hadn't really paid much attention at all until I heard a shout, "It's coming!" and then I saw Willie's folks lined up on the platform just down from me. Most of the other folks I knew, too, at least by sight. I spotted Mary Turley and I smiled to myself. Willie might insist that they were "just friends," but didn't her presence verify my suspicions?

That's nice, I thought to myself. *Mary would make a wonderful missionary's wife. She's kind and caring, even attractive in her own way.*

The train blew its whistle then and I forgot all about the crowd of people. I forgot all about Willie's family and even Mary Turley. All I could think about was Camellia. My throat got dry and my eyes moist and my knees felt so weak I felt that I might go down in a heap.

I saw Willie first. He looked about twice as big as I had remembered him. He had on a new coat. I unreasonably thought it strange to see Willie in clothes I hadn't seen before. He looked taller and broader and much more grown-up. But his smile was the same. He yelled, "Hi, Josh!" my direction; then he saw his folks and he turned from me and wrapped his mother in his arms.

I searched over the tops of heads to watch for Camellia to appear on the train steps. I was beginning to fear something had happened and she had changed her mind. Folks seemed to have stopped coming from the train, and then Willie broke from his folks and dashed back up the steps again and when he returned he was carrying a large suitcase and an armful of parcels. Just behind, looking even more beautiful than I had remembered, was Camellia.

Her coppery hair was still wisping about her face, but in a much more grown-up style than the flowing waves of her girlhood. Her coat was a soft green color and it accented her creamy cheeks and her beautiful eyes. For a moment my breath caught in my throat, and I couldn't move or speak. Her eyes sorted through the crowd that was left; then she looked directly at me and cried, "Josh!"

Somehow I managed to get my feet going, and I moved myself forward toward Willie and Camellia. Willie grabbed me first and as we hugged one another, I remember thinking that he was likely making an awful mess of the box of candy I held in my hands.

Then he let go of me and I was standing there facing Camellia. She laughed softly and reached up to my shoulder.

"You've grown, Josh," she said in a teasing voice. I just nodded dumbly.

Then she pushed herself up on her tiptoes and with one hand on the back of my head to tip it forward, she kissed me right on the cheek. I wanted to reach out and pull her to me and kiss her again, but I couldn't move. She moved back rather quickly and looked at me again.

"I gave Willie permission to tell you the good news, but I want to fill in all the details myself. I know you've prayed for me for a long time, Josh—and I thank you. But I still need your prayers. It isn't going to be easy to see Mamma."

I nodded again. I still hadn't managed to speak a word to Camellia.

"I wrote Mamma that I was coming, but I asked her not to meet the train," Camellia went on. "I have a feeling that our meeting might be a bit emotional."

I just nodded again.

"I promised her that I would go directly to her."

I swallowed and nodded the third time. Her plans were reasonable enough.

And then she laughed again and her beautiful hair swirled as she flipped her head. "We have so much to talk about," she said. "Can you come over about three-thirty? I'm just dying to tell you everything." She stopped and looked at me again. "And to hear how things have been going with you," she concluded.

Willie and Mary were chatting excitedly beside us, but I didn't hear a word they said. I was too filled with the sight of Camellia.

I finally found my voice. "Three-thirty," I promised, then remembered the box of candy that I still held in my hand. I thrust it forward. The bow was lopsided and the paper a bit crumpled, but I guess Camellia understood.

"Welcome home," I managed.

"It's so good to be home," she said softly, and her eyes were misty with unshed tears.

Before I could say anything more, Camellia and Willie were moving away. Camellia was being greeted by his family, and I knew that she and all of her belongings would be loaded in the waiting sleigh and driven off to see her mother.

I berated myself for not having the foresight to bring the team right to the station. *I* could have been the one taking Camellia home.

But three-thirty really wasn't that long to wait. And I had some shopping to do. Now the fancy jewelry not only seemed like a good idea, but a must. I hurried off down the street to give myself plenty of time. I couldn't remember being so excited or so happy in all my life.

Chapter 16

The "Call"

It took me quite a while to find the piece of jewelry that was just right for Camellia. There wasn't a necklace or bracelet in town with a ring to match, so I had to settle for something else. I finally found a chain with a cameo so delicate that it looked like it had been made just for her. It still wasn't as pretty as the wearer would be, but nothing could hope to compete with Camellia.

I had the clerk wrap it prettily, and I carefully tucked it into the inside pocket of my coat. I didn't want to take any chances on this special package getting messed up.

I finished my shopping shortly before three-thirty; feeling generous and a bit lightheaded, I decided to go buy Sarah some peppermint patties. Pocketing the candy, I headed for Aunt Lou's.

Sarah came running to meet me. "Hi, Unca Dosh," she called, then stopped and with great concentration started over. It was obvious that someone had been schooling her. "Unca-le-J-dosh," she managed, quite proud of herself for including the proper consonants. I picked her up and kissed her, congratulating her profusely for her accomplishment. She grinned, obviously pleased with the effect of her speech.

"You come to see us?" she asked.

"No, not really. I'm going to see another—lady." I blushed even as I spoke the words.

"But you're here," she corrected me.

"Not for long. I'm going to leave again."

"Why?" she asked, looking about to cry.

"Because," I answered gleefully, and even young Sarah should have caught the excitement that I felt.

"Mamma's in the bedroom feeding my brudder," she informed me.

"Well, I didn't come to see Mamma either," I answered.

"Why?" she asked again.

"Because," I said, drawing out the small bag of peppermint patties, "because I've been to the store."

She squealed when she saw the bag, knowing it was for her.

Aunt Lou called from the bedroom, "I'll be right out, Josh."

"Don't hurry," I called back. "I can't stay. I just dropped by with something for Sarah."

"You're heading home?"

I couldn't keep the excitement from my voice. "No, I'm on my way over to Camellia's. She wanted to see her ma alone first."

Aunt Lou was silent for a minute; then her voice came back softly to me.

"I'll be praying for you, Josh."

I didn't feel that I needed much prayer at the moment. All my prayers—and my dreams—had finally been answered. With a light step I started out for Camellia's, leaving the team tied in the churchyard. There wasn't much room for hitching horses outside the boardinghouse, and in the middle of the business day I was sure all of the room would be taken. I had been to see Mrs. Foggelson several times over the years since she had taken up residence in the rambling building.

I paced myself so that it was three-thirty-one when I was let into the boardinghouse hallway, and a moment later I was knocking on the door marked Number Four, my heart knocking just as hard on the inside.

Camellia answered the door. She took my hand and drew me in, exclaiming as she did so, "Mamma has just been telling me how kind you've been over the years, Josh. I will never be able to thank you."

But Camellia was wrong. The light in her eyes was more than enough to thank me for the little I had done.

She led me into the small, crowded room that served as Mrs. Foggelson's parlor, sewing room, and living quarters. It was even more crowded now, with Camellia's luggage and packages littered about the room.

"Please excuse our mess," Camellia said with a wave of her hand and pushed aside enough packages for me to find room on the sofa.

"I haven't had time to put things away," she explained, then sighed deeply. "And I have no idea where I'll find room to put it when I do get the time." A silvery laugh followed the words. It was so much like Camellia, so vitally alive— and unpredictable.

She turned to me then and looked me over carefully again. I blushed under her frank scrutiny and shifted uncomfortably.

"Oh, Josh," she began, "it is so good to be home."

I looked at this beautiful girl-turned-woman. All the things that I longed to be able to express died in my throat. I could only nod and mumble something about it being good to have her home again.

The dress she was wearing was unlike anything I had seen before. The collar was high and shaped to highlight her face; the bodice fitted her well-shaped waist and then flared out in a skirt that swirled as she moved. The sleeves came down to her wrists and tapered to a point over the back of her hand. The color was a soft blue-green, and it accented her hair and eyes beautifully.

"Where do we start?" she was saying. "We have so much to catch up on."

Then she swung toward me. "Oh, my! My manners. Let me take your coat and hat."

That special gift was secreted carefully in my coat pocket. I was twirling my hat nervously in my hands. She laid them both on a chair nearby.

"Would you like some tea?" she asked.

I nodded and said that would be nice. I really didn't care for tea, but I hoped by drinking it my tongue might be loosened.

"Mamma had to deliver some sewing," Camellia informed me as she went about putting the kettle on to heat on a electric plate on a small corner table. I hadn't even thought to wonder where Mrs. Foggelson was.

"She said she wouldn't be long."

I hoped that Mrs. Foggelson didn't hurry too much.

I watched Camellia as she put the tea in the pot and tapped her trim foot impatiently, waiting for the kettle to boil. Then she poured the water, drew two plain white cups from a small shelf, and set them on the table. There was hardly room for the cups and saucers, so after Camellia had poured the tea she brought me my cup.

"So, Joshua Jones," Camellia said in a teasing voice as she settled herself on the sofa beside me, "what have you been doing with yourself in the past million years?"

She emphasized the *million*, and I found myself agreeing. In fact, the last twelve days had seemed about that long.

"Nothing, really," I answered. "Farming."

"Mamma says that you are really knowledgeable about farming. That you are trying new things and—"

Secretly I blessed Mrs. Foggelson for saying something nice about what I had been doing at the farm. I was also excited to know that the two of them had been talking about me.

"Some," I cut in modestly. "But mostly I've been just waiting—an' praying."

Camellia's teasing eyes sobered.

"I know," she said in not much more than a whisper. "And I thank you."

She sipped her tea slowly and then set her cup aside. I was surprised to see that tears had gathered in her eyes.

"I honestly don't know why you and Willie didn't give up on me long ago. I was so stubborn. So blind. I don't know why I couldn't see that you were telling me the truth all the time. That you were only interested in my good.

"Do you know what I used to think?" she said after a pause. "I used to think, 'These people are dumb. They are unlearned and they have one thing in mind only. To get me to be just as dumb and dependent as they are so that they can chalk up points for saving the most people.' That's what I actually thought. It was a long time until Willie could convince me that he was really concerned about *me*. That he knew that without God I was lost, doomed for eternity, and he cared about *me*."

Camellia twisted a coppery curl around a finger as she spoke. With all my heart I wanted to reach out and take one of those curls in my fingers but I held myself in check.

"And then this—this thing with Mamma and Papa happened. I couldn't believe it. I just couldn't bear to think of them living in two houses, many miles from one another.

"I had always been a daddy's girl. You know that. Well, I was sure that this whole thing must be Mamma's fault. I hated her. Honestly, Josh, I hated her. I couldn't understand why she had done this to Papa. I knew that she had at one time believed God. I decided if she could do that to my papa and still pretend to have known the truth—even if Papa had forbidden her to go to church—then I wanted no part of religion."

She sighed and flipped her hair back from her face.

"Well, Willie still wouldn't give up. He kept inviting me to Bible studies and to church and we had lots of talks and arguments—" She stopped and laughed as she recalled.

"Then one day I did—I'll never know why—I did agree to

go to a Bible study with him. Well, that was the beginning."
She laughed again.

"And who would have ever dreamed the end?" she said
and her eyes shone. "I was home alone in my room one night,
reading over again the portion we had read in Bible study.
It was John 5:24: 'I say unto you, He that heareth my word,
and believeth on him that sent me, hath everlasting life, and
shall not come into condemnation; but is passed from death
unto life.' Suddenly I believed it. I really believed it! Somehow I understood. I was evil, I knew that, but I could, by
believing and accepting, pass from death to life.

"I have always been afraid of death, Josh. I wanted life.
So, alone there in my room, I turned my life over to God,
thanking Him that His Son had taken my condemnation,
just as the verse said. And now I am enrolled in Willie's Bible
college instead of working at the telephone office."

"Really?" I said excitedly. "I didn't know that."

"Really! And I am learning so much, but there is so much
that I don't know. Now I wonder how in the world I could
have been so—so stupid as to believe all of those lies."

"Blinded," I corrected.

"Blinded—and stupid," she finished with a laugh.

I set my cup aside. I had wanted to hear all about Camellia's conversion, but I wanted to talk about other things,
too. If she was enrolled in college then—

"So you aren't staying home here, with your ma?" I asked.
I didn't know if I was ready to hear her reply.

"Oh no," she answered quickly. "We only have a week."

"We?"

"Willie and I."

Of course. I had forgotten that they were both going to
the same school now. They would need to be back to classes
at the same time.

"Willie should be here any minute," she said, eying the
clock impatiently.

"Willie?" I puzzled.

She looked at me with a twinkle in her eyes. "We have

something to tell you," she said. "Willie made me promise not to tell until he came."

So Willie was coming. I thought of the gift in my coat pocket. If Willie was expected soon, I'd best get some business done. I cleared my throat.

"I was wondering," I began cautiously. "I mean, well— I've missed you so much—being friends—and I was wondering, seeing you won't be here long and will need to get back to classes, if we could make the most of the days you have, sorta get to know one another again?"

It was a long enough speech for a fellow as tongue-tied as I was, but not too articulate.

"Oh, Josh!" Camellia cried, clapping her hands together. "I was hoping we could. I might have been bullheaded and mean, but I did appreciate you, and the Christian stand you took, and your prayers over the years. I was hoping—"

"How about tomorrow?" I cut in. "Would you like to go for a ride tomorrow? Maybe visit the farm?"

Her face fell.

"Oh, Josh. I'm sorry, but tomorrow I am to go to visit Willie's folks."

Willie's folks!

"Sunday?" I asked.

She made a face. "And Sunday Willie is coming here to have dinner with Mamma and me."

It seemed that a good share of Camellia's time had already been spoken for. I was a bit annoyed with Willie. He could have her company when they got back to school. Still it was understandable that he should want his folks to spend time with her. They had been praying for her, too.

"Well—" My next invitation was interrupted by a knock at the door. And I still hadn't had opportunity to give Camellia her gift.

Camellia sprang to answer the door, and just as we had both expected, Willie stood there, a big grin on his face. Camellia took his hand, much as she had taken mine, and drew him into the room.

Only she didn't drop Willie's hand. She stood there holding it and I saw Willie's fingers curling possessively around Camellia's.

"I haven't told him," she glowed. "It was so hard, but I kept my promise."

Willie dropped Camellia's hand, and his free arm stole around Camellia's waist, drawing her to him.

"Josh," he said, "because you are so special to both of us, we wanted you to be the first one to know."

I felt my throat go dry.

"Camellia and I are going to be married," beamed Willie as a radiant Camellia reached up to place a hand lovingly on his cheek.

I was glad I was still seated on the sofa. I knew that my legs would never have held. The room seemed to whirl around and around, and I was being swept along helplessly by the tide of a dark, bottomless sea. Then, just before my head went under, I realized that I was being watched, that someone was waiting for an enthusiastic response from me regarding the announcement that had just been made.

Chapter 17

Christmas

"I do believe that we took Josh totally by surprise!"

Willie's voice roused me from my stupor. I looked toward the sound and saw Willie with his arm still around Camellia, his face lit up with a broad grin.

Camellia was smiling, too. She turned to give Willie a kiss on the cheek and then moved from his arm and came toward the sofa where I was sitting.

"Isn't it wonderful?" she enthused. When I was unable to answer she continued, "Didn't you even guess?"

I shook my head slowly, still unable to express myself in words.

Willie had joined Camellia and reached out his hand toward me.

"We wanted our good friend to be the first to know—after our parents, that is. I told my folks and Camellia told her ma, but that's all. We knew that you would be—"

"Oh, Josh," cut in Camellia, "I could hardly keep our secret. If it hadn't been for you, all the years of telling me that I was wrong, all the years of praying, I might never have become a believer."

"And I would be going to the mission field all alone," Willie added rather soberly.

The spinning room was beginning to slow down. I could

hear all the words that were spoken to me, but they still seemed unreal, and I wondered momentarily if I was having a bad dream.

Willie reached down and pulled me to my feet. He thumped me on the back and squeezed my left shoulder, and the pounding seemed to start my blood flowing again.

"I want you to be my best man," he was saying.

I found my voice then. I even managed some kind of a smile. "Sure," I said. "I'd be—I'd be honored."

Willie slapped my back again. "Caught you by surprise, eh?"

I nodded. "Sure did," I was able to respond honestly. "Sure did."

And then Willie, interrupted often by Camellia, began a full account of their courtship and Willie's proposal and Camellia's acceptance. I didn't want to hear it, not a word of it—but I could hardly get up and walk out on my two best friends. I grinned—shakily, I'm sure—and nodded from time to time, and that seemed to be enough to satisfy them.

I wondered how soon they would be married, but I didn't ask. I figured that I'd find out eventually.

"And we're going to be married right here, in our little church," Willie was saying.

I did my smile-and-nod routine. Uncle Nat would have the wedding.

"I just wish we didn't need to wait," Willie went on.

"Wait?" I echoed.

"For Camellia to finish her training. I'll be done in the spring, but Camellia is just starting. She won't take four years of straight Bible courses, but she will do a couple of semesters and then go on to take classes in nursing, so that means a long wait."

I was about to ask when the wedding would take place when Camellia cut in.

"It's going to seem such a long, long time," she moaned, "but I know God can help us. Willie will put in one term on the field; then when he comes home for furlough we'll be married, and I will join him."

"How long is a term?" I found myself asking.

"Four years," groaned Camellia.

"*Four years?*" I didn't mean to say the words. They just popped out.

Willie's arm went around Camellia again. "Four years," he repeated. "A long time—but I can wait."

I didn't see anything particularly heroic about that, though I didn't say so. I would have waited four years for Camellia, too.

"Jacob waited seven years," Camellia reminded us, and Willie added quickly, "And then worked another seven."

They looked at one another and smiled. The whole scene was getting to me. I knew I had to get out of there. I pulled my watch from my pocket and studied its face. The time really didn't register, but I tried to look surprised and mumbled something about the fact that I really had to be going.

"I know you're awfully busy," said Willie, "but we have a whole week here at home. I hope we can get together often while we're here. We really would love—"

So that's the way it was. Willie and Camellia. It was no longer *me* for either of them. It was *we* now, and I was still just *me*.

"Yeah. Sure," I said. "Lots of time. We'll—we'll get together."

"That sleigh ride, Josh," cut in Camellia. "That sounds like so much fun. I hope we can work that in."

"Sure," I said. "Any time. Just let me know when it will work out."

"Hey," said Willie, pounding me on the back again as I shrugged into my coat, "I've got an idea. Why don't we ask Mary to join us? Make it a foursome? What do you think?"

Camellia was already clapping her hands. "That would be so much fun!"

"Sure," I said, trying hard to grin. "Sure—whenever you can make it."

I managed to escape then. I found my way out of the boardinghouse into the crispness of the winter afternoon. The cold air helped me get my bearings. Already the sun was hanging very low in the sky. Snow was beginning to fall in light, scattery flakes. The cold wind promised that choring would be much harder over the next few days.

But I didn't care. In fact, I welcomed the extra work. Something good and solid and demanding would help my whirling brain to sort through the news that had just been enthusiatically shared.

I still couldn't grasp it. Here I had waited and prayed for years for Camellia to become a Christian so that—so that I could feel right about asking her to be my girl. Then she finally becomes a Christian, and what happens? My friend—my best friend Willie gets there first.

I shook my head to clear it; then I realized that I was hurrying down the street in the dead of winter with my coat flapping in the breeze instead of buttoned like it should be. I fumbled with the buttons. There seemed to be a bulge in the right pocket. Then I remembered—the cameo! My special gift to Camellia. My face felt hot, even with the wind blowing cold against it. *I would have given it to her, too!* exploded through my mind. If Willie hadn't come when he did, I would have made a complete fool of myself. To think I had been dumb enough to look for a piece of jewelry with a ring to match. My face burned with humiliation.

Aunt Lou called to me as I unhitched the horses from the churchyard, but I just waved at her and shouted that I didn't have time to stop.

The horses were in a hurry to get home to a warm barn. They had been standing in the cold for too long. I let them pick their own speed and didn't even bother driving them much.

Grandpa and Uncle Charlie were both in the kitchen when I came in from settling the horses to change my clothes for choring. They seemed to look me over real good, and I was determined that I wasn't going to let anything show.

"Your friends get home?" asked Grandpa.

I nodded.

"How's Willie? Changed much?" put in Uncle Charlie.

I shrugged. "Some," I said.

"Like how?" This was Grandpa again.

"He's—he's bigger. Broader. Almost done his schooling. More grown-up, I guess."

"Grown-up," chuckled Uncle Charlie. "Never thought that Willie would actually grow up."

I defended Willie then—after all, he was my friend. "Well, he is," I said stubbornly. "He's even gonna get married."

"Willie?"

"To whom?"

"To Camellia," I stated boldly.

I hadn't wanted to say that. In fact, I hadn't even been able to admit that truth to myself yet, and now saying it out loud made me feel like I was shutting and bolting a door to a beautiful room.

"Camellia?"

"You mean, the teacher's daughter? The one that just became a Christian?"

I nodded, my eyes dropping to my boots.

I could sense Grandpa and Uncle Charlie both studying me, and then their eyes turned back to one another. I didn't even look up, just moved toward the stairs.

"I gotta change for chorin'."

I heard a chair scrape behind me and knew that Uncle Charlie was shifting his position. Then he called after me, "When?"

I didn't even turn around, just kept right on toward the stairs. "Not for four years."

I heard Uncle Charlie shift again and Grandpa give his little, "Whoo-ee," and then I heard Grandpa say plain as day, though I knew he wasn't speaking to me. "Lots of things can happen in four years." But I kept right on going up the stairs and didn't even look back.

Not until I finished with chores and supper, alone, in my

own room in my own bed, did the truth of it all really hit me.
Camellia is getting married. Getting married to Willie. There
would never, never be a chance for her to be my girl. I had
no right to even think of her in that way again.

Before me flashed her beautiful face framed by coppery
curls. Her eyes flashed excitedly and her cheeks dimpled into
a winsome smile. I turned away from her, shutting my eyes
hard to blot out the image, and I buried my face in my pillow
and cried like I hadn't done since I'd been a kid.

And after I had cried myself into exhaustion, there was
nothing else for me to do but pray.

For seven days I would be forced to see Willie and Camellia—together. For seven days over Christmas. There
would be special parties, special services, extra outings—
and I would be expected to be there. They would be there,
too, arm-in-arm, smiling. There was no way to avoid them.

I thought of faking illness, but I knew that wouldn't be
honest. I thought of not going, but that would get me nothing
but questions to be answered. I thought of saying I was too
busy, but the farm work was so completely caught up that I
could hardly use that excuse. In the end I did what I knew I
had to do. I went. I went to the Christmas program, the Carol
singing, the party at Willie's. I even took that sleigh ride
with Willie, Camellia, and Mary Turley. Somehow I managed to make it through.

We spent Christmas with Uncle Nat and Aunt Lou again.
I thought about giving her the cameo, but I knew I just
couldn't do that. I ended up shamefacedly taking it back,
exchanging it for a brooch for Aunt Lou, cuff links for Uncle
Nat and a tie bar for Uncle Charlie. That just about finished
off my Christmas shopping. I added a tie and suspenders for
Grandpa and then went looking for something special for
Sarah and Jonathan.

I didn't call on Mrs. Foggelson on Christmas Day. I knew
she was having her own Christmas that year. With Camellia
home, she sure didn't need me. It was good to see the two of
them doing things together. Mrs. Foggelson had even joined

Camellia in church on Christmas Sunday. It turned out to be a good Christmas, after all. Maybe God really was answering my prayers. I was even able to think about other things than Camellia—but that took some effort.

Before we knew it, it was time to gather at the train station and say goodbye to Willie and Camellia. I wasn't sure when I would see them again. Willie said that he might be going overseas right after he finished his schooling, and Camellia planned to stay right on at the school, working in the summer and then going back to classes in the fall again.

Mrs. Foggelson was at the station, too. She was awfully sad to see Camellia go. They hugged one another for a long time and cried a lot. It made me feel a bit teary too, but there was no way that I would let it show.

Willie shook my hand, then hugged me. Camellia hugged me too.

"You've been such a special friend, Josh," she whispered. "I have one more thing to ask of you. Take care of Mamma. Please. She needs someone so much."

I nodded in agreement but I couldn't help but wonder why Camellia couldn't stay and take care of her ma herself.

And then they were gone. Several people stood around watching the train pull out. Some of them, I imagined, would stand right there, like they always did, until the train was just a distant dot. I didn't. As soon as the big wheels began to turn, pulling it forward, I turned my back on it and headed for Chester. I didn't need to prolong the agony. I had been through quite enough.

Chapter 18

Going On

I did a lot more growing up in the months that followed. I did more praying, too. For the first time in my life I began to realize what it really meant to turn my life—everything about it—over to God for His choosing.

As I thought about it I realized that Camellia had made the right choice. Willie was a strong Christian, intent on service for God. At first I had a difficult time picturing a woman like Camellia with her hair pulled back in a strict knot, wearing a plain dark dress and high leather boots against snakes and scorpions. Then I began to think of the real Camellia, the one that God wanted her to be—gentle, caring, compassionate—a worthy and life-enriching companion for Willie.

As I prayed and sorted through things, putting them in their proper perspective, I came to a quiet peace with the way that God was working out the situation.

I turned my attention back to the farm just in time to begin the preparations for spring planting.

I knew that we still had a long way to go in reaching maximum production, but we were on the right track. The farm looked good. The freshly painted buildings and fences glistened with each sunrise, and the fields were free of weeds and thistles—as much as we could possibly keep them. The spring calves were the best-looking bunch I had seen in my years on the farm. They looked strong and healthy, and I knew they would make good stock.

So as I entered that springtime, I began it as a more mature person, physically, emotionally and spiritually.

Grandpa seemed to pick up a bit that spring as well. He seemed to feel better, and he looked better, too. Maybe he was finally getting rested and built up after so many years of carrying the load. At any rate, he did almost as much of the farming as I did, and when I protested, he just waved it aside, saying that he never felt better in his life.

Seeing Grandpa in good form made it even harder for Uncle Charlie. He wanted so much to be as involved, but he wasn't able to do much at all.

But Sarah was allowed to pay us frequent visits, and she was good for Uncle Charlie's morale. She was going on five and quite grown-up. She spent most of her time in the kitchen with Uncle Charlie, running his errands and helping him. Being with Sarah kept his spirits up—and she was amazingly helpful, too.

A late, slow spring put everything behind for the whole growing season. Aunt Lou came out and planted the big farm garden; that saved us time and worry. And it wasn't a burden for Aunt Lou, for she loved to be involved in making things grow.

At last, some warm, dry weather arrived, and the crops took off. They seemed to sprout up overnight.

I was going through the last of the summer months thinking only of farming and a very occasional trip to the fishing hole when Grandpa caught me off guard. We were heading to town for some supplies, and I was thinking ahead, looking forward to some time with Jon and Sarah and a piece of Aunt Lou's berry pie.

"Been thinking of offering to board the schoolteacher this year."

I swung around to face him and must have given the reins

a fair jerk, for the team threw up their heads and switched their tails in protest.

"You what?" I blurted.

"The teacher," repeated Grandpa as though I hadn't heard. "I hear they need a place for her to board."

"And what would we ever do with a teacher?" I said tartly. "We can barely manage ourselves."

"That's the point," said Grandpa.

"You aren't expecting a schoolteacher to teach all day and then come home and cook supper for—"

" 'Course not! 'Course not!" said Grandpa holding up his hand and shaking his head.

"Then what did you mean? How's boarding the school-teacher going to help us out any? And, besides, where would we put her?"

"We have extry bedrooms."

"Where?"

Grandpa looked at me like I wasn't even thinking. "Well," he said. "Iffen you recall, there is one just down the hall from you."

"*Aunt Lou's?*" I threw out the words as if Grandpa was considering treason.

"Was," corrected Grandpa. "Was Lou's. Don't recall seeing her use it for some time now."

He was being a little sarcastic, but I had it coming. Still, I couldn't imagine him letting someone else use Lou's room.

"Sarah uses it," I argued.

Grandpa thought about that for a few minutes before responding. Then he nodded his head. "I've thought on that," he said. "She does come now and then, an' I sure wouldn't want to be discouraging that." He chuckled. "Isn't she somethin'?" he went on. "You see the way she helps Charlie?"

I had seen all right. And yes, Sarah was really something.

Grandpa laughed again, an outright guffaw. "The other day she was even bossin' him. 'Uncle Charlie,' she says, 'I think you are making your biscuits too stiff. Mamma adds more milk.' " Grandpa laughed again.

"So what did Uncle Charlie say?" I asked, hoping to side-track the conversation and, thus, the ideas.

Grandpa laughed again. "He winked at me over her head and said, 'You're jest like your mamma—a little take-over.' But he loved it, I could tell."

But Grandpa wasn't ready to let his wild idea drop.

"Sarah could sleep on a cot in the corner of the kitchen," he said.

"In the kitchen? What kind of sleep would a child get there in the kitchen with you and Uncle Charlie having your coffee and talking over the affairs of the day?"

Grandpa thought about that for several moments. I had scored a point.

"You're right," he admitted at last. "I'll sleep in the kitchen."

"You?"

That idea was almost as preposterous.

"I've slept on the cot before," Grandpa informed me rather firmly.

I bit my lip. I didn't want to say something that I shouldn't.

"You still haven't listened to my full idea," Grandpa went on.

"There's *more*?" I hadn't intended to sound smart, but it sort of came out that way. I felt my face getting a bit red and knew that I wasn't fair to Grandpa.

"I'm sorry," I apologized. "Go ahead."

Grandpa cleared his throat. He seemed to feel that we were finally getting somewhere.

"You know Charlie is having a bad time getting things done around the house?"

I nodded. We all knew that. *But a teacher? A teacher would have no time and no inclination to help out three—*

But Grandpa was going on. "Well, for some time now I've been a thinkin' that what we really need is a hired girl."

A teacher? A hired girl? I didn't say it, just thought it, but Grandpa must have read my mind.

"Now, a teacher's much too busy teachin' and preparin' lessons to be able to help around the house, but to get in someone else, well that poses a problem too. Can't hardly ask a young girl to be moving into a house alone with three men, now can ya?"

I agreed, but I still couldn't follow Grandpa's line of reasoning.

I shrugged and spoke to the team. Somehow I felt hurrying them might also hurry Grandpa to his point.

"So iffen we have the teacher there; then it won't be a problem getting a hired girl," he said quickly.

"What?" Was Grandpa really proposing not one woman to live in, but *two*?

"Simple!" said Grandpa.

"And where you planning to put *her*?" I said in exasperation.

"Well, we got two spare bedrooms as I see it," Grandpa said flatly.

Gramps' room! The bedroom off the kitchen. I hadn't even thought of it—and I was surprised that Grandpa had.

I guess he read my mind again, for he kept right on talking. "A room is for use, Boy. Not for a shrine. One of the girls can have the upstairs bedroom and the other the downstairs bedroom. I don't much care who takes what. They can work that all out between themselves. Thing is, Charlie needs help, and you and I just don't have the time to spend in the kitchen. Yer ideas for better farmin' have been good, real good. But they also take lots more work to put into practice— you know that. Fella can't be two places, doin' two jobs at the same time. Now—"

But I cut in. I had better control now and spoke evenly and softly. "Have you talked to Uncle Charlie?" I felt that Uncle Charlie would be on my side.

"Not yet," said Grandpa. "Wanted to run it by you first."

Grandpa gained some ground there. It flattered me that he had chosen to confer with me. But I was still far from convinced. I thought the idea an awfully dumb one but I knew that rather than arguing with my Grandpa, I should be logical.

"What makes you think the schoolboard would okay a teacher staying with us?"

"Already talked to the board chairman," Grandpa admitted.

"And if the teacher refuses?"

"She hasn't. Says that our place is right handy to the school and that it is easier to board where there aren't lots of kids."

So this wasn't some sudden idea of Grandpa's. He had already been working—behind our backs.

"Where could we find a hired girl?" I asked next, hoping that I'd stumped him on that one. There weren't many girls in our area old enough to know how to keep house who weren't already keeping their own.

"Mary Turley," said Grandpa simply.

"Mary? Mary is needed at home."

"Not anymore. Her ma is feelin' just fine now, and she has two younger sisters who—"

I was beat on that point. I tried for another. "Who says she'd be willing to come? She—"

"She did," Grandpa said frankly.

I felt anger starting to rise. There sat Grandpa throwing out this wild and crazy scheme; he hadn't talked to either Uncle Charlie or to me before, but he had been sneaking around arranging the whole thing without us even having the chance to have our say. I had never known Grandpa to do anything so—so *backhanded* before.

"Now wait," I said, holding up a hand just as I had often seen Grandpa do. "Do you think you've been fair? I mean here you are, making all these arrangements and not even asking Uncle Charlie or me what we think about the whole business. Don't you think you should have asked our opinions? After all—"

"I'm askin' ya now," Grandpa said smoothly.

"Well, it sounds to me like it's a little late," I continued. "I mean you've decided—"

"Nothin's decided."

"But you've *asked*."

"Just put out some feelers," argued Grandpa.

"Quite a few feelers, I'd say," I countered rather hotly.

"Two," said Grandpa. "Whether we could keep the teacher as a boarder, and whether we could hire some help."

"We haven't even talked about whether we can *afford* the help," I reminded him. "What if we don't get a crop? What if—"

He surprised me by chuckling. "That's the beauty of the whole plan," he said. "The teacher's board pays the hired girl."

I could only stare. He had thought of everything.

I shrugged my shoulders helplessly. I still didn't like the idea one bit. What in the world would we do with two women in the house? We'd been alone for so long, and we knew our own routine and our own quirks. How in the world would we ever make room and allowance for two women? How could Grandpa even think that it would work?

Yet it was still his house.

Then I thought of Uncle Charlie. It was true that Uncle Charlie found it difficult to care for the household, but at least he still had the feeling of being useful. Uncle Charlie would never agree to having a woman come in and take over his kitchen. Why, that would be admitting that he was no longer of use to anyone. Uncle Charlie would never be shelved like that.

"As I see it," I said, mustering my courage, "it's Uncle Charlie's decision. The house is his area."

"Exactly!" agreed Grandpa enthusiastically. "That's just the way I see it, too."

Did Grandpa know Uncle Charlie better than I did? I slapped the reins over the rumps of the horses.

Chapter 19

Arrangements

Sarah pleaded to go with me to the store, and I couldn't resist the coaxing in her eyes.

"You know your mamma and papa don't want me to buy you candy," I warned her as I led her by the hand to the waiting team.

"I know," she said cheerily. "But I like being with you anyway, Uncle Josh."

She could say her *j's* just fine now. She could also sweet-talk. I looked down at her to read her face, but she seemed so open and honest. I gave her hand a little squeeze.

"I like being with you, too," I assured her.

"Where do we go first?" she asked me as I lifted her up onto the wagon seat.

"First the feed store, then the post office, then the hardware, and finally the grocery store."

She seemed quite satisfied with our schedule.

The feed store didn't take long; I threw the two bags of supplement feed on the wagon and we moved on.

The post office was busy, and I had to stand in line for some time before the clerk handed me our mail. But it was worth the wait. There was a letter from Willie. I tore the envelope open before I even returned to the wagon and began to scan the pages.

"What you got? A letter for you?" asked Sarah from her perch on the wagon seat. I nodded and climbed up beside her.

"Are you gonna read it?" she asked further, which I thought was rather a silly question seeing as I was already reading it. And then I realized that the questions were to remind me that Sarah was there beside me, feeling a need for a little of my attention. I reached out and took her tiny hand.

"There's a new catalog there," I told her. "Would you like to look at that while I read my letter?"

Sarah responded immediately to the arrangement.

"We'll both read our mail," she said with a grin.

The first part of Willie's letter was all about Camellia and their courtship and their plans and what a wonderful person she was and how she was learning and growing. I skimmed quickly since it was still rather painful.

Then I came to a part that really interested me. Camellia had been to call on her pa.

It was really hard for her, wrote Willie. It was easy to understand that. I knew how Mr. Foggelson felt about religion of any kind, and I could imagine how he would respond to Camellia's becoming a believer.

But as tough as it was, she was glad that she went, the letter went on. *For one thing, it helped her to understand her ma more. When we were home at Christmas Camellia tried hard to pursuade her ma to go back to her pa. Her ma just shook her head but wouldn't say anything about the situation. It made Camellia very angry with her mother.*

You can imagine how surprised Camellia was to discover that Mrs. Foggelson didn't stay behind—she was left behind. Mr. Foggelson has no intention of ever resuming the marriage. He told Camellia that her mother had written him twice asking him to forgive her for not being the kind of person she should have been, and for going back on her Christian faith. She also told him that she would be willing to try again, but that she had to be free to be the person that she had been before their marriage—that is, to be a Christian.

Camellia finally realized that Mrs. Foggelson would have joined Mr. Foggelson again, but this time she would stand firm for her Christian beliefs. Needless to say, he would not agree. In fact, he had quite made up his mind long before he moved from town. He told Camellia that he had found someone "more compatible." It nearly crushed Camellia.

For a moment I was filled with such anger toward Mr. Foggelson that I could feel my whole body tensing. Then I remembered that he was a victim of lies and deceit. His false beliefs had taken him down a dark and destructive path. Only God could reach out and open his blinded eyes.

But I felt terribly sorry for Camellia. How shattering it must be to discover the truth about the father that she had idolized for so many years.

Willie's letter went on. *What I really wanted to share is my good news. I went before the Missions committee last week and was accepted. I am to leave for South Africa in two weeks' time. Of course, I go with mixed emotions—I can hardly bear the thought of leaving Camellia behind, but she is tremendously brave about it. She—*

And Willie's letter went on and on about the virtues of his betrothed.

A tug on my sleeve reminded me that I had company. Sarah's little eyes turned wistfully to me.

"Are you done yet?" she asked, handing the catalog back to me. "I am."

I nodded. "I'm done, too," I told her. I still had so much to think about, but now wasn't the time. I would reread the letter and digest the contents.

"Now where?" asked Sarah as I lifted the reins.

"The hardware store. I need some nails, and some rivets for fixing harness."

Sarah waited patiently while I made my purchases; then we crossed the street to do the grocery shopping.

As I was depositing the parcels in the wagon, Sarah looked at me with big blue eyes. "Do you need anything at the drugstore?" she asked.

I shook my head and was about to lift her up to the wagon seat when I stopped. "Why?" I asked her.

"Just wondering," she said with a shrug of her slight shoulders.

A light began to dawn. "You know I told you I couldn't buy any candy today."

"I know," she said with a sigh, then added sweetly with a tip of her head, "but I didn't know if a soda counted or not."

"Come on, you little trickster," I laughed, taking her hand. "I don't know about a soda, but an ice cream cone might be okay."

Sarah skipped along beside me, her tiny face beaming.

"I want chocolate," she chirped. "What do you want, Uncle Josh?"

When I reached Aunt Lou's to drop off Sarah and pick up Grandpa, I heard part of a conversation that wasn't really intended for me. I was not trying to eavesdrop; I just came in quietly and at the wrong time.

Sarah had not come in with me. As we pulled into the yard we saw little Janie Cromstock from two houses down. She and Sarah were good playmates, and Janie called Sarah to come play on her new swing.

"Can I please, Uncle Josh?" she pleaded.

"You have to ask your mamma," I reminded her.

"Can you ask for me? Please?" Her big eyes searched mine. "You're going in anyway," she reminded me.

"Okay," I said, "I'll ask, but if it isn't okay with your mamma I'll call you and I'll expect you to come right home."

She nodded in agreement, and tripped off after Janie.

Thinking Jon might be taking his afternoon nap, I entered the back porch quietly and upon hearing my name hesitated a moment.

". . . does Josh think?" Aunt Lou was asking Grandpa.

"He kicked about it," Grandpa said in reply and then chuckled. "But he didn't make as much fuss as I feared he might."

"So are you going to do it?"

"Have to get it past Charlie first," said Grandpa matter-of-factly.

"And do you think he'll agree?" Again Aunt Lou was questioning.

"Just depends." Grandpa sounded thoughtful. "I know Charlie needs the help, but I also know that Charlie needs to be needed. Iffen he can give up his household duties and still feel he's not just in the way, then I think he'll agree. It all depends."

I knew then that Grandpa had talked to Aunt Lou about his crazy scheme. I was about to burst in and tell Aunt Lou what I thought of the idea when I heard her say, "It would be such a load off my mind. I worry so about you—all of you. I think that it would be the wisest thing you've ever done." Then she added quickly with a chuckle, "Since you had me, of course."

I knew better than to let my feelings be known. I hesitated, made a bit of noise with the door and tapped lightly before entering the kitchen. Grandpa and Aunt Lou were sitting at the table sipping from tall lemonade glasses. Lou looked up.

"Did you sell Sarah?" she asked playfully.

"She begged to go to Janie's to try a new swing. I said I would ask your permission. Can she?"

Aunt Lou shrugged and laughed. "I guess she already has," she responded.

"Yeah, but I told her I'd call her if it wasn't okay with you."

"It's okay. At least for a few minutes. I'll call her after she's had a while to play."

Aunt Lou rose to pour me some lemonade and pushed the oatmeal cookies toward me.

"Get everything ya needed?" asked Grandpa, and I nodded.

"Got a letter from Willie, too," I said.

"Any news?"

I turned to Aunt Lou, who had asked the question. I wasn't one for sharing gossip, but I felt that she had to know some of the information Willie's letter had contained.

"I know how you have been seeing Mrs. Foggelson and studying the Bible with her and all since she started coming back to church again. I know that you are excited about the way she is seeking to let God lead in her life again." I hesitated. "But I also know that you, like me, have been a little impatient with her for not going back to Mr. Foggelson."

Aunt Lou nodded, her big blue eyes intense.

"Well, Camellia went to see her pa and found out the truth," I said. For a minute I couldn't go on. I felt like I was about to disgrace the whole Foggelson family.

I swallowed hard. "It wasn't Mrs. Foggelson's idea to stay behind. Mr. Foggelson had found a—a 'more compatible' someone."

I heard Aunt Lou's little gasp; then her eyes brimmed with tears. "The poor soul," she whispered.

"She has never breathed one word about it," Aunt Lou continued. "It must be terribly hard for her—folks all blaming her, and all."

I nodded.

Just then Jon came toddling into the kitchen. His eyes were still bright from sleep, his cheeks rosy, his hair rumpled, and his clothes slightly damp from the warmth of his bed. He dragged a lumpy-looking discarded doll of Sarah's behind him, and when he saw us his eyes lit up and he headed straight for Grandpa.

He was met by open arms and Grandpa cuddled him close and kissed his flushed cheeks.

"Thought yer goin' to sleep the whole day away, Boy," Grandpa told him. " 'Fraid I wasn't even goin' to get to see ya."

Jon pointed at the cookie plate and then squirmed to get down. I was flattered when he ran to me as soon as his little legs hit the floor. But my ego didn't stay inflated for long. It turned out I was closer to the cookie plate than Grandpa, and as soon as I picked the little boy up, his pudgy hands were grabbing for all the cookies on the plate.

I settled him back and removed all of them except one, then pushed the plate out of reach. He lay back against me, munching on his cookie.

I held him until he was finished and then Grandpa stood.

"We best be gettin' on home, Boy," he said, studying the clock on the wall.

"Have you started the harvest yet?" asked Aunt Lou as Grandpa retrieved his stained, floppy hat.

I knew that the question was directed at me. I was the one who made the major decisions at the farm now. Grandpa and Uncle Charlie, without really saying so, had handed the reins to me.

"Not yet. Hope to get going just as soon as it dries."

"Expecting a good yield?"

"Looks good so far, if the frost just stays away."

"Suppose you'll be pretty busy for the next few weeks then," continued Aunt Lou.

"Expect to be."

"We won't be seeing much of you for a while."

"Only on Sundays."

"Maybe I can sneak out and give you a hand now and then," she continued. "Sure would be nice if you had some regular help."

I couldn't help but smile. I hoped Aunt Lou didn't think that she was being subtle. It was all too obvious what she was hinting at. It was also obvious that she was on Grandpa's side.

Chapter 20

Changes

Grandpa didn't waste much time in presenting his idea to Uncle Charlie. I had wondered just how he would go about it. I figured he'd wait until I had gone up to bed and the two of them were sitting around the kitchen table having their last cup of coffee. I even had the notion that I'd like to slip down the stairs and sit on the step to hear his presentation.

But he didn't choose to do it like that. Perhaps he knew Uncle Charlie so well he decided that if it came to pick and choose, Uncle Charlie would side with him rather than me.

At any rate, we had just finished up the chores and the supper dishes and Uncle Charlie had hung the dishpan back on the hook when Grandpa came right out with it.

"I suggested to Josh today on the way to town that it might be a good idea to get ourselves a little help."

My mouth fell open at Grandpa's directness, but it didn't seem to throw Uncle Charlie a bit. He never missed a beat, just went right on swishing the dishrag over the checkered oilcloth that covered the table.

"What kind of help?" he asked.

"Cooking. Cleaning. Help with harvest and canning."

"Anyone in mind?" asked Uncle Charlie. I was surprised when I looked at him that he had a twinkle in his eye.

"Mary Turley," said Grandpa.

"Oh," said Uncle Charlie with the same twinkle, "then I take it yer dependin' on Josh to bring in the help, not you?"

I started to say something but Grandpa cut me short. "What're you aimin' at?"

"Aimin'? Why, I ain't aimin' at anything. I thought the way you started off that *you* was aimin' to bring a wife fer someone into this here house."

"A wife?" snorted Grandpa. "Fiddlesticks! Josh can get his own wife."

"I'm glad we're all clear on that," I said with a bit of good-natured sarcasm.

"Then what did you have in mind?" asked Uncle Charlie, giving the table one final lick with the cloth.

"A hired girl," stated Grandpa.

"Oh," said Uncle Charlie. Just "Oh."

"Mary Turley says she's willin' to work out fer a spell," went on Grandpa.

"Still think my idea is a more permanent arrangement," smiled Uncle Charlie. "How long do you expect a girl like Mary Turley—an' at her age—to be available to babysit three bachelors?"

"Ain't babysittin'!" protested Grandpa. Uncle Charlie didn't even seem to notice.

"How do we pay her?" he asked, and I held my breath. Here was the craziest part of Grandpa's scheme in my way of thinking. Wait until Uncle Charlie heard the whole story!

"We board the new teacher," said Grandpa matter-of-factly.

Those words stopped even Uncle Charlie. He straightened up as far as his crippled back would allow and looked sharply at Grandpa.

I could see the questions in his eyes, but he didn't voice them. Grandpa took the opportunity to hurry on.

"We got two extry rooms here. The schoolteacher gits one, the hired girl the other. That way neither of 'em are put off 'bout living in a house with three men. Then we take the board payment from the teacher an' pay the hired girl. Works good for everyone."

Uncle Charlie snorted. I knew he had some doubts.

"Where's the flaw?" asked Grandpa a little heatedly.

I could hold back no longer. I leaned forward in my chair and laid my hands out on the table. "It's a crazy scheme. A crazy scheme," I informed Uncle Charlie. "We've got no business filling our house up with women. We've gotten along all of these years, and I see no reason why we still can't. They'll just come in here and start putting on white tablecloths and asking us to take off our work boots an' starching all the shirts an'—"

I hadn't run out of steam, but Uncle Charlie moved away from both of us. I thought that he was dismissing the whole crazy idea, but he was just hanging up the dishrag.

As he approached the table I started in again. "I know it's tough for a while at harvest, but harvest doesn't last long, and we can always get help. I'll bet we can get Mrs.—"

"I hope not," cut in Uncle Charlie. "Nearly drove me crazy, that woman."

"Then we'll get someone else. There are lots of women who cook out at harvest time. We'll—"

"Name me a few," said Grandpa. "Remember the time we had finding someone last harvest?"

It was a sobering fact. We'd had a tough time. All of the neighborhood women were busy with canning and their own threshers every fall.

"Well, we still don't need someone to live in, to stay here and change everything about our lives. We have our own way of doing things. Our own routine. We wouldn't feel like it was even our house anymore."

Uncle Charlie lowered himself slowly to a chair at the table. I could see that his back was giving him pain again.

"And where would we put them?" I went on. "The upstairs bedroom is Aunt Lou's and the downstairs one"—I waved at the door of the small room off the kitchen—"is Gramps'."

Uncle Charlie didn't seem to be listening to me and Grandpa wasn't saying much.

"We don't even know what this here new teacher will be like. She might—she might be—disgusting."

I couldn't think of anything specific to charge her with.

Uncle Charlie raised his eyebrows at that and turned his gaze toward Grandpa. Grandpa understood his unanswered question and responded.

" 'Course I checked her out. I wouldn't want her spittin' tobaccy through the cracks, now would I?"

Uncle Charlie's mustache twitched slightly, and I knew he was hiding a smile.

"She's from a good Christian home over near Edgeworth. She's got high recommendations, and hopes to become part of our church. She asked about stayin' in a Christian home when she applied here," went on Grandpa.

Still, Uncle Charlie looked a bit doubtful for a moment. He spoke for the first time for several minutes.

"Her folks would okay her staying on here?"

"We been checked out," said Grandpa frankly.

"What family would let their young girl stay with three old bachelors?" I argued. "Surely they—"

"Let's do it," said Uncle Charlie.

I couldn't believe my ears.

"What do *you* think, Josh?" Uncle Charlie surprised me by turning to me. Hadn't he been listening to a thing I'd said?

"He said it was your kitchen, and your decision," Grandpa answered on my behalf.

"Did ya?" Uncle Charlie looked squarely at me.

"Yeah, but—" I began.

"Then let's do it," Uncle Charlie said again, emphatically. "I think it's time we had a woman here in this house."

I was stunned. I couldn't believe Uncle Charlie had let Grandpa talk him into something so foolish. Then it began to dawn on me that Grandpa really said very little. I had been doing most of the talking, and I might have just talked myself right into a corner.

I was even more sure of it when I was preparing for bed and Uncle Charlie's voice drifted up the stairs to me.

"I'm worried some about Josh," he said.

"Meaning?" asked Grandpa.

"Did ya hear 'im? Sounded like he was scared of women— or else thinks thet they are a curse rather than a blessin'. Talked all thet silly stuff 'bout them messin' up his routine."

"Yer right," sighed Grandpa. "Guess Lou is the only woman Josh has really had much to do with."

"Hope we ain't too late," said Uncle Charlie and there was genuine concern in his voice.

I reached out and closed my bedroom door. Uncle Charlie's words made me angry, but I began to feel a little scared, too. Did I really feel that way about women? Was it too late? It was true that I dreaded the thought of sharing the house with two of the opposite sex. But why? I loved Aunt Lou. I loved little Sarah. I loved—or *had* loved—Camellia. What was I afraid of—fighting against?

And then it hit me. Uncle Charlie hadn't been so fond of the idea, either. I could see it in his face. But without even arguing, he suddenly said, "Let's do it." And I was the reason. Uncle Charlie might not like a woman coming in and taking over his work and putting him aside. He might even feel useless and not needed any longer, but he was willing to sacrifice the way he felt because he was worried that I was developing unhealthy attitudes.

I decided that I wouldn't say any more about the arrangements and when Grandpa asked me straight out, I told him to go ahead and do whatever he thought it wise to do. I was pretty sure what that would be.

Mary moved in first. Grandpa went over with the wagon and fetched her. She came with a small suitcase and a worn trunk, and I helped Grandpa haul it in.

I didn't feel too uncomfortable with Mary. After all, we had known one another since we were kids and she was a member of our church and all. It wasn't like a complete stranger coming into our home. Still, it was hard to adjust to having someone else around.

She chose the downstairs bedroom because she said it made more sense for her to be close by the kitchen, seeing as she would spend most of her time there.

We didn't need to worry about Mary knowing how to do household chores. She had been tending house since she had been a young girl. She moved in and took over that kitchen, yet I had to admire her—she didn't push Uncle Charlie aside. She asked this and praised that until she had him wrapped around her little finger. Didn't take long, either. And she found him more little jobs to keep him busy than I would have ever thought possible.

They worked there in the kitchen together. I could hear them chatting and chuckling each time that I came near the house. It upset me a bit at first; then I began to realize how good it was for Uncle Charlie, and I started being thankful for Mary and her sensitivity.

Special treats began to show up at the table, too—green tomato relish and fresh butter tarts and oven-baked squash. Uncle Charlie had done his best, but Mary's best was definitely better.

Mary had been there only a week when the new teacher moved in. Mary had already busied herself cleaning Aunt Lou's room until it sparkled. She even put in a small bouquet of fall flowers and a tiny basket of polished apples.

Mary may have been excited, but I was dreading the thought of sharing a house with a finicky schoolmarm. I made myself scarce the day Miss Matilda Hopkins was to arrive. I wanted to be as far away from the house as possible. It wasn't hard to do. We were already into harvest, and I had lots to keep me busy.

Miss Hopkins was to arrive by train, and Grandpa volunteered to go to the station to meet her.

I worked late. The supper hour came and went, but I purposely paid no heed to it. It was still light enough to work the field, so I just stayed working. Even though my stomach was complaining bitterly, I disregarded it. I was in no hurry to get to a kitchen overrun by women.

When it finally got too dark to see any longer, I unhitched the team and headed for the barn. I took my time watering and feeding the horses and giving them a good rubdown. A quick check around told me that Grandpa had already cared for the other chores. Normally I would have been thankful for that but tonight it just irked me a bit. I would have no excuse to escape the kitchen.

I finally headed for the house, grumpy and dirty. I knew that introductions would be in order and I also knew that I sure didn't look my best. Well, I didn't care. What difference could it make to some old-maid schoolteacher anyway?

I stomped my way across the back veranda and pulled open the door. The kitchen was empty, except for Grandpa and Uncle Charlie.

"Working kinda late," Grandpa observed.

I stared around rather dumbly, but I wasn't going to ask any questions. I crossed to the corner basin and poured myself a generous amount of water. Then I set about sloshing it thoroughly over my hands and face. When I looked up I noticed that I had also sloshed Mary's well-scrubbed floor and spic-and-span washstand. I pretended not to notice and moved toward the table.

"Where's supper?" I asked, trying to sound casual.

"Supper was over a couple hours ago," said Grandpa, not even looking up from the paper he had gotten from somewhere.

"Yours is in the warmin' oven," said Uncle Charlie around his section of the paper.

I crossed to the warming oven and found a generous serving. I hadn't realized how hungry I was until I saw and smelled the food. Even so, my good sense told me that it had been much better a couple of hours earlier. Well, that wasn't Mary's fault, I had to admit.

"Where'd you get the paper?" I asked around a mouthful.

"Matilda," said Grandpa.

"Matilda?"

Grandpa just grunted.

"You mean Miss Hopkins?"

"She wants to be called Matilda," Grandpa spoke again.

There was silence as the two men pored over their sections of paper. We didn't often see a daily paper in our house, and they seemed to find this one awfully intriguing.

"So she arrived, huh?" I tried again.

"Yep," said Uncle Charlie; then he began to read aloud to Grandpa some bit of interesting news that he found in the paper. Grandpa listened and then they read in silence again. Soon it was Grandpa's turn to read some little bit to Uncle Charlie. I expected they had been sitting there doing that all evening, and I also expected they would keep right on doing it. Some exciting evening this was going to be!

I finished my meal and pushed my plate back. "Any dessert?" I asked.

Grandpa waved a hand that still clutched the paper. "On the cupboard," he said and never even looked up.

I found fresh custard pie—my favorite—and helped myself to a large piece. That was one nice thing about having Mary around—she sure could bake a pie! I had a second piece.

The two men still hadn't stirred except to read to one another every now and then. They were really enjoying that paper.

My eyes traveled to Mary's bedroom door. It was open a crack and I could see a neatly made bed and the small desk in the corner of the room. It was clear that Mary was not at home.

Finally I could stand it no longer.

"Kind of quiet," I said. "Where is everyone?"

Grandpa lowered his paper just enough to look over it at me. "We're here," he said simply.

I blushed and ran a hand through my unruly hair. But Grandpa still didn't pay much attention to me.

Uncle Charlie folded his section of paper carefully and

laid it on the table beside him. He removed his tiny round reading glasses.

"You know," he said to Grandpa, "I think Matilda's right. A man does need to read the daily paper to keep up with what is goin' on in the world. I can't believe all the things I've learned in just one night."

Grandpa grunted his agreement and shuffled through some more paper.

I carried my empty pie plate to the cupboard and piled it with my dinner plate—more out of habit than consideration. I was about to say I was going up to bed when Grandpa looked up.

"Oh, Josh," he said, "Mary took Matilda over to her folks to introduce her. I let them hook Chester to the light buggy. Hope you don't mind."

I just stood there letting the words sink in. Not only were they taking over my kitchen and my house, but my horse as well! Anger welled up within me, but at the same time I realized how juvenile it was to feel the way I did. I calmed myself, muttered some kind of reply to Grandpa, and started to climb the stairs.

"Goin' to bed already?" Uncle Charlie called after me.

"Yeah," I replied, not even turning around. "It's been a long day."

"Sure you don't wanta read a little of the paper here?" Grandpa asked.

I was in no mood for reading Matilda's paper, I can tell you that, but I didn't say so to Grandpa. At least not in those words.

"Think I'll just go on to bed," I said instead.

But I couldn't sleep. I lay there tossing and turning and listening for the sound of buggy wheels.

They finally came. Then I could hear their whispering voices as they approached the house after putting Chester in the barn. They sounded like two young kids sneaking in the back door, but they weren't kids and they weren't sneaking in. Grandpa and Uncle Charlie were waiting right there at the kitchen table where I had left them.

I could hear the rattling of cups as Mary made them their before-bed coffee and then there was general chatter and some soft laughter and finally footsteps on the stairs, and then the house was quiet for the night.

I still couldn't go to sleep. It seemed that life was out of control. All the old familiar ways seemed to be changing. Even our familiar routines seemed to be gone.

Then I thought of Grandpa and Uncle Charlie and that last cup of coffee, and I realized that things weren't really so different after all.

Chapter 21

Harvest

I wasn't in a much better mood when I awoke the next morning. I hadn't had much sleep, but mostly I had my mind set to be ornery.

I got up early and went out to get a start on the chores. First, I went to check out Chester. I couldn't find anything to get upset about so I went on down the lane to let the cows up for milking.

It wasn't long until Grandpa joined me at the barn.

"Yer up early, Boy," he greeted me. "You musta had a good sleep last night."

I didn't make any comment.

"How's the cuttin' comin'?" Grandpa went on.

"Fine," I answered truthfully.

"Does it look as good as we hoped?"

I had a hard time keeping the excitement out of my voice. The crop was a good one. It looked like it would beat any yield we'd ever had.

I forgot my sour mood momentarily and concentrated on sharing the report of the field with Grandpa. His eyes took on a twinkle as I talked and his mustache twitched in satisfaction now and then.

By the time I had finished raving over the crop, Bossie was bellowing to be milked. We parted ways; I went on to slop the pigs and Grandpa grabbed the milk pail.

I had almost forgotten my dread of going in to breakfast and was thinking instead about the tractor I was dreaming of purchasing. I was walking toward the chicken coop with my head down when I unexpectedly bumped into something.

Now I had walked that path many, many times over the past years, and I knew very well that there shouldn't be anything in that spot one could bump into.

My head came up and my hand reached out at the same moment. And there, standing with her back to me and looking around as startled as I had been, was a slip of a girl.

"I—I'm sorry," I mumbled, pulling my hand back from her shoulder where it had landed. "I wasn't watching where—"

What's she doing standing there in the middle of the path, anyway?

She was shaking her head back and forth, the startled look giving way to mirth. "It's my fault. I shouldn't have been standing here in the way—I've been drinking in the sunrise."

Drinking in the sunrise? I had never heard it expressed like that before. My eyes shifted to the east and was astonished to realize the sunrise was worthy of such an expression. I stood staring at it—seeing it like it was the first time.

"It is pretty, isn't it?" I mumbled. "Could I help you?" I asked. "Are you looking for someone?"

She looked puzzled at my question, then began to laugh. "You must be Josh," she said, rather than answering my question.

I nodded, but I didn't see what that had to do with anything.

"I'm Matilda," she said simply, extending a small hand.

My mouth must have hung open at that. I had expected an older woman, with hair swept severely back from her face and a dark blue, long-skirted dress with lace at the throat and sleeves. But I was facing a girl who looked no more than seventeen, with bouncing, light brown curls and sparkling eyes. She wore an attractive dress of green calico.

"Matilda Hopkins," she said again. "The new teacher."

I still couldn't speak.

Then Matilda changed the subject completely, her enthusiasm spilling over in a candid fashion. "I love your horse, Chester. He's just bea-u-ti-ful." She stretched the word out, emphasizing each of the syllables.

"I've never seen such a beautiful horse," she went on, "and Mary says that he is saddle broken too. I'd love to ride him sometime. I'd just love to!"

She took a breath and finished more slowly, "If you wouldn't mind, that is."

I found myself shrugging my shoulders and saying "of course not," and Matilda was beaming her joy and thanking me profusely.

"But I must get in. I'll be late for school on my very first day if I keep dawdling."

And she was gone, tripping down the path in a most undignified way for a schoolteacher.

I could only stare. And then I began to laugh. What had I been so upset about? Why had I been so scared? There was absolutely nothing to fear from this child. It wouldn't be much different than having Sarah around.

I chuckled all the way to the chicken coop.

Friday night there was a Youth Group meeting at the church. Grandpa suggested, rather slyly, that I might want to break from the field work a bit early and take the girls. At first I was going to decline, and then I figured that it really wouldn't hurt. I knew Uncle Nat felt that the farm work shouldn't really come before my church commitments, so it might be wise for me to follow Grandpa's suggestion.

I should have taken the team, but I guess I just wanted to show Chester off a bit. The light buggy would be faster than the heavy wagon, but the light buggy also was very crowded for three people. It was really only made for two.

Grandpa raised an eyebrow when he saw me hitching up. I knew what he was thinking.

"Won't be a problem," I said before he could comment. "Both those girls are so small I could fit four like 'em on that seat."

Grandpa didn't say anything.

When I went in to do my last bit of slicking and polishing Uncle Charlie looked at me good-naturedly.

"Figure you might take a bit of teasin' showin' up with two girls, Josh?" he asked me.

His question caught me completely off guard.

"Girls?" I said. "One of them is Mary and the other—well, she's just a kid."

Uncle Charlie looked surprised at my assessment but he didn't say anything.

I was ready before the girls were, which was always a puzzle to me. I had put in a full day in the field, helped with chores, hooked up Chester, and still had to wait.

Mary showed first. She really did look nice, and I remembered thinking again that Willie really had missed out—until I also remembered just who Willie had ended up with.

What is taking young Matilda so long? I fidgeted mentally, and then she came down the stairs and I couldn't believe my eyes. Her hair was gathered up away from her face and her dress was much more grown-up and I suddenly realized that she wasn't a kid after all. I also realized that Uncle Charlie had been right. I might be in for some ribbing.

But it was too late to unhitch Chester and hook up the team. The girls had already expressed their delight in the light buggy. I gathered up the reins and climbed aboard. I wasn't sure how to arrange the seating.

Mary took charge.

"Why don't you sit in the middle, Josh, and one of us will sit on each side," she suggested.

I don't exactly know why I agreed, except I didn't know what else to do, so I sat down in the middle, a girl on each side of me. It was crowded, and I guess they feared they might get bounced right off the seat with Chester moving along like he always chose to do. Each grabbed an arm and hung on for dear life. I was hard put to handle the reins.

I began to sweat. I didn't know if I had the right to pray over such things or not, but I sure was tempted. I hoped there would be no fellas outside watching me arrive. But it was a warm fall night, and the fellas always stood outside and laughed and talked and watched everybody as they came.

Oh, boy, I thought, *have I gone and done it now!*

I wanted to put the blame on the girls. What did Mary go and fix herself up like that for, and why had Matilda chosen *this* night to look her age? How old was she, anyway? And why hadn't she warned me?

But I couldn't blame them. Chester and the buggy had been my idea. I'd wanted to show off my horse—and look where it had gotten me!

Mary and Matilda didn't seem to have any problem with the arrangement at all. They laughed and chatted all of the way to town, with me right there in the middle.

At one point a big jack rabbit sprang from the grass in the ditch, making Chester shy to his right. It wasn't dangerous; Chester was a well-trained horse, and it only startled him.

But it was enough to give the girls quite a scare. They grabbed hold of me with both hands. Matilda screamed. Mary was the first to recover; her face got a bit red and she released her firm grasp and mumbled some sort of apology.

Not Matilda. I think she actually enjoyed the excitement and would have been glad to repeat it again. She wasn't like any schoolteacher I'd ever had!

When we got to the church, a whole yard full of fellas were standing there waiting. I could feel my face color and knew that I was really in for it.

The girls didn't seem to notice.

"Josh!" one of the group called out. "Got your rig pretty full, don't you?" But to make matters worse, I knew I had to get the three of us down from that buggy seat. I didn't know quite how to be gentlemanly about my situation. I mean, how was I to hold Chester and assist two young women—one on each side of me—to descend in ladylike fashion?

Uncle Nat arrived to save the day. He was just coming from the parsonage to the church, and he stopped and greeted us cheerily, then took Chester's bridle and eased him in to the hitching rail. When I was able to release the reins, I excused myself and crossed in front of Mary so I could jump to the ground; then I was able to help the girls step down one at a time.

While the boys were still shuffling and gaping, Mary was calmly introducing Matilda to Uncle Nat, a job that I should have been doing.

The entire evening was pretty much what I expected. The fellas razzed me the total time. I sweated my way through the social, vowing to myself that I'd never be caught in the same predicament again.

When we were about to go Aunt Lou called me aside. "I'm so glad you brought the girls, Josh," she said. "I hope that you can do it again. Matilda seemed to fit in well with the group."

I nodded. She had, in fact, rather been the life of the party.

"And, Josh," went on Aunt Lou, lowering her voice to a whisper, "don't pay any attention to the 'pack.' " She nodded her head slightly in the direction of the boys, who had given me razzing for bringing two girls. "There's not a one of them who wouldn't give his right arm to be in your position to-night."

I looked dubiously back at my circle of friends and I began to grin. Aunt Lou was right. I walked over to the two young ladies who had shared my crowded buggy and extended an arm to each of them.

From then on things began to change at our house. My lot wasn't really so bad, after all. In fact, many would have envied my situation.

Mary was probably one of the best cooks in the whole

neighborhood. What's more, she was gentle and caring and thought of many little ways to brighten the days for each one of us.

And Matilda? Well, Matilda was Matilda. She was vivacious and witty and bright—a real chatterbox, about as different from Mary as a girl could be. Each added to our household in a special way.

I wasn't chafing anymore. There were still times when our big farm kitchen seemed a bit too small and I longed for a bit more space and a little more quiet, but generally speaking we all began to adjust to one another.

And then we went full swing into harvest. All I could think about was getting that bumper crop from the field to the grain bins, and I blocked everything else momentarily from my mind.

Chapter 22

Fall

Harvest went fairly well that year. We had the usual weather set-backs, but nothing that lasted more than a few days at a time. As the weather permitted, the grain was cut and stooked; then we had to wait on the warm sun to do the final drying of the stooks.

It was my first year to drive a team on the neighborhood threshing crew. We traveled from farm to farm working the fields. A strict tally was kept of our days worked; we were allowed one day of labor, a man and his team, for every day that we put in. If I worked for eighteen days, I would be allowed three days of a six-man crew with no money changing hands. I figured that three good days would about finish our threshing, and that eighteen to twenty-four days would be the maximum of good weather needed to take care of all of the crops in our area.

It was hard work, and long days for both the teams and the men. It was especially hard when the farm being threshed was several miles from home. Most of the farms were bunched in within a radius of a few miles, but one of them was seven miles away and another was six and a half. On those days I had to leave home early to get there in time to start the day with the rest of the men, and on the same days I got home well after dark.

Some of the men took their bed rolls and bedded down in the stack of fresh straw, tying their teams to a nearby fence post. I didn't want to stay, but rather than driving a tired team the additional miles each day, I decided to tie Chester on behind my rack first trip out. Then I left the team resting and feeding and rode Chester home each night and back again in the morning. It worked well. Chester could shorten my time on the road and also get a bit of a workout. He got too frisky when he wasn't ridden frequently.

The threshing crew represented an assortment of fellas— big and small, old and young, quiet and loud—all working together for a common goal. There were usually about six of us at a time, plus Mr. Wilkes, the man who operated the threshing machine. Some of the men worked for two or three days at a time and then sent out a replacement so they could get on home and get their own crops cut and ready for thresh- ing. I was lucky enough to have all my fields cut before I left home.

Mitch Turley and I were the youngest two on the crew. We had gone to school together back in our little one-room school—the very school where Matilda taught now. Mitch was Mary's older brother, so he kept asking me strange ques- tions about Mary. I soon caught on that he was really fishing for information about Matilda. It seemed that Mitch had seen her once or twice and been quite impressed.

I wasn't sure I wanted to help Mitch get acquainted with Matilda. At one time he had attended Sunday school with Willie and me. At that point he never missed a Sunday, even though he hadn't had much encouragement from home at the time. But now he never went, even though Mary tried her hardest to talk him into it. I didn't offer him much in- formation—or much hope.

The oldest member of the crew was Mr. Smith. I think that Mr. Smith had been threshing most of forever with Mr. Wilkes. In fact, his team of bays was so familiar with all of the nearby fields that I think Mr. Smith could have stayed at home and the team could have made the proper rounds—

except that they wouldn't have been much good at forking bundles!

Barkley Shaw and Joey Smith were both on the crew part time, too. Barkley and Joey were about the age of my Aunt Lou. I had never cared that much for Barkley—always considered him a show-off. But to his credit, he had settled down a lot since he had married SueAnn Corbin and become the father of four little ones.

All of the crew were neighbor folks I had known all of my growing up years. There wasn't much said around the table about world events. Mostly it was who had lumbago, and who had the best seed grain, and who was seeing whose daughter. I learned a lot just listening to the conversation.

During the time that I worked with the crew Grandpa did all of the choring. Uncle Charlie did whatever he could, and Mary did more than was expected. Even Matilda pitched in with feeding the chickens and carrying some wood.

I didn't see too much of the household during harvest. But when I got home late at night, they would all be waiting up. Matilda would sometimes be preparing her next day's lessons while Mary mended or worked on some fancy things that Uncle Charlie and Grandpa teased her about, saying it was for her hope chest. Grandpa and Uncle Charlie would often be reading the latest edition of Matilda's paper.

They'd all ask politely about my day, and Mary would quietly prepare a snack and the evening coffee for Grandpa and Uncle Charlie while Matilda told us amusing stories about the happenings at school. As soon as we finished we'd all head for bed. Some nights I was so tired I could scarcely drag myself up the creaking steps. But then I would be off again in the morning before anyone else was even up.

For eleven days we worked that way; then it was our turn for the threshing rig. I was so nervous and excited that I could hardly stand it. This was my first year to be completely in charge of the operation on our farm. I had to make all the decisions and handle all the arrangements.

We had always hired at least two women to work in the

kitchen preparing the food for the crew, but this year Mary informed me that she was sure she and Uncle Charlie would be quite able to care for things. I must have looked a bit doubtful. I remembered some of those farm homes where the food had been a little short and the unspoken disgust of the men around the table. I sure didn't want them feeling that way about us.

When Uncle Charlie sided with Mary, I decided to let them give it a try, wondering if Uncle Charlie was simply saying what he did because he hated extra women in the kitchen.

I needn't have worried. Before the three days were up Mary had established quite a name for our kitchen. Her meals were wonderful, and she also brought refreshments to the field—steaming coffee, cold milk, sandwiches, cakes and cookies. She fed the men so well, in fact, that it was a good two hours after each meal until they were really able to work well again.

The first night we went in for supper, I could see Mitch Turley straining to get a look in the kitchen window before we entered the room. At first I supposed he was looking for his sister, but I noticed that his glance slid right past Mary, who was at the stove serving up heaping bowls of corn on the cob.

Matilda appeared just then, a big white apron nearly circling her entire frame, making her look even tinier than she actually was, and I heard Mitch suck in his breath.

Mitch didn't say much at the table, but I saw him stealing glances Matilda's way. Seeing Mitch watching Matilda made me look at her a little more closely. She seemed to belong in our country kitchen, and I suppose I was getting used to her. But now I watched, and noticed that she didn't just walk, she floated around, her full-skirted dress swishing about her legs and her hair swishing about her cheeks. She served and smiled and dished out food and witty conversation, making all the men feel that they weren't quite as tired as they had been when they seated themselves at the table. Some of them even began to make funny remarks and tell ridiculous stories on one another.

Mary worked just as fast—only it didn't look that way. She moved with a quietness and grace that I hadn't noticed before. But then, I had never noticed anything about the way Mary moved. She did nothing to draw attention to herself. She had a poise—a serenity that people felt rather than saw. In fact, Mary had a way of making people feel comfortable, at home with themselves.

But Mitch never looked once at his sister—at least, not that I observed. And if Matilda knew that she was being studied, she never let on.

Mitch wore a clean, fancier shirt the next day when he came to work. Usually we wore old, patched, faded work-clothes in the fields, because the work of pitching bundles was hard on clothes as well as bodies. Sweat drenched our shirts and straw stuck to them. Wagon wheels sometimes had to be greased and horses curried. A shirt could look pretty bad by the end of the day and nobody wanted to wear a shirt that he had to worry about. But here was Mitch looking like he was heading for town or going to the school picnic.

I guess the other fellas noticed it, too, and having been young once themselves, they pretty well knew the reason for his fancying up. I saw some whispering going on and heard a few laughs, and I knew that something was up. Barkley Shaw seemed to be the instigator; maybe he hadn't settled down all that much after all.

The day was almost over and we were just finishing up the last couple of loads. I had forgotten all about my suspicions by then, so I wasn't being very cautious. Mr. Smith was the second last wagon in, with Mitch following right behind him. As the other racks were all unloaded, I sent up an extra two men to help each team driver. Barkley and Joey were standing by, awfully anxious to give a hand to Mitch. I didn't think a thing of it at the time. Just figured that they were in a hurry to get in for supper.

Smith was soon unloaded and moved his rack out of the

way for Mitch to pull up. The unloading went well, and before we knew it Mitch's rack was empty. Then Mitch went to drive his team on, when there was a thump and one back side of the wagon dropped down much lower than the other.

He halted his team and leaned over to look. To his surprise, his back wheel had come completely off. He said some questionable words, tied the lines securely over the middle post of the rack and climbed down. That was when Joey and Barkley both pressed in, seeming to be awfully concerned about Mitch's misfortune.

They talked about the wheel for a few minutes and then Barkley moved over to his rack and came back with a can.

"I got some real good wagon-wheel grease here," he offered. "Might make the wheel work back on a little easier."

Now if Mitch had known Barkley like I knew Barkley, he would have been suspicious right there. But he didn't seem to think Barkley was up to anything. He just thanked him and started to pry at that can to get it open.

"Here, use this," Barkley said, offering him a piece of metal to pry with. Mitch went to work. I could see the lid gradually coming loose as Mitch worked his way around it with the lever. Just as it opened, Barkley tripped forward over a rough bit of ground that had been there all of the time and smacked right into Mitch's extended arms. The can flew up, along with its contents, and Mitch stood blinking through a covering of dirty black oil.

"Oh, man!" exclaimed Barkley, snapping his fingers and shaking his head in fake exasperation at his mistake. "I must a' got the wrong can."

Mitch stood looking down at his fancy shirt. It was streaked and splotched with dark patches.

"Here, fella," spoke Joey in a sympathetic voice, "let me clean ya up some," and he grabbed a handful of straw and began to wipe at Mitch's chest.

At first Mitch just stood there silently and let Joey wipe away—until he saw that the straw also contained clumps of exposed soil. Every swipe that Joey took left a smeared streak of Jones's farmland behind.

By then others had gathered and were guffawing at Mitch's expense. I figured that things had gone quite far enough.

"Okay, fellas," I said as quietly, yet authoritatively, as I knew how, "let's not keep supper waiting."

Most of the men moved on then, and I turned to help Mitch get the wheel back on his wagon.

"I'll lend you a shirt when we get to the house," I promised quietly, then added as an afterthought, "It won't be fancy, but it'll be clean."

Chapter 23

Settling In

I spent several more days back on the road with the threshing crew, and then we were finally finished for another fall. As usual, after the harvest was over things settled down considerably. There still was lots to do, but we were at least allowed a decent night's sleep in between the doing. I was glad to be home instead of on the road, and I think Grandpa and Uncle Charlie were glad to have me at home, too.

As soon as the grain was portioned out—for sale, for feed, and for seed—we got out our pencils and scraps of paper and began to figure what our profits would be.

We all worked on it. Matilda was a real whizz in math and even outfigured me at times. Mary hadn't had as much book learning but she had an uncanny sense of rough calculations. More than once she surprised us at how close she came to the correct answer—in just seconds, too.

There were many reasons to be concerned with the year's profit; my primary goal was to establish whether we had made enough to be able to purchase the tractor I had my heart set on. I had discussed it with Grandpa and Uncle Charlie, and they seemed almost excited about the idea.

After a great deal of figuring and working things one way and then another to try to cover all of the possibilities, it was decided that there was money, with some left over. With the decision finally made, I could hardly contain myself.

The tractor had to be ordered for delivery and would be shipped in on an incoming freight train. While I waited, I busied myself with other things.

Matilda decided to have a school social and worked hard to talk us all into going. I really don't think that any one of us could have turned her down, but we teased along, letting her think we still hadn't made up our minds. By the time the night came she was all in a dither. It was rather a big undertaking for her first community affair. There would be games, some special music, and refreshments, and Matilda had to organize it all.

I think she was relieved to come down from her room to find us all waiting for her in the kitchen, dressed in our best and ready to go. She gave a glad little squeal and threw her arms around Grandpa's neck.

Uncle Charlie and I just looked at one another and grinned. We had known all along that we'd be going.

This time for sure there were too many of us for the light buggy, and we still didn't have snow so we couldn't take the sleigh. Taking the rather cumbersome wagon meant we had to leave early so Matilda could be there to make the final preparations. When the crowd began to arrive, we were ready.

I noticed Mitch as soon as he came in the door. He had been at our house a few times over the past weeks—to visit Mary, he said. Uncle Charlie and Grandpa would just smile and wink at that. Mary always seemed pleased to see him. I knew she was praying for him and hoping that he was ready to show some interest in church again. Tonight he was dressed all up in a brand-new suit that I figured he must have purchased with his harvest money. He looked pretty good, too. For a moment I wished I hadn't ordered that tractor. I could have done with a new suit myself.

Matilda started the evening with some "mixers" just to get folks moving about and talking to one another. Harvest had kept everyone too busy for visiting.

After spending a half hour or more playing the games, Matilda went on to her program. Several of the school children sang songs or recited pieces. Some of them were good, some not so good. But we all clapped anyway, and some of the young fellas lined up across the back of the room, whistling shrilly.

I found it awfully hard on the ears, and then I remembered times when I and my friends had done the same thing because it seemed like the thing to do. Now it just seemed loud.

The last item on the program surprised me; Matilda sang. I had no idea that she had such a voice. In fact, I could hardly believe it as I listened to her. To think such a full, melodious sound was coming out of such a little frame was almost unbelievable. I guess that others felt that way too; the room was totally quiet. Even the babies seemed to stop their restless stirring, and when it was over there was thunderous applause and more shrill whistles. People kept crying "Encore! Encore!" until finally a flushed Matilda sang us another. But she wouldn't sing a third number though, no matter how we coaxed.

When the refreshments were served, several neighborhood women gave Matilda and Mary a hand. They had all brought sandwiches and pastries from their own kitchens.

We all assured Matilda that her evening was a complete success as we bundled up against the cold and started off for home. It was a bright night with a full moon, and the horses had no trouble at all seeing where they were going.

Once again I was on the front seat driving with one girl on each side of me. Grandpa and Uncle Charlie had crawled up on the back seat and bundled themselves into heavy quilts. The cold made Uncle Charlie's arthritis act up, so Mary had made sure that we had lots of blankets along.

At first the ride was rather quiet, with only an occasional comment followed by some laughter. A shooting star caused some oohs and aahs from the girls. Mary told Matilda she had a lovely voice and begged her to sing the song again.

Matilda began to sing, softly at first, and then Mary joined in, and the beautiful sound drifted out over the moon-drenched countryside. It was a well-known hymn, and by the time they got to the second verse I could hear Grandpa humming along with them. Then he stopped humming and began to sing, and then Uncle Charlie joined in, softly, shyly.

Matilda gave me a little poke, and I sang, too—a bit hesitantly at first, and then much more bravely. Soon we were all singing, full voice. We finished the song and went on to another one and then another and another. As soon as we had completed one, someone would lead out in another.

All the way home we sang. I had never had an experience like it in all my life. Somehow in the singing we had drawn closer together against the coldness and the darkness of the world around us. It all seemed so natural, so right.

For the first time I was sorry to see our farm come into view. I could have gone on and on just driving and singing and being close to those I cared about. Just as we pulled up to the house a star fell, streaking its way downward, then burned out and was gone—and the spell was broken.

Sarah came to visit. It had been a long time since she had spent time with us at the farm, and we had missed her.

"Oh no!" said Uncle Charlie in mock horror. "What am I gonna do with *two* bosses in the kitchen?"

Mary and Sarah both laughed.

I came home from town midafternoon to find Mary and Sarah elbow-deep in flour as they rolled and cut sugar cookies. Uncle Charlie sat in his favorite chair by the window working a crossword puzzle, but every now and then he would steal a peek at the activity. I knew that he was enjoying their fun almost as much as they were.

"What would you like us to make for you, Uncle Josh?" Sarah called. Without hesitation I answered, "A tractor." It had seemed like the tractor was taking an interminable time to come.

Sarah laughed at my response but Mary gave me a sympathetic smile.

"I don't know how to make a tractor," Sarah giggled.

"That's too bad," I said shaking my head. "If you could make me one I could cancel my order."

Uncle Charlie's head lifted from the crossword.

"No word?"

I shook my head in disappointment.

"I thought you didn't need a tractor 'til spring," Sarah offered as she patched up the leg on a cookie dog.

"I don't."

"Then why are you so apatient?"

She tipped her head to the side and sucked some cookie dough off a finger as she waited for my answer. I waited too. I wasn't sure how to answer her. At last I had to smile.

"I'm 'apatient,' " I said honestly, borrowing her word, "because I *want* it so much, not because I need it so much."

"Oh!" nodded Sarah. She could understand that.

She thought for a moment and then her face brightened. "Then I know," she said matter-of-factly. "Pray. Pray an' ask Jesus to help you wait. Before I had my birthday one time I was apatient an' Mamma told me to pray, an' I did, an' Jesus helped me wait."

It sounded so simple. Maybe it was simple. I ran a hand over Sarah's curly head. "Maybe I'll do that," I said huskily.

She seemed perfectly satisfied that the matter had been taken care of and could be dropped.

"Would you like a horse?" she asked.

"I've already got a horse," I informed her.

She giggled again. "Well, this one don't need hay, or oats, or anything," and she handed me a slightly damaged horse with crooked legs.

I ate the horse in two bites.

"Mamma don't let me do that," said Sarah seriously, her eyes big. "She says I might choke and throw up."

I wanted to tell Sarah that such talk wasn't very ladylike

and then I was reminded by a little glance from Mary that I had provoked the whole thing.

"I shouldn't have done it, either," I admitted. "I promise not to do it again."

I gave Sarah another pat, grinned sheepishly at Mary and went on up to my room.

The question of where Sarah should sleep at our house hadn't really been solved. I offered to sleep on the cot, but Grandpa refused. He didn't say so, but I think it had something to do with him having gotten two boarders for our extra bedrooms. Uncle Charlie said he would, but it was hard enough for him to get a decent night's sleep in his own bed.

Grandpa ended up on the cot that first night. He looked awfully tired the next morning.

We talked again about letting Sarah take the cot. The idea didn't seem like a good one—not that the cot wouldn't fit Sarah better than it had Grandpa, but simply because she would be kept awake so late. Sarah would never go to sleep as long as there was stirring in the kitchen, yet none of the rest of us were ready for bed at seven-thirty.

Mary finally worked it all out. "Move the cot into my room," she suggested. "There's plenty of room; Sarah can go to bed at the proper time and the rest of us can keep our own beds."

"That's awfully kind of you, Mary," Grandpa started to protest, "but you shouldn't have—"

"Nonsense," she said. "I love her company and you know it."

So the cot was moved into Mary's room and Sarah was tucked in for the night. It was a much better arrangement. After Sarah had returned home the next day, I offered to move the cot out, but Mary wouldn't hear of it.

"Just leave it there," she said. "It's not in my way, and it will be all ready for the next time she comes."

The snow came softly at first, then heavier and heavier

until there was a deep ground cover. I didn't like the idea of tiny Matilda heading off for school across the open field. It was already knee deep and there would be no path.

"Take Chester," I urged her.

"I'll be fine," she insisted. "A little snow won't hurt me. The walk does me good. Besides, there'll be worse storms before the winter is over. I might as well get used to it."

I stopped arguing, but I will admit I cast a glance out the window now and then until she passed out of sight, just to be sure that she would make it to the schoolhouse.

Storm followed storm, and we settled into another winter. Soon we all had adjusted to it, and I no longer fretted when Matilda left for school, her high boots clearing a way through the drifts and her arms full of textbooks.

Shortly before Christmas the tractor finally arrived. The station master sent word out to us with one of our neigbors. Mr. Smith seemed to be quite pleased to have been chosen to bear the news. There weren't too many tractors in our part.

I rushed off to town to pick it up and it looked like the whole town was there to watch me take delivery.

I had thought from reading the manuals that a tractor would be easy enough to handle. But we had a real time getting it fired up, and by the time the blacksmith came to give me a hand, my face was red and my fuse short.

Then I had to back the big monster up in order to get it turned around. That seemed to be harder than backing a horse and buggy. We had to start it twice more, because I kept killing the engine. I finally did get it heading the right direction, with all eyes of the townsfolk upon me. But then, not wanting to hog all the road, I got a little too close to the edge of the roadway. Those big steel wheels just seemed to pull me right on down into the ditch, and the tractor stalled again. When the helpful blacksmith and I did get it started, I wasn't sure how I was going to get myself out of there. But to my amazement, those same steel wheels that took me down so unexpectedly also took me back out, and I was off down the road heading home.

It was a cold ride. The thing moved along at a crawl, and it was made all of steel, so there was nothing warm about it—at least not back where I was sitting.

By the time I got it home, I sure was glad to pull it up beside the granary and climb on down. It wasn't nearly as easy to handle as a team, I can tell you that, and it took me most of the afternoon to get the chill out of my bones.

I did some thinking about that tractor that I hadn't done before. Getting the tractor was fine, but I hadn't thought much of where to go from there. I could tell just by looking that the farm machinery we had used behind the horses wouldn't work behind that tractor. We'd probably need to replace nearly all the equipment we owned.

I wrote Willie a long letter that night, the first one in a while. I'd had a few letters from him, and I knew he was just as busy there in South Africa as I was back home.

He was pretty excited about his new life. Oh, he still missed Camellia terribly—and his family and friends, too, I guess, but he sure was excited about getting into the work he had been trained to do. God had given him a deep love for the black Africans he was reaching out to. They were so friendly and open, he said, and he knew he was going to love being a missionary among them.

I had already told him about Grandpa's wild idea of moving two women into our house. I had even written later, admitting that it really wasn't as bad as I had expected. But I hadn't told him about the community social or our good harvest or the new tractor.

I told him, too, that Mrs. Foggelson was really doing well since she had reestablished her faith. Not that she was running around town preaching or singing on the street corner

or anything like that, but she was growing in a quiet, ma-
turing way.

I miss you, Willie, I wrote, *and I'll be glad to see you again.
Four years, after all, is a long, long time. God's blessing on
your work; my warmest regards. Your best friend, Josh.*

Chapter 24

Winter Ills

Another Christmas was approaching. We all went together to the school Christmas program. Matilda had labored long and hard over it. The youngsters performed well, and the crowd of neighbors insisted that Matilda sing again. She sang two lovely songs and then she asked Mary to join her for one. Mary did, without protest, and the people clapped even more enthusiastically after the duet.

The program at the church on Sunday night was mostly Aunt Lou's responsibility, though she had help from Matilda as well.

Little Sarah sang her first solo, "Away in a Manger." She was doing fine, too, carrying the tune just perfectly until Jon jumped down from the bench beside Mrs. Lewis, who was supposed to be looking after him, and ran to get in on his sister's act.

Aunt Lou didn't know what to do. To dash after Jon would interrupt the song, but leaving him alone proved to be even more disruptive.

At first he merely stood beside Sarah, looking up in her face and rocking gently back and forth to the music. Then he decided to sing, too, but Jon didn't know the words. His song was "Ah-ah-ah" at the top of his healthy lungs. Sarah frowned at him, but went on singing. It wasn't long until

Jon's "Ah-ahs" were drowning out Sarah's voice. She finally stopped mid-phrase.

"Go to Mrs. Lewis!" she hissed loudly at her brother.

He shook his head and started to sing again.

"Then go to Mamma," Sarah insisted, giving him a push.

Jon still refused to budge. I could hear some snickers and caught a glimpse of Uncle Nat heading for the platform, but Sarah hadn't seen him. "Go!" she insisted and gave Jon another push, a bit more forcefully.

"No!" hollered Jon. "Sing!" As he whirled around to escape his sister, he entangled himself in the decorated tree. It came down with a crash and Jon, frightened by it all, began to bellow as loudly as he could. By the time Uncle Nat arrived, his two offspring were both crying and the platform was a mess.

"Preacher's young'uns!" Uncle Nat said to the amused congregation, rolling his eyes heavenward half in jest and half in exasperation, and scooped up his two errant family members while Aunt Lou tried to restore some order to the front of the church.

On Monday we took Matilda to the train; she was to spend her holidays at home. She was in a dither about seeing her family again, but that was normal—Matilda lived life in an air of excitement. She and Mary had become very close friends, and they hugged one another over and over. In fact, the only one who didn't get a hug was me. I would have been embarrassed about it if I had. Us being right out in the eyes of people and all. I knew that few would understand how it was at our house. The house seemed a bit quiet when we returned. Mary served us a tasty dinner, washed up the dishes and then went to her room. Soon she reappeared with her small carpetbag in her hand.

"Your Grandpa has given me Christmas week off. With Matilda gone he says you can get along just fine by yourselves."

I was a little doubtful. We hadn't been doing much cooking for ourselves lately, and it would be rather hard now to fit back into the old rut.

"I've done extra baking," went on Mary. "You'll find it in the pantry."

I nodded.

"If you should need me—"

"We'll be fine. Just fine," I assured her with more confidence than I felt.

She pulled on her heavy coat, and I finally realized it was cold out, and it was over a mile to the Turleys'.

"I'll get Chester and give you a ride home," I offered.

I didn't wait for her to answer, just grabbed my coat and cap and headed for the barn.

I hooked Chester to the one-horse sleigh, and we set off. The afternoon was crisp and bright and the snow crunched under the runners.

"I'll miss Matilda," sighed Mary after a long silence.

I was on the verge of saying that I would too but checked myself just in time.

"She's so—so alive," went on Mary.

That was the truth. I was reining in Chester—as usual, he wanted to run.

"It won't be long till she's back."

"Oh, I hope not!" Mary gave a deep sigh.

I didn't go in when we reached the Turleys', though Mary asked me to. "I've got to get home and start in on the chores," I told her. Then I added, feeling suddenly shy, "We'll see you in a few days. Have a real good Christmas."

She turned to me. There were no rows of eyes watching.

"Thank you, Josh," she whispered. Then she reached up, gave me a quick embrace, and she was gone.

It turned out that we did need Mary. Two days after Christmas Uncle Charlie became ill. We could have handled that, but the next day Grandpa, too, was down. I didn't know what to do. I still had all the chores, and the two men were sick enough that they needed someone to care for them. In desperation I finally saddled Chester and headed back for Mary.

Mary flushed a bit when she saw Chester, but she laughed, too. "Well," she said, "does he ride double?"

"How stupid of me!" I blushed. "I should have brought the sleigh. He can carry two, but—"

"It's fine, Josh," she assured me. "If Chester doesn't mind, I don't."

She rode behind me, her arms around my waist as though it was the most natural thing in the world.

In the next few days, Uncle Charlie worsened, and though Mary nursed him with all of her skill and prepared him broths and chicken soup, he still couldn't keep anything on his stomach. I saddled Chester up again and went after Doc.

After a few days on the medicine that Doc left, Uncle Charlie seemed to be able to make some headway. But by the time Grandpa and Uncle Charlie were beginning to show a bit of improvement, Matilda was back, and Christmas was over.

Things seemed to be fine for about two days, and then Matilda came down with chills and fever. School was cancelled until further notice, and Mary started her nursing again.

When it finally hit me, I couldn't believe that anyone could feel that bad. My whole body ached, and I broke out in sweats and then shivered until the bed shook. The mere thought of food was unbearable, and I was so weak that I could hardly turn my head on the pillow.

I don't know how Mary made it through those days. She did send for Mitch to do the choring, but even so, I don't think she got much rest day or night. Whenever I stirred restlessly, cool cloths were pressed against my fevered forehead and sips of water held to my chapped lips.

I drifted in and out of reality. Sometimes I had strange dreams where I was in heaven and the angels were flitting about me, brushing back my hair and cooling my face. Sometimes I was quite rational and Mary or Matilda would be there sponging off my face or back and chest. I think that Doc was there once or twice. I don't remember seeing him; I just remember his voice giving somebody instructions.

I had no idea how many days were passing by. I only knew that when I was finally aware enough to ask, I couldn't believe that so much of the month of January was already spent. From then on I had almost constant company. Mary came with broths and soups and Pixie lay at the foot of the bed. Uncle Charlie just sat there quietly and cleared his throat now and then. Matilda came with books and read to me for what seemed hour after hour in a voice filled with energy and excitement.

By the time I was able to sit up for short periods in the kitchen, Grandpa and Uncle Charlie were almost as good as new, and Matilda had been back to her classes for a couple of weeks.

I had never been that sick before in my whole life. And after those days in bed, helpless and sick and flat on my back, I was ready to admit one thing—I was glad there were women in the house.

It turned out that Mitch had to do our chores for the whole month of January and half of February. I maintained that I was well enough to get back to work, but Doc wouldn't hear of it. My recuperation time did give me a good chance to get back into some books. I had been so busy using my muscles that I had almost forgotten how to use my brain.

I discovered, too, that the daily papers that arrived for Matilda to the post office weekly weren't all that bad. To relieve the boredom, I began to sort through them and found some terrific articles under "Farm News and Markets."

There was so much more to farming than mere sowing and reaping. I could see the possibility of the farm turning a tidy profit in the future, and the thought filled me with energy and excitement. Folks like Willie needed support in order to stay on the mission field. I didn't say anything to the family yet, but I did do some talking to God. I was beginning to get a vision of the farm being used in God's work by helping meet the financial needs of missionaries—especially Willie. I intended to do all I could to make the farm produce so that he would never need to worry about support while he served on the field.

Chapter 25

Chester

I was sitting at the table talking to Matilda about some strange ideas, to my way of thinking, I'd found in one of her books. I heard a commotion and went to the kitchen window to look out toward the barn.

I smiled. There was nothing to be concerned about. The horses were just frisking about. I looked at the sky, thinking that another storm must be moving in.

"Why are they running?" Matilda asked at my elbow.

"Just feeling frisky," I answered. "Or could be a storm coming in. Horses often run and play before a storm." We stood there to watch them for a minute.

Chester was really worked up. He loved to run, and any excuse for him was a good enough one.

Mary crowded in on the other side of me, her face lightened by a smile. "I love to watch them."

The three of us stood there watching the horses rear and kick and race around the barnyard.

"He is so beautiful!" exclaimed Matilda. She held Pixie in her arms, gently scratching under one of the dog's silky ears. But I knew that it wasn't Pixie that she referred to. It was Chester, showing off out in the barnyard. "Look at him, his head thrown back, his tail outstretched—" The word ended in a gasp.

Chester, who had been doing a tight circle around the end of the barn at almost full speed, had suddenly gone down, apparently hitting a patch of ice under the snow where the eaves dripped in milder weather.

I didn't even wait to comment; just turned and ran from the house. I guess I knew I should have stopped for my coat, especially since I had just been sick, but I didn't.

As I raced toward the barn, Chester was still floundering in the snow, pulling himself up, then tossing back down. His feet were thrashing, the snow flying, and as I ran I kept wondering why he wasn't back up on his feet.

I was almost to him when, with a snort and a flurry, he righted himself. I took a deep, relieved breath—and then I saw it. Chester's right front leg wobbled at an awkward angle. He had broken a leg in the fall!

I skidded to a halt and whirled around with my back to the horse. My arm came up and I buried my head against the fence, not wanting to see. Dry sobs wrenched my throat; then someone was gently nudging me. "Here put this on." It was Mary, helping me into my coat.

Then she, too, looked at Chester and I could hear her soft gasp.

I'm not sure when Matilda joined us. She came scurrying up beside us, her breath preceding her in little shivery clouds.

"Is he okay?" she gasped out.

Chester attempted to move, and I heard his pain-filled cry and Matilda's answering scream.

"No! No!" she kept saying over and over. I put my arms around her. She clung to me, sobbing convulsively.

When Grandpa came, we were all still standing in a huddle trying to comfort one another.

"Hurt bad?" I heard Grandpa ask.

I muttered in answer, "His front leg."

This brought a fresh burst of tears from Matilda. "I can't bear it!" she cried. "I can't bear to see him like that!"

I cast another glance toward Chester. He hadn't taken

another step. He stood there, shaking his head and snorting, totally confused by the pain.

Somehow I got control of myself. "Here," I said to Mary. "Take Matilda to the house."

Mary led Matilda, still crying, away.

For the first time I took a good look at Chester. His heaving body was still covered with snow. He trembled with each breath he drew and his leg just dangled there, supporting none of his heavy frame.

I moved toward him and reached out a hand to run down his smooth neck. He quivered at my touch, then tried to take a step. His whole body reacted to the pain, and I thought for one awful minute that he was going to go down again. Sick at the sight, I turned from him, and wretched. The illness I had just come through probably had something to do with it. But I had to get control of myself. I had to help Chester.

Grandpa hardly knew whether to go to Chester or to me. I nodded at him that I was okay and he moved toward the horse. He spoke to him in soft tones, rubbing his neck and trying to calm him, his hand moving gently down toward the injured limb.

Chester threw himself back, and the pain of the movement made him squeal again in anguish.

I whirled and headed for the house. I didn't go to the kitchen, just to the back porch, and stopped there only long enough to check that there were shells in Grandpa's big old Winchester. I was turning to leave again when I heard the door open and close. Quick footsteps dashed after me and I could feel a hand on my arm.

"No!"

I jerked my arm free and tried to keep on walking.

"Josh, listen!" But I still didn't stop. Just as I reached the door Mary pushed herself ahead of me. She stood there, her back against the door, her slight frame heaving. She had been crying, too; the traces of tears were still on her cheeks.

She stood there, defying me, shaking her head and blocking my way.

"Don't!" she pleaded again.

I reached out a hand and pushed at her. "Do you think I want to do this?" I almost screamed.

We both knew the answer.

"Then don't," she said again, not budging from the spot she guarded.

"He's suffering!" I cried. "Can't you see that? He's suffering!"

Mary reached out and placed a hand on my coat front. Her eyes looked wide with fright and determination. "Yes," she said and her voice rose to almost the pitch that mine had been. "Yes, he's suffering. But life is full of suffering, Josh. You've suffered. I've suffered." She took another deep breath and her whole body heaved. "For years—for years I watched my mother suffer—day after day—week after week. I loved her, Josh. I loved her. But I didn't give up. I fought. I fought to save her. Chester is a fighter, Josh. A thoroughbred and a fighter. Chester isn't done yet. He hasn't given up. And we can't either—not without a fight."

With her final outburst, Mary took the gun from my unresisting hands and moved away from the door. I heard the sound of metal on metal as she hung it back on the pegs. The world was whirling around me and I was afraid I was going to be sick again.

Mary brushed past me and went out the door.

It was several minutes until I got myself under control. When I could think straight again, I thought of Mary's plea to fight for Chester's life. It would never work. Chester's leg was broken; anyone could see that. There was no way we could save him now. If we tried, he would suffer and suffer and then we would need to destroy him anyway. Better to relieve his suffering now.

I looked back at the gun and then let my shoulders droop in resignation as I turned my back on it and headed for the barn.

Somehow Mary and Grandpa had managed to get Chester

into his stall. They were talking in quiet tones as I entered the barn.

" . . . a good clean break," Grandpa was saying. "No protruding bone."

"We need to keep his weight off it," Mary replied, beginning to gentle Chester with her hands and voice.

"How?" It was only one word from Grandpa, but it spoke for both of us.

"We need to construct some kind of sling—to hold him up, off his feet."

Grandpa eyed the stall. It wouldn't be easy.

"I saw Pa do it once with a critter," went on Mary. "Worked it on a pulley system."

Grandpa chewed on a corner of his mustache as he thought deeply. "Might work," he said at length.

"You keep him warm and try to quiet him, and I'll go get Pa," said Mary. I wasn't sure if she was talking to Grandpa or to me.

It was an awfully long time until Mr. Turley got there. Mary didn't come with him to the barn, but went right on to the house. I had spent the time soothing Chester. We had thrown a heavy horse blanket over him and rubbed his body down with clean straw. He was quieter. The fright seemed to have left him. He still quivered every now and then and snorted loudly when he tried to shift his weight.

Mary's pa went right to work. He called out orders so quickly that I was running to keep up. In a couple of hours we had Chester fitted with a body sling, and then with the pulley system Mr. Turley had rigged up above him, we gently hoisted him until his three feet just barely touched the floor. Chester's right front leg was raised just a shade higher so that he couldn't put any weight on it at all.

Chester, of course, didn't understand the arrangement. He snorted and pitched, trying to get proper control of his circumstances. It was some time until we were able to quiet him, and by then I was just sure it wasn't going to work.

As soon as Chester was settled down, Mr. Turley began

to work on the leg. It had swollen a good deal, so it was difficult for him to feel the break. And any pressure on the area sent Chester flailing again.

At length Mr. Turley stood up. "A real shame!" he said soberly. "Such a beautiful horse."

I thought he was going to agree with my first response, to say that nothing could be done for Chester—but he didn't.

"Good clean break," he said instead. "Should heal nicely, barring any unforeseen complications."

The breath I had been holding came out slowly.

Then with the help of Grandpa and me, Mr. Turley got a leg support on Chester. By the time we were through, we were all worn out.

Grandpa invited Mr. Turley up to the house for a cup of coffee and I slumped down in the straw, my back to the manger and one hand on Chester. I just sat there—wondering, praying, hoping with all my heart that this beautiful animal would be all right.

I didn't even hear the door open.

"Josh?" It was Mary. She spoke in a whisper. "Josh?"

The barn lantern flickered with the slight movement of air from the door, the wavering flame sending the shivers of light dancing cross Mary's face. She stood there, holding out to me a steaming mug of chicken soup. I took it in still-trembling hands.

Then without another word she lowered herself to the straw beside me and laid a hand on my arm.

"He's gonna be okay," she whispered. "He's gonna be fine."

I tried a weak smile.

"How's Matilda?" I asked, wanting to forget just for a moment the pain of Chester.

"She's okay now. She's making dessert for supper. She's been praying—steady—ever since it happened."

I sighed and turned back to Chester.

"You really think he'll be all right?" I asked Mary.

Her smile was a little wobbly.

"Look at him," she said rather than making me any promises. "Pa says his leg felt real good. The bone seems straight—it's just a matter of time."

I looked at Chester. He was much calmer now. I almost believed what Mary was saying to me.

I turned to her. "Thanks," I said, taking her hand. "Thanks."

I should have said a lot more. Thanks for stopping me from doing something foolish. Thanks for riding old Maude through the cold and snow for your pa. Thanks for bringing me the hot soup. Thanks for your support. But all that I could say was "thanks."

She gave my hand a slight squeeze, rose to her feet, and returned to the kitchen.

Chapter 26

Willie

Chester adapted remarkably well to his body harness. Maybe he enjoyed the extra attention. I spent a great deal of time in the barn with him, and Matilda visited him often with treats of apples and sugar lumps. Mary inspected his entire body at least once a day, watching for any sores that might result from the harness straps.

The swelling began to go down in the leg, and after Mr. Turley had taken a look at it a few times, he suggested putting on a new leg brace. Chester hardly complained at all as it was done.

After a few weeks the brace was taken off altogether, but Chester was still not allowed to put his weight on it. I began to massage and exercise it. I wanted to be sure that the knee and ankle would still work well. Chester was able to move it with no problem—with my help, of course.

Finally the day came when we lowered the hammock and let him test his weight. He seemed reluctant at first and snorted his concern. I rubbed his neck and spoke to him 'til he calmed down.

We didn't leave him on all four legs for long. We didn't want to tire him. But every day he was allowed to stand for a longer period of time.

At last I began walking him. At first he had a bit of a

limp, and then even that disappeared. It was almost too good to be true, but it looked like Chester was going to be just fine.

As the winter wore on, we all went about our daily chores. I fired up our new tractor every once in a while, just to make sure it was still working. Then Grandpa had the bright idea of dragging a log behind it to clear snow on our road. Uncle Charlie got in a bit of teasing about my "new toy."

We spent the evenings together in the big farmhouse kitchen, Pixie curled up contentedly on the lap of one or another. Those evenings were special times. On such nights, we were comforted by the thought of being snuggled in the kitchen, a warm fire crackling in the big cookstove. We could often hear another storm as it swept through, the wind howling and raging and rattling the loose tin on the corner of the eaves trough. Every time I listened to it, I reminded myself to fix it come the first nice day. But when the nice days came, I was always busy with something else.

Every time I went to town—and I didn't go any more often than absolutely necessary on those cold days—I picked up another bundle of Matilda's papers to help pass the boredom of the winter days. It had been several weeks since I had heard from Willie, and I had been watching for a letter from him—but the letter didn't come.

Then one day I heard the farm dog bark a greeting, and I looked out the frosted window to see Uncle Nat flip the reins of Dobbin over the gate post. He came toward the house in long, quick strides, and I wondered if he was cold or just in a hurry.

I met him at the door with enthusiasm. It had been a while since he had been out.

Mary pushed the coffeepot forward and added fuel to the fire so that Uncle Nat could warm himself a bit, and Grandpa and Uncle Charlie pulled up chairs to the table, getting ready for a good visit.

Uncle Nat sat down and indicated the chair next to him.

I pulled it up and leaned forward, eager to hear how things were going in town.

"How's Chester?" asked Uncle Nat.

I beamed. "He's doing fine. I can't believe it. You should see him. He can move around almost as good as before."

Uncle Nat smiled and nodded his head.

"How're Lou and the kids?" asked Grandpa for all of us.

"Busy," laughed Uncle Nat. "Real busy. That Jonathan! Lou hardly knows how to keep him occupied in this cold weather."

We all laughed, knowing enough about active Jon to feel a bit sorry for Aunt Lou.

"You out callin'?" Grandpa asked.

"No," said Uncle Nat slowly. His head lowered and his face sobered. We all waited, knowing instinctively that there was more. He lifted his head again and looked directly at me.

"I'm afraid I have some bad news," he said. "I thought you should know. It's Willie."

"Willie?"

"He's gone, Josh."

I didn't understand.

"Gone? Gone where?"

"Word came to the Corbins by telegram this morning. Willie died a couple of days ago."

"But there must be some mistake!" I hardly recognized my own voice, hoarse with shock. "Willie is in South Africa. How do they know—?"

"The Mission Society sent the telegram."

"But there must be some mistake," I repeated, not wanting to accept or believe what I had just been told. I started to get up from my chair. Uncle Nat put a hand on my shoulder and eased me back down.

"There's no mistake, Josh," he sorrowfully assured me. "The Mission Board sent their deepest regrets. Willie is dead."

I heard someone crying, and then I realized that it was

me. I buried my head in my arms and cried until the sobs shook my whole body.

"Not Willie!" my voice was saying over and over. "Dear God, please, not Willie."

And all the time a part of my brain kept saying, *It's all a mistake. You'll see. They'll soon discover that they were wrong. It was someone else—not Willie.*

In the background I could hear voices, but the words never really registered. Someone was comforting a weeping Mary. Someone was trying to comfort me.

It was a long time until I was able to get some measure of control. Grandpa was asking more questions.

"How did it happen?"

"Some kind of fever—malaria, they expect."

"Was he sick for long?"

"They still don't know."

"How are his folks?"

"Taking it hard."

It seemed so unreal, senseless. Willie had hardly arrived out there, and now he was *gone*.

And then I thought of Camellia. And I began to cry again. "Poor Camellia. Poor Camellia," I muttered over and over.

That storm passed, too, and I sat, head bowed, shuddering and hiccuping as I wiped my eyes and blew my nose on the handkerchief I found in my hands.

"Would you like to go to your room?" Uncle Nat asked, and I must have nodded. Uncle Nat helped me up the stairs and to my bed. I threw myself down there and began to weep again, but it seemed so useless. I started to pray instead. For Willie—though I don't know why. Willie was safe enough. For the Corbins; I knew the whole family would be devastated. I had to go to the Corbins. I had to let them know that I too shared their suffering over the news of Willie's untimely death.

I prayed for Mrs. Foggelson; Willie was to have been her son-in-law. But mostly I prayed for Camellia. How would she ever bear it? She was all alone at the college, preparing herself to serve with Willie in his Africa.

She would come home now, broken perhaps, but she would come home.

I went back to the kitchen and splashed water on my swollen face. Uncle Nat had already left, but Grandpa and Uncle Charlie sat silently at the kitchen table. Untouched cups of cold coffee sat before them. They looked at me without saying a word. Mary was nowhere to be seen, but her bedroom door was closed tightly.

"I'm going to the Corbins," I said quietly, and Grandpa nodded.

I wasn't sure Chester's leg was well enough, so I put a bridle on old Maude.

I didn't bother with the saddle; just grabbed up the reins and rode bareback. Maude wasn't the easiest horse in the world to ride, but maybe I took some satisfaction in my discomfort.

I found the Corbin family tear-stained and desolate. Mrs. Corbin sat in a rocker by the kitchen stove, saying over and over as she rocked, "My poor boy. My poor boy. My poor Willie." When she saw me she held out her arms and I went to her. She held me so tightly that I could scarcely breathe, and I knew she was trying to hold on to a little part of Willie.

Mr. Corbin paced back and forth across the kitchen floor, his face hard and his hands twisting together. Other family members huddled in little groups here and there, whispering and crying by turn.

And then a very strange thing happened. SueAnn, who had been crying just like the rest of them, wiped away her tears, took a deep breath and managed a weak smile.

"I know God doesn't make mistakes," she said. "There will be good, some reason in all this, even if we can't think of any right now."

They began to talk, in soft whispers at first, with frequent bursts of tears, but gradually the tears subsided and the praise became more positive. There was even an occasional chuckle as someone recalled a funny incident from Willie's

life. Soon the whole atmosphere of the room had changed.
Mrs. Corbin had stopped rocking and moaning, and Mr. Corbin was no longer pacing. Someone brought the family Bible
and they began to read, passing the precious book from hand
to hand as they shared its truths.

Later, when I left for home, the Corbin family was still
grieving, but each member had found a source of comfort
beyond themselves.

I waited a day or two before I called on Mrs. Foggelson.
I didn't think I could manage it earlier. I still felt a dull ache
deep within me, and I was afraid if I tried to talk about Willie
I would break up again.

Mrs. Foggelson met me at the door. "Oh, Josh!" she said
with a little cry and she moved quickly toward me, her arms
outstretched.

I held her for a few minutes. She was crying against my
shoulder, but when she moved back she quickly whisked
away the tears and motioned me to the sofa.

We talked about Willie for a long time; we both needed
it. I asked about Camellia.

"How is she?" I asked.

"Crushed!" said Mrs. Foggleson. "Crushed—but she'll
make it. We've talked on the telephone a couple of times."

"When will she be home?"

"Today. On the afternoon train. That was the soonest she
could come."

There was a pause; then she added, "It seems like such a
long way to come for such a short time, but we both felt it
important that she be here for the Memorial Service."

"Short time? What do you mean?"

"She has to go back right away. She's writing important
exams next week."

"You mean she's going to stay on in school?" I couldn't
believe it. Why? Willie was no longer there to draw Camellia
to South Africa.

Of course, I reasoned, *Camellia would not want to quit*

classes halfway through a year. I admired her for that. *But she quit the Interior Design course before she had completed it.* I was puzzled, unable to understand the difference.

"If she doesn't write these exams, she loses a whole semester. That would set her back considerably."

I nodded, a bit surprised that Camellia still wanted to be a nurse.

I went with Mrs. Foggelson to meet Camellia's train. Some of the Corbin family were there as well. There were more tears. Camellia went from one to another, being held and comforted. When it was my turn there was nothing that we could say to each other. I just held her and let her weep, and my heart nearly broke all over again. The three of us walked on home through the chill winter air and Mrs. Foggelson set about making us all a pot of tea.

"Your ma says you need to go back soon," I said to Camellia.

She nodded slowly, a weary hand brushing back her curls.

"You're still set on nursing?"

"Willie said that is the biggest need out there—and who knows? If there had been a nurse there, Willie might not have died."

I could understand that much but not what it had to do with her situation.

"I just wish I hadn't wasted so much time," she went on as though talking to herself. "If I had started my training at the same time Willie did . . ." She left the statement hanging.

"But you didn't know."

"No, I didn't know." Her tone was tired, empty; then she smiled softly. "But at least I'll have the joy of serving the people that Willie learned to love."

It finally got through to me then. Camellia was still planning on going to Africa.

"You're going to go after *this*?" It seemed out of the question.

"Of course," she said simply, as though I shouldn't even need to ask. "They need me."

Chapter 27

God's Call

The three of us made it through the Memorial Service; Mrs. Foggelson asked me to sit with her and Camellia. And then we saw Camellia off on the train again. She held her mother a long, long time as the tears flowed.

"Mamma, I love you so much," she sobbed. "If I didn't *have* to go, I'd stay with you—you know that."

Mrs. Foggelson seemed to understand. She looked Camellia straight in the eyes and said earnestly, "Remember—always, always stand true to your convictions, to what the Lord is telling you."

They hugged one another again, and then Camellia turned to me.

"Thank you, Josh, for always being there. For being such a dear, dear friend to Willie and me." I couldn't say anything in repiy. I just held her for a brief moment and then let her go.

I was restless over the next several days. I couldn't seem to think, to sleep, I didn't care to eat—I couldn't even really concentrate when I prayed. My prayers were all broken sentences, pleas of isolated words, fragments of thoughts.

I walked through the days in a stupor. I went through the motions of chores each day. The animals were cared for. Chester got his daily massage and exercise. I moved. I functioned. I spoke. Occasionally I even heard myself laugh, but it was as though another person were existing in my body.

I had to make a trip to town. We needed some groceries and the whole household seemed anxious for a new set of papers.

I went the usual route, picked up the papers at the post office, shuffled through the mail, and my eyes lighted up as they fell on an envelope from South Africa. It was from *Willie*! And then my whole body went numb.

But Willie is dead! Willie is no longer in South Africa!

I looked at the postmark. It was dated several weeks back. Somewhere the letter had been held up.

I put the letter in my coat pocket, *I wonder if I'll even be able to read it,* I thought. But at the same time I knew that there was no way on earth I could keep from reading it.

I didn't open the letter until after I had arrived home, cared for the team, done the chores, had my supper, and retired for the night. I didn't tell anyone about it either—I wasn't sure how its contents were going to affect me.

At last I opened it slowly and let my eyes drift over the familiar script. My hands were shaking as I held the pages to the light of the kerosene lamp.

Willie, in the usual fashion, wrote about the people he was getting to know, how they were learning to trust him and listen when he talked to them about Jesus. His love showed in every word he spoke. You could tell Willie was happy that God had called him to South Africa.

He made comments about my last letter and asked questions about my family and the community. He sent his love to Mary and even teased me a bit about having *two* eligible young ladies in the household.

Then he began to talk about Camellia. *How happy and blessed I am that God brought us together! I always cared for Camellia—right from the first day that she came to our school.*

I watched silently as you and Camellia became friends, both sad and happy at the same time.

And now God has turned everything around; Camellia is going to be my wife. I can hardly believe the way I have been blessed; I hope with all my heart that you haven't been hurt. It will be a long time yet before Camellia can join me; I'm counting every hour, but God is making the busy days pass quickly, and before we know it, she will be at my side.

And then Willie said, *Josh, I don't have to tell you this, but the most exciting thing in the world is to live day by day in the will of God. He has a perfect plan, and if we are obedient to Him He will accomplish it, whether it takes fifty years, twenty years or a single day.*

A sob caught in my throat. I read the paragraph again. Then I went on.

I am thankful that God gave me a good home, a good church, and good friends so that I could learn that truth without fighting it. I know that you have often wondered why the Lord hasn't called you to the pastorate or to the mission field. The important thing isn't where *we serve, but* how. *The question is not "what does He have for me in the future?" but "Am I obedient to Him right now?" And you can walk in obedience, Josh, wherever you live and serve.*

May God lead you, Josh, in whatever He has for you. You're the greatest buddy a fellow ever had. Love, Willie.

I cried many tears over that letter. I read it so often in the next several days that I could have repeated it by heart, yet I had a hard time getting to the truth of it.

I was in the barn one morning exercising Chester when the door opened and Uncle Nat came in. After warm greetings, Uncle Nat came over to check out my horse. He was nearly as pleased as I was to see how well Chester was progressing.

"He looks real good, Josh," he said to me. "Soon he'll be running at a full gallop again."

I grinned.

"Well, I sure hope the ice and snow are off the ground before then," I said. "Don't want it to happen again."

"Oh, it will be," said Uncle Nat with confidence.

I shook my head. "Seems to me this winter has hung on and on," I said soberly.

Uncle Nat looked at me evenly. I could read questions in his eyes. He pulled forward a barn stool and sat down.

"So, how's it going, Josh?" I knew that it wasn't just a passing question or a social pleasantry.

I let Chester drift back to his own stall, and I sank onto a soft mound of straw.

"I don't know," I said honestly. "It's been a tough winter."

Uncle Nat nodded.

"Tough times make us grow, Josh," he said simply.

I thought about that. I hoped I had done some growing.

"The farm's doing well," Uncle Nat went on, encouraging me to talk.

"Yeah," I nodded, thinking of the good seed grain in the granaries, the fine stock in the pasture, and the tractor waiting for spring.

"You should be real proud of yourself," Uncle Nat continued. "I know we all are."

"You are? That's good, but I still—"

"You unhappy with farming?" Uncle Nat's question brought me up short.

"Oh no," I was quick to inform him. "I like it—*love* it. It's great to watch things grow—and change—and to know that you've been a part of it."

"But something is bothering you."

"Well, I mean—I still don't know what God wants me to do in life. I expected by now that He would show me, but He hasn't yet. By the time a fella is past twenty-two, he should have some clear direction about his life, he should know what he's supposed to do."

Uncle Nat gave me a playful poke on the arm. "I thought

maybe you had girl troubles," he teased. "Couldn't make up your mind about which one of those fine ladies—"

"Naw," I answered, "not girl troubles." But I pondered Uncle Nat's words.

"I wouldn't even dare to choose a girl now," I added defensively. "Not 'til I know what God has in mind for my life."

"I see," said Uncle Nat.

We were both silent for a few minutes.

"But you enjoy farming?" said Uncle Nat, as though to clear up a point. "You don't feel any kind of guilt for being here for the last several years?"

"I *had* to be here," I said, surprised that Uncle Nat didn't understand that. "Grandpa and Uncle Charlie needed me. There was no one else to help them."

"And with your hard work and good management you have turned the farm around—it's better now than ever."

I appreciated Uncle Nat's lofty compliments, and I had to admit that there was some truth in what he said.

"And you think that the two men will be able to handle the farm now by themselves?"

It was a foolish question. Anyone could see that Grandpa and Uncle Charlie wouldn't do much farming in the future.

"You know they couldn't," I said rather abruptly.

"So they still need you?" Uncle Nat left the question hanging in the air between us. I didn't even try to answer it.

"Have you ever considered the fact that God might want you to go on farming? That farming might be His call for you?"

"*Farming?*" I paused for quite a while. Then I said, "Not really. I just supposed—" I shook my head.

"But you do enjoy farming?" pressed Uncle Nat.

"Sure I do. But it all seems kind of pointless. I've been trying hard to build up the farm so that it would be productive, make money." I lowered my head and picked absently at some straw. "I had even promised God that the money I made would be used to support missionaries—like Willie.

And now—now it all seems wasted." My speech ended with a sob caught in my throat. Uncle Nat sat silently for several minutes until he could see that I had control of myself again.

"I suppose Willie's early death seems a waste to you, too, Josh."

Uncle Nat had tied up my confused feelings into a neat package. I said nothing.

"I don't understand about Willie's death," went on Uncle Nat. "It is sad and it causes us all much pain, but it wasn't wasteful. God doesn't make mistakes, Josh."

"That's what SueAnn said the day we got word of his death. But, Uncle Nat, that's really hard for me to swallow. Look at Willie—if anybody was being faithful to God, he was. So why did God let him die like that, so young, with so much ahead of him?"

Uncle Nat looked intently at me. "Josh, none of us can know for certain *why* these things happen. We may never know. Because God gave man a free will and he chose to sin, we now live in a world marred by sin—"

"But Jesus' death sets us free from sin!" I protested.

"As individuals who trust Him—yes. From the *judgment* of sin. But as long as we live on this earth, we will have to live with the effects of sin."

"Like evil?"

"Evil, and sickness, and accidents, and untimely death— all those things that don't quite seem fair. We live in a sin-damaged world, Josh. People do get sick and die. We may not understand it, but we do know—"

"That God loves us and wants the best for us," I finished for him. Somewhere, in the darkness of my grief and confusion, I felt a light beginning to dawn.

"We have to believe that or life has no meaning," Uncle Nat agreed in a soft, firm voice.

"Now, I don't know the reason for what happened. But there is a purpose. God can make 'all things work together for good'—those aren't just words, Josh. I'm sure of that.

Willie's life accomplished what it was meant to accomplish. Willie was obedient to God. He was right where God wanted Him to be at the time that God wanted him to be there. He wasn't running away; he wasn't fighting God's plan. He was obedient. God can always—and only—fulfill His plan for us when we obey Him—about the daily decisions and the big ones."

Parts of Willie's letter flashed back into my mind. That was what Willie was trying to tell me. All that was really important was that I obey God now, this very moment, at this very place. Tomorrow could be left in God's hands.

Uncle Nat was talking again. "Do you feel that you are disobeying God in farming, Josh?"

"No," I was able to answer honestly. "I really don't."

"Then if you are not disobeying Him, could it be that you are *obeying* Him?"

I stared at Uncle Nat, thinking. Then I began to chuckle. "It seems so simple," I said, tossing a handful of straw into the air.

"Maybe it is. Maybe we're the ones who make it complicated."

I felt as if a great burden had suddenly been lifted from my shoulders. Uncle Nat and I hugged each other and then he held me away and said softly, "Josh, there are other missionaries who will still need to be supported. Camellia, for one."

Tears filled my eyes. I guess there was no other missionary I would rather support than Willie's Camellia. I nodded, too choked up to speak.

"You ready to go?" asked Uncle Nat.

I was ready all right. I had been spending too much of my time hidden away in the barn lately. Chester was doing just fine on his own. He didn't need me that much anymore. *At least for now, God wants me to be a farmer—the best one possible,* I thought. *Unless or until He shows me something else* . . . And I had the big issue settled. I was ready to get on with some of the other decisions that a fellow has to make. I gave Uncle Nat a smile—the first in a long time, it seemed. We left the barn and I fastened the door securely behind me.

As we headed for the house, I lifted my eyes to study the farm I loved. A distinct feeling of spring filled the morning air.

SPRING'S GENTLE PROMISE

SPRING'S GENTLE PROMISE

JANETTE OKE

BETHANY HOUSE PUBLISHERS

MINNEAPOLIS, MINNESOTA 55438

A Division of Bethany Fellowship, Inc.

Published by Bethany House Publishers
A Division of Bethany Fellowship, Inc.
6820 Auto Club Road, Minneapolis, Minnesota 55438

Printed in the United States of America

Library of Congress Cataloging-in-Publication Data

Oke, Janette, 1935–
   Spring's gentle promise / Janette Oke.
      p. cm. — (Seasons of the heart ; 4)
   Sequel to: Winter is not forever.

   I. Title. II. Series: Oke, Janette, 1935–
   Seasons of the heart ; bk. 4.
   PR9199.3.038S67   1989
813'.54—dc19   89–22
ISBN 1-55661-059-9   CIP

To all the men and women
of the soil,
past and present,
who have fought against the elements
and the changing times
to maintain their roots
and to pass on a heritage.

We need you.
We cheer you on.
God bless you.

BOOKS BY JANETTE OKE

SEASONS OF THE HEART Series
    Once Upon a Summer
    The Winds of Autumn
    Winter Is Not Forever
    Spring's Gentle Promise

LOVE COMES SOFTLY Series
    Love Comes Softly
    Love's Enduring Promise
    Love's Long Journey
    Love's Abiding Joy
    Love's Unending Legacy
    Love's Unfolding Dream
    Love Takes Wing
    Love Finds a Home

CANADIAN WEST Series
    When Calls the Heart
    When Comes the Spring
    When Breaks the Dawn
    When Hope Springs New

The Father Who Calls—spiritual insights
    from the Canadian West Series.

JANETTE OKE was born in Champion, Alberta, during the depression years, to a Canadian prairie farmer and his wife. She is a graduate of Mountain View Bible College in Didsbury, Alberta, where she met her husband, Edward. They were married in May of 1957, and went on to pastor churches in Indiana as well as Calgary and Edmonton, Canada.

The Okes have three sons and one daughter and are enjoying the addition to the family of grandchildren. Edward and Janette have both been active in their local church, serving in various capacities as Sunday-school teachers and board members. They make their home in Didsbury, Alberta.

Contents

Characters

Joshua Chadwick Jones—The boy raised by his Aunt Lou, Grandfather and great-uncle Charlie. Josh is now an adult, farming the family farm.

Grandpa and Uncle Charlie—The menfolk who shared Josh's home and life.

Matilda—The neighborhood schoolteacher who boards with the Joneses.

Mary Turley—Housekeeper and neighbor girl who helps the men with the kitchen duties. In Grandpa's thinking, two girls in the house made the arrangement more "respectable."

Willie—Josh's boyhood friend who went to Africa as a missionary and died of a native disease.

Camellia—Josh's first love, but she loved Willie instead.

Chapter 1

A Beautiful Morning

I was whistling as I left the house. It was early. The sky had brightened, but the sun had not as yet lifted its head above the tree line that marked the border of the Sanders' place—new neighbors in our community.

Even in the dimness of early morning I could see field after neighborhood field as I let my gaze wander around me. First there was ours—I supposed I would always think of the farm as *ours*—Grandpa's, Uncle Charlie's and mine—though in truth it really was just mine now. Guess that was one of the reasons I was whistling. Just yesterday Grandpa and Uncle Charlie had signed all the official papers to make the farm mine—really and legally mine. *Joshua Chadwick Jones* the papers read, clear as could be. The full impact had yet to hit me. But I was excited. Really excited. I mean, what other fella my age had a farm his own, title clear and paid for?

I sobered down a bit. It was a big responsibility 'cause I was the one who had to make the farm "bring forth" now. Had to support Grandpa and Uncle Charlie and myself and Mary, our housekeeper, and even Matilda, our boarder, though she did pay us some board and room.

I was the one who had to make the right decisions about which crops to plant and which field to plant them in, which livestock to sell and which ones to keep, and where to find the particular animal that would help build up the herd. I would need to keep up the fences, repaint the buildings, work the garden, keep the machinery in working order, watch out for weeds, put up the hay for winter feeding. . . . The list went on and on—but that didn't dim my spirits. It was a beautiful morning. I was a full-grown man with a place of my own.

I lengthened my stride. I'd been dawdling somewhat while I looked all around. The fields, the tree line, the wooded area where the crick passed through, the pastureland, and then the fields of the Turleys, Smiths, Sanders, the faraway hill that marked another Smith, the road to town—I knew it all. And I loved it more than I would ever have been able to say.

My roots were buried deep in this countryside I had known since a child. This was my life. My whole sense of being and knowing and living and growing were somehow wrapped up in the soil that stretched away before me.

I opened the gate at the end of the lane and took a break in my whistling to speak to the milk cows. The little jersey, one of my most recent purchases, rubbed her head against me gently as she moved to pass by. I reached out and ran my hand over her neck. She seemed satisfied then, and I smiled. *She's a great little cow,* I gloated. *Can fill the milk pail with the richest milk I've ever seen.* She was a mite spoiled though. Her former owners had treated her as the family pet.

I hurried ahead of the cows to open the barn door for them. I knew they were right behind me, anxious to reach the milking stall where their portion of morning grain waited. They also wished to find relief from the heavy load of milk that swelled their udders and slowed their walk.

I began my whistling again. A bird joined me, off to the right, and I turned my head to look for it. It was high in a poplar tree by the hen house, and by its vigorous song I imagined that it was just as happy with the early morning as I was.

From somewhere in Turleys' pasture a cow bawled and

another answered. Perhaps a mother had become separated from her baby and was calling it for breakfast.

I opened the barn door for the cows and turned right back to the house for the milk pails. I knew the three cows would find their own way to their stalls and be appreciatively feeding on the chop when I returned. I could have gone the entire milking time without fastening the bars that held them in position, but I never did. I knew they wouldn't move from their places, heads between the stanchion bars, bodies motionless except for the ever-flicking tails and an occasional shift of a foot; but when I returned with the milk pails I fastened the bars just as I always had. It was pure habit I guess—but it was the way Grandpa had taught me.

The jersey gazed back at me with soft brown eyes as I hooked a toe under the milking stool and pulled it up to her side.

"What's the matter?" I chuckled. "You think I'm too lazy to bend over?"

I rubbed her side and eased myself onto the stool beside her, then reached out to brush off her taut bag, wash it a bit, and gently start the flow of milk.

"Well, maybe I am," I conceded. "But a fella has to conserve all the energy he can. I've a busy day ahead. I start plantin' today. Just as soon as I get the chores done. My own fields. Never planted 'my own fields' before."

I grinned and began the steady stream of milk that would soon fill the pail with rich, warm, foamy liquid.

I would never have been able to explain to anyone why I talked to the cow. I mean, no one would understand if they hadn't spent time in a barn at 5:00 in the morning doing the milking.

A barn cat, meowing, brushed itself against my pant leg. I didn't know if the soft sound was my welcome or an urge for me to hurry. I stopped long enough to squirt some milk in the cat's direction. It immediately sat back on its haunches, front paws batting in the air as though to capture every drop of milk and direct it toward its open mouth.

We were rather good at this—the gray tom and I. But then, we'd had a few years of practice. He sat there guzzling contentedly as I gave him squirt after squirt.

"Go on, now," I said at last. "I've got chores to do. You'll get your fill as soon as I'm done here."

The cat seemed to understand. He walked off a few feet and sat down to begin carefully grooming his spattered face.

The milking didn't take long, so after giving each cow a final pat on the flank, I left them, and carried two brimming pails of milk to the house. I would need to return for the third one, which was now hanging on a peg beyond the reach of the barn cats.

In spite of the early hour, Mary was moving briskly about the kitchen when I entered with the milk. I thought I noticed a certain gleam in her eyes—but perhaps it was just fanciful on my part. The fact that I was feeling so good seemed to be affecting my whole outlook on life.

Pixie was there too, rubbing against my legs, looking for her share of attention. I reached down and scratched her soft, silky ear. She was no longer the puppy I had learned to love. The years had passed by and Pixie was now old in dog years. She had remained behind, curled and contented, when I'd left my bed that morning. And I had been happy to let her sleep on. I rubbed her soft side and she licked at my hand.

"Mornin', Josh," Mary said cheerily. And without even waiting for my reply she went on, "My, you're up early. Don't know how you can even see out there in the barn."

"I waited for some light," I answered with a smile. "At least it was gettin' light when I went out." Then I added, "True, the barn stays dark a bit longer than the outside world, but I know my way around out there well enough that I don't need much light."

Mary smiled, adding to the brightness of the morning.

"Do you want to eat early?" she asked.

"I still have some chores to do."

Mary's eyes lifted to the kitchen clock, and mine followed.

"Guess I will be ready before the rest of them," I admitted.

"Want to start plantin' just as soon as I can."

"I'll git your breakfast," Mary said simply and moved toward the pantry.

"Thanks. I—I hate for you to get breakfast twice, but I'm kind of anxious—"

I needn't have tried to explain. As Mary tied her apron around her slim waist, without even turning to look at me she answered, "In plantin' and harvest time, a man doesn't want to lose any time gittin' to his fields. An early breakfast is no problem—an' we sure don't need to be wakin' the rest of the house."

I hadn't missed Mary's reference to "a man" and "his fields," and my heart beat a little faster. Then my thoughts hurried on to Grandpa, rather old and tired out after all his years of farming, then to Uncle Charlie, all crippled up with his arthritis. I wondered sadly just how much sleep he had been able to get over the night hours. My thoughts went on to Matilda. She was testing her pupils again at the nearby schoolhouse, and I knew she had been staying up late marking papers for a number of nights in a row. I nodded my head in agreement with Mary's simple statement. They all needed their sleep, all right.

"I'll only be another half hour or so," I reported to Mary and then went to strain the milk into the bowl of the cream separator.

"You go on," Mary prompted. "I'll tend to that."

My eyes questioned her, though it was true that Mary had often stepped forward to help with such tasks in the past.

Her eyes held mine steadily, and I knew she wished to take over the chore.

"At least let me strain it," I urged. "These pails are heavy to lift."

Mary did not argue with that. Her eyes followed the stream of milk from the pail into the large bowl of the separator.

"The jersey's?" she asked me. But she didn't wait for my reply. "My, such rich milk. I think I'll separate it by itself and keep the cream aside. Just think of the butter it'll make!"

I could hear the smile in Mary's voice even though I was too busy to look at her face.

I positioned the pail under the separator for Mary and turned to go back to the other chores. On my way to the barn to pick up the remaining pail of milk, I stopped by the tractor and ran a hand over its still-shiny fender. I could hardly wait to crawl up into the seat and begin passing back and forth over my fields, dropping the seed that would mean a bountiful harvest. I lifted my eyes toward heaven, and an unspoken prayer of thanks welled up within me. I'm not sure, but there could have been a few tears in my eyes.

I turned back to the chores at hand. I was whistling a tune I had learned some time back in my childhood, a tune I had sung frequently over the years. But it swelled in my heart in a new way now: "Praise God from whom all blessings flow. . . ."

Chapter 2

Togetherness

I was tired and stiff when I climbed down from the tractor that evening. Already the sun was disappearing in the western sky and there was a slight chill in the air. It was, after all, still early spring. I had been riding the tractor almost constantly since sunup. Mary had brought my noon meal and an afternoon snack to the field to save me time. I was glad I wasn't driving a team that would need to stop for a rest and nourishment. The tractor didn't complain about the long hours, though I did need to stop to refuel now and then.

I was a bit surprised at the aches and pains in my back and legs. But then I remembered I'd been bouncing and jostling my way over the field for several hours, and it always took a few days for my body to readjust.

I moved toward the smell of roast beef, my feet reluctant to proceed as quickly as my stomach was demanding. I hadn't realized just how hungry I was until I smelled supper in the air.

"Are you finally stopping for the night?" Matilda good-naturedly asked.

I tried to disguise my stiffness as I stepped up onto the back porch. Matilda was seated on the porch swing, a cup of tea in her hands.

"I was beginning to think we'd never eat," she continued.

"This is all Mary would let me have to tide me over till supper."

I stopped mid-stride. "Why?" I asked, surprised. Mary wasn't one to withhold victuals from anybody.

"Well—" laughed Matilda. "Guess I'm exaggerating some. Truth is, Mary would have let us go ahead, but we all opted to wait for you."

"I'm sorry—" I began. "If I'd known—"

But Matilda interrupted me. "We all know how important it is to get the crop in. We didn't mind waiting." She stood to her feet and took another dainty sip of the tea, then looked at me, her eyes sparkling. "Honest!" she said frankly, and I believed her.

I held the kitchen door for Matilda and followed right behind into the aroma-filled room. Grandpa was reading a paper in his favorite chair by the window. Uncle Charlie sat on the couch along the west wall gently massaging his gnarled hands, and I knew without asking that they were paining him again. As soon as he felt my eyes on him, he stopped the rubbing and let the hands drop idly into his lap.

Mary was at the big kitchen stove spooning food into serving bowls. She turned, glanced over her shoulder and gave me a smile. I thought she would ask a question, but she didn't—at least not vocally. Maybe her eyes found their answer, I don't know, but she smiled softly again and turned back to the stove.

"We're ready as soon as you wash, Josh," she said.

I crossed to the corner sink with its big farm basin and noticed that it had already been filled with warm water. I didn't know who had thoughtfully supplied the water, but I did think, with appreciation, that I sure was well looked after.

It didn't take long to scrub my face and hands clean enough to appear at the supper table. By the time I'd re-hung the towel, the rest of the family had gathered around the table. I took my place beside them and bowed as Grandpa asked the grace.

When we lifted our heads and began to help ourselves from Mary's heaping bowls, Grandpa spoke for the first time.

"How'd it go, Boy?"

He still called me "Boy." Guess to Grandpa I would always be Boy no matter how old I grew or whether I was a farm owner or not. I didn't mind. It made me feel "belongin'."

"Good," I replied around a mouthful of fresh bread.

"Tractor workin' right?"

I nodded, my mouth too full to venture an answer.

Uncle Charlie took a long draft of his coffee. "Thet there noise must nigh burst yer eardrums," he ventured. "Think I'd rather drive me a team."

I grinned. Uncle Charlie had a bit of a hard time adjusting to farm machinery that didn't require four-footed horsepower.

I swallowed sufficiently to make a decent reply. "It's noisier but faster, and one needn't stop for restin' or feedin' either."

Uncle Charlie chuckled a bit. "I had my eye on the field, Josh," he reminded me, "and seems to me I saw ya stop different times today to feed thet critter's iron belly."

I laughed along with Uncle Charlie. He'd made his point.

"I think I'd like to drive a tractor," put in Matilda, and I chuckled again at the picture that little bit of a woman would make up there on the seat of the big tractor.

Matilda must have misread my laughter, for her chin went up stubbornly. "I could, you know," she argued. "Bet I could. All you have to do is to put your foot on that—that thing, and move that lever now and then and turn the wheel where you want it to go."

Even Grandpa was chuckling now.

Matilda looked to Mary. "We could—couldn't we, Mary?" she challenged.

Mary fidgeted slightly. "I—I don't really know, but I—I think I'd just as soon leave the tractor to Josh."

Her eyes met mine for an instance. I noticed the slight color flush her cheeks before she lowered her head. For some silly reason I couldn't have explained I felt that I had just been given a compliment. Mary often affected me that way—with just a look or a word she could make me feel like a man—a man in charge and capable. I felt my own cheeks warm slightly.

"Someday—" began Matilda, and I looked at her, waiting for her to go on. I was hoping to be able to tease her good-naturedly just a bit; but she would not meet my eyes, and she let the rest of her comment go unsaid.

Supper finished up with Mary's bread pudding, one of my favorite desserts. There was thick whipped cream for the topping, and I was sure this was how some of the jersey's cream had been used.

After enjoying a man-sized portion, I reluctantly pushed back from the table and got slowly to my feet. Uncle Charlie moved at the same time, and I knew he was getting set to give Mary a hand with the dishes.

"I can help tonight, Uncle Charlie," Matilda spoke up.

Now there was nothing new about Matilda calling him Uncle Charlie. Both she and Mary called him such, just like they did when talking to my grandfather. It seemed to please everyone all around. Guess we felt more like family than employer and employee and boarder. What had caught my attention was Matilda's offer. Not that Matilda didn't often help Mary with her household chores, but lately Matilda had been too busy to do anything but correct papers and prepare lessons.

"What happened to the classroom work?" I asked her.

"All done. Finally! And believe me, I feel like celebrating."

Matilda swirled around, her long, full skirt flowing out around her. In one hand she held the sugar bowl and in the other the cream pitcher.

Uncle Charlie looked at her with a twinkle in his eyes. "Seems like ya oughta find a better way to celebrate than with the cream and sugar," he teased.

"Well, Josh is always too busy to celebrate," Matilda

teased back, pretending to pout. And she looked deliberately at me and exaggeratedly fluttered her long, dark eyelashes.

Laughter filled the kitchen. Matilda was always bringing laughter with her lighthearted teasing, but for some reason this time her teasing did not have me laughing. It gave me a funny feeling way down deep inside, and I moved for the peg where my farm jacket hung beside the door.

"Where ya goin'?" asked Uncle Charlie, and when I turned to look at him I caught his wink directed at Matilda. "Gonna feed thet there tractor agin?"

"I've got chores," I answered as evenly as I could.

"The chores be all done, Boy," cut in Grandpa.

I stood, my outreached hand dumbly dangling the jacket, my eyes moving from face to face in the kitchen. They all seemed to be in a jovial mood, and I wasn't quite sure if they were serious or funnin' me. It was to Mary that I looked for the final answer. She just nodded her head in agreement.

"All of them?" I had to ask.

"All of 'em," said Grandpa.

For a moment I wanted to protest. It was my farm. I could do my own chores. But then I quickly realized how foolish that was—and how tired I was—and my hand relinquished my coat to the peg again. I turned and smiled at the household of people.

"Thanks," I said simply and gave my shoulders a slight shrug. "Thanks to whoever did them."

"We all pitched in," replied Grandpa. "Little here, a little there and had 'em done in no time."

"Thanks," I said again.

"So you see," teased Matilda, fluttering her eyelashes again, "you will have time to help celebrate."

I was ready for the challenge now. "Okay," I answered, "checkers—right after dishes." And I reached for a tea towel and stepped up beside Mary. "I'll dry—you put things away," I dared order Matilda.

"Checkers?" Matilda commented. "Not exactly a corn roast or a pie social—but I guess it'll have to do," and to the accompaniment of chuckles from the two older men, she moved quickly to put away the dishes as I dried them.

When the last plate was on the shelf, Matilda and I turned to the checkerboard, and Mary picked up some handwork that always seemed to appear when she had what she called a "free moment." Grandpa and Uncle Charlie spent a little more time poring over newspapers. I wasn't sure if we had received a new one or if they were just rereading an old one, but I didn't ask. Beside us on the bureau squawked the raspy radio. I enjoyed the soft music but paid little attention to the commentary that interrupted it at intervals.

It wasn't too hard for me to beat Matilda at checkers. She had a keen mind and could have offered some real serious competition if she hadn't been so impatient. As it was, she played more for the fun than for the challenge, and for three games in a row I turned out the victor.

At the end of the third game I stood and stretched.

"Is that enough 'celebratin' ' for one evening?" I teased Matilda.

"It'll do," she answered with a flip of her head that made her pinned-up curls bounce. "But next time I'll insist on lawn croquet."

Matilda was an expert at lawn croquet. In fact, whenever there was a matchup, I always hoped Matilda would be my partner. Now I just smiled and tried to stifle a yawn.

Mary laid aside her handwork. "Would you like something to eat or drink before bedtime, Josh?" she asked me and started to leave her chair for the cupboard.

"No, thanks. It's been a long day. I think I'll just go on up to bed." As soon as I said the words, I realized the day had been equally long for Mary. "You must be tired, too," I said, studying her face. "You've been up 'most as long as I have."

Mary brushed the remark aside and went to put on a pot of coffee for Grandpa and Uncle Charlie.

There was the rustle of paper as Grandpa put down what he was reading and took off his glasses.

"I'm plannin' to go on into town tomorrow, Josh," he said, folding up his glasses and placing them on the bureau beside the sputtering radio. "Anything you be needin'?"

I tried to think but my head was a bit foggy. I finally shook it. "If I think of anything I'll leave a note on the table," I promised. "Can't think of anything now."

"You got a list, Mary?" went on Grandpa. "Or would ya rather come on along and do yer own choosin'?"

I stood long enough to watch Mary slowly shake her head. "It takes too much time to ride on in and back," she said. "I'll just send a list."

I took three steps toward the stairway and then turned. "I've been thinkin'," I said, half teasingly but with a hint of seriousness; "maybe when we get in this year's crop, we oughta get us one of those motor cars. We could be in town and back before ya know it."

I don't know just what I expected, but I sure did get a reaction. Grandpa raised his shaggy eyebrows and studied me to see if I was serious. Uncle Charlie stopped rubbing his gnarly fingers and stared open-mouthed. And Mary stopped right in her tracks, one hand reaching out to set the coffeepot on the kitchen stove. But Matilda's response was vocal. "Yes!" she exclaimed, just like that, and she clapped her hands and ran to me. "Oh, yes, Josh!" she said again, her cheeks flushed and her eyes shining. "Get one, Josh. Get one." And she reached out impulsively and gave me a quick hug that almost knocked me off balance.

"Whoa-a," I said, disengaging myself from her arms. "I said 'maybe'—after the crop is off. I'm just plantin' it, remember? We've got a long time to wait."

Matilda stepped back, her eyes still shining. She clapped her hands again, not the least bit daunted. "Now, that's what I call really celebrating, Josh," she enthused, her hands clasped together in front of her.

I let my eyes travel back over the room. Mary had finally set down the coffeepot. Uncle Charlie had closed his mouth and was chewing on a corner of his mustache, and Grandpa's eyebrows were back where they belonged.

I shrugged my shoulders carelessly. "It's just something to be thinkin' on," I repeated lamely and headed for the stairs and my bed.

Chapter 3

Visitors

The spring planting went steadily forward. The tractor chugged on with only minor adjustments and repairs. The family continued to help with evening chores and work about the farmyard. Only one rain slowed me down and then it was just a few days—enough for me to sort of catch my breath and do a few little extras that always seem to need doing around a farm.

Matilda never gave me a moment's peace about the motor car. I began to wish I hadn't mentioned it. Still, her enthusiastic arguments in favor of the vehicle may have gone a long way toward influencing Grandpa and Uncle Charlie. At any rate, I never did hear much opposition to the idea, and everybody seemed to be holding their breath—waiting to see what the harvest would bring.

About the same time I finished the planting, the school doors closed for another year and Matilda left for her home again.

"Oh, Josh," she enthused on before departing, "I can hardly wait for fall—and the car. It'll be such fun, Josh!" She emitted a strange little sound like a combination sigh and groan.

"I haven't promised," I reminded her. "Just said I'd be thinkin' on it."

"I know. I know. And it will be such fun!" Apparently Matilda didn't want to hear of the possibility of *not* getting a car, so I let the matter drop.

As usual, Matilda and Mary's goodbye was rather emotional. They had grown to be like sisters in their affection and missed each other during the summer months.

"Oh, I'll be lonely without her," Mary half-whispered after Matilda was gone, and she slyly wiped her cheek with her handkerchief.

"Summer will pass quickly," I tried to console her.

"The house is always so—so *quiet* when she's gone," she responded.

It is quiet without Matilda's bubbly enthusiasm, I mentally agreed.

"You'll be busy with the garden," I reminded Mary.

She nodded; then after a moment of silence she said wistfully, "Maybe Lou will let Sarah Jane come visit for a while. She is 'most as chattery as Matilda."

I smiled at the thought. Sarah Jane was getting to be quite a little lady. And it was true that she was "chattery."

"Maybe," I responded, "for a few days. Lou counts on Sarah for running errands and entertaining her two little brothers."

Mary thoughtfully spoke as though to herself. "Lou does need her more than I do. It was selfish of me to—"

But I interrupted. "It wasn't selfish. Grandpa and Uncle Charlie—and me—we all look forward to her coming."

"Maybe we could have Jon come to the farm, too," Mary brightened. "That would leave Lou with just the baby."

I wasn't sure Mary wanted to take on the lively Jon plus all of the household and garden chores of farm life. I was about to say so, but she placed a hand on my arm, seeming to know just what I was thinking.

"It wouldn't be so bad," she argued. "Sarah would help with Jon, and there is lots for a boy to do on the farm, and the garden isn't ready for pickin' or cannin' yet, and he's usually not *too* rascally." She looked a bit doubtful about her last statement. "Besides," she hurried on, "it sure would make the house more—more—"

I looked at the small hand resting on my arm. It was hard for me to argue against Mary, but I did wonder if she was thinking straight to figure that Jon wouldn't take much time or trouble.

"It would help the summer pass more quickly," she finished lamely.

"Why don't you try it for a few days—to start with? Make sure you aren't gettin' in over your head," I advised.

Mary smiled, and I knew she was pleased with my qualified consent.

It wasn't that Jon was a bad boy, and it certainly wasn't that I didn't love my young nephew, but he was one of the busiest and most curious children I had ever known. His poking and prodding into things invariably got him into some kind of trouble.

"Keep him away from the tractor," I added quite firmly, remembering the time Jon had poured dirt in the gas tank.

Mary just nodded. "I'll check with Lou next time I'm in town," she promised. I couldn't help but think that a break from Sarah and Jon might be a welcome change for my Aunt Lou.

True to her word, Mary made arrangements with Lou. And before the week was out, Sarah and Jon had joined us at the farm. Sarah busied herself with copying the activities of Mary. She helped bake bread, churn butter and wash clothes. She even spent time in the garden pulling weeds— along with a few carrots and turnips—and washed dishes, very slowly, doing more playing in the soapy water than scrubbing the plates and cups. But Sarah seemed to fit very nicely into the farm life, and we all enjoyed her chatter and sunny disposition.

Grandpa and Uncle Charlie tried their best to keep young Jon entertained. They whittled him whistles and slingshots, fashioned him fish poles and found him a barn kitten. But, still, Jon seemed to be continually slipping out from under supervision, off finding entertainment of his own making.

In the few days he was with us he got into more scrapes and mischief—not out of naughtiness but "just tryin' to he'p." He dumped all the hens' water and filled their drinking dishes with hay—he said they looked hungry. He tied the farm dog to a tree with so many knots that it took Grandpa most of an afternoon to get him released again—he said he was afraid "Fritz might get runned over by the tractor." He shot a rock through the front room window with the slingshot he was not to play with around the house—he said that it "went off" when he wasn't ready. He picked a whole pail of tiny apples that were just beginning to form nicely on the apple trees—he wanted to help Mary with an apple pie. He visited the hen house and threw a couple dozen eggs at the old sow who fed in the nearby pen—he wanted to teach her a trick, "like Pixie," of snatching food from the air.

And, as far as I was concerned, the worst stunt of all was helping himself to a bottle of India ink from Matilda's supply desk and sneaking up on unsuspecting Chester, climbing the corral fence and pouring it all over the horse's back. He wanted to "surprise Unc'a Josh" with a pretty, spotted horse like one he had seen in a picture book.

We had a family council that night. I was ready to send Jon on home, but Mary argued that he really wasn't naughty and needed a chance to learn about the farm. Grandpa sided with her. How could the boy learn what he could and couldn't do if he wasn't given the chance to do a little exploring? So Jon stayed on, but we gave the four-year-old more rules and tried to watch him even closer.

I was busy repairing the back pasture fence when Jon joined me one afternoon

"Hi, Unc'a Josh," he greeted me warmly. I looked at the bright eyes and mop of brown hair.

"Hi, fella," I responded a bit cautiously. "Does Mary know you're here?"

Jon did not answer my question but held a little red pail

as high as his short arm could hoist it.

"Brought ya a drink," he announced. "Are ya thirsty?"

The summer sun was hot, and I *was* thirsty. I stopped to wipe the sweat from my brow and reached for the pail the boy held out to me.

"Auntie Mary said ya would be thirsty," Jon continued. Lou had her children refer to Mary as "auntie" as a term of respect.

My eyes shifted to the nearby farmhouse. I was close enough that I didn't need to be waited on—I could walk to the house or the well for a drink. Still, maybe Mary thought a bit of a stroll and an "errand" would do the small boy good. I sat down on the grass and pulled Jon onto my knee, one hand supporting the pail.

"Where's Mary?" I asked him, looking at the dirt streaks on his hands and face.

"Busy doin' some'pin," he answered.

"So you brought me a drink?"

He nodded.

"That was mighty nice," I complimented Jon. "Thank you."

I lifted the pail to my lips. The water was not as cool as usually comes from our deep well, and I couldn't help but wonder just how long Jon had been on his journey. At least it was wet. I took another long drink.

"So what have you been doing today?" I asked Jon.

He thought about that for a few moments before answering.

"I he'ped Grandpa hoe the garden," he said brightly and then added more soberly, "but he said, 'Thet's enough, Jonathan,' and sent me back to Auntie Mary."

I tousled his hair. "And why did he do that?" I questioned. "Did you mix up weeds and vegetables?"

Jon nodded his head, his eyes thoughtful. "I guess it was peas," he said somberly, and I had to hide my smile.

"Then I brought in the clothes for Auntie Mary," he began, but ended with a shrug of his small shoulders. "But she hada take 'em back agin. They wasn't dry yet." Then Jon added quickly as though with great relief, "But Auntie Mary din't scold me. Jest took the clothes and hung some back up an'—" His eyes lowered and then lifted again to mine. He finished with a grin that told me everything was all right. "An' washed some of 'em agin an' then hung *them* back up, too."

Poor Mary. She had enough work without re-doing the wash.

"Here comes Aunt Mary now!" Jon excitedly pointed toward the farm buildings.

He was right. Mary and Sarah were coming our way.

"We brought you something, Uncle Josh," Sarah called before they reached us.

I looked at the small container in Sarah's hands and then to Mary. Both young ladies seemed pleased with themselves.

"Do I have to guess?" I asked Sarah.

Puffing, she reached the spot where Jon and I still sat on the ground.

"It's a drink," she said proudly.

"A drink? That's nice. But Jon here"—I ruffled the boy's hair again—"he already beat you to it. But I guess another drink would—"

But I stopped. The mention of the drink brought to me by young Jon had made Mary's face blanch, her hand went to her mouth and she stood staring down at the red pail.

"Is something wrong?" I asked Mary, but it was Sarah who answered the question for me, though in a rather roundabout fashion.

"In that?" she squealed, pointing her finger at the red pail in the grass. Before I could even answer her she went on, "Jon was botherin' Grandpa in the garden—hoeing up things—so Grandpa gave him that pail and sent him to water the flowers."

That didn't sound so bad. I didn't mind sharing water with the flowers. But Mary's face was still pale and she hadn't said one word except for a gaspy little, "Oh, Joshua."

"But—" went on Sarah, "Jon was dipping water from the stock trough!"

For a moment my stomach rebelled. I even thought I might be sick. The thought of the horses and cattle slurping and snorting in my drinking water made my insides heave. I looked up at Mary's white face and agonized expression. And then the whole thing struck me funny, and I pulled Jon closer into my arms, rolled over in the grass and began to tickle him and laugh. Not just little chuckles, but outright guffaws. Mary's color returned to normal, and I saw she was trying to hide a snicker behind her hand. Then she looked at Jon and me tumbling on the grass together and began to laugh right along with me. Now my stomach hurt from laughter.

When we finally got ourselves under control, we all sat down on the ground together and shared the cool lemonade Mary and Sarah had brought.

"I guess if I can drink with the cows and horses, I can use the same cup as family," I said and began to laugh again.

"We have cookies, too," Sarah informed me importantly. I think she was trying to get me to settle down. She didn't seem to understand why I thought my drink from the stock trough was so funny. I tried to respond properly to Sarah's announcement.

"Cookies? What kind? Where did you find cookies?"

"They're sugar cookies and I made 'em—myself." And then she quickly corrected her statement. "Auntie Mary and me made 'em."

"Can I have one? Can I have one, Sarah?" Jon was asking. Sure enough, there were some for all of us.

I guess the lemonade and the sugar cookies had a settling effect on my stomach. At any rate, I suffered no ill effects from drinking water out of the stock trough, though I did determine that in the future I would carefully check any food or drink offered me from the hand of my young nephew.

Chapter 4

Summer

Things settled down again after Sarah and Jon went off to their home. I think even Mary was glad for the peace and quiet, though she never admitted it. She had much to do, with the garden now in full swing. Her hands never seemed to be empty nor her body still.

The summer was busy for me as well. There was haying, the war with farm weeds, the continual care of the stock and fences; and before we could scarcely turn around, the summer would be drawing to an end.

I was glad for Sundays. It was the one day of the week that, with a clear conscience and no guilty feelings, one could actually take a bit of a break. It was good to be driving into town for the church service—though I must confess that as I sat behind the slow-moving team, I kept thinking more and more of the time we'd save in traveling if I had that motor car.

On a couple of Sundays we stayed on to dinner with Lou and Nat and their three. That was about the only chance we really had to catch up on the happenings of one another's lives.

Baby Timothy was growing so fast it was hard to keep up to him. He celebrated his first birthday in June and was busy with the task of learning how to walk—how to run might more aptly describe it. Timmy wanted to be in on the fun with his older brother and sister and tagged around after them as fast as his sturdy little legs would allow.

"The crop's looking good and seems to be a little ahead of schedule," I told Nat over one of our Sunday dinners. "It might well be our best crop yet," I admitted.

But I went from day to day with one eye on the sky and the other on my fields. I knew without being told that one good hailstorm could change everything, and deep inside me, I kind of wished there was some way I could make a little bargain with God. But of course I didn't try. I had the good sense—and faith—to know that He knew all about our needs and my wishes, and that in His love He would take care of our future. But oh, my, how I did hope that the future didn't include hail.

In next to no time Matilda was breezing in again. The two girls hugged and squealed and laughed like they'd been apart for years. Even Grandpa and Uncle Charlie got enthusiastic squeezes. I accepted a small hug myself, then backed up and looked at Matilda's glowing face.

"How's the crop, Josh?" she burst out before I had a chance to open my mouth. No "How are you?" or anything like that, but "How's the crop?" and I knew just what she was thinking about. I was prepared to tease her a bit.

I shrugged my shoulders and put a glum look on my face. "It might pay for the cuttin'," I informed her drearily. "That is, if we don't get any hail or such."

Matilda's mouth went down at the corners, and a sound of disappointment escaped her lips.

"Look on the bright side," I said, patting her shoulder. "With good weather and no more problems, we'll have a bit of seed grain for next spring."

Matilda looked awfully disappointed, even shamefaced.

"I told all my friends that you'd be getting a—a motor car," she said softly, her voice catching on the last word.

"Well, now, I didn't make me any promises on that, did I?" I said, keeping my expression somber. "Maybe you shouldn't'a been tellin' tales out of school." But when she looked like she might cry, I decided I had gone far enough.

"I'm just joshin'," I grinned at her. "The crop looks good. Real good." And as Matilda was about to exuberantly throw herself at me I hastened on, "Now remember, I'm still not promisin'. Just been thinkin' on that automobile. No promises."

But Matilda didn't seem one bit worried about the results of "thinkin' on it." Guess she knew me well enough to know I wanted that motor car too.

She punched me on the arm with a little fist, but her eyes were shining. "Oh, Josh," she scolded, "you're mean!"

Grandpa chuckled and Uncle Charlie just grinned.

When the school year started again, it was rather a traumatic time for Aunt Lou. Sarah Jane started off to first grade. I hadn't realized how tough it was on mothers to see their first baby go off into a whole new world. Lou wanted to be enthusiastic for Sarah's sake, but I knew that if it had been in Lou's power to turn back the clock a year or two, she could not have refrained from doing so.

Mary went into the final stages of putting up summer fruits and vegetables. As I watched the stacks of canning jars fill and refill the kitchen counter top, I wondered how in the world the five of us could ever consume so much food. Part of the answer came when I saw Mary and Grandpa load a whole bunch into the buggy and send it off to town to Aunt Lou. Lou was too busy with her little family and being a pastor's wife to do much canning of her own, Mary reasoned. Lou was deeply appreciative. After all, a pastor's salary didn't leave much room for extras, though I'd never heard Lou complain.

I began to find little pamphlets and newspaper advertisements scattered about the kitchen telling about this motor car or that automobile and the merits of each. I didn't have to guess who was leaving them about, but I did wonder how Matilda was collecting them.

I read the descriptions—just like she knew I would. In

fact, I sneaked them off to my own bedroom and lay in bed going over and over them. My, some of them were fancy! I hadn't known that such features existed. Why, you could start the motor without cranking it in the front! Then I would look at the listed price. I hadn't known that they cost so much, either, and doubts began to form in my mind. The same number of dollars could do so many things for the farm. I began to realize that Matilda's little campaign might well come to nothing. It could be sheer foolishness for me to buy a car.

I went into harvest with my mind debating back and forth. One day I would think for sure that I "deserved a car." The whole family deserved a car after all the years of slow team travel. *And think of how much valuable time we'd save,* I'd reason. Then the next day I would think of the farm needs, of the church needs, of my promise to support Camellia in her missionary service, of the stock I could purchase or the things for Mary's kitchen; and I would mentally strike the motor car from my list. Back and forth, this way and that way I argued with myself. Even all of the praying I did about it didn't put my mind at rest.

It did turn out to be a good crop. Even better than I'd dared hope. I watched the bins fill to overflowing with wonderfully healthy grain. I had to purchase an extra bin from the Sanders and pull it into our yard with the tractor. I filled it, too. The good quality grain brought good prices as well. God had truly blessed us.

Now, how did He want me to spend what He had given? How could I be a responsible steward?

I was still busy with the farm duties during the day, but in the evenings I spent hours and hours poring over the account books. I figured this way, then that way. With every load of grain I took to town, the numbers in my little book swelled. There would be a surplus. But would there be enough for the motor car? And if so, was a motor car necessary? Practical? The right thing for the Jones family?

I knew everyone was waiting for my decision. Grandpa

and Uncle Charlie did not question me. Mary never made mention of the vehicle, but I could sense that she was sharing my struggle over the decision. Matilda stopped cajoling me about it, but her eyes continually questioned, and I knew she was getting very impatient waiting for me to make up my mind.

I went to my room one night and took out all the advertisements again. I laid aside the one showing the shiny gray Bentley. It was far too fancy and costly for me, though I did allow myself one fleeting mental picture of me purring down our country road at the wheel. I laid aside a few more as well. As the pile of discarded pamphlets grew, a bit of the pride and envy of Joshua Jones was also cast aside. At last I was left with a plain, simple car made by the Ford company. There was plenty of money for the Ford—with a good deal left for other things we needed. I would get the Ford. My conscience could live with that.

I breathed a sigh of relief, laid aside the pamphlet and blew out my light. In the darkness of my room I knelt by my bed to pray. With the decision finally made with the seeming approval of my Father, I welcomed a sense of peace. I slept that night like I hadn't slept in weeks.

The next morning at the breakfast table I cleared my throat to get the family's attention. "I decided to get a car," I announced, and before I could go further there was a squeal from Matilda, a smile from Mary, and a nod from Grandpa. Uncle Charlie just grinned a bit. The long, jarring buggy rides were hard on his arthritic bones.

"Now wait. Now wait," I protested, holding up my hand and directing my words to Matilda. "We can afford a motor car—no problem. But I decided that it won't be a fancy one. No need for that, and it would just set us back. We'll get a simple, practical Ford—none of the gadgets and gizmos."

Matilda sobered.

"But it will have wheels—and get us to where we need to go," I assured them.

Matilda's face brightened again.

"When?" asked Grandpa, and though he tried hard to hide it, I caught the excitement in his voice.

"I'm goin' to town to order it today," I answered, and I had a hard time controlling my own excitement.

Matilda squealed. "Oh, Josh. It's so-o exciting!" she bubbled.

Uncle Charlie's smile widened.

I looked at Mary. Her face was flushed, her eyes shining. Then she did a most unexpected thing. She reached over and gave my hand a squeeze.

If Matilda had done it, I would have thought nothing of it. In fact, I would have thought nothing of it if Matilda had thrown herself wildly into my arms or flung her arms about my neck and squeezed with all her might—that was just Matilda. But Mary? That quiet, little gesture of shared excitement somehow set my pulse to racing.

I flushed slightly as I pulled my eyes back to the other members at the breakfast table and rose slowly to my feet. It was a moment before I found my thoughts, my tongue.

"I—I'll order it—today, but—but I have no idea how long it might be before it comes."

Matilda brought things back to normal. "Oh, I hope it arrives *soon!*" she exclaimed, bouncing up from her chair. "I hope it hurries. We don't have much time. We need it before winter so we can learn to drive it before the snow—"

Matilda caught herself and stopped mid-sentence. Her eyes met mine and she looked like a small child coaxing for a treat. She had been using a lot of "we's," which was rather presumptuous on her part, but I just smiled and gave her a quick wink. I understood.

After we shared our morning devotions together around the breakfast table, I went back to my room and folded the Ford pamphlet and slipped it into my pocket. As soon as I had finished the last of the morning chores, I would saddle Chester and head for town.

Chapter 5

The Ford

Like Matilda, I was hoping the car would arrive before snowfall. I wanted the chance to learn to drive it while the roads were still clear.

I managed to keep myself busy with no problem. I must admit I made a few more trips to town than normal. I pretended that I needed things or wanted the mail, but in fact I stopped in to check—with regularity—if there had been any word on the car.

On one such trip to town I found a long, newsy letter from Camellia. She had received word from the Mission Society that she would be leaving for Africa in the spring. She was so excited that her penmanship, usually in character—neat and attractive—was rushed and almost sloppy. This letter conveyed intense excitement.

"I can't believe it, Josh!" she wrote. "After all these years I am finally going to Willie's Africa. To the people he learned to love so. I will be stationed near enough to the village where Willie served that the mission has promised a trip to the grave site. I will be able to see the spot where Willie's body is lying. I know that it might not seem like much to others, but I think you will understand. I want to personally be able to lay some flowers on Willie's grave. And it will be very

41

special for me to be able to kneel there and ask God to help me in carrying on Willie's ministry.

"I won't be staying in the area. At least not for now. They say it is much too primitive to leave a woman all alone, and there is no other young lady available to live and work with me at present. But I am praying that if it is God's will, He will provide me with a working companion so that we might be able to live there before too long and have a chance to reach Willie's people.

"He used to write me all about them. I can almost see them. There was the chief—a small man by our standards— but, my, he had power! Willie said that the people didn't question his word for one minute. And there was one old woman—I do hope she is still there. She fed Willie from her own cooking pot, even though there was scarcely enough for her own family. Willie was sure she herself must have gone without food numerous times. And the little children. Willie said they followed along behind him, curious as to what this strange white man was going to do. And then there was Andrew. That was not his African name. That was the name Willie gave to him after he became a Christian. He was Willie's only convert. I can hardly wait to meet Andrew."

Camellia's letter went on, but I couldn't continue reading for the moment. It was some time before my eyes were dry enough to see the words on the page. If I missed Willie this much, I couldn't imagine what the loss was like for Camellia.

Camellia wrote about not wanting to leave her mother all alone. Then she chided herself. Of course her mother would not be alone—she had the same Lord with her who would be with Camellia on the mission field.

"You've always been such a dear friend, Josh, to both Willie and me. I appreciate your friendship now more than ever. And I can never thank you enough for helping with my support so I can go to Africa as Willie and I had planned. I pray for you daily. May God bless you, Josh, and grant to you the desires of your heart, whatever or whoever that might be."

Camellia had underscored "whoever," and I could picture her face with the teasing gleam in her eyes as I read the little message. I felt an emptiness inside of me. Would there ever be anyone else who would take the place of Camellia in my heart? I pushed the thought aside. Camellia was headed for Africa, and for some reason, still a mystery to me, God had chosen for me to stay on the farm.

I read the last paragraph again. "May God bless you, Josh, and grant to you the desires of your heart, whatever—"

I stopped there. I had come into town to check on the Ford again. As my eyes traveled back over the pages of Camellia's letter, the idea of a motor car paled in comparison.

"Lord," I admitted in a simple prayer, "I've got things a bit out of perspective. We need a car. I've weighed the purchase this way and that way, and for all involved it seems like the right move—but help me, Lord, not to get too wrapped up in it. A car is, after all, just a way to get places. These people—these Africans of Camellia's—they are eternal souls. Brothers. Remind me to spend more time in prayer for them as Camellia goes to minister the gospel to them."

I carefully folded Camellia's letter and tucked it in an inside pocket. I didn't even bother to go on down the street to check on the arrival of the car. It would be here when it was here! Instead I turned Chester toward Lou's. The children would welcome a little visit, and it would be nice to sit and share a cup of coffee with Lou.

When we awakened the next morning the ground was covered with snow. I won't pretend it didn't give me a bit of a start. I had so hoped. But I dismissed the thought. Surely a car could be driven in a few inches of snow.

When Matilda came downstairs, she didn't seem to be able to dismiss the snow quite as easily.

"Oh, no-o," she wailed. "What will we do? What will we *do*, Josh? The snow is already here, but the motor car isn't! Oh-h-h." She crossed to the window, swept back Mary's carefully ironed white ruffled curtain and groaned again. "We'll have to learn to drive it in the snow. It would have been so much easier—"

"Guess there's no problem," I was quick to cut in. "We don't have the car yet anyway."

"But it'll be here just any day now and the snow . . ."

But the snow had all disappeared by noon, and two days later the Ford arrived. I thought I had prepared myself for the role of motor-car owner, but when the news reached me I felt a thrill go all through my body. This was followed by a cold sweat. My hands got sticky and my mouth dry and my knees fairly shook with excitement—and just a little fear.

We hitched up the team, and Grandpa and Uncle Charlie drove with me on into town. I couldn't just ride Chester to pick the car up because I needed to drive it back.

We drove right up to Mr. Hickson's, and I pretended nonchalance as I stepped into his office and said I was there to pick up the car. I had the rest of the payment in my coat pocket, pinned in so I wouldn't accidentally lose it. I began to carefully unpin the coat in order to get at my money, but Mr. Hickson rushed right on by me, calling as he went, "It's this way, Josh, an' she's a beaut! Come on in an' git a look at 'er."

I followed, with Grandpa and Uncle Charlie right on my heels.

She was a beaut all right. Never had I seen so much shiny metal. There she stood, black paint gleaming and window glass sparkling. I slowly sucked in my breath. She was beautiful!

I was quite familiar with the few motor cars on our town streets. Several of them were quite fancy, too, but to me this Ford—this car that was mine—was the nicest of the lot.

I moved forward and ran a hand over the shiny fender. Mr. Hickson opened a door.

"An' look in here," he urged. "See them leather seats. Looka that. Looka that."

I moved to look. Sure enough, leather seats—finest black leather one ever saw. I let out the breath I had seemed to be holding. I heard Uncle Charlie say something to Grandpa and Grandpa answer, "Well, whoo-ee!" and I wheeled to look at them. Both of them were grinning. *Standin' there a gazin' at that car like they've never seen nothin' like it before*, I chuckled to myself.

"Whoo-ee," said Grandpa again, and he lifted a hand to stroke the black leather. Uncle Charlie's mustache was twitching. He reached out one gnarled hand to touch the shining glass of the window. For a moment I wondered if there could ever be anything more exciting in life than this—standing there getting a good look at your first car and brand new at that.

I came back down to earth in time to hear Mr. Hickson saying, "Just a few things to take care of, an' you can drive her right on out of here."

Mr. Hickson was moving back toward his little office, and I turned to follow, though I was feeling a moment of panic. I could "drive her right on out," said Mr. Hickson. But surely Mr. Hickson knew I had never driven a car before. Surely he wouldn't just put me in it and expect—

"Ya got some 'struction papers with this here new Ford?" Grandpa was asking Mr. Hickson very matter-of-factly, and I knew I should have asked the question.

"Of course. Of course," Mr. Hickson answered, nodding his head vigorously. "Everything thet ya need to know is right in here in the office."

Whew! Maybe I wouldn't embarrass myself after all.

"Joe Hess, down the street, has got him a Ford. Much like this one, only not as new," Mr. Hickson was saying. "He'd be glad to come on over here and take Josh for his first run."

"Thet'd be good. Real good," Grandpa agreed. Then added quickly, "Just till he gets the hang of it. He'll catch on real quick. Been driving thet big ol' tractor now fer quite a spell."

Mr. Hickson nodded his head again. "I'll send Mickey right over fer Joe," and making good on his word he called a young fellow from the back room and sent him on his way.

For some reason the rest of them seemed to have forgotten

that I was the buyer. Grandpa and Mr. Hickson were busy making plans without me. But they soon turned back to me when it came time for the final payment to be made. I pulled the money from my pocket and Mr. Hickson counted it out.

"Right," he said. "Just right."

That was no news to me. I had checked the money out carefully—three times—before I left home.

By the time we finished with the paperwork Joe was there. He seemed properly impressed with the new car and walked around and around it, studying each feature, especially those that his older model did not have. He didn't say much, but he grinned and he admired and he ran a hand over the black metal now and then.

We all climbed in for our first spin around town. I sat up front with Joe so I might learn all the procedures for driving. Grandpa and Uncle Charlie settled in the back. It was hard to tell who was the most excited.

Mr. Hickson gave it a good crank, we started off with a bit of a jump, and I heard Grandpa gasp, but then we moved out onto Main Street past all the stores and people.

We made quite an impression, you can be sure of that. Heads turned, people stopped, store owners came out of their shops, curtains fluttered at windows and dogs barked and chased us on down the road.

The farther we went the faster we went. It wasn't long until we were whizzing along. It fairly took the breath out of me, but Joe seemed to know just what he was doing, and he maneuvered the car like it was no problem at all.

When we got out in open country he suggested that I give it a try. I was so nervous that my hands shook, but I crawled behind the steering wheel and did just like Joe had showed me. Well, almost. I let the clutch out a bit too quickly, and the Ford bucked like she'd been spurred. It killed the motor and Joe had to get out and give it a crank again. The next time worked better and soon I was steering down the road like I'd been driving all my life.

By the time we got back to town and dropped Joe off, I

was getting pretty good. We decided to wheel around to Nat and Lou's and show off just a bit. I was hoping Nat would be home. A car like this would sure save a pastor some calling time.

Nat was there all right, and we had to show him everything on the Ford that moved. He studied it over and over again, making contented clicking noises and grinning from ear to ear. I felt my buttons pushing at my shirt front. I felt pretty proud and even more grown up than when the farm was signed over to me.

At last we pulled away from our admirers and headed back out on the street again, Jon howling behind us. He wanted to go too. I had already taken them all for a little spin, but I guess that wasn't good enough for young Jon. He wanted to go wherever the car was going.

When we got back to Hickson's, Grandpa climbed out and went to untie the horses from the hitching rail. Uncle Charlie began to climb out too, maybe a little reluctantly. I guess Grandpa must have sensed it. "Why don't you jest go on home with Josh?" he said. "Don't take two of us to drive this poky ol' team."

Uncle Charlie didn't argue. He settled back on that leather seat and took a big breath of the autumn air. Then he pulled out his pocket watch and sat studying the face of it.

"Okay, Josh," he said, and there was a glint in his eye. "Let's see how long it takes 'er to make the trip to the farm."

I grinned, then nodded. I put the Ford into gear and we started out. Once we cleared the town streets I opened her up a bit more. The breeze fairly whipped in the open windows. Way back at the edge of town we could see Grandpa just turning the team and buggy onto the road for home. Then the dust from our wheels blocked him from view, and Uncle Charlie and I were off.

We didn't try to set any records. I drove as sensibly as I knew how. But even with my caution at the wheel, the trip home took only eleven minutes and thirty-seven seconds.

Uncle Charlie chuckled gleefully as he held the watch out for me to see.

We turned into our lane. I could hardly wait to show the girls the new car. Then I looked with dismay at the dust that already clung to her shiny exterior and wished there was some way I could quickly polish her up before the introduction. But I realized that would never work, for already Mary was running to meet us.

Chapter 6

A Caller

I had plenty of time to show Mary the car, take her for a ride, and wash and polish all the metal and leather before Grandpa pulled into the yard with the team.

I had learned one lesson on the way home. The feel of the fresh autumn air blowing in the open windows might be invigorating, but on our dusty country roads it was not practical. I decided that from now on when the car was on the move, the windows would be kept up. I said as much to Uncle Charlie as he watched me polish and clean.

After Grandpa had gone off to Mary's kitchen with the groceries she had ordered, I settled the team and went back to shining the car. Reluctant to leave the new Ford, I was finally coaxed into the kitchen for tea and cornbread.

As soon as the kitchen clock told us that school would be letting out, we all climbed into the car and set off to pick up Matilda.

"I can hardly wait to see her face when we pull into the school yard," Mary said warmly.

I drove very slowly. I didn't want to get the car all dusty again before Matilda had a chance to see it. Even so, we got a bit ahead of ourselves according to Uncle Charlie's pocket watch and had to pull to the side of the road just over the hill from the schoolhouse. We didn't want to arrive before

Matilda was free to dismiss her students.

At last Uncle Charlie gave us the go-ahead, and I hopped out to give the car a crank while Grandpa pulled and pushed the necessary buttons and levers. Joe had said a man could start the car all by himself, but we weren't sure we had the hang of it yet.

We met some of Matilda's students as we chugged up the last hill to the school yard, so we knew that school was over for the day.

If we had expected Matilda to be excited, we weren't disappointed. As we pulled into the school yard, we saw her appear at the window. She probably wondered what the strange sound was. For a moment she stood as though stunned, her eyes wide and hands over her mouth. At Mary's wild waving, Matilda finally came to her senses. She fairly exploded from the door and took the front steps as though they weren't even there.

"It's here! It's here!" she was screaming as she ran toward us. "Oh, Josh, it's here." I decided not to point out that I was well aware of that fact.

She never even stopped to admire the shiny metal I had just worked so hard to polish. She didn't look at the gleaming glass windows. She never slowed down for a moment, just hurled herself at the door, climbed right over Mary in one swift motion and shuffled to settle herself right between the two of us.

"Show me!" she squealed. "Quickly—show me."

"You can't see much scrunched in here," I said a bit sourly, trying to shove over enough to give Matilda room. "You gotta do most of your lookin' from the outside," and I moved to open my door.

But Matilda was shaking her head so vigorously that her curls were coming unpinned. "No," she wailed, grabbing my hand from the door handle. "Show me how to drive."

Grandpa snorted and Uncle Charlie chuckled. Mary just shrugged her slim shoulders and smiled. I was stunned. I sure wasn't prepared to give Matilda a driving lesson in my new car. I'd barely learned how myself. I stalled for time.

"We've come to take you home," I informed her. "Are you ready to go?"

For a moment she seemed not to understand. She took a few gulps of air and then answered me almost sanely, "No, I have to get my books and clean the blackboards and lock the school."

We all piled out. Mary cleaned the blackboards while Matilda gathered her books. Uncle Charlie and Grandpa studied a map on the wall, but I just wandered around picturing the room as it had been when I was a student there.

In the row over by the windows had sat Avery, then me, then Willie—I could see him yet. His mop of unruly hair spilling over his forehead, his freckles scattered across the tip of his nose, his face screwed up in a frown as he worked on an arithmetic problem.

I turned abruptly and walked from the room. Even yet the memories were too painful.

"I'll wait outside," I said with as steady a voice as I could manage and I closed the schoolhouse door rather firmly on the memories.

It didn't take Matilda long and we all climbed back in the car and started down the country road.

We rearranged our load. Mary climbed in the backseat between Grandpa and Uncle Charlie. It was a bit crowded but they didn't seem to mind. Matilda rode in the front by me. Her eyes did not travel over the polished leather upholstery. Instead, they stayed glued to the steering wheel and the controls, watching every movement I made. I knew Matilda would never let me rest until she had been taught how to drive my car.

However, I was not ready to share the driving with anyone just yet. Not even Matilda.

"Why don't you settle back and enjoy the ride?" I urged her. "Remember, it won't be every day that we come and pick you up from school."

I guess she got the message. She sighed and did sit back. Sort of. Though I could still feel her eyes on my hands.

It wasn't long before I relented and did give Matilda a few driving lessons. We did not venture out on the road, only up and down our long farm lane. She caught on quickly, I must admit. I offered to teach Mary how to drive, too, but she just smiled and said she would just as soon let me do it.

The car was certainly an asset and time saver in driving back and forth to town. We looked forward to the family drive each Sunday. It was a bit crowded, but no one complained.

And then the winter snows came deep enough that the car was no longer practical. I drove it into the shed I had built for it and we started using the team again. Never had the trip to town seemed longer than when we were forced to travel it again by sleigh.

The dog was making an awful commotion one evening, and we all rose from our places to look out the window. We hadn't been expecting any callers. The evening was chilly, but not inhuman. There was no sharp wind blowing and the moon was bright. Still, we couldn't figure out why anyone would be making house calls on horseback at such an hour. I had a momentary pang that something might be wrong in town and Uncle Nat had come to inform us.

But it wasn't Uncle Nat. Relieved, I realized the traveler was a stranger. Well, not exactly a stranger. I had seen him once or twice, and from the greetings later in our kitchen, I came to realize that both Mary and Matilda had met him before.

But when Grandpa had answered his knock and opened the door, he didn't seem to know who the young man was. He extended his hand cordially anyway and offered for the young fella to come in.

"Don't believe I've had the pleasure," Grandpa was saying as he shook the hand firmly, and the man answered cheerily enough, "Sanders. Will Sanders. We bought the place just over yonder," and he nodded his head to the east.

"Sanders," repeated Grandpa. "Thought I'd met Sanders." Grandpa looked a bit perplexed. "Thet weren't yer pa, were it?"

"No, sir. My oldest brother. He bought the place. My pa's been gone for nigh unto seven years now."

"Sorry to hear thet," Grandpa said sincerely. "Come in an' sit ya down. Is there something we can be a helpin' ya with?"

The young man smiled easily. "Thank you, no," he answered evenly. "Just callin'." He made no move toward a chair.

All of this conversation had taken place while the rest of us looked on. I guess Will figured it was time to change all that. His eyes traveled around the room. He nodded briefly to Uncle Charlie, studied me for a moment and then turned his gaze toward the two girls. That was the first he smiled. He reached to remove his hat and with a slight nod in the girls' direction said, "Hello, Miss Turley, Miss Hopkins."

That was when I began to study the man before me.

A little taller than me, his shoulders were broader, hips slimmer. Even in the lamplight I could see the waves of dark hair and the deep-set dark eyes. His jaw was rather square and his nose straight. When he smiled he showed a row of even, white teeth. Even I was smart enough to know that ladies would consider him a good-looking man. I stirred uneasily as Mary and Matilda acknowledged his greeting. Both of them had a flush on their cheeks and shine to their eyes.

Mary was the first to move forward.

"Won't you come in, Mr. Sanders," she greeted him cordially. "Here, let me have your hat and coat."

Will Sanders passed Mary his hat and took off his heavy winter coat. Mary took both to a peg reserved for visitors' wraps in the corner.

I had never seen Matilda silent for so many minutes before.

"I didn't realize you were staying on," she finally ventured with a shy look in Sander's direction.

"Well, I had thought about going back to the city for the winter, but my brother said he could sure use some help with the choring."

I shifted uneasily again.

"Have you met Josh?" asked Mary, returning from hanging up the man's hat and coat.

The eyes shifted to me. He studied me for a moment before saying slowly, rather deliberately, "I don't believe I've had the privilege," and he smiled a bit too familiarly, I thought.

I stepped forward and extended my hand. It seemed like the neighborly thing to do. He shook it firmly. I wondered if he was trying to make me cringe under his grip. I found my fingers tightening around his. I wanted the man to know that other men had strength in their hands as well.

For a moment our eyes locked, and I could see in his expression some sort of challenge. I wasn't sure what it was all about, but I sure felt ill at ease.

After just sitting around for a spell thinking up things to talk about like weather and cattle feed, Matilda suggested that we play some Chinese checkers. We moved our chairs into position around the table. The game went well enough. For some reason I can't explain, it was very important to me that I win. I did. But just. Then the next game was won by Mary. That didn't bother me a bit, but it did bother me some that young Sanders came in second.

Mary fixed a little snack, and Grandpa and Uncle Charlie joined us around the table. Matilda carried most of the conversation. She and Sanders chatted on merrily, and occasionally he turned and offered some comment to Mary and she responded. I didn't pay too much attention to it all. I couldn't see where it concerned me much anyway. Then a comment of Matilda's caught my ear.

"Josh has a new Ford, but with the snow so deep he has it put away for now."

I felt my pride swell a bit. Here was one area where I had an edge on the city slicker fella. But his words quickly cut me down to size again.

"I have a silver Bentley, but I left it in the city. I wasn't sure of the country roads and I didn't want it damaged. I'm thinking of bringing it on out in the spring."

I had a sinking feeling in the pit of my stomach.

Mary said nothing but Matilda swooned. "A silver Bentley! I saw one of those in an advertising pamphlet. They are just gorgeous."

The young man nodded matter-of-factly as though a silver Bentley was really the least of the "gorgeous" things he possessed.

After a lot of small talk, mostly centered on Will Sanders, he finally decided to go. If he expected an argument from me, he sure was mistaken. But as he took his leave, he promised to be back. Not "may I" or "by your leave" or anything like that. Just "I'll drop back again the first chance I get." I cringed inside.

After he'd finally gone I went up to bed as soon as I could tactfully excuse myself. Even with my door closed I could hear Mary and Matilda talking and giggling like a couple of schoolgirls. The whole thing disturbed me so much I could hardly concentrate as I read my nightly Bible passage and tried to pray. Yet I couldn't put into thoughts or words just why I felt as I did. I tried hard to shove the uneasy feelings aside and get to sleep, but it was too big a job for me. I tossed and turned until I heard the clock strike three—still sleep eluded me. I slammed my fist into my pillow and wished fervently that I had never laid eyes on the guy.

Chapter 7

Changes

I awoke still tired and grumpy from my lack of sleep. I had never felt quite so disturbed in my entire life, and I couldn't make heads or tails of it. I knew it had something to do with that young whippersnapper Will Sanders, but what he might have done to merit such feelings on my part I had no idea. He seemed like a decent enough chap, and he certainly had behaved himself in gentlemanly fashion while he had been a guest—though an uninvited one—in our home.

No one else seemed to take offense at his sudden appearance, and *some* members of the household actually seemed to favor his visit.

Somehow I knew he had touched on a raw nerve. After pondering the situation, I realized I resented the attention that Matilda and Mary had given to him. I had no reason to resent it, but the feeling was there. I felt challenged—backed up in my own corner. But what was I trying to defend? And why did the presence of the new neighbor put me on the defensive?

I shoved the whole thing aside, for it was more than I could deal with in my present mood.

I finished the chores and returned to the house for breakfast. I was later than usual in coming in and the table was nearly cleared and empty.

"Matilda had to eat so she could get to school on time," Mary explained without a hint in her tone that my lateness had made it difficult for anyone else.

Mary dished out two plates of pancakes and bacon and poured two cups of coffee, which she brought to the table.

"Grandpa and Uncle Charlie joined Matilda," she continued. She did not comment on the fact that she had waited for me.

I just nodded to Mary, and when she joined me at the table I said the table grace as usual.

"Anything wrong at the barn?" she questioned.

For a moment I didn't follow her, and then I realized she noticed I had taken an unusually long time with the chores.

"No," I replied hurriedly. "Just the usual. Guess I was just plain slow this mornin'. I didn't sleep too good last night for some reason."

I figured the matter was explained sufficiently and could be dropped, but Mary's eyes searched my face.

"You're not comin' down with somethin', are you?" she asked, her eyes troubled.

"Me? No, just—just somethin' I ate, I s'pose. I'm not used to eating so much before I go to bed."

Mary let it go but I could still feel her eyes on me. I didn't dare leave any of my breakfast on the plate like I wanted to.

We continued the meal in silence—there wasn't much I wanted to talk about anyway. Mary, sensing it, didn't try to involve me in meaningless conversation.

"Where's Grandpa and Uncle Charlie?" I finally asked, realizing it was strange for the two menfolk to be missing from the kitchen at that hour on a wintry day.

"Uncle Charlie went back to his room. To read, he said, but I've a notion he didn't get much sleep last night either. And Grandpa went out to the shed to work on that toboggan he's makin' for Sarah and Jon. He says the weather could turn bitter any day now, and then he won't be able to work outside."

I nodded. Yes, the weather could turn bitter. We were nearing the end of November.

After some more silence, Mary removed our plates and poured fresh coffee. She returned to her chair and sipped the hot liquid slowly. Then she put down her cup.

"Mitch stopped by while you were chorin'," she said simply and my head came around, wondering if Mitch had brought bad news. It had been some time since Mary's brother had paid us a call, and he certainly wouldn't be making neighborly calls at breakfast time.

Mary met my gaze.

"He's tired of the farm," she went on evenly, but I could see pain in her eyes. I didn't know if she was thinking of Mitch or of her ma and pa.

"He's off to the city to find himself a job. Was goin' on into town to catch the mornin' train."

I forgot my own small problems for the moment. I knew Mary needed all the sympathy and support I could give her. I could see tears glistening in her eyes, but she didn't allow them to spill over. I wished there was some way I could comfort her—give assurance that I knew it was hard for her and cared that she was hurting. But I just sat there, clumsily trying to find words, not knowing what to do or say. Finally I made a feeble attempt to reach out to her, if only by letting her talk about it.

"Did he say for how long?"

Mary's eyes lowered. "He's not plannin' to come back," she said quietly.

"I'm—I'm sorry," I muttered, reaching out to take Mary's hand resting on the checkerboard oilcloth.

"Can—can your pa manage the farm without him?" I went on.

Mary turned to me and the tears did spill over then; she clung to my offered hand as though it were a lifeline. "Oh, Josh," she said in a whispery voice, "it's Mitch I'm worried about. I've been prayin' and prayin' that he might become—become a believer. What ever will happen to him if—if he gets in with the wrong crowd in the city?"

I reached over to cover Mary's hand with my other one. "Hey," I comforted, "we can still pray. Prayer works even over long distances. There are 'right' crowds in the city too, you know. Maybe God is sending Mitch to just the right people—or person—and he will listen to what they have to say in a way that he might never listen to us."

Mary listened carefully. She was quiet for a moment and then she turned to me and tried a wobbly smile through her tears. She pulled back her hand and searched in her apron pocket for a handkerchief. After wiping her eyes and blowing her nose, she had control of herself again.

"Papa will manage—I guess," she said softly. "Mitch never did care for farm chores anyway. But Mama will be heartbroken." And another tear slipped down her cheek.

I sat there thinking of Mary—thinking of her ma and pa and their concern over Mitch.

"Did they have a row?" I asked carefully, knowing full well that it was really none of my business.

Mary smiled. "That's exactly what I asked Mitch," she answered, "but he said 'no,' he just announced that he was leaving and they didn't even try to argue him out of it much. He said that Mama cried some—but he expected that."

Mary left the table and began preparing for washing up the dishes.

I thought about her words for a few minutes. There didn't seem to be much I could do about the whole thing.

Then an idea came to me. "Hey, why don't you go on home for a few days?"

Mary whirled to look at me, her eyes wide.

"Oh, I couldn't!" she exclaimed.

"Why not? We could manage for a few days."

"But—but the meals an' all—"

"We've made meals before." I was sure now that it was just the thing for both Mary and her mother.

"But—but Matilda—her lunch an'—"

"We'll fix Matilda's lunch. I'll do it myself—if she'll trust me."

"But I—I don't know what to say."

"Then go. Really. We can manage—as long as you don't stay away too long."

Mary was torn—I could see that. She wanted desperately to go to her mother, but she felt a deep responsibility to us.

"I mean it, Mary," I prompted further and left my chair to take the dish towel from her hands.

"Now you run off and pack yourself whatever you need for the next few days, an' I'll go out an' hitch Chester to the sleigh."

"Are you sure?" Mary asked one last time.

"I'm sure," and I turned her gently around and urged her toward her bedroom door.

Mary left then but turned back to say over her shoulder, "But the dishes—I haven't even finished the dishes."

I looked at the dishes that remained. Mary had already washed up from the first breakfast.

"I'll do the dishes the minute I get back," I promised her, and Mary went.

As soon as she had disappeared I lifted my winter coat and hat from the peg by the door and went out to harness Chester as I had promised. Mary was out, valise in hand, just as I pulled up in front of the house. I helped her tuck in and we were off. Chester was feeling frisky, not having been used much, and he headed for the road at a fast clip. I had to slow him down to make the turn at the corner.

Mary and I didn't talk much on the way over. But we both enjoyed the brisk run in the cutter. I could sense the tension leaving Mary's body and see the shine return to her eyes. I was pleased that the idea of her spending some time at home had come to me.

As we turned down the Turley lane Mary spoke for the first time.

"How long should I stay?"

"Well—as long as you think you should," I responded slowly.

Mary smiled mischievously. "Are you trying to get rid of me, Josh?"

"Truth is," I answered, matching her mood, "I'm sorta hopin' that you'll get to missin' us real soon."

Mary's face flushed slightly, and I couldn't help but laugh.

"Seriously?" she said when her composure had returned.

"Seriously—how about until Sunday?"

"That long? This is only Wednesday."

"I know—an' I'll be counting every day—so don't be late." Mary flushed again.

"I was wonderin'," she said after a moment, "if Matilda might like to come join me on Friday evening. She's never spent time at my house before an'—an' I think that her—her cheery mood might be good for Mama."

I pulled Chester up to the front of Mary's house. "I'll tell Matilda," I promised. "I'm sure she'd love to come and I'll bring her over."

I helped Mary out and then lifted Chester's reins again.

"Will you come in, Josh?" asked Mary.

"I think you and your mama need to meet alone," I said thoughtfully. "Besides," I went on in a lighter tone, "I've got to get on home to those dishes, remember?"

Mary laughed softly, and then grew more serious.

"Thanks, Josh," she said. "For understandin'—an'—everythin'."

I nodded and climbed back into the sleigh.

"And, Josh," Mary called softly. I turned to look at her. A few scattery snowflakes were falling about her. Some of them rested on the hair that escaped beneath her fur-trimmed hat. Her eyes ere shining, her face lightened by some impulsive but pleasant thought. I waited, thinking what a picture she made as she stood there, valise in hand.

"Josh," she said again. "A motor car is nice. Really. But—but you sure can't beat a wintry sleigh ride behind Chester, can you?"

I chuckled. Mary had summed up my own feelings.

"We should do it more often," I answered. "Remind me."

And with one last grin I turned Chester around and left the lane at a fast clip. Mary was quite right. You couldn't beat a wintry sleigh ride behind Chester, and I was all set to enjoy it to the full.

But for some reason, the ride back home wasn't as pleasant as I had anticipated.

I didn't need to do the dishes when I got home. Uncle Charlie had already washed and put them in the cupboard. He had also made a fresh pot of coffee, and Grandpa had joined him at the kitchen table for a cup. When I walked in both pairs of eyes turned to me.

"Somethin' wrong, Boy?" asked Grandpa.

I poured myself some coffee and joined them at the table before explaining all about Mitch leaving and Mary's concern for her ma.

"You done right, Boy," said Grandpa. "We been hoggin' too much of Mary's time. Her ma needs her too."

Uncle Charlie just slurped his coffee and then tilted his chair on the two back legs.

"What about Matilda?" he asked at length.

"Mary wants her to come and spend the weekend," I answered. "I'm sure Matilda will be glad to."

"This is Wednesday," went on Uncle Charlie.

"We'll manage until Friday," I assured them both, and Grandpa nodded.

"I don't have anything pressing right now. Just chores. I can help in the house," I added.

Uncle Charlie hid a smile. "Never did cotton to yer cookin', Josh," he teased.

I just grinned. "Then you cook an' I'll do dishes," I challenged him.

Uncle Charlie nodded. "It's a deal," he agreed.

"We'll manage," Grandpa concluded, but I could tell by his tone of voice that he was a mite doubtful. I guess none of us realized how much we'd come to depend on Mary till she wasn't there.

Matilda was looking forward to spending the weekend with Mary and her family. The plan was for us to have our Friday supper, do up the dishes and then I'd drive Matilda over to Mary's house.

We were just finishing the cleaning up when the dog announced a visitor. It was Will Sanders again. This time he'd come by sleigh. I grinned to myself when I saw him. He certainly hadn't lost any time in making good on his promise to return, but this time he had been outfoxed. We were almost ready to leave for the Turleys'.

Grandpa opened the door and welcomed him. He came in confidently and took in the whole kitchen scene with one sweeping glance. I don't know if I just fancied it or if he really was amused to see me wiping the dishes.

"What a shame!" exclaimed Matilda. "We are just finishing up here, and then I am off to the Turleys' to join Mary for the weekend."

"I understood that Mary lives here," he responded.

"Well, she does," hastily explained Matilda, "but she's been spending a few days at home with her folks this week. She doesn't get to see much of them even though she lives so close, so Josh sent her on home for a few days."

Matilda gave the last bit of news with a hint of pride in her voice, but I think Will Sanders might well have missed the meaning of it all. At any rate, he let it go by completely and surprised me by saying to Matilda, "Then let me drive you."

Now just a minute here, I wanted to cut in, but instead I said as calmly as I could, "I already have my horse ready and waiting in the barn. All I need to do is hitch him to the sleigh."

"But mine are already hitched and waiting. No use for you to go out in the cold when I can just run Matilda on over."

He ignored my scowl and hurried right on, "I wanted to see Mary anyway."

I couldn't argue much about that.

"That's very kind," Matilda responded. "I'm sure Josh and Chester will appreciate not having to go out."

Well, I couldn't speak for Chester, but I sure knew how Josh felt about the matter. I didn't say anything, though. There didn't seem to be much point.

"Go ahead," I told Matilda. "I'll finish the dishes."

"Oh, thank you," she responded, reaching up to give me one of her impulsive little hugs right there before the eyes of Will Sanders. I was both embarrassed and smug. *So what do you think of that, Mr. Sanders?* I wanted to say, but I bit my tongue and turned back to wipe the table and rinse the dishpan.

Matilda was soon back, bag in hand and her warm coat wrapped securely around her. I didn't even watch them go, and when Matilda called, "Good night, Josh," I only mumbled in reply.

I was grumpy all evening. It was almost nine o'clock before I remembered Chester still waiting in the barn, harnessed and ready for travel. Grumbling, I lit the lantern and pulled on my heavy coat.

"Well, fella, sorry about that," I apologized as I slipped the harness from his back. "I near forgot about you. Guess— guess you an' me sorta got—stood up."

I flung the harness with extra intensity to hang it back on its pegs, and it made Chester jump.

I crossed back to him and began to gently rub his neck and his back. The ink that Jon had splashed over him had finally faded away in the sun and rain.

"Sorry, fella," I soothed. "Guess I'm just a little out of sorts. First, we've been needin' to do without Mary. It isn't easy for three fellas to batch anymore when we've been used to somethin' else. An' then this here fella comes along and takes—just takes right over with Matilda—with Mary, too."

I don't know why I expected a horse to make any sense

out of what I was saying, but I went right on talking to Chester for the next five minutes. By the time I got back to the kitchen, I had settled down enough to think that I might sleep.

"Guess I'll make it an early night," I said to Grandpa and Uncle Charlie, and they didn't seem surprised. They both said good night without really looking up and I headed on up the stairs to my room.

Chapter 8

Troubling Thoughts

But I couldn't sleep this time either. I tossed and turned and roughed up my pillow, but my mind just wouldn't let my body rest. Pixie got rather impatient with me. She left the warm spot where she always slept curled at my feet and scrambled up beside me. She whined softly, her little body wiggling slightly and her tail thumping. Then she took a lick at my face. I don't know if she was sympathizing with my misery or telling me to settle down and let her get some sleep, but I did find a bit of comfort in her seeming concern.

I reached out and ran my hand across her silky back. She let me stroke her a few times and then returned to the foot of the bed, turned a few times and lay down. I heard her yawn as she tucked in for the night. I guess she felt she had done all she could.

At last I stopped even pretending. I reached out to my night stand and felt around for the small container that held the matches, struck one and lit my lamp. Matilda had just received a stack of new dailies. I decided to get one from the kitchen and read for a while.

I was surprised when I started down the stairs to see the kitchen light still burning. I wondered if someone was ill. Then I thought of Uncle Charlie. He often got up and sat alone by the warm stove if his arthritis got too painful during the night. I decided I'd just join him for a while in the kitchen. Maybe make some hot chocolate or something.

But as I neared the bottom of the stairs, I heard voices and realized that Grandpa was up, too. I guess I hadn't been tossing for as long as I'd thought. It had just seemed like hours and hours.

"You think he's 'callin' '?" Uncle Charlie was asking.

There was a moment's silence before Grandpa responded; then I heard a chuckle. "Thet's the way I figure it, but I'll be hanged iffen I can figure out, callin' on *who*."

"Matilda?"

"Thet was in my thinkin'—at first—but he paid considerable attention to Mary the other night too. An' did ya hear him say tonight thet he wanted to see Mary?"

"Yeah—I heard 'im."

I heard a coffee cup being set on the table. A chair moved slightly on the linoleum floor. Then Uncle Charlie spoke again.

"Maybe he's jest sorta lookin' 'em both over."

"A man don't git hisself nowhere a doin' thet," observed Grandpa.

Uncle Charlie snorted. He'd been a bachelor all his life. Maybe he knew the truth of the statement. I had never thought to wonder if there had ever been a young lady or ladies in Uncle Charlie's life way back when.

"Nowhere. Thet's it exactly—nowhere," said Uncle Charlie.

" 'Course they're both awful nice girls," put in Grandpa.

"Yup. Both awful nice girls," agreed Uncle Charlie.

"Don't rightly know which one I'd pick myself."

Uncle Charlie seemed to be giving the matter considerable thought. I heard the coffee cups again.

"You know anythin' 'bout this here fella?" Uncle Charlie asked, and I could follow his line of thought. No good-for-nothin' was gonna come along and make things miserable for one of *his* girls, no siree.

Grandpa let out his breath in a raspy little sound. Finally

he said slowly, "Checked a bit in town," then added quickly to try to justify himself, "Jest fer the record ya know. They say they're a fine family. Three boys. Lost both folks when the youngest was jest a tyke. Thet's Henry. Will is a couple years older. The oldest son an' his wife took in the two younger boys. Will went on to school an' then worked in the city fer a spell."

There was a moment of silence while the two men thought about Grandpa's information. Grandpa broke it.

"Couldn't find no skeletons a'tall," he admitted.

More silence. I didn't know what the emotions were down there in that kitchen—but my stomach was churnin' and my mouth went all dry. I hadn't realized it until my palms began to hurt, and then I noticed I had my fists curled so tightly that my nails were digging into them.

"Anyways—as I see it," went on Grandpa, "Josh better hurry an' make up his mind as to which girl he wants—or he's gonna be takin' the leftovers."

I felt all the air leave my lungs.

"Maybe he don't want neither," responded Uncle Charlie.

Grandpa snorted. "Iffen he don't," he said matter-of-factly, "he's dumber'n I took 'im fer."

I had long since forgotten about Matilda's newspapers. I had even forgotten about the hot chocolate. The conversation down below had my blood boilin' and was givin' me the chills—both at the same time.

"Hard choice," Grandpa was saying reflectively. "Real hard choice."

"Can't have 'em both," spoke up Uncle Charlie.

"Maybe it's been the wrong thing to have 'em both here," said Grandpa after a pause. "I mean, seein' both girls—so different—yet so—so special, an' gittin' to feel like they was more like family than—than young women to court." A long pause. "An' how in the world does a fella go about courtin' a girl thet lives in the same house as he does anyway?"

"Yeah," agreed Uncle Charlie, "an' when ya like 'em both,

how do ya court the one 'thout the other feelin' left out an' such?"

"Well, this here Will don't seem to have 'im no problem—he's courtin', an' thet's fer sure."

There was silence for a minute.

"Do ya think the girls—?" began Grandpa but Uncle Charlie cut in.

"You seen an' heard 'em same as me. Any girl is flattered by courtin'."

"Do ya think they know which one he's picked?"

"I dunno. Maybe. Women have an uncanny sense 'bout thet," mused Uncle Charlie.

At the time I didn't even stop to wonder where Uncle Charlie got all his knowledge about the fairer sex.

A chair scraped against the floor. Someone was standing to his feet. I moved quickly to make my escape back to my bed, but Uncle Charlie—or was it Grandpa? no, it was Uncle Charlie, I could tell by the shuffling steps—just moved to the stove for the coffeepot.

I heard the coffee poured and Uncle Charlie sit back down. They sipped in silence for a few minutes, each busy with his own thoughts.

"Maybe Josh really doesn't care," said Grandpa.

"He cares," Uncle Charlie affirmed flatly.

"Yeah—'bout which one?"

"Can't answer thet. But he cares. It's nigh been eatin' his insides."

He sure seemed to know a lot—maybe more than I did.

"Hadn't noticed," admitted Grandpa. "How's thet?"

"Little things. He can spend the whole night tossin' on his bed. I can hear 'im. Then he gets up as touchy as a bear with cubs. I see 'im lookin' from one girl to the next—an' when thet there fella showed up tonight, Josh fairly bristled."

"Thet right? Thet right?" said Grandpa, and for some strange reason there was a bit of excitement in his voice.

I'd heard about enough. The whole thing was leaving me

with a sick feeling. I moved back a step, intending to return quietly to my bed. Then a word from Grandpa caught me a blow right in the middle of my stomach.

"Jealous, huh?"

Jealous? Me? Of course I'm not jealous, I fumed. Jealousy was an evil emotion. It went right along with covetousness. My whole being rebelled against the thought.

"Iffen he's jealous—then maybe he does care. Or maybe he's jest plain-out possessive of 'em both," went on Grandpa.

"I think he cares."

" 'Bout who?"

Uncle Charlie thought for a minute. Then answered slowly, "I'm not sure thet even Josh has got thet sorted out yet."

"Well, he'd better start 'em a sortin'," Grandpa replied very seriously, " 'cause thet there young Will ain't gonna waste 'im no time."

"Yeah, he's courtin'. Fer sure he's a courtin'."

"He's a courtin' all right," agreed Grandpa again, then repeated on a still-puzzled note, "but I'll be hanged iffen I can figure out which one."

I crept back to my room, my stomach still churning and my body tight with tension. Pixie didn't even move as I eased myself back into my bed. I had been repelled by every word I'd heard. I guess that was what an eavesdropper could expect. Still, I hadn't planned to eavesdrop—it had just happened, and after the first few words I had overheard, I sure wasn't going to give myself away.

So Will is courtin'? Matilda? Or Mary? I sure hadn't been able to discern which one. *And if he's courtin', then we might lose one of the girls.* The thought was not a comforting one. Matilda and Mary seemed to sort of come as a set. And furthermore, they *both* belonged to us somehow.

But no. That was ridiculous. Even I knew that. The day would come—maybe much sooner than I liked to think—that we would lose one of the girls, or maybe both of them. We couldn't possibly keep the two of them forever. *Maybe we couldn't keep either one of them*, was a startling thought. Will would cart one of them off and then some other young buck would come along and take the other.

The very thought made my blood boil.

But *jealous*? Why would I be jealous? I mean, I had no claim to the girls—no personal claim. I'd never courted either one of them. And they certainly had not flirted with me. Well, not really. Only in a teasing sort of way.

I thought of Matilda's impulsive little embraces and my face flushed in the darkness. Then I remembered Mary reaching out to gently touch my hand, and the deep look of concern and understanding in her eyes as she did so, and I colored even deeper. *Maybe they do like me—sort of. Not just as family.* The thought was a new one and one that I had not consciously entertained before. But if—if they did—if there was any chance that they did—then I should do something about it. I mean, I didn't particularly enjoy the thought of spending my whole life as a bachelor like Uncle Charlie. I wanted a wife—love—a family.

But first—there came the courting.

I had no idea how to go about courting a girl. Oh, if it was like this here Will fella handled it, there wasn't much to it. I mean, he just came over whenever he took the notion and just sorta hung around and teased and complimented the girls some. Any fella could do that.

But, I knew that wasn't the way that I'd do it. A girl deserved more consideration than that. I thought she had a right to expect more than that. If I was courting I'd try to think of nice things to do that she might enjoy.

Take Matilda—*she loves flowers—an' sweet smellin' perfume—an' trips to town an' pretty new pieces of jewelry*, I listed off. *She likes music—and laughing and picnics in the country and drives in the motor car.* Wouldn't be too hard at all for me to think of ways to court Matilda.

What if I courted Matilda? How long did a fella have to "court" before he could properly ask a young woman to marry him? I mean, courting could take a good deal of time and expense. True, a fella could get a lot of enjoyment out of it. Especially if the young woman really enjoyed the courting—like Matilda would. Maybe she'd just want it to go on and on. *Matilda would like courtin' all right,* I decided.

But what about after the courting? I couldn't really picture Matilda in the kitchen, working over a hot stove, baking bread and canning the garden produce. I couldn't really see her leaning over the scrub board, hair in disarray while she scrubbed at dirty farm socks. Oh, Matilda fit into the courting picture just fine—but the marriage picture wasn't so easy to visualize.

Now, Mary—I could see Mary doing all those kitchen things. I had watched her perform all the household tasks dozens of times. It seemed so—so *natural* for Mary. She did it without fuss—without comment—and even seemed to somehow enjoy the doing. Mary in the kitchen seemed right reasonable. *But courtin'?* I couldn't think of a single way that one would properly court Mary. I mean, she never fussed about perfumes or pretty jewelry or lace hankies or anything like that. She never coaxed for rides in the motor car or asked for picnics. I couldn't honestly think of a thing that would make Mary impulsively throw her arms around my neck or giggle with girlish glee.

I lay there, struggling with questions I'd never faced before—working them this way and then that way. No matter how I tried I couldn't come up with any answers. But I knew instinctively that I could no longer just push the matter aside. I had to get it sorted out. My whole future depended on it.

Chapter 9

Eying the Field

Even if I had wrestled with the problem for half the night, I was no nearer an answer when I got up to go choring the next morning. This much I knew, I had two girls right at hand who most young men in the area considered first-rate candidates for a marriage partner, and I had been taking them for granted.

I also knew that if I was going to choose one of them— and I figured I would be pretty dense not to—then I was going to need to decide which one and get on with the courting. The trouble was deciding. They were so different—yet both special.

Matilda's energy and enthusiasm made the house seem alive. We all enjoyed her company. Even Grandpa and Uncle Charlie counted the days until she returned from her trips home. The world just seemed like a nicer place when Matilda was around.

Then I thought of Mary. Mary was quiet—not bouncy. But Mary was—well—supportive. She was dependable and sort of comfortable to be around. I'm not sure how we would have managed without Mary.

Matilda or Mary? How was one to decide? And just what kind of tension would it put on our household if I started to court the one and left behind the other?

Now, I had no reason to think that either girl was sitting around holding her breath waiting for Josh Jones to start calling. Neither of them had led me to think they were interested in me in any other way than as a member of our household. I was maybe being presumptuous to even think that one of them would accept my small gifts and attention.

Then a new thought hit me. What if I picked a girl—Matilda or Mary—and decided to court her and she flatly turned me down? It could happen.

The thought scared me. I remembered what had happened when I had the foolish notion that I could just walk back into Camellia's life and she had announced instead that she was marrying Willie.

The idea of being rejected was so frightening that I decided, as I slopped the pigs and cared for the cows, that I would just hold back for the next several days and sorta look things over. I wanted to put out a few feelers to see if it appeared that either of the girls might favorably respond to being courted by Joshua Jones.

I was more sensitive to little things as I gathered around the breakfast table with the family that morning.

Matilda was telling a funny incident from school. One of the children had written a composition about winter. He had said in part, "The best thing about winter is that the 'moskeytoes' "—Matilda spelled it for us—"fly south to bite other people."

Matilda laughed merrily as she told it and Grandpa chuckled and Uncle Charlie grinned. Matilda was a lot of fun.

Matilda began to gather her school supplies and reach for her heavy winter wraps as soon as Grandpa had finished with our morning devotions. I had a sudden inspiration.

"Chester's in his stall," I said. "How would you like me to hitch him to the sleigh and drive you to school?"

She looked at me, her eyes big with unasked questions; then she threw her arms around my neck with a little squeal of delight.

I took that as her yes, and I grinned to myself as I shrugged into my heavy coat and headed for the barn while she finished her preparations. Maybe courting wasn't so hard after all.

It was colder and another storm was dumping more snow. I was glad I had thought of driving Matilda to school. It would have been rather miserable walking.

I tucked the heavy lap robe closely about her and we started off, Chester tossing his head and snorting, anxious to get out to the open road for a good run. Matilda leaned into the wind, anticipating the speed of the open cutter skimming over the frozen ground.

I watched her face. She loved a good run. If she had been holding the reins, she no doubt would have given Chester his head and let him run at a full gallop. As it was, I let Chester do a bit more running than I normally did, just so that I could watch Matilda's enjoyment.

When we got to the school I helped gather her things and climb from the sleigh. Her face was flushed—whether from excitement or the cold wind, I couldn't tell.

"I'll be back to pick you up after school," I promised and she flashed a beautiful smile.

I waited long enough to see her into the school building, noting as I did so the smoke curling up from the brick chimney. The Smith boy had done his work and the potbelly stove would be spilling its welcome warmth into the room.

Matilda turned and gave me a bit of a wave just before she closed the door. I waved back and clucked to Chester, who turned smartly around and headed back out the school gate.

I felt good about the little drive to school. Oh, I hadn't made any kind of open statement or anything, but Matilda certainly had not been adverse to my company. I would just sort of keep my eyes open and see what the future days might bring.

But maybe while I was waiting, I should come up with some plan to sorta "test out" Mary.

My plan might have worked just fine had it not been for Will Sanders. I mean, the "wait and see" didn't seem too practical when he turned up on our doorstep every few days.

I still didn't care much for the guy. Grandpa's midnight discussion with Uncle Charlie kept running through my head. *He's courtin' all right,* I decided—but like Grandpa, I couldn't figure out which girl he had his eye on.

I didn't have much to say when he arrived, just sat back watching the situation. He teased and flirted with Matilda, but then he turned right around and asked Mary to a Pie Social in town. It happened to be on the night of Matilda's annual school program, so Mary turned him down. He smiled and said, "Next time" and Mary nodded her head.

When Christmas came, along with it came Will Sanders as well. He brought each of the girls a gift, a pair of warm gloves. After he finally left for home that night, the girls openly talked about it.

"I never dreamed we'd be on his Christmas list," said Matilda. "I never even thought to put his name on mine."

"Me neither," said Mary, studying the fingers of the gloves absent-mindedly. "What do we do now? I s'pose it would be terribly rude not to give a gift in return."

She looked imploringly at Matilda as though she wished her to say that it wouldn't be rude at all. Grandpa said it.

"Seems to me that one shouldn't feel obligated, things bein' as they be."

I wasn't quite sure what Grandpa meant, but I was willing to agree.

The girls kept on mulling over the problem.

"I know," said Mary suddenly. "Let's give him a gift together!"

"Together?" echoed Matilda.

"One gift—from both of us."

Matilda's face brightened. "Let's!" she squealed.

A few days later they were wrapping up a pair of socks and putting both names on the card. I won't pretend I didn't get a bit of satisfaction from the arrangement. Then it hit me—perhaps the girls didn't care too much either for the fact that Will had not openly made known whom he was courting.

On Christmas morning I unwrapped my own gifts. Matilda gave me a pair of fine cuff links. Mary gave me a hand-knit scarf and gloves set. I don't know when she ever found the time to do it without my knowing, but I sure did take pleasure in the gifts, realizing how special they were and how they bespoke the two givers.

Will Sanders, I breathed, but not aloud, *it's your turn to be jealous!*

The winter storms began to abate, and I could sense another spring just around the corner. I could hardly wait. I wanted to get back on my land. I wanted to get the Ford out again and feel the thrill of covering the miles so quickly, the wind whipping around me. As it was, I dreaded each trip to town since I had gone from the motor car back to the slow-plodding team. I put off every journey for just as long as I could.

On one such day I returned home a bit out-of-sorts because of my impatience with the snow-covered road. After caring for the team, I bundled the groceries into my arms and headed for the kitchen and a hot cup of coffee with a bit of Mary's baking.

No coffee greeted me. Grandpa and Uncle Charlie sat at the table. It appeared that they had been there for hours, not because they wanted to but because they didn't know what else to do with themselves. It was so untypical that it threw a scare into me right away.

"Where's Mary?" I asked, my eyes quickly darting about the room.

There was silence; then Grandpa cleared his throat, while Uncle Charlie shuffled his feet.

"She went on home," explained Grandpa. "Word came her ma was sick."

"Sick?" I repeated, letting the word sink in and thinking

of all those years that Mary's ma had spent in bed. "How sick?"

"Don't rightly know," said Grandpa. "The youngest girl jest came a ridin' over here—nigh scared to death, and hollered fer Mary to come quick. Mary did. Without hardly lookin' back—jest jumped on up behind her an' the two of 'em took off agin."

I put the groceries down and wheeled back toward the door.

"Mary should've taken Chester," I mumbled as I went.

Grandpa called after me, "Where you off to?" Then he added as kindly as he could, "Josh, at a time like this, sometimes folks only want family."

But I didn't even slow down. "Mary's about as 'family' as you can get," I flung back over my shoulder, and Grandpa didn't argue anymore.

I didn't even wait to saddle or bridle Chester. Just untied the halter rope and led him out of his stall. In a wink I was on his back. He wanted to run and I let him. He was hard to hold in with just the halter; I guess I rode him rather recklessly. We were soon in Turleys' yard, and I flung myself off and tied Chester to the gate before hurrying to the house.

I rapped politely before entering the back porch. There was no answer so I just eased the door open and let myself in. Once in the kitchen, I took a deep breath and the doubts began to pour through me. Who did I think I was that I could intrude upon a family in such a way? Why did I dare come without invitation?

I knew instinctively that the answer to all of the questions was, "Mary." For some reason I felt she might need me. Still—I shouldn't have . . . I turned back to wait outside, but just then the younger girl, Lilli, entered the kitchen. She was wiping tears as she came, and at the sight of me she stopped short, sucking in her breath in a little gasp. Then she seemed to realize who it was and took another step forward.

"I—I'm sorry," I apologized. "I—I thought that I might—

that Mary might . . . Could I go for the doc or anything?"

She shook her head slowly, the tears pouring again down her cheeks. I moved toward her but she turned her back on me, not wanting me to see her fresh outburst of tears. I hardly knew what to do or say so I just stood there, carelessly crunching my hat in my hands.

"Josh?" The little gasp that bore my name came from Mary. I wheeled to look at her, my eyes full of questions.

"Josh," she said again.

I looked into her tear-filled eyes. Her hair was disarrayed and her long skirt spattered with road grime, attesting to the fact of how she had traveled to get to the side of her ailing mother.

I moved forward. "How is she?" I asked. "Could I—"

But Mary cut me short with a tremulous voice. "She's gone, Josh."

And then I was holding her close, letting her sob against my chest. I don't know which one of us moved toward the other. Perhaps we both did.

I just held her and let her cry, and I guess I wept right along with her while my hand tried to stroke some of the tangles from her normally tidy hair. I heard my voice on occasion but all I said was, "Oh, Mary. Mary. I'm so sorry. So sorry."

At last Mary eased back from my arms. We were alone in the big farm kitchen. I looked at Mary, wondering if she was okay, wondering if I should let her go, but she just gave me a little nod and moved toward the cupboard.

"Papa needs some coffee," she said matter-of-factly, and began to put the pot on.

But Mr. Turley did not drink the coffee. I'm not sure that anyone drank from that particular pot. The whole house was too stunned—too much in pain to think of coffee or anything else.

At last I found something useful to do. I was sent to town to fetch Uncle Nat. I was both glad to go—just to get away from the intense sorrow—and sorry to go, for I hated to leave Mary in such pain.

The funeral was two days later. Mitch came home, but he stayed only a couple of days afterward and then returned to the city. Mary stayed at her home for an entire week. It seemed forever. Even when she did return to us I hardly knew what to say or do. I knew she was still sorrowing. But how did one share sorrow without probing? The only thing I could think of was to make things as easy for Mary as possible. I made sure the woodbox and water pails were kept full. I helped with dishes whenever I was in the house at the right time. I was extra careful about leaving dirty farm boots outside her kitchen—even stepped out of them before I came onto her back porch.

Whenever I saw tears forming in her eyes, I wanted to hold her again—just sort of protect her from her pain and sorrow—but it didn't seem like the thing to do. Matilda slipped her arms around her instead, and I left the room, confused and sorrowful.

Somehow we managed to get through the days until spring was finally with us again.

Chapter 10

Spring

I gave my full attention to the land and the planting. I didn't even have time to wonder and worry about which girl I should be courting. Except on those evenings when Will Sanders showed up at our door. He still called at least once a week. I guess getting the crop in didn't cause Will as much concern as it did me.

He asked Matilda for walks and paid Mary elaborate compliments on her pies and cakes. He suggested picnics and drives. He kept promising to bring out that silver Bentley from the city. I tried to ignore him and go about my daily tasks. I was busy enough that I didn't have too much time to fret—even about Will Sanders.

Matilda began to coax about the Ford again, so on Sundays we used it to go to church and then sometimes went for a little drive in the afternoons. Matilda always wanted her share of driving. She handled the car quite well, too. Pretty soon she was asking to take it to town on her own or to take Mary home for a visit. I couldn't think of any good reason that she shouldn't, so I let her use the car. It seemed to please Matilda mightily to be behind the steering wheel.

Mr. Turley wasn't doing too well since his wife's death. In May, Faye got married as had been planned. Mary was her maid-of-honor. We were all invited to the small wedding.

Mary wore a gown of soft green that brought out the reddish highlights of her hair and matched the green flecks in her eyes. I thought it most becoming on her.

Everyone tried to make the wedding a happy occasion, but we all knew that it really could not be. It was the first "big" family event that Mrs. Turley had missed, and I guess we were all thinking of her.

It was especially hard on young Lil. She knew that she would be the only girl at home now, and I think she dreaded the thought. She also was likely wondering about when it came her turn to wed—would she feel right about leaving her pa at home all alone?

I suggested to Mary that she might want to spend a few days at home after the wedding, and without argument she accepted.

She stayed for three days, and when her pa drove her back to our farm to resume her duties, he carried a large box in and set it down just inside the kitchen door.

We were all glad to see Mary back. As soon as she removed her hat she tied on her apron. The next thing she did was to stir up the fire and put on the teakettle. Mr. Turley watched her move about the kitchen. I wondered what was going through his mind. Perhaps Mary reminded him of her mother. At any rate he sure did seem to be studying her.

When the tea was ready and Mary served it up along with what was left of her orange loaf, Mr. Turley sat a long time. Grandpa and Uncle Charlie kept trying to engage him in conversation, but he answered each query scantily. He didn't seem in any hurry to leave though, and I guessed he was just stalling, hating to return to his empty house. They had dropped Lil off with a friend for a few days, Mary explained.

"Why don't you just stay on to supper?" I heard Grandpa asking.

"Got chores," mumbled Mr. Turley, and he seemed to stir himself to leave.

"Chores work up a lot faster on a satisfied stomach," argued Grandpa.

Mr. Turley nodded and settled in again.

It ended up with Uncle Charlie and Mr. Turley having a few games of checkers while Mary fixed supper. I didn't see the games, being out with my own chores, but I understand they were played rather absent-mindedly by Mr. Turley. However, they did help to pass some time.

After he had eaten, Mr. Turley still didn't seem in too big a hurry to leave. He sat toying with his coffee cup and thinking. Finally he spoke out.

"Been thinkin' on sellin' off the livestock. Mitch is gone an' there jest don't seem to be no point in spendin' time out at the barn."

I guess we all sort of looked at him, surprised at his statement. But then, we shouldn't have been.

"Anythin' over there thet you might want fer yer herd, Josh? Got one real good milker. She's had her three sets of twins already in jest five years of calvin'."

It sounded good. I nodded. "Might take a look at her," I agreed.

"Got one first-rate brood sow, too. Averages nine per litter. No runts. Though she's big, she's careful. Never laid her on a piglet yet. You know how some of 'em big sows just go 'plop' right down in the middle of the litter. Well, not this one. Coaxes 'em all off to the side 'fore she goes down."

That sounded impressive all right. I nodded again.

"Come over some time, Josh. See if there be anythin' ya'd like. Rather sell 'em to you than off fer slaughter."

I stood to my feet when Mr. Turley stood.

"You're sure you want to sell?" I asked. I still found it hard to believe.

He sighed deeply. "Yeah," he said at last. "Been thinkin' on it fer some time. Just don't cotton to the idee of spendin' hours out chorin' when the winds start to howl agin. Best time fer sellin' is when they're nice an' fat on summer grass. I'll sell 'em off gradual like an' be done with 'em by fall."

"Sure," I nodded. "Sure. I'll be over first chance I get."

"No hurry," went on Mr. Turley. "Come as soon as yer crop is all in."

Then he kissed Mary on the cheek, thanked Grandpa for supper and picked up his hat.

I felt so sorry for the man that I ached inside. I was glad I had more chores of my own that needed doing. At least they would keep me busy for a while and out of sight of Mary's sorrowful eyes.

When I came in from chores Mary had the big box up on the kitchen table and was carefully lifting something out from the wrappings to show Matilda.

"Oh," I heard Matilda gasp. "It's just beautiful!"

"I think so," Mary said softly. "Even when I was a little girl I used to admire them. They sat in Mama's buffet, and I'd look at them and look at them. Mama wouldn't let me touch them. She didn't want fingerprints all over them. Then when I got older Mama taught me how to handle them carefully. I was even given the privilege of cleaning each piece."

"How many are there?" Matilda asked.

"The large tray, a smaller tray, the coffeepot, teapot, creamer and sugar bowl, plus a sugar spoon and a cake server."

"They are beautiful!" Matilda said again.

I watched as Mary lovingly ran a hand over the silver pieces sitting before her on the table.

"Pa found a note Mama left in her Bible," she stated, tears in her eyes. "She said that I was to have the silver. She left Mitch her Bible, Lil her ruby pin, and Faye her china."

"Oh-h-h," murmured Matilda. I could tell she wanted to say how fortunate Mary was, but that hardly seemed appropriate under the circumstances.

We didn't have to wonder how special the silver was to Mary. After fondly gazing at each piece, she polished them all once more. Then she began to carefully wrap them in the soft pieces of cloth they had been snuggled in and, with tears in her eyes, placed them tenderly back in the box.

Grandpa cleared his throat. "Would ya like to put 'em

there in the corner china cupboard," he ventured, "where ya can see 'em?"

Mary hesitated, looked across at the cupboard and then went to give Grandpa a little hug. I don't know what she whispered to him, but Grandpa's mustache twitched a bit and Mary began clearing a spot for her silver on the middle shelf. It did look pretty there, and it sure did dress up our farmhouse kitchen.

I guess we got rather used to it after a while, but I noticed Mary frequently glancing that way. She even used the set for tea when Aunt Lou dropped out one day, and the Sunday of Uncle Charlie's birthday she served us all our afternoon coffee from the shiny coffeepot when she served his birthday cake. Sarah thought it was just wonderful.

"Where did you get it, Aunt Mary?" she asked, her eyes shining. And Mary's eyes shone just as much as she answered.

"It was my mama's."

"I have never seen anything so pretty," went on Sarah. "Where did your mama get it?"

"It was her grandma's—a wedding present from an elderly lady she worked for. Mama said it was a shock to everyone. The older lady was usually sour and tight with her money, and no one could believe it when she gave Great-grandma such a beautiful gift."

Mary chuckled softly. It was the first I had heard her laugh for some time. She smiled often, sincerely, almost sadly, but she did not laugh. With the soft laughter a heavy weight seemed to lift from me deep down inside somewhere. I looked around the circle, wondering why there was no celebration, but no one else seemed to have noticed that Mary was laughing again.

Still I tucked the sound of that laughter away inside and replayed it over and over during the next days.

As soon as I finished the spring planting, I went over to see Mr. Turley. I ended up buying the cow he told me about plus a couple of her heifers. I also bought the sow along with the recent litter. We decided we shouldn't move her at the present, so Mr. Turley agreed to feed her for a few more weeks.

Mr. Turley carried through with his plans to sell off all his livestock, and neighbors dropped by to look over the animals and buy what they figured they could use. I thought it strange for a farmer to be without stock. But I guess the fields were enough to keep one man busy, and, as Mr. Turley had said, Mitch didn't seem inclined to come back home. It sounded as if he liked city life and was happy with the job he had found.

Lilli was restless, though. She didn't even plant much of a garden. Mary planted even more and prepared herself for a busy canning season. She went over to her ma's cellar and brought back some boxes of canning jars so she could fill them for her pa and Lil.

Matilda suggested to me that Mary might like another trip over to see Faye before her busy summer began. Mary didn't get together with her sisters nearly enough, I knew.

"I'll see what I can do," I nodded to Matilda as we sat idly swinging on the back porch swing.

It was the first we had spent any time together for several months, and with school almost out I immediately thought ahead to Matilda being gone for another summer. I wondered if I had allowed my busyness to interfere with courting again. *If I keep on at my present rate, I'll never get around to findin' myself a girl*, I concluded.

Maybe I'd lost my sense of urgency. Word passed around the neighborhood that Will Sanders had decided he preferred city living and had left his brother's house to return there. I felt a bit of smugness when I reminded myself of it.

My thoughts were interrupted by Matilda.

"You needn't do anything about it, Josh," she was saying. "I can drive Mary over to Faye's."

I was about to object when I realized that there was really no reason why Matilda couldn't. She could drive the car as well as I could. And Mary might not feel as rushed if I weren't hanging around, impatient to get back to some farm chores.

I nodded without saying anything, wondering if I was about to get another impulsive hug. Rather shamelessly I wondered if this time I should do some huggin' back. But the hug never came. Just then the back door opened and Mary stepped out with a tray of cold lemonade.

"Guess what?" squealed Matilda. "Josh says I can take the car and drive you over to see Faye before I leave for the summer."

Mary's eyes shone in the soft darkness, and I could see her appreciative smile. She didn't speak, but her eyes met mine and I read the thank you there. For a moment I wondered what it would be like to get a hug from Mary. And then I remembered the time when I had held her—not like Matilda, bouncing in and out of my arms with a quickness that took one's breath away. Mary had lingered, had leaned against me like a lost child, drawing strength and understanding from me. I had felt protective, needed. In spite of the sadness of that moment, I treasured the memory. Yet I couldn't really explain—

My thoughts were interrupted.

"When should we go?" Matilda was asking Mary.

Mary put the tray down and handed each of us a glass. "We don't have long," she reminded Matilda. "You have only another seven days to teach."

Had time really slipped by so quickly? It seemed that the year had just started, and here we were heading into another summer vacation.

"I know," moaned Matilda.

"I think we should go at a time when we don't have to worry about darkness," went on Mary. "Maybe Saturday."

"Saturday," said Matilda. "That sounds great!" Then she had the good grace to turn to me. "Will you need the Ford for anything on Saturday, Josh?"

I shook my head. I still had field work to do.

"Then we'll leave on Saturday morning," agreed Matilda.

Mary seemed to think carefully about it. "I guess we could," she said at last. "I could leave dinner all fixed for the men, and we'll be sure to be back in plenty of time for supper."

When Matilda went to school the next day, Mary sent a note for Faye, and Matilda sent the note home with one of the students who rode past Faye's new home. A reply stated that Faye would be watching for the two of them the next Saturday.

Saturday morning I moved the car from the shed, filled it with gas and checked the tires. One needed more air so I got out the pump and pumped it up until I was sure it was okay. Then I left the keys on the table for Matilda and went off to the field to do some summer-fallow work that needed doing.

I was interrupted midafternoon by a sudden rain squall. I studied the dark clouds for a few moments and headed in with the tractor.

I hope the girls aren't on their way home now, I thought, but the shower passed over. When the girls did not arrive, I dismissed the incident from my mind and started some evening chores.

By suppertime there still was no sign of an approaching car. I remembered Mary's words about being home in plenty of time to get supper, and I felt just a little aggravated that her visiting had put us hungry menfolk from her mind.

I went on to further chores and was surprised when Grandpa joined me at the pig barn. After making small talk for a few minutes, he turned to me. "The girls aren't home yet, Josh."

It wasn't news to me. I nodded rather glumly.

"It's past suppertime," went on Grandpa.

"Guess we can get our own supper," I grumbled. "We've done it before."

I wondered why Grandpa or Uncle Charlie weren't in the kitchen doing just that. Why should I need to do the chores, then—?

But Grandpa kicked at a fluff ball; then his eyes met mine. "It's not like Mary, Boy."

It finally got through my thick head. Grandpa was worried. I threw a look at the sky. It *was* getting rather late. *I* should have been worried. I just hadn't been thinking straight.

"I'll get Chester," I said, throwing my slop buckets down beside the pig pen. But I hadn't even gotten the saddle on Chester's back before I heard voices. Someone was "yahooing" my grandpa. I left Chester and went to see who had come and what news he had brought. It was one of the young Smiths, but he had already delivered his message, whirled his horse and was on his way back down the lane.

I started to holler at him to come back; then I noticed Grandpa still standing there, his hands lifted helplessly to the gatepost as though to steady himself. I hurried to him. His face was shaken.

"The girls—" he choked. "There's been an accident. The car flipped."

Chapter 11

An Awakening

I just stood there, staring at Grandpa, trying to get his meaningless words to make sense to me. I couldn't get them to connect somehow.

"Wh-what?" I finally heard myself stammer.

There was no response from Grandpa. He still clung to the post, weaving slightly as though fighting against a strong wind.

Uncle Charlie seemed to bring us both back to reality. He had hobbled out with his two canes to see what the commotion was about. He had heard the galloping horse—and I knew he realized it meant some kind of trouble. I could read it in his face when he demanded an explanation.

"What is it? Is it the girls?"

"They—they flipped the car." I mouthed the words but still did not really understand them. "The Smith kid—" But that was all I knew. I reached out a hand and squeezed Grandpa's arm.

"What did he say?" I insisted.

Grandpa shook his head as if to clear it. Still, it was a moment—a long moment—before he got his dry lips to form words.

"He said they—flipped the car."

"I know—I know," I heard myself agreeing impatiently, "but are they hurt?"

My own common sense told me that they would be hurt. I began to shake. "How—how badly—?" but I couldn't finish.

"I—I don't know," Grandpa said with a shudder. "The older boy went fer Doc. Thet's—thet's all he said."

I came alive then. Spinning around I ran for the barn, calling over my shoulder, "Where are they?"

Grandpa called back, "At Smiths'," and I raced to get to the barn and Chester. My insides felt as if they were in a vice. I was frantic for both girls, but I heard only one word escape from my lips. "Mary!"

Maybe it shouldn't have surprised me, I don't know. I probably should have been smart enough to know it all along, but it was painfully clear to me as I ran that if anything happened to Mary, I—I wouldn't be able to bear it.

Chester had stood stock-still. I guess he sensed I hadn't finished the job of properly putting on his saddle. If he had moved at all it most certainly would have fallen down under his feet somewhere. I jerked it off and thrust it aside now. I sure wasn't going to take the time to fuss with a cinch.

I threw myself across Chester's back even before we left the barn, ducking low to miss the crossbeam of the barn door. I didn't stop even to fasten the door behind me as I had been taught. I put my heels to Chester, and we were off down the lane.

It was the first time in my life that I let Chester run full gallop for any distance, but I didn't check him. He seemed to sense my agitation and took advantage of the situation. But even with the Smiths being fairly close neighbors and Chester running at full speed, the trip still seemed to take forever.

I wanted to cry but I was too frightened—too frozen. Even the whipping wind failed to bring tears to my eyes. All of my being seemed shriveled and deathly cold with fear. All I knew was that Mary had been hurt—maybe badly hurt—maybe even—*I need to get there—need to get to Mary!* my mind screamed at me.

When we came to the Smiths' lane, I forgot to rein Chester in and we very nearly didn't make the turn at their gate. Because of his speed, Chester swung wide when I turned him and ended up almost running into the fence rails. That near-accident sharpened my senses a bit, and I began to think rationally again.

I pulled Chester in and was able to get him under control as we entered the farmyard. I flung myself off his back and flipped a rein carelessly over a fencepost. I could see Doc's horse tied to a post down by the corral. I breathed a prayer for him and the girls as I raced toward the Smiths' back entry.

I guess I didn't knock—I don't know, but there I was in the Smiths' big kitchen. Mrs. Smith was clucking over the tragic event.

"—such a shame," she was saying. "Such nice young ladies, too. Just to think—"

"Where are they?" I cut in, completely ignoring any manners.

"Doc is with them," she replied, not seeming to take any offense at my rudeness.

"How—how—?" But I still couldn't ask the question.

Mrs. Smith just shook her head, motherly tears of concern filling her eyes. I couldn't stand it any longer. I wanted to scream. Mrs. Smith was busy pouring a cup of coffee, and I knew without her even saying so that she expected me to sit down at her table and drink it. I turned my back on the table and the coffee cup, biting my lip to get some kind of control. I had to know! I had to know!

"Where are they?" I asked Mrs. Smith again, fighting to control my voice.

"The young schoolteacher, Miss Matilda, is in Jamie's room," she said slowly. "We thought that—"

"Where's Mary?" I cut in.

But I didn't get an answer. Right at that moment Mr.

Smith entered the kitchen. He eased himself to a chair at the table and took the coffee that had been poured. Mrs. Smith just reached for another cup.

"A shame, Josh, just a shame," Mr. Smith said, shaking his head in sympathy. "Here ya only had thet there new car fer such a short time, an' I'm afraid thet it won't never be quite the same." At the look of horror on my face he hurried on. "Oh, Jamie and me pulled it outta the ditch with the team. Got it back right side up—but the frame—"

I couldn't believe it. Mr. Smith was bemoaning my motor car, and the girls were somewhere in the house in a condition I could only guess at, with the doctor trying to piece them back together.

"I don't care none about the car," I fairly exploded and then knew I wasn't being fair. "I—I'm sorry," I apologized. "It's just—just—what about the girls? You see," I went on, nearing Mr. Smith's chair as I spoke, "I don't even know what happened. How badly—?"

"I'm sure Doc will—" started Mrs. Smith, but I didn't even turn to hear the rest of her sentence.

Mr. Smith interrupted her. "Near as we can figure it," he said, "they was headin' home when thet there storm hit. The road likely got slippery. You know how it gets."

I nodded and Mr. Smith stopped for another sip of coffee. I urged him on with another nod. *That storm was hours ago!* my brain was telling me.

"Well, they went off the road. The car flipped over. Miss Matilda wasn't able to go fer help. I suspect thet she has a broken leg—along with other things."

"Mary?" I asked numbly.

"She—she was pinned under the car—she couldn't go fer help either."

Pinned under the car. The words sent my world spinning. She was pinned under the car. She might be—she could be—

"Mary," I heard myself say again, but this time I was pleading. "Please, dear God, don't let Mary—"

"Too bad they had to lay there in the wet fer so long," Mr.

Smith was saying. "Not many folks travel along thet road. Jamie an' me jest happened to—"

But I couldn't stand it anymore. I knew the rules. One was supposed to wait patiently until the doc had finished with the patient and given permission for you to go in to call at the bedside. *But this is Mary!* I had to know.

I headed for a door that would lead me to the inner part of the house. There were no sounds coming from anywhere but the kitchen, so I had nothing to guide me. "Josh," Mrs. Smith was calling from behind me, "Josh, you should—"

There was a stairway—and I took it. It led me to a hallway with doors leading off it. Four doors, in fact. I assumed them to be bedrooms and opened the first one. No one was in the room. I hurried on to the second. Doc was there. He was bending over the bed where someone lay quietly. I moved forward, part of me demanding that I turn tail and run.

It was Matilda. Her hair was wet and matted. Her face was bruised and had several tiny bandages. One leg, which lay partly exposed outside her blankets, was wrapped in whiteness. I guessed that Mr. Smith's diagnosis had been right.

I had never seen a human all bruised and broken before. She looked just awful.

At the sight of me she began to cry. "Oh, Josh. I'm so sorry," she sobbed. "The rain—the road just—"

Doc didn't scowl me out of the room. He even moved aside slightly. I knelt down beside Matilda and ran a hand over her tangled hair.

"It's all right," I said hoarsely. "It's all right. Don't cry. Just—just get better. Okay?"

I wanted to cry right along with Matilda, but I couldn't. My eyes were still dry—my throat was dry. I could hardly speak. I just kept smoothing her hair and trying to hush her.

Matilda seemed to quiet some. I stood to my feet and looked Doc straight in the eye. "How's—" I began. "How's—?"

"Mary?" he finished for me.

I nodded mutely.

"She's in the room across the hall," Doc said and turned his attention back to Matilda's arm.

I swallowed hard and turned back to the hallway. The first few steps made me feel as if I had lead boots. I could hardly lift my feet, and then I almost ran.

The door was closed and I shuddered as I turned the handle. Seeing Matilda had really shaken me. How might Mary look? She had been—had been *pinned* under the motor car. I didn't want to go into the room—but I had to know. I had to be with her.

I opened the door as quietly as I could. A small lamp on the dresser cast a faint light on Mary's pale face. There was a large white bandage over one eye, and another covering most of an arm lying on top of the sheets, which were pulled almost to her chin. Two heavy quilts were tucked in closely about her body. *What are all those blankets hiding?* I asked myself. *She was pinned—*

My eyes went back to her face. So ashen. So still. Her eyes shut. Was she—? *Is she already gone?* And then I saw just the slightest movement—almost a shiver.

In a few strides I was beside her, kneeling beside her bed, my hand reaching to gently touch her bruised face.

"Oh, Mary, Mary," I whispered.

Her lashes lifted. She focused her eyes on my face. "Josh?" she asked softly.

"I was so scared," I admitted as I framed her cheek with my hand. "I was afraid I'd lost you—that—"

"I'm fine," she whispered, moving her bandaged arm so that she could reach out to me.

"Don't move," I quickly cautioned, fearing she might come to more harm.

"I'm fine," she assured me again in a whisper.

"But—but you were pinned—"

"Miraculously pinned," Mary responded and she even managed a weak smile. "Oh, it caught me a bit on the arm—

but it was mostly my coat sleeve. Doc says I'm a mighty lucky girl."

"You're—you're not hurt?"

Mary moved slightly, and groaned. "I didn't say I'm not hurt," she admitted; then seeing the look of panic in my eyes, she quickly went on, "But nothing major and nothing that won't heal."

"Thank you, God," I said, shutting my eyes tightly for a moment. Then I turned my full attention back to Mary. "I was so scared—so scared that—that—I didn't even know until—until Billie brought the word—"

"I'm sorry, Josh. We had no way of getting help. No way of letting you know. We couldn't get to a neighbor's. Couldn't even get to the road an'—your supper—?"

I stopped her. The memory of my impatience over our meal not being ready made me flush with shame. I looked at Mary's face, swept soft and pale in the lamplight. "I should have known. I should have realized before," I admitted. "I don't know how I could be so dumb."

"You had no way of knowin'," argued Mary. "Sometimes we are later than we plan. Things—things just happen that delay us. But to miss the supper hour—No one could have guessed that we were lyin' there in the ditch," Mary explained and I realized that once again she was finding excuses for me. She was always doing that. Getting me off the hook when I did or said something stupid.

I brushed a wisp of hair back from her face. "Maybe deep down inside I knew all the time," I murmured, "but it took something like this for me to realize—"

Mary's eyes were puzzled. "You couldn't have known 'bout the accident," she said.

"No," I answered. "I'm talkin' 'bout me—us. I was scared to death, Mary, that I'd lost you—before I'd really found you. I didn't realized until—until—" I stopped with a shudder.

"Josh," said Mary softly but insistently, "what are you talkin' about?"

I looked at her—my Mary, lying there white and quiet on

the neighbor's borrowed bed. *She could have been killed!* My heart nearly stopped even at the thought. *I could have lost her. But she is still here—*

I tried to speak but I choked on the words. I swallowed hard and tried again, looking directly into Mary's eyes.

"I—I love you," I managed to blurt out. "Maybe I always have—at least for a long time, but—but I was just too blind to see it—until now. I—"

But Mary's little whisper stopped me. "Oh, Josh," she uttered, her hand coming up to touch my cheek, and I could see tears filling her eyes.

My own tears came then. Sobbing tears. I laid my head against Mary's shoulder and wept away all the pent-up emotions of the past dreadful hours. Mary let me cry, her hand gently stroking my head, my shoulder, and my arm.

I didn't bother to apologize when I was finished. Somehow I knew Mary wouldn't think an apology necessary.

"I love you," I repeated, conviction in my voice.

"Bless that ol' car," Mary said with a little smile.

"What?"

"Bless that car. An' the rain. An' the slippery road. An' our upendin'." Mary was smiling broadly now, but her words made no sense at all. I wondered if she maybe was hallucinating.

"Oh, Josh!" she exclaimed, her eyes shining, "you don't know how long I've wanted to hear you say those words."

"You mean—"

"I have loved you—just *forever*," she stated emphatically. "I began to think that you'd never feel the same 'bout me."

I felt as if there was a giant explosion somewhere in my brain—or in my heart. *I love Mary. Mary loves me back!* She would get better. We could share a life together. I could ask Mary to be my wife.

I had to put it in words—at least some of it. "You love me?"

Mary nodded. "Always," she stated simply.

"And I love you—so much."

Mary nodded again, her face flushed with color.

"Then—" I began, but stopped. I hesitated. It didn't seem fair to her somehow. Slowly I shook my head.

"No, no," I said. "I'm not gonna ask you now. Not yet. I'm gonna court you properly. Give you a little time."

A small question flickered in Mary's eyes.

"But not much time," I hurried on. "I couldn't stand to wait long now—now that I know. And one thing you can be sure of—I'm gonna come askin'—so you'd best be ready with an answer."

"Oh, Josh," Mary whispered.

Doc's timing couldn't have been worse. I had just kissed Mary—for the first time—and found it quite to my liking. Knowing now that she wasn't seriously injured, I drew her a little closer. Mary's eyelashes were already fluttering to her cheeks in anticipation of another kiss, her arms tightening about my neck. I don't know if it was the opening of the door or Doc's "Ahem" that brought me sharply back to reality, but I sure did wish he could have delayed just a few minutes more.

Chapter 12

Courtship

When I got back down to the kitchen, Grandpa and Uncle Charlie had arrived as well as Uncle Nat. Everyone was concerned about the girls, and the talk in the room was hushed and stilted.

But I wanted to shout and skip around the room like Pixie used to do. It seemed impossible that just a half hour earlier I'd had the scare of my life. Now I was walking on air. With all my heart I wished that I could share my good news—but I knew that wouldn't be right. Especially when Mary couldn't be with me. Yet I was fairly giddy with my newfound love. I felt several sets of eyes on me, and I wondered if they could see right through to my heart. I fought hard for some composure.

"They're fine," I said as nonchalantly as I could. "Both of 'em. Only scratches and cuts and bruises and a broken leg."

I knew that description didn't exactly go with "fine"—but I guess the group around the kitchen table was willing to chalk it up to my relief.

"Thank God!" said Grandpa, and Uncle Nat echoed his words. Then we were all bowing our heads while Uncle Nat led us in a prayer of thanksgiving. As soon as we had finished our prayer they wanted a more complete report.

"So Miss Matilda's leg *was* broken," Mr. Smith pointed

out with a knowing glance around the room.

I nodded.

"What else?" prompted Grandpa, referring to Matilda again. "What other injuries? Is she hurt bad?"

"Just cuts and bruises. Nothin' that won't quickly heal. She was worryin' about the motor car." I was still uncomfortable that she would even think about that when all I wanted was for the two girls to be alive and well.

"An' Mary?" asked Uncle Charlie, his voice quivering a bit.

At the mention of Mary's name, my heart leaped in my chest and I was sure my face must be flushing.

"She's fine—just fine." I couldn't keep some excitement from creeping into my voice no matter how hard I tried. "She—she has some cuts—one above her eye, one on her arm. Lots of bangs and bruises—but not even a broken bone." They were all so intent in their worrying over the girls that they missed my intensity. Anyway, no one looked at me like I expected them to look. They just muttered words of relief and joy and glanced at one another with a great deal of thankfulness.

"She was pinned," insisted Mr. Smith, who must have told them that Mary, having been pinned under the automobile, could be in serious condition.

"Doc says she was lucky," I explained. "It was mostly the sleeve of her coat that was pinned to the ground. Oh, her arm is cut some—but it could have been bad—really bad."

There were murmurs again.

"Now, Josh, you just sit yerself right down here and drink a cup of coffee," Mrs. Smith was saying. "You are 'most as pale as a ghost."

All eyes turned back to me. And then the funniest thing happened. The whole world began reeling and spinning like you'd never believe. I felt myself a reeling and spinning right along with it. But I didn't seem to be keeping up somehow—or else I was going faster. I tried to walk to the chair that Mrs. Smith had indicated, but my feet wouldn't work. Besides, the chair had moved. I didn't know what was happening to me.

I guess Uncle Nat caught me. I really don't remember. I came to my senses on Mrs. Smith's couch with Doc bending over me and a whole cluster of people hovering near. It took me awhile to realize what was going on, and then I felt like a real ninny. I mean, it was the girls who had been hurt in the accident and here I was doing the passing out.

I struggled to sit up, but Doc reached out a restraining hand.

"Take it easy, Josh," he cautioned. "You've been through quite a bit tonight."

Was it my imagination or was there a bit of a chuckle in Doc's voice? I remembered the scene that he had walked in on upstairs, and I felt my face flush. But no one else seemed to notice.

"Mrs. Smith is bringing some broth and crackers," Doc said. "You probably didn't have any supper."

I refused to be fed like a child, though I did obey Doc and sat up slowly. Then I carefully spooned the broth with its crumbled crackers to my mouth. My head soon began to clear and things came into focus again. With the return to awareness came the recollection of my recent discovery, and I could scarcely conceal my excitement.

As soon as I was able to convince Doc that I could walk a straight line, I stood to my feet.

"Can I see Mary—the girls—again?" I asked.

"Matilda is already sleeping—and Mary might be, too. I gave her a little medicine to help. You can peek in on her—but just for a moment. You hear?"

There was a twinkle in Doc's eyes and I caught a quick wink. I flushed and nodded, then headed for the stairs.

Mary was almost asleep when I crept quietly to her bedside.

"Doc says I can say good night," I whispered, "but I'm not to stay long."

Mary gave me a dreamy smile—brought on more by the

sleeping powder than by my presence, I was sure.

"How are you feelin'?" I asked, taking her hand.

"Sleepy," she murmured.

I kissed her fingers.

"You're not backin' out on me, are you?" I teased. "Haven't changed your mind, now that you've had a little time to think on it?"

Mary tried a smile. It was weak and lopsided in her relaxed state. Fighting hard to keep her eyes open, she squeezed my hand. "You don't get off that easy, Josh," she teased back. "I'm holdin' you to your word."

I leaned over and kissed her. "I love you, Mary," I told her again. "That's never going to change."

She stirred and tried to smile again. Sleep had almost claimed her.

I knelt down by her bed, my arm around her blanketed form, my other hand still holding hers.

"Go to sleep," I whispered. "I'll stay with you until you do."

She moved her head so her cheek rested against mine and then she sighed contentedly. It was only moments until her even breathing told me she was sleeping soundly. I leaned to kiss her forehead before standing to my feet.

She slept so peacefully, so beautifully. *Even with bandages and bruises, she's the most—the most lovely girl in the world, my Mary,* I thought. I could hardly wait for the time when she would be well and whole again—for the real courting to begin.

"Good night, Mary," I whispered. And then after a quick look around to see if Doc was lurking in the doorway, I tried a new word I'd never used before, just to see how it sounded. "Good night, sweetheart."

It sounded just fine.

Matilda's folks hired a motor car to come and take her home where her mother could nurse her back to health again. Since school was nearly out for the summer anyway, they just let the kids go a little earlier than usual.

Mary went back home to her pa and sister Lilli. I missed her something awful at our house, but it did make things a bit easier for me in regards to courting. Like I said before, how does one go calling on someone who is right there in your own house? Mary said that her being home with her pa right now was working out good because it would help to keep tongues from wagging. I hadn't even thought on that, but if it made Mary feel more comfortable with the courting, then I was quite happy to put up with batching it for the summer months.

I was in for a great deal of good-natured teasing when family and friends learned that I was actually courting Mary. I didn't mind. In fact, I rather enjoyed it. I didn't see Mary objecting much to it either. It was rather nice to be known as a couple. Made us feel that we really belonged to each other in some way.

I took a hammer and mallet to the frame of the Ford and to the fender dents. It wasn't a good job, but when I was done she could at least stand on four wheels and make it slowly down the road again. I even bought some paint and touched up the scars, but she never did shine and sparkle the same. I will admit that I sure didn't like the way she looked, but to my surprise it really didn't matter as much as I had thought it would. *And*, I reminded myself, *the accident, dreadful as it was, had brought Mary an' me together.*

In the absence of Mary, Uncle Charlie took over the kitchen duties again. His cooking wasn't near as good as it used to be. I suppose there were times I might've even been tempted to complain a bit—but I wasn't noticing much what I was putting in my stomach anyway. I was far too busy thinking of Mary.

Every day that I was able to finish up my work early enough, I chugged over in my beat-up Ford to call on her. I brought her field flowers that I knew she admired. I kept finding little things in town to bring a shine to her eyes. I picked the produce from her garden and toted it over so that she and Lilli could can it for fall. I tucked a member of the new litter of kittens in my shirt as soon as its mama had weaned it and took it over to Mary as a surprise. I brought news of Grandpa and Uncle Charlie and shared bits of information about the farm and clippings on garden care from the farm paper. And we spent hours just talking—about our plans, our dreams, our goals, and getting to know each other better.

I was hoping for a fall wedding. Just as soon as the harvest was in and the fall work was done. But I hadn't yet mentioned that to Mary. I was waiting for just the right time. It seemed to me that the right time would be somewhere in the first part of August—after the haying was done and before I went full tilt into harvest. That would give me time to shop carefully for a ring—maybe even go into Crayton. It would also give Mary time to make her wedding plans after she had said yes.

But before all that could take place, I had to ask her pa for Mary's hand in marriage. I wasn't worried about the prospect. I was confident that Mr. Turley would not hesitate in giving us his blessing. He had already indicated as much on more than one occasion. Still, I planned to fit in with all of the social obligations and do my courting in the proper fashion.

I fervently hoped and prayed that all the farm work would move along properly so that as much of my time as possible could be spent with Mary and so that none of the fall work would delay our plans. Things did go along quite well until we hit mid-July. I had been sweating over the haying, hurrying it up so that I might pass on to the next stage of the work. Just getting from one task to the next seemed to somehow hurry the days along until I could be with Mary.

But rain stopped the scheduled progress. Gazing at the foreboding sky, I sensed it was going to be more than just a shower. I felt awfully agitated as I steered the tractor through the gate and headed for its shed. I cast another look at the sky. From one horizon to the other, dark, ominous clouds hung above me with no break in sight.

I thumped a fist against the steering wheel. *The dumb weather is going to go and throw everything off schedule!* I fumed.

I did the chores in a sullen mood and went in for supper. Uncle Charlie was serving up his tasteless stew—again. I couldn't help but think of Mary's cooking. The roasts, the biscuits, the gravy. Then my eyes noticed big pieces of peach pie sitting on the counter.

"Where'd the pie come from?" I asked, knowing without asking that it wasn't Uncle Charlie's doing.

"Mary brought it over. She came to pick the beets."

Mary had been here—and hadn't even waited to see me.

"She was goin' to take ya some lunch in the field, but thet dark cloud came up an' she knew she had ta beat it home," explained Grandpa.

I nodded then, simmering down some.

I ate the stew, all the time thinking ahead to that pie. It was just as good as I knew it would be. My longing for Mary increased with each mouthful, not because of the pie itself. It was just a reminder of how much I missed her.

After supper I sorta kicked around. I helped with the dishes, noticing how careless we were about keeping the big, black stove shined up. I made a hopeless botch of sewing a patch on my faded overalls. I tried reading the farm magazine, but the words wouldn't sink into my thick skull. Finally I gave up. Scooping up Pixie, I headed upstairs for bed. But I couldn't sleep. I just kept thinking about Mary. Pixie seemed to know that something was bothering me. She licked at my hand and whimpered softly.

"Sorry, Old Timer," I said, swallowing my frustration. "I just miss her. So much. I know that courtin' is s'posed to be a special time—yet I keep thinkin' that if it wasn't for courtin', she could be here now where she belongs—with us. I don't know how much longer I can stand this—this waiting."

It wasn't that Pixie was unsympathetic—but she was getting old. I guess she figured that she deserved a good sleep even if I couldn't manage one. She took one lick at my cheek and then excused herself, settling in at her customary spot at the foot of the bed.

I lay there in the darkness, hurt and lonely, angry with the rain that still relentlessly pounded the roof above my head. *It's slowin' down everything*, I reasoned unrationally. *I'll have to wait even longer for Mary.*

The next day it continued to rain. I wanted to go to see Mary, but I decided my mood was so sour that I'd better keep to myself.

In the evening I moped around again. I don't know how Grandpa and Uncle Charlie put up with me. Finally I motioned to Pixie and headed for bed.

She didn't spend much time sympathizing that night. She must have figured it was my problem. After one lick on the cheek she found her way slowly to the foot of the bed and settled herself in with a deep sigh.

I lay there listening to the wind and the rain and hating both of them along with my own feelings. I couldn't sleep. I tossed and turned and sweated and shivered by turn. Grandpa and Uncle Charlie finally went to bed. I saw the light pass by my door, and then I was in total darkness. At last I could stand it no longer. I crawled from bed and pulled my pants back on. I shrugged into my shirt and grabbed my socks and shoes. I knew I would be quieter going down the stairs barefoot.

I heard Pixie stir and whine a bit as though she was asking what in the world I was up to, but I didn't even stop to stroke her soft head. I couldn't stand it one minute longer. I was going to see Mary.

Chapter 13

Plans

I didn't even have the good sense to put on my slicker. Before I reached the barn I was soaked. The water ran down the brim of my hat and dripped down the back of my neck. The wind lashed against my body, sticking my pant legs to my limbs and whipping my chore coat tightly against me.

I didn't dare try to drive the car in this weather. Chester had been given the freedom of the pasture and rarely ever fed near the barn. But one of the work horses was humped up against the corral fence, back to the storm and head hanging down. I called to him and moved to open the barn door. The horse was only too glad to hurry in out of the wind and rain.

I felt almost like a traitor when, instead of producing a scoop of grain, I slipped a bridle over his unsuspecting head. He didn't fight it but he must have been disappointed.

I had to walk him every step of the way. As I had guessed, the road was already slippery and he wasn't nearly as sure of foot as Chester. Besides, the heavy clouds made the night so black one could scarcely see the trees by the side of the road.

"Why didn't I just walk?" I mumbled to myself as we trudged along, but even with my question I knew that the horse was better at picking his way through the mud than I would have been.

There was no light in the Turleys' windows when I turned old Barney down the lane. I knew they would have all retired long ago, and half my mind kept urging me to turn the horse around and go home in sensible fashion. But I couldn't. I just couldn't. The other part of me said I had to see Mary.

I slipped the reins over Barney's head and flipped them around a fence post. Even to get across the yard was a chore. I slipped and slid my way to the house. My teeth were chattering and my whole body drenched. I'd probably catch my death of cold—but now wasn't the time to be worrying about that.

Rather than pounding on the door and waking the whole household, I went directly to Mary's window. I tapped with my fingers on the glass, wondering if she would hear as she slept.

But the blind responded almost immediately and the curtain was lifted back from the pane.

"Who is it?" Mary called softly.

As should have been the case long before now, I felt like a complete fool. *What in the world am I doing? What on earth will Mary think?* my thoughts and emotions tumbled together. *And her pa?* If he had been willing to give his consent, he surely would change his mind now. I wanted to bolt and run for cover, but I didn't. I just couldn't. I had to see Mary.

"It's me. Josh," I said as clearly and quietly as I could, so Mary would hear me but her pa wouldn't.

"What is it? What's wrong?" Mary's voice faltered, and I realized for the first time that of course she would come to that conclusion.

"No. No, nothing," I quickly assured her. "I—I just had to see you—that's all."

Mary hesitated for just a moment. "Go to the door," she told me. "I'll be right there."

And she was, with a heavy housecoat wrapped firmly about her. She held the door for me and then gasped.

"Oh, Josh. You are soaked to the bone. You'll catch your death!"

I couldn't deny it, so I just shrugged.

"Get out of those shoes and socks," she ordered, just the right amount of authority in her voice. "An' that coat!" she added. "I'll be right back."

I laid aside my dripping hat and pulled myself free of the rain-heavy coat. I pulled off the soggy shoes and tugged away the sodden socks. Embarrassed, I noticed the terrible mess that I was making of the Turley entry.

Mary was back just as the last sock came off. In her arms were some dry clothes and a rough towel.

"Mitch left them," she explained. "Use his bedroom and get out of the rest of those wet things. I'll put on some coffee."

"But—but I'll leave a trail all across your floor," I said hesitantly.

"A trail I can wipe up. Now hurry," urged Mary.

I hurried. Actually it was rather fun to be bossed by Mary.

It didn't take me long to towel myself dry and slip into the borrowed clothes. But I was still shivering as I headed back to the kitchen.

"Your pa's gonna want my hide," I said through chattering teeth as I held my hands up to the newly fanned fire.

"My pa would sleep through a hurricane," answered Mary as she placed the coffeepot on the stove.

"He would?"

"He would."

Mary had returned to her room while I had been changing and was now fully dressed. She'd even taken the time to tie her apron carefully over her kitchen frock. I noticed, though of course I didn't comment, that Mary was not wearing one of her Sunday frocks as she normally did when I came calling and that her hair was not as neatly groomed as usual. She had simply tied it back from her face with a ribbon.

"If nothing is wrong—with anyone," she said carefully, not looking at me from her place at the stove, "do you mind telling me what brings you out on such a night as this?"

I held my breath. Was there just a trace of scolding in Mary's voice? Was she angry with me? She had good reason to be. I waited a moment. Mary waited also.

"I—I couldn't sleep," I answered lamely.

Mary swung around to get a look at me. She must have thought I'd taken leave of my senses. The scar across her forehead from the accident showed faintly in the lamplight. It reminded me of how close I had come to losing her.

"You—you couldn't *sleep*?" she echoed and turned back to put another stick in the fire and needlessly shift the coffeepot.

There was more silence. Mary broke it. "That seems— seems like a rather—rather poor reason to be out ridin' in a drenching rain, Josh," she said quietly.

"It—it is," I admitted. Then I hesitantly went on, "Except that I knew the reason I couldn't sleep was because—because I needed to see you."

Mary stirred slightly but she didn't turn around to face me.

"I—I missed you," I stammered to a conclusion.

I saw Mary's back stiffen slightly. "You could have told me that at a sensible hour, Josh," she reminded me.

She *was* angry with me. Mary, who never got angry with anyone—who always found some reasonable explanation for the dumb things I did—who fought for me, defended me. She was angry—and I had never had Mary angry at me before.

Rooted to the spot, I was unable to decide what to do next. I should never have come—not at such an unearthly hour, not in the rain that dripped muddy puddles all over her floors. I had been inconsiderate and stupid. I had been thinking only of my loneliness—not the feelings and rights of Mary.

But Mary was speaking again—and there was a tremor in her voice. "I waited for you all last evening—all this evening. I knew you weren't busy. There was nothin' you could do in the rain. But you didn't come. An' finally I—"

But I had stopped listening to the actual words and was hearing the meaning loud and clear. Mary wasn't angry with me because I had come. She was angry with me because I hadn't come *sooner*.

I looked at her straight, slim back with the neatly tied apron, the gently sloped shoulders set in a plucky line, the head stubbornly lifted. It was enough to propel me forward silently, swiftly. I slipped my arms around her and buried my face in her hair. Tears came to my eyes, though I don't really know why.

"Mary," I whispered, "I came because I couldn't stand being without you any longer. I was so upset about the weather I didn't want to come and burden you with it all. But I—I can't bear it without you. I—I want you to marry me—as soon as possible. I can't stand being apart like this. Please, please forgive me for coming so late but—"

Mary turned in my arms. She was looking directly at me when I opened my eyes.

"Oh, Josh!" she cried. "Yes. Yes," and her tears mingled with mine as she pressed her cheek against my face.

I don't know how long I might have gone on holding her, kissing her, had not the coffeepot boiled over. With a little cry Mary jerked away from me and rescued the pot.

"Sit down," she said, wiping her eyes with a corner of her apron and nodding toward a kitchen chair. She hurried to clean up the stove and pour the coffee.

She pulled her chair up next to mine and rested her chin in her hand. "Now, sir, you were saying—?" she teased.

I laughed right along with her. Then I sobered. "I—I guess I was asking you to marry me and not in the most orthodox way," I admitted. "Not at all like I had planned. I've just gone and ruined the whole thing. I—I mean—I had these great ideas. I spent hours thinking about it. Selecting just the right words. Not just—just blurting it out." I stopped and shook my head. "I'm—I'm sorry," I whispered.

Mary reached out a hand and touched my cheek. "Sorry? Sorry for missing me? For loving me?"

"For spoiling what should be one of your most treasured

memories. For blundering into something that should be very special."

"Josh," said Mary softly, her eyes filling with tears and her voice soft with emotion, "I have just been told that I am loved. I have been asked if I will share your life—for always. Josh, it doesn't get any more special than that."

A tear slid unchecked down Mary's cheek. I reached out a finger and brushed it away.

"I don't even have the ring," I confessed.

"You'll get it soon enough," Mary defended me.

"I—I haven't even spoken to your pa."

"He'll give his blessing."

Then I took a deep breath. "That's not all," I admitted slowly as Mary waited. "I—I don't want to wait," I burst out. "Not till after harvest. Not a month. Not even a week if—"

Mary's eyes flew wide open.

"I know it's not fair. That it's terribly selfish. But you won't come home until we are married and I guess I couldn't bear it even if you did—but honestly, Mary, I don't want to wait any longer to get married. I know—I know it's not reasonable, that a girl needs lots of time to make her dress and sew her pillowcases and—and do whatever else it is that girls do, but—"

"Sunday?" said Mary.

"We really don't need a big fancy cake an' all the trimmings, and we've got pillowcases, an' you could wear that pretty blue—"

"Sunday?" said Mary again.

I frowned, not understanding.

"I think I could be ready by Sunday if you can," Mary said calmly.

"Sunday? Which Sunday?"

"Next Sunday."

"*Next* Sunday?"

"This is Tuesday," said Mary, laughter in her voice. "That leaves us Wednesday, Thursday, Friday and Saturday. Then comes Sunday. I can be ready by Sunday."

"By Sunday? Next Sunday?" I stammered.

"Are you trying to back out?" she teased.

"Of course not. I—I just supposed that you'd need—"

"You told me already that you planned to propose—remember? Well, there is no cake or dress ready—*yet*. But Lou said she would bake the cake, and I did find a piece of lovely material and I'm really quick with a sewing machine. Both Faye and Lilli will help. They promised. And as for the pillowcases, Josh—that is the *one* thing that *is* ready."

Neither of us had paid any attention to the cups of coffee that now sat cool and unwanted before us. I pushed my cup farther away so I wouldn't tip it over when I put my arms around Mary.

"Sunday," I grinned. "Sure. Sunday." Then my mind began to whirl. I had a few things that needed doing before Sunday, as well. How in the world would I get it all done in time? First thing in the morning I'd need to head out for that ring. Two rings, in fact. Then I'd—I'd—well, I'd talk to Uncle Nat and Aunt Lou, that's what I'd do. They'd have a whole list of things I needed to attend to. I had no idea.

Mary stirred. "Pa?" she said.

"You said he'd sleep through a hurricane," I reminded her.

"And so he would," Mary smiled, ruffling my still-wet hair, "but not through the marriage of one of his daughters. You'd best try to get a comb through that hair while I go wake him," and she kissed me on the nose and went off.

My head started working again. "Barney," I muttered. "I didn't care for Barney." I looked about the kitchen for a slicker, not wishing to get a soaking again. Mitch might not have left anything else behind.

I spotted a slicker belonging to Mr. Turley and took the liberty of borrowing it just long enough to lead the horse in out of the rain and toss a bit of hay in the manger.

When I returned to the kitchen I managed to comb my hair and smooth some of the wrinkles out of Mitch's worn shirt. There was nothing I could do about the short legs on my pants. Mitch wasn't quite as tall as I was.

Mary and Mr. Turley arrived in the kitchen together a few minutes later. He still looked sleepy and confused, but Mary was radiant. She had changed her dress to the pretty blue one I had referred to earlier. Her hair was carefully pinned up, too. She gave me an encouraging smile, and I took a deep breath and began my little speech.

"Sir, I realize that this is an untimely hour, and I apologize for that—but I would—would like to ask for your daughter Mary's hand in marriage, sir. I—I love Mary deeply and she has—has honored me by returning the love, sir, and—"

I guess Mr. Turley had heard enough or maybe he was just anxious to get back to bed. He reached out and shook my hand vigorously. "I'd be proud, Son," he said huskily. "I'd be proud." Then in a slightly choked voice, he added, "It woulda made her mama very happy."

Mary slipped an arm about me and gave me a squeeze and then she ran off to waken Lilli and tell her the good news.

No one went back to bed that night, not even Mr. Turley. We stayed up until the sky began to lighten. The sun never did come out because of the clouds, but I didn't mind them anymore. We talked the night away, making our plans for the coming wedding. Then with the daybreak I kissed Mary goodbye, borrowed Mr. Turley's slicker again and mounted Barney for the trip back home.

I got home before Grandpa or Uncle Charlie had left their beds. Pixie was waiting for me, though, sniffing at the door, a confused look in her eyes.

I picked her up and held her close. "Pixie," I told her, "I'm getting married. Not 'sometime,' but Sunday. *This* Sunday." Then I threw all caution to the wind and bellowed for the whole house to hear. "I'm getting married! Sunday! This *next* Sunday. You hear! *I'm getting married!*"

Chapter 14

Sunday's Comin'!

I sure was relieved when it stopped raining. I had lots of plans to make and traveling to do, and it would have been most miserable trying to do it all in the pouring rain.

As it was, the roads were rutted and muddy, so it was out of the question to use the motor car. Mostly I rode Chester, and the horse heard many declarations of love that week. Even if they weren't meant for him.

I don't know what I would ever have done without help from Uncle Nat and Aunt Lou. Even Grandpa and Uncle Charlie lent a hand—mostly doing up my chores while I ran about. They were 'most as excited as I was.

I asked Avery to be my best man. A lump came into my throat as I made my choice. I knew Willie would have been standing at my side had things turned out differently.

Mitch would have been my second choice—mostly for Mary's sake, but Mitch sent back word that he wouldn't be able to make it by Sunday, and he gave Mary and me his best wishes. So I went to call on Avery and he grinned from ear to ear as he accepted my invitation.

Mary picked Lilli to be her maid of honor, and she was pretty excited about it too.

True to her word, Aunt Lou made the cake. She also organized some of the church ladies who offered to serve a meal following the ceremony. Everyone seemed anxious to help out, and I knew that some of the reason was because Mary had lost her mama.

Even Sarah got involved. "Mama says I can serve the punch, Uncle Josh," she informed me and I gave her a hug and told her I knew she'd do a great job.

On Thursday I made the long trip to get the rings since our little town did not have what I considered suitable for Mary. How I wished for better roads and the automobile, but Chester did the best he could. We were both tired when we got home that night; even so I cleaned up and headed for Mary's house. I figured Chester had used his legs enough for one day, so I walked. It wasn't that far to Mary's if you cut across the pasture.

She looked a bit surprised when she opened the door to my knock.

"Expectin' someone else?" I bantered.

"No, Josh," she laughed, drawing me in. "But I wasn't expectin' you either. I thought you'd be far too busy to come callin'."

"I was," I teased. "I am—but I thought you might like to have this before Sunday." I held out the little box that held her ring.

Mary gave a little gasp and reached out her hand. I pulled the box back. "Not so fast," I told her. "You haven't yet told me what a wonderful guy you'll be marryin' come Sunday."

Mary glanced back at the table behind her. I could see bits and pieces of soft white material scattered over it.

"If you don't stop pesterin' me and be on your way, there won't be a wedding," she warned me. "No dress—no wedding."

I turned to look more closely at the table, but Mary put a hand over my eyes.

"No peeking," she commanded. "It's not fair to see the dress before the ceremony."

"Then come out to the veranda," I suggested.

"For only a short time," Mary insisted, pretending she

wasn't interested in the little box, as she allowed herself to be led to the veranda bench.

I seated Mary, then dropped to one knee in front of her. I reached for her hand and spoke softly, "Mary Turley, would you do me the honor of becoming my wife—Sunday next?" I added with a hint of a smile.

Mary reached out to ruffle my hair, then changed her mind and let her hand fall to my cheek. "That would make me the happiest girl in the world," she said, her gentle smile saying even more than her words.

I caught her hand and kissed the palm—then opened the small box and removed the ring. Carefully I slipped it on Mary's slender finger. "Oh, Josh," she murmured, lifting the ring to study it and then brushing it against her lips, "it's beautiful."

She leaned forward to kiss me as I knelt before her.

"Now go finish that dress," I prompted. "I don't want any excuses come Sunday."

But we lingered for a while, just talking about our plans and comparing progress. It was dark before I headed back across the fields for home. I whistled as I walked in the light from the moon. I had never been happier. I had just placed my ring on Mary's finger, and Sunday promised to be the greatest day of my life.

We were to be married immediately following the Sunday morning service. Everything, as far as I knew, was in readiness. I would wear my wedding suit to church. Mary and Lilli would slip out and change at Lou's just as soon as the service ended. Lou had things well in hand for our reception dinner with the help of the parishioners. Mary's silver service had been polished to perfection and stood ready and waiting to serve the guests. I knew the silver pieces were far more than a teapot and coffeepot to Mary. They were a small symbol of her mother at our special occasion. I also knew that Mary would miss her mama even more intensely on her wedding day.

On Sunday I was up long before daylight, polishing and licking and patting for almost an hour. Something unheard of for me. Grandpa and Uncle Charlie didn't even tease me. They themselves were far too busy licking and polishing.

At last we were ready to go. We had decided the road was dry enough to take the motor car. I'd attempted to polish it up the day before, though it still bore the dents and scars of the accident.

We climbed in, I started up the Ford, and we headed down our long farm lane. I wouldn't be doing any speeding, even though I could hardly wait to get to town. Here and there along the road, mud holes waited for the unwary. And we sure didn't want mud stains on our carefully groomed Sunday suits and shoes.

We were there lots early, and I paced back and forth as I waited for Mary and her family to arrive.

Matilda came, though her leg was still in a walking cast. "I wouldn't have missed this day for the world!" she exclaimed and gave me one of her hurried, impulsive hugs. "I'm so happy for you, Josh," she bubbled. "Happy for both of you."

She welcomed Grandpa and Uncle Charlie with hugs as well. "Oh, I miss you," she cried. "All of you. The summer has seemed so long." There were tears in Matilda's eyes. "But I have good news," she hurried on. "I got the school I applied for near home."

"Ya mean yer not comin' back—?" began Grandpa.

"Oh, I couldn't," Matilda said softly. "I—I mean—I'm happy for Josh and Mary, but it wouldn't be the same now. I—mean—it wouldn't be fair to newlyweds to have someone—"

Grandpa nodded but I could see sadness in his eyes.

I had to admit that I hadn't even thought of Matilda's dilemma. But she was right. It would be better for Mary and me to get a good start on our own without an extra person around. It was going to be enough for us to share the house with Grandpa and Uncle Charlie. I would talk with Mary later about the new teacher, but as far as I was concerned it was just about time that one of the other neighbors took on boarding duty.

"But they've found a new teacher to replace me," Matilda's voice interrupted my thoughts, "and I've found a new school—so everything has turned out just fine."

At that point another interruption, and a welcome one—the Turleys arrived. Mary gave a squeal at the sight of Matilda and ran to meet her, her arms outstretched. They hugged and cried and hugged some more. I didn't mind. After all, Mary and I could look forward to a whole life together, beginning today. I just stood back and watched the goings-on.

Then I realized that I should be welcoming Mr. Turley. I had never seen him at church before, except of course for his wife's funeral. I shook his hand and smiled, not knowing exactly what to say. He gave a lopsided grin in return, looking a trifle uneasy. By then the girls had settled down, and Mary came over to me and slipped a warm little hand into mine. I whispered "Good morning, sweetheart," into her ear and made her blush prettily. It was time for the service, so we all moved inside the church doors and found places to sit.

The service seemed unusually long. It was probably a very good sermon—Uncle Nat's always were. But for some reason I had a hard time concentrating on it. When I took a peek at the pocket watch I had gotten from Uncle Nat and Aunt Lou, I was astounded to discover it was even earlier than usual when the service was dismissed! Then I again felt Mary slip her hand in mine for just a moment, and I squeezed it gently in return. It was our little message to each other that it wouldn't be long until we'd be standing before the minister pledging our vows of love and commitment—and also that we were anxious for that moment.

Mary slipped away to Aunt Lou's as soon as she could, and I paced about checking to see that everything was in readiness. There certainly was no need—a lovely bouquet from Aunt Lou's garden graced the altar, and candles had been lit on either side. I straightened my tie—again—and smoothed back a wayward lock of hair.

At last Sally Grayson took her place at the organ and Uncle Nat stepped to the front of the church. That was my cue to join him. I gave Avery a bit of elbow and wiped my hands again on a handkerchief Aunt Lou had provided. I moved awkwardly forward down the aisle that looked as long as our farm lane. Boy, was I nervous. I tried to swallow but there was nothing there. Eventually Uncle Nat's reassuring smile came into focus, and I turned beside him along with Avery, cleared my throat and waited, trying hard to avoid all those eyes looking right at me.

Lilli came down the aisle next. She looked just fine. I'm guessing Avery noticed, too, for even in my mental fog I thought he was watching her progress rather carefully.

And then there was Mary, poised at the door on the arm of her father, ready to take those few steps that would bring her down that aisle to me.

Her dress was simple but very appealing, and suited Mary perfectly. Her veil fell forward over her face, partly concealing her smile and her bright colored hair. But I could see her shining eyes, and they told me all I wanted to know.

"Dearly Beloved . . ." Uncle Nat's firm voice was an anchor for my whirling emotions. The ceremony was a short one—but I meant every word of the promises I made to Mary before God and many witnesses. From her expression and the directness of her answers, I knew she meant the promises to me as well.

"For richer, for poorer, in sickness and in health . . ." The words rang in my ears long after they were spoken.

But the words that really caught my attention were "to love and to cherish—till death us do part."

I had heard much about love. And I felt I understood it. I had no doubt in my mind about my love for Mary. But did I know what it meant to *cherish* her? Not much had been said in my presence about cherishing. I determined to do some looking into the meaning of that word at my first opportunity.

When the vows had been spoken, Uncle Nat indicated that I was to slip the wedding band on Mary's finger. And almost before I knew it he was pronouncing us man and wife. I lifted Mary's veil then to give her the expected kiss and could see fully the shine in her eyes and the flush to her cheeks. She was beautiful, my bride!

Uncle Nat presented us to the congregation. "Mr. and Mrs. Joshua Jones!" What a ring those words had! Mary and I looked at each other, and I felt an astonishment and excitement I'd never experienced before. I wished I could stop and kiss her again, but we had to go outside so folks could hug us and kiss us and give us their congratulations and throw rice and take pictures and all those usual things. I went through the whole thing in a daze. What a shame, too, because I wanted to always be able to look back with clear memories on this incredibly important day in my life.

We were finally ushered back into the church basement for the dinner. Guess folks were fairly hungry by then. For some reason I still hadn't felt hunger pangs. I went through all of the motions of eating, though, so Avery wouldn't rib me about being "lovesick."

Our friends gave little speeches and the Squire twins sang "Bless This House" and Matilda sang a lovely song based on a scripture text from the story of Ruth. Little Sarah played a piano piece. Lou said she'd worked hard on it all week. There were a few jokes here and there, and I guess they were funny—I mean, folks all laughed. All in all, the afternoon passed in fine style. Then we had gifts to open. In spite of the short wedding notice, the congregation did themselves proud. We got some real lovely things. Mary was thrilled over the linens, quilts, tea towels and such for our home, and that made me happy also.

At last people began to drift off to their homes, and finally it was just the family members who were left. I took off my suit coat and began to pack the gifts away in the car and help with the cleanup. Mary, still excited and happy, was also looking a bit tired.

We finally got everything cleared away or stacked in a corner. Then we slipped over to Aunt Lou's for a cup of hot tea and some slices of pumpkin bread. Mary took the opportunity to change from her wedding gown back into her Sunday dress, still looking like the pretty bride she was.

Mr. Turley excused himself as soon as Lilli and he had finished the light lunch. As he kissed Mary goodbye, he held her close. I saw tears in his eyes as he turned to go, and I wondered what it would be like to raise a daughter you loved so much only to give her over into the keeping of another man—particularly when her father had so recently lost his wife. I felt a pang of sympathy for Pa Turley. I followed him out to his team.

"Thank you, sir," I said sincerely, "for all you have done to make your daughter the beautiful person she is. I will love her always, I promise you."

Then we moved toward each other and I have never had such a bear hug. It suddenly hit me—*I have a pa! I mean, a real pa!* I hadn't had one of my own since I had been a small boy. I stepped back and looked at this man who now was a part of my life. I couldn't express all I was feeling. Instead I said, rather hoarsely, "How about comin' for supper—Wednesday night?"

He nodded his head and climbed into his wagon. "And Lilli, too, of course," I called after him. I watched him go until he turned the corner, and then I hurried in to tell Mary of my invitation to her pa—*our pa*—before I forgot.

It was late by the time we got home. We unpacked the car of the gifts and things Mary hadn't wanted to leave in town—things like her ma's silver tea service. We also had Mary's suitcases, although many of her belongings still waited in her downstairs bedroom, not having been moved back to her home after her accident.

There would be no honeymoon—at least not at the present. I was sorry about that. Mary and I had talked it over, and she had assured me she didn't mind. But still I felt she was a bit cheated out of what she rightfully deserved.

"After harvest," I'd promised her.

"Josh," she insisted, "the important thing is that we will be together, not *where* we will be together." I loved her even more for that.

As we carried Mary's personal things into the house, it became apparent that we menfolk, in all our hurrying and scurrying on short notice to prepare for the wedding, had given no thought to the room arrangements.

"Where should I put these?" Mary asked innocently.

"I—I—in—in my room, I guess," I began, but even as I said the words I knew that wouldn't work. I had the smallest room in the house. My tiny closet was already crowded with my few things. Mary's would never fit there too.

Grandpa cleared his throat. "The master bedroom," he said. "I'll git my things right outta there," and he moved to do just that.

"Oh, no," insisted Mary. "I wouldn't think of putting you out of your room, Grandpa."

A debate ensued, but Mary prevailed. It was finally decided that Mary and I would use Lou's old room. It was much roomier than mine and had a much larger closet. I carried Mary's things up to the room, and while she unpacked I busied myself making the evening coffee.

Mary was soon back down and took over in the kitchen. "Boy, is it ever good to have you back!" I teased.

"So you just wanted a cook!" she teased right back.

I looked around at Grandpa and Uncle Charlie. They both wore a very satisfied expression, and I figured that bringing Mary permanently into our family was about the smartest move I had ever made.

Chapter 15

Beginnings

With the weather turned for the better, our household back in order and my wife nearby, I got back to the haying again. Mary immediately took over her kitchen. My, how she did scrub and clean. I'm embarrassed to admit we menfolk had let things get even worse than I had realized.

She organized the rest of the house too—like moving the rest of my belongings from my old room to our new one, straightening the pantry, properly patching my worn overalls, sorting out the canning jars in the cellar and all sorts of other tasks. Every time I came in she was busy with something, though she often stopped to give me a hug and a kiss.

On Wednesday night the Turleys came for supper. Mary did herself proud, but then I guess her pa and Lilli were used to Mary's good cooking. I had to remind myself that Mary had likely cooked Pa Turley more meals than she had cooked for me.

Mary made life totally different for me when she was there. I could hardly wait to get in from the field at night—and I'd always enjoyed field work. I looked toward the house a dozen times a day just to see if I could catch a glimpse of her. And she often slipped out with a drink of cold water or fresh buttermilk. She even came to the barn when I was milking and laughed as I squirted milk to the farm cat, chatting about her day, her plans for the house or garden while I did my chores.

Of course Grandpa and Uncle Charlie were awfully glad to have her back as well. Uncle Charlie seemed to walk a little jauntier, and Grandpa took to chuckling a good deal more. Though I was quite willing to share Mary's return with them, I marveled at the fact that she was really mine—just mine—in a very unique and special way. Every day the word "marriage" took on a new meaning for me, and I thanked God over and over for her and that He had thought of such a wonderful plan.

Friday night after all the chores had been done, the supper dishes washed and back in the cupboard, and we were gathered around the kitchen table enjoying various activities, I suddenly remembered my resolve to look up the word *cherish*.

My dictionary was up in my old room, I thought. But when I climbed the stairs to get it, I found that Mary had moved my few books as well. I went to Lou's room—I had to get that change made in my mind, to stop thinking of that room as Lou's—it was mine now, mine and Mary's. After rummaging around for a bit I found the dictionary. I flipped through the pages and came to the word.

"Cherish—to hold dear, to treat with tenderness, to nurse, nourish, nurture, foster, support, cultivate."

Wow! I read it again—and again. *I had promised before God to do all that!* I marveled. It had seemed to me that my loving Mary was sort of beyond my control. I mean, who could help but love Mary? But "cherish"—that was different. Most of the words in the definition were words of choice, of action—not feeling.

I knelt beside our bed with the dictionary open before me, and I went over each word in the list one at a time, promising God in a new way that with His help I would fulfill my promise to Him and to Mary. I even did some thinking on just how I might keep the promises. I prayed that God would help me to be a sensitive and open husband for Mary.

When I had finished my rather lengthy prayer, I heard a stirring at the door. It was Mary.

"I—I'm sorry, Josh. I didn't mean to interrupt. I—I—"

But I held my hand out to her.

"I want to show you something," I said, indicating the open book before me.

I rose to my feet and sat down on our bed. Mary crossed the room and sat beside me.

"Do you know what 'cherish' means?"

"Cherish?"

"Yeah. What we promised to do for each other last Sunday."

"Oh!" Mary exclaimed, her eyebrows lifting.

I traced the dictionary meaning of cherish while Mary read the words for herself. When she finished, her eyes met mine. We just looked at each other for a few minutes and then Mary spoke.

"Rather scary."

She was so serious, so solemn, that I began to laugh. I laid the dictionary on the bed beside me and reached for her. She snuggled into my arms and put her head against my shoulder, but I gently turned her face so that I could look directly into her eyes.

"Mary Jones," I said, enjoying the sound of her new name, "before God and with you as my witness, I promise to love you, to hold you dear, to treat you with tenderness, to nurse you, nourish you, nurture you, foster you, support you and cultivate your individuality—till death us do part."

I had needed to refer to the dictionary beside me a few times during my little speech, but I meant each word in a new way. When I finished there were tears in Mary's eyes.

"Oh, Josh," she murmured softly, "I love you so much."

That was really all I needed to hear.

I kissed her again.

"When you left the kitchen and didn't come back, I was a little worried," she admitted. "I thought—well, I don't really know what I thought."

"It took me awhile to find the dictionary," I confessed, "and then when I did, I needed some time to think it through and to pray for God's help."

I shifted so I could gather Mary more closely to me. The dictionary fell unheeded to the braided rug. I was through with it for the moment anyway.

"I need to go make the coffee," Mary murmured, but she didn't sound too convincing.

"Uncle Charlie knows how to make coffee," I reminded her.

"Yes—" But I stopped her protest with another kiss.

"We don't get much time alone," I reminded her. "I want you to tell me all the ways you can think of for me to keep the promises I've just made."

It was some time later that the smell of fresh-perked coffee drifted up the stairs and into our room, and Mary and I smiled at each other. It seemed that Uncle Charlie had found the coffeepot.

I finally finished the harvest. It wasn't a great crop, but it would get us through. The fall had been a dry one. In fact, the last moisture we got was what had come in July to delay my haying. I smiled every time I thought of that rain. It had speeded up my marriage to Mary, and for that I owed the rain a great deal.

We decided to further postpone our honeymoon. Mary said it was silly to spend the money when it might be needed elsewhere.

Mary got all her garden taken care of, and we settled in for another winter—one totally different for us, for now we had each other.

Matilda and Mary kept in touch by way of letters. Matilda's leg had mended well and she was enjoying her new school. There were even hints that some young man she had met was becoming rather special to her.

In November Lou gave birth to another girl, Patricia Lynn, her coloring darker than Sarah's. This little mite demanded a bit more attention than Sarah had as an infant. I looked at Lou with her family of four and wondered what it must be like. Certainly it meant work and sacrifice—but I figured it would be more than worth it.

With Matilda gone we had decided to subscribe to our own paper. I guess we had all become intrigued with the reading material that kept us informed of the world's events. Many evenings were spent sharing the paper around the kitchen table.

We were saddened and horrified by the news reports of the stock market crash. It seemed to be of great significance to many people—even causing suicides and such things. I couldn't understand how that whole financial world worked, though I did feel sorry for those who were directly affected by it all.

It sure didn't have much affect on our life, however. I mean, no one in our small community ever had money to invest in any stocks or such. The results of that crash would have little, if any, repercussions in our town, I reasoned. We were a bit relieved when the newspaper stopped screaming horrid headlines about the crash and went on to something else.

Winter came—according to the calendar—though the look of things didn't change much. There was no snow to speak of. The weeks trailed on, following one right after the other, and the world outside was just the same—brown and bare. Mary kept talking longingly about snow, and I must admit I was wishing for a good snowfall, too.

Christmas was nearing, though it was hard to get in the holiday spirit without a white world outside. But family members began to sneak around on their way to hide something somewhere. Secret whisperings and plottings made life rather interesting and fun. Then the whole house began to smell like a bake shop as Mary turned out special cakes and cookies. I wondered if we'd finish eating all those things even by Easter time.

Mary talked about trimmings for the tree, and I hoisted

the boxes down from the attic and she went through them. I'd never realized before what a sorry lot they were. Mary set to work making new ones and even spent some of her egg money in town to replace several items. I could see that she received a good deal of pleasure out of making Christmas something special for all of us.

I looked forward to Christmas—but it sure would be nice to have some snow.

Chapter 16

Christmas

One little skiff of snow dusted the ground a few days before Christmas, and Mary got all excited over it. But it sure didn't last long. Before it had even covered the ground it began to melt off again. Mary was disappointed and I was disappointed for her. There wasn't anything I could do about snow for her Christmas, though.

"Josh," Mary said on the Saturday before Christmas, "we need to get a tree."

That was no problem. We had lots of small trees down along the crick that would look good with Christmas decorations.

"I'll get one," I promised.

"I thought maybe we could go together," offered Mary, and I grinned in appreciation.

"Great! When would you like to go?"

"Right after dinner—if that's okay with you."

"Fine."

And so the two of us headed out for the crick bottom right after the noon dishes were done.

It was colder than it had looked. I wondered if Mary might not be bundled up warmly enough, but I guess the vigorous walking helped keep her warm. Anyway, each time I asked her, she assured me that she was just fine.

The farm dog went along with us. Truth was, any time one of us went out, we didn't get far without Fritz at our heels. We didn't mind. It would have been fun to have Pixie along too, but she couldn't run very well anymore. She seemed to have arthritis like Uncle Charlie. Anyway, she didn't do any more walking than absolutely necessary. I even carried her upstairs each night. Most of her day was spent curled up in her little box behind the stove.

The pond in the pasture was frozen, and we took some time to slide back and forth. Sorta like being a kid again.

"We should have a skating party," enthused Mary, but I really didn't know who would want to come. All our old friends were either married with youngsters to care for or else had moved away.

For some reason I thought of Willie—maybe because he had skated with me on this very pond. Boy, I missed the guy. It still didn't seem real to me that he was gone—actually in heaven. I could see his face so plainly, could hear his banter and laughter—could sense his feel of mission and commitment when he spoke intensely of the needs of African villages for the gospel. Boy, I missed Willie.

I thought of Camellia. She had gone across the ocean to Willie's people now. I put money for her support in the collection plate the first Sunday of each month, and Uncle Nat forwarded it on to the Mission Society. We got an occasional prayer letter from Camellia, too. She loved Willie's Africans. She was kept busy with her nursing, for they were a poor people and many of them, old and young alike, had physical needs. Camellia was glad God had called her to this work. I still had a hard time picturing Camellia, the golden girl, trudging through destitute villages, visiting dirty, unkempt huts with medicines and love. But God did wonderful things with those who obeyed Him. Used people in ways we would have never dared suggest. Mary and I prayed daily for Camellia.

Mary brought my thoughts back to the present with a jerk when she lost her balance and ended up on her back in the middle of the ice. I was afraid she might have hurt her-self, but she was laughing as I bent to help her and soon we were both down on the ice rolling and laughing.

It was fun until old Fritz jumped right into the middle of the fracas. He was barking and prancing and taking quick licks at our faces. By now Mary and I both decided we'd had enough, so we scrambled to our feet and started off again on our Christmas tree quest.

I'd figured it would be a quick, easy task. But with every tree I pointed out, Mary was sure we could do just a bit better. So on we walked, checking out tree after tree.

I was beginning to worry about getting home to do the choring when Mary at last found the very one she was look-ing for. It was about my height, with full, even branches.

"It will fit just fine in the parlor," Mary exclaimed and then added matter-of-factly, "Of course I will need to trim it up a bit."

I smiled wryly. She could trim it all she pleased just as long as we could cut the thing and get on home.

It wasn't hard to cut it down. It was a bit harder to get it home. There was no snow, so we couldn't drag it because Mary was afraid of damage to some of the branches—*probably the ones she'll eventually trim off anyway,* I thought but didn't say. That meant we had to carry it. Mary insisted on sharing in the effort. I lifted the big end and she took the small one, but carrying a tree, particularly one that has large, full branches and sways in the middle, is not an easy task.

We tripped about as much as we walked. The dog didn't help matters. He kept running around the tree and our feet, constantly getting in our way and tripping us up even more.

"Why don't *I* carry it?" I finally suggested.

"Oh, Josh. It's too heavy for one person."

I could have told her that it was too heavy for *two* peo-ple—but I didn't.

"I think it would be easier," I dared insist.

Mary looked reluctant. "Do you want it on your back—

or your shoulder?" she finally conceded.

"My shoulder," I decided.

"I'll help you lift it up."

It didn't work very well that way either. Possibly it would have if Mary had allowed me to trim off some of the bottom branches—but she wanted the branches to come right down to the parlor floor. It was prettier that way, she said. So I was trying to carry a tree on my shoulder with branches right down to the bottom of the trunk. They poked me in the face and knocked off my hat.

I finally dumped the thing to the ground, and Mary gave a little gasp, fearful that I had broken some of her precious branches—which there were far too many of anyway.

"Look," I said, a little out of patience, "why don't I just get the team and wagon and come and haul it home?"

"Can you drive back in here with the team and wagon?" Mary wisely asked. I would have had to cut my way in and out again. There were no trails except those the cattle had made, and they were too narrow for a wagon to travel.

"Then I'll hook Barney to the stoneboat," I threw out, keeping my voice even.

Mary tipped her head slightly to consider it.

"It should work," she nodded in agreement. "You can sorta snake your way in and out among the trees."

I didn't like her description. "Snaking" didn't seem like much of a way for a man to travel.

"We need to put it someplace so you can remember where to find it," Mary continued, and I got even more huffed at that.

"I'll remember," I said flatly. "You think I'm an old man or somethin'?"

Mary looked a bit hurt by my response. "Of course not," she assured me apologetically; "but the trees all look alike an' *anyone* can forget."

She stressed the anyone.

"You forget that I was raised on this land," I reminded her loftily. "I know this crick bottom like the back of my hand. Roamed through here all my life—fishin' and huntin' cows."

Mary nodded but said nothing more.

We stashed the tree up against two anchored ones and started off for home. I checked the sky. The sun was already low on the horizon. I would need to hurry to get back for the tree before dark.

Mary reached out and slipped her mittened hand into mine, and I gave hers a bit of a squeeze. I wanted her to know I really wasn't mad at her or anything. We walked in silence for a while and then Mary began to chat about how she was going to decorate the tree and how pretty it would look. I could sense how special it was to her, and I was glad I hadn't insisted on lopping off some of the lower branches. "Nourish and nurture her" flashed through my mind, and I gave her hand another squeeze.

At home Mary went right on to the kitchen to get busy with supper, and I went to the barn to get old Barney.

It didn't take me long to get down to the crick bottom with the stoneboat, and I figured out how I'd slip right in, pick up that bulky tree and get back to the farmhouse in a jiffy.

I drove directly to where we had left it—but it wasn't there. Nor were the two trees we had braced it against. I couldn't believe my eyes. I started looking around, this way, that way, and the more I looked the more confused I got. I had to use the axe a few times to untangle the stoneboat from the brush, and that didn't make me so happy either.

All the time that I was searching, it was getting darker and darker. And I was getting madder and madder. I don't know why. It was my own dumb fault, but I was mad at Mary. I don't really know what she had done. Just been right, I guess. Anyway, I kept right on looking, too mad and too proud to give up. At the moment I couldn't think of anything more humiliating than showing up at home without that tree.

But in the end I had to give up. I was so confused I didn't

even know which direction to point old Barney to get him back to the barn again. That made me even madder. Not being any snow, I didn't even have tracks to follow—though I was glad for that in a way. I sure wouldn't have wanted anybody to have followed my tracks through that brush. They'd have laughed at me for sure.

I finally conceded defeat and just gave Barney his head. He weaved in and out—*snaked*, if you will—and finally came out into the open again. There across the field were the welcome lights of the farmhouse.

Mary ran to meet me as soon as I pulled into the yard. If she was disappointed about me not finding her tree, she didn't voice it.

"I was worried," she said instead.

"Too dark," I sorta growled. "I'll have to go pick it up later."

"Supper's ready," she told me. "Do you want to eat before you chore?"

I nodded—which she probably couldn't see considering how dark it was. Mary started back to the kitchen. "I've fed the pigs and chickens," she called over her shoulder, "and Grandpa carried the wood and water."

It should have made me feel great. Here I was coming in late without having accomplished my errand and chores still ahead of me, and I found them half done already. But it didn't make me feel great. It made me even madder. *Don't they think I can even do my own work?* I fumed.

I put Barney back in the barn and fed him. No soft words or appreciative pats for him tonight. I pushed a barn cat out of my way with a heavy-booted foot. He was lucky. I felt like kicking him.

On the way to the house it hit me. I was acting like a spoiled child, not a married man—and certainly not like a Christian husband who had promised to *love* and *cherish*, with all that it meant. Mary had done nothing to deserve my wrath. She was trying to make Christmas special. For me, for Grandpa, for Uncle Charlie. She had wanted a special tree. Had tried hard to help with the work of getting that tree. It wasn't her fault I couldn't find my way around my own woods.

But she had been right, she would likely—likely look at me with I-told-you-so in her eyes. *If she does—*

But I stopped right there beside the woodshed and prayed, reminding myself of all of my promises and asking God again to help me keep them. It didn't change my circumstances any, but it did make me a better supper companion.

The tree was not mentioned or the tree ornaments that sat waiting in the parlor either. Nor did Mary look at me as I had expected her to. She found something to busy herself with that Saturday evening and chatted away as if everything was just fine.

I loved her for it. It seemed that Mary was doing a much better job of keeping her promise to "cherish" than I was.

On Monday morning I hooked Barney up again. I still didn't know how I was ever going to find that tree, but I'd find it if I had to spend the whole day looking.

Then Mary complicated things. She came from the house, all bundled up, and smiled sweetly at me. "Thought I'd ride along," she stated in a matter-of-fact tone.

My head was spinning. *I'm going to be humiliated again.* I'd boasted of knowing my own crick bottom, of having a near-perfect memory. Both statements had proved to be false. I took a deep breath, gritted my teeth and directed Barney to head for the woods.

Halfway there I got this brilliant idea. I gave Mary a big grin and motioned for her to scoot up beside me.

"Wanna drive?" I asked her. Her face didn't brighten as I expected. For a moment I feared she might turn me down. Mary had her own little code of what rights belonged to the man of the family. But when I passed Barney's reins to her, she grinned and accepted them without further comment. I inwardly sighed with relief.

I was afraid as we neared the brush that she might pass

the reins back to me. I had to do something to prevent that. I leaned over and lifted the axe to my lap.

"You drive," I said as casually as I could, "an' I'll cut any little shrubs that get in our way."

Mary just nodded.

We reached the woods, and she began to "snake" her way through with that stoneboat. Not once did she get hung up on anything, so I never got a chance to use that axe.

And would you believe it, she drove straight to that tree.

I made no comment as I loaded it. It filled up the stoneboat, so Mary and I had to walk back. She didn't seem to mind, and I sure didn't. On the way home she left the driving to me. I never even thought to share it. I was too busy wondering just how she had done what she had done. I mean, dead on! Right to where that tree stood waiting.

When we got back to the farmyard Mary went in to finish the washing. I put Barney away and went to do up a few odd jobs. I knew that in the evening we would be decorating the tree in the parlor. I looked forward to it now that we finally had the thing home.

We ran into another snag the next day. I didn't see it coming, though I should've been smart enough to sort it all out beforehand. You see, ever since Lou and Nat had married, we had always spent our Christmases with them. Lou had made the arrangements, cooked the dinner and everything. All we fellas ever did was show up.

Well, that's not quite true. We did our own shopping, wrapped our own gifts—in a manly sort of way—raised the turkey that we chopped the head off and plucked. But other than that, Lou took care of everything. I have no idea why I expected it to just remain that way.

Anyway, I should have been alerted when Mary said one morning as Christmas neared, "Do you mind if I invite Pa and Lilli for Christmas dinner?"

Of course I didn't mind. It sounded like a good idea to me,

and Lou always cooked plenty of everything. We ate leftovers for days after Christmas was over.

So I heartily agreed to the arrangement. I even rode over to the Turleys and extended the invitation myself. I stayed awhile too. Just to chat with Pa Turley and to play a couple games of checkers. He didn't have much male companionship now that Mitch had left home, and I guess he missed it. Mary was happy when I returned with the news that they would be glad to come.

The next day Mary spoke about Christmas again. "I think you can bring in the gobbler now," she informed me. "I want to get it dressed and out of the way so everything won't need to be done at the last minute."

That made perfect sense to me. We men had always left it to the last minute simply because nothing else needed doing then for us. I had no idea what Mary's many tasks were going to be, but she was always powerful busy with something.

I killed the gobbler, plucked off the feathers and carried him to Mary's kitchen. She took over from there and soon he was ready to be hung outside in the shed where he would be kept frozen until needed further.

That night as we retired, Mary spoke again—and this time the truth of her Christmas plans finally got through to me. "Would you like to invite Nat and Lou?"

At first I couldn't understand the question at all.

"Invite—to what?" I asked innocently.

"For Christmas."

"We don't bother none with invitations," I said to Mary, tossing another sock in the corner. "We've done it so long now everybody just knows without invitations."

I figured in my ignorance that Mary had just reversed the order without meaning to.

But Mary hadn't reversed the order. She had known exactly what she said. "What do you mean?" she asked, stopping in the middle of pulling the pins from her hair.

"Well, I suppose the first few Christmases Lou invited us.

After that—well, we just knew that every Christmas we would go there. Oh, not always 'there.' A few Christmases Lou's packed everything up and had the Christmas out here at the farm. But mostly, unless it's planned beforehand, we go on into town."

There was silence for a few minutes. Mary started to slowly unpin her hair again. "That was before you had a wife," she said softly.

I looked up then. Something in her voice was sending me funny messages.

"What do you mean?" I asked, wondering if I should have caught it already.

"That was before you had a wife," she repeated slowly as though I was dense or something.

"What does that have to do with it?" I dared ask.

Mary's voice raised a bit and she answered rather quickly, "It has a good deal to do with it, I should think."

"It hasn't changed the fact that we are still family—that Lou—"

But Mary swung to face me and I could see a stubborn set to her chin and a hurt look in her eyes. I didn't get any further. At least not just then.

The silence hung heavy again.

Finally Mary broke it. She fought to keep her voice controlled—even.

"Josh," she ventured, "what do you think has been goin' on around here for the past several days?"

I shrugged. I couldn't follow her.

"The bakin'? The plannin'? The tree? The turkey?" Mary went on.

I shrugged again. I had the feeling that no matter what I said I was going to be in trouble.

"Christmas, Josh. Christmas," Mary said with emphasis. "I have been gettin' ready for our first Christmas. Now, if I wasn't going to be allowed to *have* Christmas—why've I been allowed to *prepare* for it?"

"It's—it's not that you aren't allowed," I stammered.

Mary ran a brush through her hair. "Good," she said simply. "Then we will have Christmas as planned. Do you want to invite Nat and Lou?"

Oh, boy! Talk about not communicating. We were running full circle.

I stood to my feet and crossed to stand in front of her. Somehow I had to get things cleared up.

"Mary," I said in exasperation, "we always—Grandpa, Uncle Charlie and me—go to Aunt Lou's each Christmas. Every year. We—"

But Mary had turned her back on me. It made me angry. I wanted to reach out and turn her around again. Make her face me.

"That was before," she insisted.

"Before? What does that have to do with it? Before! It doesn't change Christmas. We are all *still* family. Families are to be together at Christmas. Not just—just little chunks of them. All of them. Can't you see? Don't you understand?"

Mary wheeled around then. There were tears spilling down her cheeks. "No," she stated with a sob, "*you* don't see. I've worked for days, Josh, no—*weeks*, to get ready for this first Christmas. Always before I've had to leave you at Christmas and go home to my family. Well, now *we* are family, Josh. You and me. I wanted this Christmas to be ours. To be special. I thought you wanted it, too," she sobbed. "But now—now you say that Christmas is to be a trip to town— to Lou's to have dinner together. Well, I care about the family as much as you do, Josh. I love Lou and Nat—and the kids— but that's—that's not the way I had planned our first Christmas."

Mary was crying hard by the time she finished her speech. I found myself wondering if Grandpa and Uncle Charlie were hearing every word. The walls certainly were not soundproof. Well, let them hear. This was our business.

I tried one more time.

"It's not that I don't want our Christmas to be special," I argued. "To me it is always special to be with Nat and Lou."

Mary reached for a corner of her nightgown and wiped away her tears. She didn't cry any further, and I thought I had won. That she had finally listened to reason.

She didn't say "very well," or "fine," or anything like that. In fact, she didn't say anything at all. She just laid her brush back down on the dresser and walked around the bed to slip into her side. She even allowed the customary good-night kiss after I had put out the light.

It was some time in the middle of the night that I awakened. I had the feeling that I'd heard something, but as I lay there in the darkness, straining to hear whatever it had been, there was total silence. And then it came again. Just a shaky little sob from Mary's side of the bed.

I rolled over then and reached out a hand to her.

"Mary?" I questioned in a whisper. "Mary, is something wrong?"

"Oh, Josh," she sobbed, slipping her arms about me. "I'm so sorry. I shouldn't have—shouldn't have been so insensitive. I—"

"What are you talking—?" I began, not understanding, completely forgetting our little tiff at bedtime.

"Of course you want to be with your family, like always. I'm sorry that I—"

So that was it.

I held Mary and let her cry. All the time I thought on what had transpired. For the first time I began to see and understand Mary's thinking. We were family now—Mary and I, and with the years we might be blessed enough to have other family members join us. We had the right and the responsibility to make our own traditions—our own Christmases. Sure, the rest of the family would always be dear to us—and we could share and be with them—but not *lean* on them. Not depend on their traditions anymore.

My hand patted Mary's shoulder, and I lay staring into the dark thinking and praying a bit, too.

I had slipped again. I had failed in cherishing Mary. I had

not been sensitive to her needs, had not nurtured nor supported her. Would I ever learn?

"Mary," I whispered against her hair, "you were right and I was wrong. I'm sorry. Truly sorry."

There was silence again. I dared to continue.

"We should have our own Christmases. *We* are family. It's important to—to both of us."

Mary tipped her face in the blackness. "It's all right," she said. "I don't mind. Really."

But I wasn't turning back now. "I'll go see Aunt Lou tomorrow," I informed Mary. "Grandpa and Uncle Charlie can still go. We'll have Lillie and Pa here."

"No," said Mary. "We'd be splitting up family. That wouldn't be right."

"I'll talk to Lou," I insisted. "She'll understand."

"*I'll* talk to Lou," said Mary. "We'll work it out."

"But—" I began. Mary reached one finger out in the darkness and placed it on my lips.

"Trust me?" she asked simply and I nodded my head against her finger to assure her that I did.

Chapter 17

Adjustments

Grandpa drove Mary in to see Lou the next day. He was looking for an excuse to go into town anyway. I figured he had some more Christmas shopping to do.

Everything worked out just fine. It was decided that Christmas would be at our house with Uncle Nat, Aunt Lou and family, Pa Turley and Lilli, all around our table. Mary would take care of all the arrangements for the dinner. Grandpa confided to me that he felt Lou was a bit relieved. The new baby was still keeping her up nights a good deal.

Lou and Mary also agreed that in the future each would take turns having Christmas dinner. That sounded like a sensible arrangement to me. It gave both women a Christmas "off" and yet allowed each to have Christmas just her way on the Christmas when it was her turn.

I was proud of Mary. She had been sensitive and caring— and yet had shouldered her share of family responsibility.

That Christmas turned out to be the best I had celebrated up to that point in my life. Mary did a fine job with the dinner—just like I'd known she would. The turkey was cooked to perfection, the potatoes fluffy and the gravy as smooth as silk. All the good things she had been baking over the previous days appeared on the kitchen sideboard—right along with the honored silver tea set from which she served the tea and coffee.

The weather was fine—though we never did get our Christmas snow, nor any other snow, for that matter. The families arrived early and left late, and we all had a great time together.

Of course Lou's four little ones added a lot of spark to the occasion. Sarah was too grown-up now to be relegated to the children's status. Jonathan too had matured a lot over the summer months and wasn't nearly as hard to keep track of, but Timmy more than made up for him. Someone had to watch the boy every minute. I finally had to carry Pixie up to the bedroom and shut the door on her. Timmy insisted on petting her and holding her, and poor old Pixie's bones were too fragile for Timmy's kind of handling. He tried to be careful, but being a small boy he was pretty awkward at showing his affection.

Baby Patty slept a good share of the day. Aunt Lou ruefully commented that it might mean a long, wakeful night. I had no idea what that was like and wasn't particularly interested in finding out.

Pa Turley really seemed to enjoy being with the family. He watched the antics of the children with loud guffaws and slaps to his knees. I couldn't help but wonder, *What'll he think of having grandchildren of his own?*—though I felt I knew.

Lilli was quiet. She helped Mary in the kitchen, but her mind didn't seem to be on it much. I wasn't too surprised when along about midafternoon Avery appeared at our door. I invited him in but he declined. Said he'd come to take Lilli for a bit of a drive. We teased them some, but they just flushed and bundled up to get away from all of us.

When they returned Avery accepted our invitation to share leftover turkey and homemade buns. We formed a little foursome and played dominoes. Mary and I won, hands down, but I don't think our opponents were doing too much concentrating on the game. Avery and Lilli were the last to leave that evening.

We were all tired but happy when we retired. Mary and I cuddled close in Aunt Lou's old bed and talked over each of the day's happenings. It was fun to go over it all again.

"You know which gift I liked the very best?" Mary asked me.

"Which?"

"The mirror. The new mirror."

I wasn't really surprised. I'd noticed her stretching or stooping, trying to see herself in Lou's old mirror. The gilt was wearing off at just the wrong place.

"What was your favorite?" asked Mary.

"Oh, boy! That's tough. I liked them all."

But Mary wasn't to be put off so easily.

"Come on, Josh. Favorite."

I reviewed the gifts Mary had given to me. "I guess the pullover sweater," I said after much thought.

"The sweater?"

"And do you know why? Because you made it yourself. For me." I paused a moment and then went on with a chuckle, "And you know why else?"

"*Why* else?" teased Mary. "Is that proper English?"

"Of course it is. *Why* else would I say it?" I bantered back and Mary gave me a little jab in the ribs.

"Okay—so *why* else?" she asked me.

"Because it actually fits," I laughed. "It has two arms—and they are the same length. It has a hole up top for my head and one at the bottom for my waist."

By now Mary was chuckling too but she gave me another playful jab. "Are you saying you didn't think I could knit?" she accused me.

"No," I answered, dodging away from another jab, "but I have seen a few sweaters in my day that were made by girlfriends or new brides. You had to ask to be sure what the thing was."

Mary gave me one more jab. That one I figured I deserved.

On a cold, windy day near the middle of the month, I came in one morning to find Mary in tears. I couldn't think of anything I had done, and I was sure Grandpa or Uncle Charlie wouldn't do anything to make her weep. For a moment I feared Mary might be ill, and that scared me something awful.

I didn't ask questions. I didn't have time. Mary threw herself into my arms and sobbed against my shoulder. By now I was really worried. My eyes traveled to meet Grandpa's across the room, but he wouldn't look at me. He was busy staring out of the window at the bleak, sunless day. Uncle Charlie was nowhere to be seen.

In my mind I frantically reviewed family members, wondering if bad news had come in some way while I'd been out. But I hadn't heard a horse, and the farm dog had been with me all the time. His ears were sharper than mine, and he most certainly would have heard if someone had come.

"Sh-h-h. Sh-h-h," I tried to quiet Mary, brushing aside strands of fine hair from her tear-streaked face.

"Sh-h-h. Tell me. Tell me what's wrong."

Mary swallowed hard and tried to get control. "It's Pixie," she finally managed to gasp out. "I found her in her box behind the stove."

"Pixie?"

Mary burst into fresh tears and clutched me even more tightly.

I wanted to free myself and check on Pixie. The little dog might be in need of some attention. But I couldn't just leave Mary. Not the way she was feeling now. I held her more tightly and rubbed her shoulder and patted her back.

When her tears finally subsided, I put her gently from me and went to kneel beside the stove to check on Pixie. It was far worse than I had feared, and my whole being rushed to deny it. The little body was lifeless. There was nothing I could have done. She was already stiff and cold.

Tears came to my own eyes. I picked her up as gently as I could and ran my hands again over the silky sides and let my fingers toy with the floppy little ears. *She's been a good dog—a good friend,* I mourned. Pixie had been with me ever since my dearly loved Gramps had found her for me so many years ago. Boy, would I miss her. It reminded me of how much I missed Gramps.

I knew Pixie was old, that she had been stiff and arthritic and in pain much of the time. She was far better off having just slept her way out of life. But I still fought against the reality of it. If I'd had the power right then, I'd have brought her back.

I didn't have that power, so all I could do was hold her up against my chest. The small body sure didn't feel like it usually did. I was used to her little tail wagging gently as I petted. I was used to a little lick with a pink tongue every now and then. I was used to warmth and energy. And now there was only the quiet, stiff, lifeless little form. I felt almost repelled by it—but I couldn't put her down. I just kept running my hand over her, speaking to her as though I thought she should awaken.

Mary came to where I knelt and laid a hand on my head, running her fingers softly through my hair.

"I'll fix a box," she said quietly.

For a moment I wanted to protest. Pixie had been *my* dog. I would fix the box. And then I remembered how much Mary had loved her too and I nodded in agreement, the tears flowing again.

I pulled Pixie's small bed out from behind the stove and laid her gently back down. Without a backward glance I arose, pulled my heavy mittens back on and left the kitchen.

I found the shovel and a pick and chose a spot in the garden. I wanted her to be down under the trees beside the grave of my first little pup, the one I had named Patches. *Gramps brought me that puppy too,* I remembered as I raised the pick above the frozen ground. It was hard digging. Maybe that was good. I needed something difficult to concentrate on for the moment. I put my full strength behind each swing of the pick. Then I shoveled out the frozen clumps of dirt, making a hole big enough to hold a small box. A small box with an even smaller dog.

Tears froze on my cheeks as I worked. *She might've been small,* I thought, *but she was all heart.* All heart and love. I'd never known anyone who had loved me like my small dog had. She asked no questions, demanded no apologies. She just loved me—Josh Jones—just as I was.

I guess I got a little carried away on the size of the hole. I made it bigger than it needed to be, but perhaps I wasn't ready to go back to the house yet. I needed a little more time to be alone. With Pixie's death went my last visible memory of Gramps. Oh, I had lots of memories. Things that I treasured as I pulled them out and thought on them—which I did often. But with Pixie those memories had been different, more vivid. Each time I picked up the little dog I could see the age-softened hands of Gramps as he handed her to me for the first time.

I remembered Aunt Lou sharing with me how Gramps had walked into town after my first puppy was killed and searched the town streets until he had found me another puppy. I remembered too how small Pixie was, and how Gramps had told me that she would need special care and love.

Pixie had been my little love-gift, that's what she had been. It was Gramps special love for me that prompted the giving, and it was Pixie's and my special love for each other that had helped us share so many things over the years.

And now she's gone. I had known all along that one day it would happen, but I had just kept pretending in my heart that I could hold it off somehow.

I finally stopped my digging, wiped the frozen tears from my cheeks and went to put away the pick. I would still need the shovel.

Mary had the box all ready. She had lined it with some soft material that made Pixie look as though she were all cuddled in and snug as she liked to be. The lid was next to it, and I knew Mary expected me to put that in place after

I'd told my little dog goodbye one last time.

I ran my hand over the silken fur and then placed the lid on the box. I pulled on my heavy mitts and looked at Mary.

She had wiped away all her tears, but I could still see the sadness in her face.

"I thought you might like to be alone," she said softly to explain why she didn't have her coat on. I nodded, surprised that she knew me so well so soon, and then I picked up the little box and went back to the garden.

After I had completed my sorrowful task, I stayed outside for a while finding little chores I could do. Mary didn't come looking for me. When I finally decided I was ready to face the family and go on with life, I went back to the kitchen. I could smell the coffee brewing even before I opened the door, and I realized just how chilled I was.

Mary's eyes met mine and we spoke to each other even without words. She smiled then, just a tiny little one, and I gave her a bit of a nod.

Uncle Charlie reappeared. We tried to talk normally at the table. Didn't seem much to talk about, save the weather. It worked for a time. By then I had thawed out a bit and was feeling some better, though I knew it would be a long, long time until I got over my hurt. Mary knew it too. I could feel her love and understanding even when a whole room separated us. It was a marvel, this being man and wife. I began to wonder how I had ever functioned before Mary had changed my whole life. I hoped and prayed I would never need to function without her again.

For the first time in my life I began to realize what Grandpa had suffered over the years without Grandma—and why Gramps had commented to me about being anxious to get to heaven. It gave me a new respect and sympathy. And I think it opened up a whole new understanding of the word *love* for me too.

Chapter 18

Life Goes On

I came in from the morning chores expecting breakfast on the table as usual. It was—after a fashion. The pot of rolled oats still simmered on the stove, the coffee bubbled in the coffeepot. Thick-sliced bread was toasted, the table set, but it didn't take sharp eyes to know that something was amiss.

"Where's Mary?" I asked Uncle Charlie, who gave the lumpy porridge another stir while Grandpa poured the coffee.

"She's not feeling well," Uncle Charlie informed me and went on quickly when he saw the look in my eyes. "Nothin' serious. Jest a tummy upset, she said. Bit of the flu, I 'spect."

I didn't even wait to remove my outside wraps but headed for the stairs.

Mary was lying on the bed in her clothes, so I knew she had been up.

"I'll be fine," she assured me wanly. "Just—"

I'd already heard that little speech from Uncle Charlie. I sat on the bed and laid a hand on her forehead.

"I don't have a fever, Josh," Mary protested. "I already checked it myself."

"You feel hot to me," I argued.

"As cold as your hand is from chorin', anything that isn't

freezing would feel hot," Mary reminded me. "Go on," she prompted. "Go have your breakfast."

"Aren't you going to eat?"

"It would be pointless," insisted Mary. "I'd just bring it right back up again."

"Could I bring—"

"Josh," said Mary with a bit of impatience, "I can't even stand the *smell* of it."

I tucked a blanket about her and left her then, though I was still worried even with her assurances that she'd be up soon.

True to her word, Mary came down later. She still looked pale, but she insisted that she felt just fine. She proved it by taking over her kitchen chores.

For the next three mornings the scene was repeated. I was getting kind of tired of Uncle Charlie's version of our breakfast porridge—even though I'd eaten it most of my life. I was also getting very concerned about Mary. One morning she didn't make an appearance until almost noon, and even then she looked as if she should be back in bed. I tried to talk her into staying in for the day so she could lick this thing, whatever it was. But who was I to argue with a woman who's made up her mind?

When it happened the fifth morning in a row, I decided something must be done. Without saying anything to Mary, I saddled Chester and headed off to town. I figured it was about time Doc was consulted about the matter.

Doc arrived at the farm soon after I had returned home again. By then Mary was up and about. She looked pale and often turned her face away when she lifted the lid to stir a pot, as though she couldn't bear the sight or smell of whatever she was cooking.

Mary looked surprised when I ushered Doc into the kitchen. Then she set about putting on the coffeepot, probably assuming that he had just popped in to warm up on his return from a neighborhood call. Doc was content to wait, visiting with Grandpa and Uncle Charlie, but I could see that he was watching Mary carefully out of the corner of his eye.

"Hear you haven't been feeling so well, young lady," Doc said as he stirred in some cream into his cup.

"A bit of a flu bug, I guess," Mary answered off-handedly as she passed him a plate of cookies.

"Maybe," agreed Doc. "It sure is making the rounds again. But Josh thought I should check it out, just in case."

All eyes turned to me. I was especially aware of Mary's.

"It's not always flu when the stomach acts up," Doc went on. "Josh is right," he said in answer to Mary's expression. "No harm in checking."

After we had finished our coffee, Doc sent Mary up to our room to prepare for the examination.

"Do—do you think it's serious?" I ventured before Doc went up to join her.

He put his hand on my shoulder as he rose. "No point in worrying about it till you have something to worry about, Josh," he said, while Grandpa and Uncle Charlie nodded solemnly in agreement.

He wasn't gone long. When he appeared in the doorway I was all ready for the explanation of Mary's illness. I started to ask but Doc stopped me. "Mary is waiting for you," he told me, and I felt my heart constrict with fear. I ran up the stairs two at a time and flung the door open.

Mary was propped up on two pillows. Instead of pale, now her cheeks were a trifle flushed and—I crossed quickly to her after swinging the door closed behind me. I wanted privacy if I had to hear the worst.

"Sit down, Josh," Mary said gently. I did so and took her hand in mine.

"Is it—? Are you really sick?" I managed.

"No," Mary answered and her eyes were shining. "I'm just fine."

"Then—then—?"

Mary began to smile, then giggle. Here I was about to die of worry and she sat there giggling like a silly schoolgirl.

"Josh," she began, and took a deep breath to try to calm herself. She seemed about to explode with excitement. "How would you like—like to be a father?"

"I'd like it," I stammered. "You know I would. We've talked about it—"

"Good," squealed Mary, "because you are going to be one!"

Her words didn't make much sense, but the way she was pulling on my arm and beaming made me realize that something good was happening—something extraordinary. I started sorting through the conversation again, looking for the answer and finally it got through to me.

"You mean—now?" I yelled back, grabbing her by both shoulders.

"Well—well—" she teased, but I had already jumped up from the bed. I ran down the hall and bounded down the stairs two or three at a time. "We're gonna have a baby!" I shouted to Grandpa and Uncle Charlie, who were both on their feet and hollering along with me before I could make full circle. Then I ran back up the stairs again and grabbed Mary. I held her close and we laughed and rejoiced together.

I finally stopped rocking her back and forth and held her at arms' length. "You didn't know—?" I questioned, gazing into her face. Somehow I thought that women automatically knew these things.

"I suspected," she admitted, "but I still wasn't sure."

"When?" was my next question.

Mary screwed up her face. "The timing's not great," she said slowly. "The baby will arrive right in the middle of harvest."

"We'll manage fine," I quickly assured her. "We'll find you some help."

"So this is why you've been feelin' sick?" I went on.

She nodded.

"I don't remember Lou being sick like that. It scared me," I admitted.

"Some women are. Some women aren't," Mary explained

matter-of-factly. "Anyway, it shouldn't last for long, Doc said."

But Doc was wrong. Mary continued to feel sick for many weeks. Months, in fact. She lost weight and looked pale and fragile. It tore me apart to hear her in the mornings. I felt responsible for the way she was feeling and I sure would have gladly taken her place.

We menfolk took turns cooking breakfast. I even hung a blanket over Mary's door so the odors from the kitchen wouldn't bother her as much. Other than that, it seemed we simply had to wait it out.

In March we had a visit from Lilli and Pa Turley. They brought both good and bad news. Lilli brought the good news. Bubbling as she shared it, she told us that Avery had asked her to marry him and she had said yes. The wedding was set for June.

Pa's news brought sadness to Mary's eyes.

"I've decided to put the farm up for sale," he informed us.

I saw Mary start and wondered what thoughts were going through her mind. She didn't speak them then; she simply nodded.

"I've given it a lot of thought," went on Pa Turley. "Mitch isn't interested in farmin'. He has him a good job in the city now." Pa Turley sat twisting his coffee cup this way and that as he looked into the steaming interior. "Don't 'spect he'll ever return home to the land . . ." His voice trailed off.

"Never was no good at batchin'," he mused after a moment of silence.

"What will you do?" Mary finally found voice to ask. My thoughts had already jumped ahead, and I was about to call Mary aside to suggest that we offer Pa the downstairs bedroom.

"Emma—yer aunt Emma over to Concord—has been after me fer some time to move in with her. She'd like someone about the house to keep things in order like—an' she knows

I don't wanna be alone. She thinks thet it would work best fer both of us."

"And what do you think?" Mary asked calmly.

"I've no objections," Pa Turley answered a bit quickly. "Always got along with Emma the best of any of my sisters."

Mary looked at me and I nodded. She took a big breath as though in relief, her eyes thanking me as she said, "You're welcome here, Pa."

Pa Turley pushed back his chair and waved the offer aside in one quick motion. "Oh, I couldn't," he protested.

"And why not?" questioned Mary. "We've got the room. We'd be glad to have you, wouldn't we, Josh?"

"Sure would," I assured him. "A room right there," I said, pointing to the downstairs bedroom, "or one right up there at the head of the stairs. Take your pick."

Pa Turley seemed to be having a mental debate. He finally sighed deeply and pulled his chair closer to the table and his cup.

"Much obliged," he said with feeling. "Guess it's always good to know thet yer wanted. But—I think thet we'd best leave things be. I—I would be welcome here. I know thet. But Emma—Emma needs me. There's a difference there, ya know? No, I think thet we'd best let things be as planned."

Mary and I looked at each other, and we knew that we had to let him decide the matter. "Well, as long as you know you're more than welcome, Pa," I told him.

"You'll visit?" asked Mary.

"Oh, why sure," he promised. "Got three girls all a'livin' here. 'Course I'll visit. 'Sides, I sure wanna keep up on the grandchildren."

Mary and her pa smiled fondly at each other.

That night Mary and I lay in our bed talking over the day's events. I decided to tell her what had been churning through my mind ever since the Turleys' visit.

"I've been thinkin'," I said softly into the dark, "I'd like to buy Pa's land."

I felt Mary move slightly in order to see my face. It was too dark in the room, so she settled back in her spot beside me.

"You need more land, Josh?" she asked.

"Not—not really. Not right now. But—but it was your home, your family's land for as long as I can remember—as long as *you* can remember. I thought—I thought it might be hard—that you might sorta like to keep it."

There was silence and then Mary said softly into the night, with a break in her voice, "Thank you, Josh."

I ran my hand over her soft hair and traced the scar over her eye with one finger. "Besides," I went on slowly, "who knows? Maybe we'll have a son and he'll need the land. I'd be pleased to give him his grandpa's farm to work."

Mary chuckled at the thought and put her head on my shoulder. "If you can—if you can work it out, Josh, I'd be most happy about it," she whispered, and a sob caught in her throat. "It would only seem right, wouldn't it—and it would make Papa so happy."

I decided on a trip to town the very next day to see what arrangements could be made.

The banker was agreeable, and Pa Turley sure was. It took some time to get all the paperwork sorted out and processed. But in the end the Turley farm belonged to the Joneses. Pa acted like a heavy burden had been lifted from his shoulders when I handed him the check for the farm. He couldn't say anything. He just reached out and gave me a big bear hug, and I knew he felt that he wasn't really giving up the land—just handing it on to his family.

He had a farm sale then and packed his few belongings for moving on to his sister's. Lilli went to live with Faye to await her wedding to Avery.

Mary and I drove Pa into town to catch the train for Concord. He'd already said goodbye to his other two daughters. He didn't have much to say on the way, but his eyes sure did study out every farm and field as we traveled along. *It's like he's closing the door on his past life,* I thought, *and getting ready to open a new one.*

When we got into town he excused himself and said he'd like to take a bit of a walk before the train pulled in. Mary had groceries to purchase and I had some harness parts to pick up, so we let him off and promised we'd be there at the station when the train arrived.

I wondered what the little walk was about. Figured he might have some old friends he wanted to say goodbye to or something—and then I saw him head off in the direction of the cemetery.

He was going to say his goodbye to Mrs. Turley. Guess he missed her far more than any of us knew. More than he'd ever miss the farm. Maybe sister Emma would be good for him—though of course I knew she'd never take the place of the one he had shared life with for so many years.

Like we'd said, Mary and I were both there when the train pulled in. 'Course the tears flowed some with the goodbyes. I knew it was hard for Mary, but she was brave about it. And then the train was pulling off and we were alone on the platform, the wind whipping Mary's coat about her small form. I took her hand and led her from the station. More than ever, she was mine to care for now. She had neither ma nor pa to lean on when she needed them. I was really all she had.

Chapter 19

Happiness

With the addition of the Turley farm, I had even more fields to plant that spring. I knew Pa Turley had been a good farmer in his day, but perhaps he'd sorta lost heart since the death of Mrs. Turley. Anyway, there was a lot of catching up to do in working up the land.

Mary was patient about my long, long days. Many times I saw her only at breakfast and for a few minutes at supper before I fell into bed exhausted. She didn't make many trips to the fields, either, with refreshments as she had usually done. Partly because it was more difficult for her with the baby coming, but mostly because some of the new fields I worked were so far away. Instead, she packed a lunch for me each morning.

We didn't get much rain at all that spring, so I wasn't slowed down any with the planting. In fact, it was so dry that neighboring farmers were all talking about it and wondering if the seed would have enough moisture to sprout.

The crash of the faraway stock market did affect us. I guess it affected the whole world. Everyone sorta held their breath, waiting to see just what calamity would strike next. I prayed that there wouldn't be one and that I would be able to take care of the family members who were my responsibility.

Lilli married in June as planned. Pa Turley came back for the wedding and spent a few nights with us before returning to Aunt Emma. Mary was so glad to see him. While he was there, he and Grandpa and Uncle Charlie all worked on a cradle together. They seemed to take great pleasure in the project, and Mary of course was thrilled.

The grain did start to grow. Here and there green shoots began to poke their heads through the soil, and I felt more relaxed. With a good rain I was sure we'd be well on our way. But the rains still didn't come, and pretty soon the small spears began to turn kind of yellow and wilt in the sun. I guess I should have faced the facts then, but I still kept hoping that with a good rain the grain could pick up again.

The summer was a hot one too. I felt sorry for Mary, being heavy with child as she was. The heat was especially hard on her. But she didn't complain. Just slowed down with the many jobs she had. Without rain her garden wasn't looking near as good as it normally did, and that bothered her. She and Grandpa carried pails of water to some of the plants, but it was too much work to try to water the whole garden.

When haying time came, the crop was thin and stunted. I worried about how we'd make it through the winter for feed as I put what hay we had up into stacks. Wasn't near as much as most years.

I guess the thing that kept me going that summer, the knowledge that brought excitement to both Mary and me, was the anticipation of the arrival of our child. The whole family was waiting for the baby, and now that Mary had gotten over her morning sickness and seemed to be feeling fine except for the heat, we were all sorta counting the days.

What harvest there was that year was so thin and runty, I wondered if it really merited cutting—but like all the farmers around me I went to work in the fields anyway. Lilli came to help Mary. It sure was decent of Avery to allow her to come, them being newlyweds and all. Mary was grateful for the help, and she and Lilli seemed to get along real good in the kitchen together. They didn't even need to talk about certain things—seemed to just understand what each one was supposed to do without saying so.

While Lilli was there, most of the canning was done. I had our little bit of grain ready for the threshing crew. Mary was hoping we'd get the crew out of the way before our little one decided to join the family. For her sake, I was hoping so too.

Mary and I talked a lot about our coming baby. Of course we talked "boy or girl." I told Mary I'd be happy with either one—but I think she knew I figured a son would be pretty nice. I mean, I had this extra farmland and all, and I sure did hope that someday a son would be farming it. *But a girl would be nice, too,* I decided as I thought of Sarah and little Patricia. Patty was walking now. She was over her fussiness and was a cuddly, lovable, contented little darling. I didn't mind the thought of a daughter one little bit.

The threshing crew had just moved in and set up, and the first load of bundles had been placed on the conveyer belt, when I glanced toward the house and saw Lilli standing in the yard waving her apron back and forth like the house was on fire. For a moment I couldn't understand her action, and then I realized the waving was meant to get my attention. Even so it took a while for me to understand what Lilli was trying to tell me.

"Go ahead, Josh. I'll take over here," said a voice beside me, and I turned to see Avery also watching the waving apron.

Then I understood what it was all about. It was Mary. *It must be time* . . . I dropped the pitchfork right where I was standing and took off for the farmyard on the run. Lilli saw me coming and turned to hurry back into the house.

Puffing from the run, my chest heaving and my lungs hurting, I just looked, wild-eyed, around the little circle in the kitchen, hoping that someone would give me information.

Lilli was stoking the fire and putting the kettle on. Her back was to me but she spoke anyway—evenly, controlled, just as though nothing out of the ordinary was happening.

"It's time to fetch Doc, Josh."

I headed for the stairs. I had to see Mary first.

She was lying in our bed, her face damp with perspiration, her hair scattered across the pillow. When she saw me she managed a weak smile, but I could see relief there too.

"It's time, Josh," she whispered.

I went to the bed, knelt beside it and took her hand. For a moment I couldn't speak. I pressed her fingers to my lips. She reached out and gently brushed at my cheek.

Before I could even tell her that I would hurry, her hand tightened on mine and she squeezed my fingers until they actually hurt. Her face drained of all color and her breath caught in a ragged little gasp.

It scared me half to death. I was sure something was dreadfully wrong. And then she began to relax again. I could feel the tension on my fingers lessening, and Mary let her head roll back on the pillow so that she could look at me again.

"Go, Josh," she whispered. "You'd best hurry."

I nodded and was gone.

I hadn't been using the Ford much, but I ran directly to it now. I prayed that it had enough fuel to get me to town and back. I also prayed that it would start right off after sitting for most of the summer.

It did start. I thanked God all of the way down the lane, and then I wheeled onto the road and headed for town just as fast as I could push that thing.

Doc wasn't home. I nearly panicked. Thanks to his wife, I found him in the barber shop getting his monthly haircut.

"It's Mary!" I gasped out. You would have thought I had run all the way to town. "Mary needs you. Now."

Doc didn't fool around any. He jerked the white cloth from around his neck.

"I'll be back, Charlie," he flung over his shoulder and left with only half a cut. Then we were off for his house to pick up his bag and whatever else he needed.

The trip home was a fast one. I turned once to look at Doc to see if I was scaring the living daylights out of him, but he was grinning just a bit as he held on to his hat, and I got the feeling he was actually enjoying the ride.

We wheeled into the yard and screeched to a stop right before the picket fence. Doc grabbed his bag and headed for the house. I wasn't far behind. Only Grandpa and Uncle Charlie were in the kitchen when I entered.

"How's Mary?" I asked, and Grandpa told me that Lilli was up with her and she seemed to be doing fine.

I started pacing. Back and forth across the kitchen. I knew Uncle Nat had been with Lou when some of their babies were born, but that was one detail Mary and I had forgotten to talk about.

I wasn't sure I'd be good company in the birthing room. I was afraid I'd go and pass out or something right when Mary needed me the most. Oh, if only—if only there was some way that I could help her!

Lilli came down, her face a mite pale. She spoke as she walked right on by me to poke at the stove again.

"Mary wants you."

For a minute my feet wouldn't even move. I stood there, staring blankly after Lilli, licking dry lips and trying hard to swallow. And then I suddenly found my legs and propelled myself forward and up the steps.

Doc was bending over Mary, talking to her, calming her. I didn't want to get in his way so I went around to the other side. Mary, her face damp from her exertions, turned to look at me. She didn't say anything, just reached for my hand. I leaned over and kissed her on the forehead—right on the scar from her accident. Mary sort of buried her face against me for a moment, and then another contraction made her stiffen and pull away.

I looked at Doc. How could he stand this? She was—she was—

"She's doing fine. Just fine. You're doing just fine, Mary.

Won't be too long and it'll all be over," Doc was murmuring, his voice more a drone than speech.

According to Doc, things progressed quickly. For me it seemed to take forever. But it did eventually come to an end. Like a wondrous miracle—one minute we were in the throes of birthing agony, and the next minute we were parents. *Parents.* I could hardly believe the fact even though I'd been waiting for it for months. But there he was—*our little son*—mine and Mary's. Red and wrinkled and wailing his head off.

I heard Mary chuckle and I wondered if she was totally aware or under the influence of some of Doc's ether. But she looked at me, her eyes big with wonder and then tears began to form and run down her cheeks. "A boy, Josh," she whispered. "A boy." And at that moment I knew that Mary had wanted with all her heart to present me with a son.

I leaned over to kiss her and smoothed the tangled hair back from her face. Oh, how I loved her. How I loved that new little bundle she had just presented to me. A son. Our very own son.

"William Joshua," I whispered, for that was the name we had already chosen.

"William Joshua," echoed Mary, and her eyes shone, the hours of pain totally forgotten. Just then Doc placed the still-squalling little bundle in Mary's arms.

"Isn't he beautiful?" Mary was crooning and I had to admit that he was. *There's different kinds of beauty,* I thought with a smile as I looked into the little face all scrunched up with his efforts to cry.

Mary began to pat the baby and croon to him and the crying ceased. "I'll bet he's all tired out," she whispered. "It's hard work being born."

I hadn't thought of that. I had some idea now of how tough it was for Mary—for me—but for William Joshua? Maybe it was, I admitted.

I kissed Mary again—almost delirious in my happiness. Then I bent down to kiss the top of the head of our little child. He stirred a bit, and I pretended that he looked right at me and knew just who I was.

Mary pretended right along with me. "So, you are getting acquainted with your papa, William. You are one lucky boy. You have a wonderful papa. He'll take you fishin' an—"

Tears were on my cheeks. I hugged Mary and our son closer.

There was a tap at the door and I looked up, realizing then that Doc had quietly slipped from the room. It also dawned on me that there were some other anxious family members who were waiting down in the kitchen below.

Mary called, "Come in." And they were all there. Lilli and Grandpa and Uncle Charlie. The color was back in Lilli's cheeks and Grandpa was grinning like the world had just turned rightside-up and Uncle Charlie looked so relieved and proud at the same time that I wanted to chuckle.

They tiptoed in to peek at the small baby resting on Mary's arm.

"It's okay," said Mary. "He's awake."

Then they all started talking at once, saying what a fine baby he was and who he looked like and how alert he was and asked what we were going to name him and all that.

We had to slow them down and sort things out and finally were able to announce that his name was William Joshua. Grandpa looked across at me and nodded in understanding and agreement.

Doc returned and told us that Mary needed some rest. In spite of all the commotion, William Joshua had already fallen asleep. Lilli lifted him tenderly from Mary's arm and placed him in the nearby cradle. I went to look at him again, suddenly torn. I wanted to be near Mary, but I wanted to study my son. Doc settled it for me.

"Out with you, too, Josh," he informed me. "You can come back again when she's rested a bit."

I gave Mary one more kiss, took one last look at my son and reluctantly left the room. I didn't realize until I fell into one of the kitchen chairs how emotionally drained I was. I was glad for a cup of Lilli's coffee to sort of perk me up.

"How's the crop?" Grandpa asked, making conversation, and that brought the threshing sharply back to mind.

"I don't know," I admitted. "They were just starting to run some through."

I decided I'd best get back to the field and find out just what was happening.

Chapter 20

Tough Times

Unfortunately, the crop was even poorer than I expected. I should have known that it wouldn't be worth much, but I'd kept hoping that something might be in those near-empty heads. There wasn't much grain in the bins. It had me concerned, for a heavy farm payment was due at the bank. I knew it was going to be tough to cover it. We'd all have to tighten the belt. Considerably. But I hoped I wouldn't need to bother Mary with the worry of it.

Lilli stayed with us until Mary was back on her feet. Avery came whenever he could and spent the night. I knew he was anxious to get his wife home again.

William was an easy baby to have around. He scarcely cried at all, it seemed to me. But then I was in the fields or the barn a good deal of the time. Besides, William didn't have much need for fussin'. If Mary wasn't available, Grandpa or Uncle Charlie were. I figured as how they'd have that youngster spoiled long before he cut a tooth.

I put it off as long as I dared, and then one day I went out to make an honest assessment of the way things stood. I'd hated to face the truth, but the bank note was due the next Monday. I knew I had to figure out just how I was going to make the payment.

The picture wasn't a rosy one. There was barely enough

seed grain to plant again come spring.

"If I can just make it through to another crop," I told myself, "then we'll be back on our feet again."

I reached a hand down into the bin and let the kernels of grain trickle through my fingers. Dwarfed and skimpy, they were nothing like the seed I had worked so hard to build up. But I was sure that with a couple years of good rains, I could be right back with good seed again.

I pulled a piece of paper from my hip pocket and a stub of a pencil from my shirt and started figuring. I had a little money laid aside, but it was nowhere near enough. There wasn't any grain to sell. I'd need every bit of it for seed come spring and to feed the cattle and hogs through the winter.

I jabbed at the paper with my pencil. Who was I trying to kid? There wasn't nearly enough grain to winter the stock. Some of the stock would have to go.

I had worked so hard to build up those bloodlines—some folks were saying I had the best breeding stock in the county. I sure didn't want to part with any of them.

But on the other hand, I reasoned, that would make them easier to sell—and at better prices.

I really got down to figuring then. After I had it all worked out on paper, I went back to the house.

Mary had dinner on the table. I crossed over to the cradle in the corner and looked down at my sleeping son. For once he wasn't being held by someone. He sure had changed already. His face was round and smooth and his nose and eyes were no longer red and swollen like they'd been when he was newborn. He had lost some of his dark hair too, but Mary didn't seem concerned about it. Babies did that, she said. Actually he was getting prettier and prettier—if boy babies don't mind being called "pretty." Lots of folks said he favored me, but every time I looked at him I saw glimpses of Mary.

"Been sleepin' like that most of the morning," boasted Mary. She had come to stand beside me. I slipped an arm around her waist and gave her a squeeze. The future didn't look nearly as bad with her beside me and our son to love and nourish.

"Your dinner's gettin' cold," Mary reminded me. I joined Grandpa and Uncle Charlie at the table, and we bowed our heads while I sincerely thanked God for His many blessings.

I could have discussed my plans over our noon meal, but I chose to wait until Mary and I were alone. William had awakened and insisted on being changed and fed immediately, and Mary cooed and smiled and went off to oblige. I went up to see them as soon as I had finished my bread pudding.

"He's been good, huh?" I asked, sitting beside Mary and lifting one of William's wee hands in mine. It looked rather lost there.

"Real good," said Mary, kissing his soft head.

We sat and admired William for a few minutes longer. He sure was growing fast.

"I'm going to be gone for most of the afternoon," I informed Mary.

She looked up, waiting.

"We'll need most of the crop for seed. I decided to sell off some of the stock so we don't need to worry none about winter feedin'."

"Couldn't we just buy us some more grain?" Mary asked innocently.

"I think it's better this way," I said without emotion. I didn't add that we didn't have money for more grain. Didn't even have enough money for the payment at the bank.

Mary nodded, quite willing that it would be my decision. She trusted me. That very fact made my stomach knot up.

"You going to ship?" she asked, knowing that market hogs and cattle were shipped from town by train.

"Think I'll give the local farmers a chance. They're always talkin' about my herds and wishin' they could add some of my stock to theirs."

Mary nodded again and I could see the pride in her eyes.

I kissed them both and went on down to saddle Chester.

I rode all afternoon—from farm to farm, and the story was always the same. No one had feed. No one had money. Over and over I heard the same words.

"Boy, I'd like to, Josh. Been wantin' to get some of yer stock fer a long time. But right now ain't a good time. Crop too poor. No feed. No money. Maybe next year after we git 'nother crop in the bins."

But next year wouldn't help my dilemma. I needed cash *now*.

By the end of the day I was about spent. It wasn't just that the ride had been tiring. It was the whole emotional drain of the process. And I'd been unsuccessful. I would need to resort to shipping the stock, and I knew the price I got for slaughter animals would not be nearly as good as that paid for breeding stock.

I hated to go home and face Mary. I was afraid she would read in my eyes the fear I felt inside.

I tried to shake off my foreboding. We'd make it. It would just be tough for a while and then the crops would get us on our feet again. All we had to do was make that bank payment and ease our way through the year until the crop was up again. We could make it. It would be good for us to have to cut back a bit. Make us even more appreciative of the good harvest—the bountiful times.

Before I went into the house I sat down on a milk stool and pulled out my paper and pencil again. It would take more critters than I had first counted on to make the payment. It was really going to cut into the herd to meet that bank commitment. And I'd have to go see the banker the first thing in the morning and ask for a few days' extension. There was no way I could get my payment in the mail in time for the original deadline. I hoisted myself off the stool and tucked away my figurings.

Mary gave me a smile when I entered the kitchen, but she didn't ask about my day. I was glad. I didn't have an answer quite ready yet.

It wasn't until we were retiring that night that the subject was discussed. Mary waited until William had been changed and fed and tucked in for the night. After we had finished our regular devotions together, I stretched out full length beneath the fresh-smelling sheets and was about to shut my eyes, hoping for early sleep and maybe postponement of a difficult discussion. But Mary slipped her hand into mine.

"How'd it go, Josh?" she asked me.

I hesitated for just a moment and then answered honestly, "Not good."

She was silent, giving me a chance to go on.

"Oh, everywhere I went folks were anxious enough to buy. They just don't have any feed either. I should've thought of that. Whole country was dry this year."

"Any way to get the stock to where folks *do* have feed?" asked Mary, and I wondered why I hadn't thought of that. I lay there thinking about it now—but came up empty.

"I wouldn't know how," I admitted. "From the reports in the paper and on the radio, the dryness has covered a large area. I have no idea where folks might have more feed than critters." I sighed deeply and Mary's hand tightened on mine. "Besides," I went on, "I would have no way of making contacts or of getting the animals beyond the county."

"What are you going to do?" asked Mary.

"Ship. Market them. There's another market day on Thursday. I'll get 'em in for that."

I had to round up a crew of neighbor boys to help me drive my stock to town. It seemed that every farmer in the whole area was like-minded. When I arrived with my cattle, the holding pens were already filled to near bursting. I knew without thinking on it that I needed to knock a few more dollars off the price I would get for the animals. It always happened that way when the market was flooded. I wished I'd brought along a few more yearlings.

The bank manager was decent enough. He admitted that it had been a tough year—that all the area farmers were having a hard time. He said the same thing that I had been saying to myself—over and over. Things would all straighten out next year when the crop was taken in.

There was nothing for me to do then but to wait for that stock payment to arrive in the mail. I thought of it constantly. Prayed that it would be enough. But it wasn't. Not quite. I took it to the banker and promised to sell a couple more cattle. He nodded solemnly and applied to the loan what I had brought.

Mary knew I was troubled. She left me alone for several days, and then I guess she decided we needed to talk about it.

"How bad is it, Josh?" she asked and I knew that she wanted, and deserved, an honest answer.

"Pretty bad," I admitted. "But it'll be all right. I made the loan payment. I was sorry to sell as much stock as it turned out I needed to, that's all. It was good stock. Too good for slaughtering. It should have been used to help other farmers build their herds. But it couldn't be helped. Everybody's having a tough time. No feed. Prices down. It just couldn't be helped. We get these cycles from time to time—and then things bounce back. We'll be all right with another crop."

"Anything I can do?"

I could have said, "Economize. Watch each dollar. Skimp all you can." But I didn't need to say those things. I knew Mary would do that without me asking.

"We'll make it," I said instead.

We lay in silence, each with our own thoughts.

"We have the egg money," Mary offered.

I drew her up against my side. I knew she'd stretch that egg money for all it was worth.

Chapter 21

Planting Again

Winter dragged by on reluctant feet. I guess I was just too anxious for spring to come so that I could get to the planting again. I was weary of trying to make each dollar stretch and of seeing Mary skimp and save. She never complained though. Nor did anyone else in the household.

The little snow that did fall was soon blown into small, dirty piles mixed with top soil from the parched fields. I'm sure if we'd had seven feet of snow that winter, none of the neighborhood farmers would have complained.

Our William gained weight steadily and became more interesting—more of a "real person"—with each day. He was our bit of sunshine over a bleak winter, and the hours of playing with him and hearing his squeals and giggles more than brightened our lives.

The whole household doted on him, but thankfully he didn't seem to get spoiled. He contentedly lay in his cradle and talked to himself as he tried to catch his chubby toes or the items that Mary dangled over his head.

At last the days began to warm into some kind of spring. I finally decided I could start work on the land. I didn't need to wait for the snow to melt—there was none. I didn't need to wait for the fields to dry either. The stubble was dry as tinder. I didn't use the tractor. There was simply no money for fuel, so I hitched up the farm horses and began to farm the way the land had been farmed for many years before me.

I'd forgotten how much slower going it was with horses. Often my eyes would wander to the shed where the tractor sat silent. The row of shiny, unused farm machinery I had bought over the past few years to pull behind it seemed to mournfully becken me. I longed to return it all to use. There was no use moaning. This spring it was not meant to be. As I planted I told myself that things would be better next spring.

I came in from the field each day dusty, tired and sometimes a bit out of sorts. The ground I turned with the plow was powdery or chunky hard; and as my eyes watched the clouds, I saw no sign of spring rains.

Mary tried to keep everyone's spirits up with talk of how well the chickens were laying and how perfect the new calves were and what a good litter the last sow had given us. I knew I should be thankful. I really was thankful, but in the back of my mind was the nagging doubt that all those things might not be enough.

I'd hoped for a rain before I actually did the spring planting, but when all of the land had been tilled and still dry as a bone, I decided to plant anyway. If I got the grain in the ground and the rains quickly followed, I'd be even further ahead. Yes, I decided, that was a good plan.

So I planted the seed—every last kernel I had. Placed it right there in the dry ground with the faith that every farmer must have each spring—the faith that at the proper time, within the structure that God has ordained for seed time and harvest, the rain would come, the seed would germinate and a harvest would result.

The grain lay for a week before a cloud even appeared in the sky. It didn't develop into much, but we did get a light sprinkle. I knew it had scarcely dampened the ground. Still, it brought hope. The whole town was buzzing with talk of it when I drove in to pick up groceries and the mail. Everyone was hopeful that there would be more clouds coming with spring rains in the normal fashion, and I came home in much better spirits. I guess all the jovial bantering and lighter chatter had helped.

Mary smiled as I placed the few staples on her kitchen table.

"Did we get a letter?" she asked hopefully. I was usually excited when we received one of our rather rare letters. I shook my head but grinned at Mary in my new-found cheer.

Grandpa wandered over to the table and listlessly turned over the two small sales pamphlets. He missed his daily paper—as we all did. The paper was just one of the things we needed to forego during our belt-tightening time.

"Farmers are pretty excited about the shower," I reported to Mary but including Grandpa and Uncle Charlie also.

"Say that it's most certain to stir up some more storms," I went on.

Grandpa nodded. "Gotta be rain up there somewhere," he agreed.

Uncle Charlie used his two canes to lift himself from his chair by the window and join the rest of us at the table.

"They reportin' how much they got?"

This was common talk when farmer met farmer. "Had three quarters of an inch over our way, but Fred says thet he got a full inch." Or, "That heavy shower dumped two an' a half inches at my place." Always the rains were measured, the amount that fell of utmost importance.

I shook my head. "No one seemed to get more'n we did—didn't measure much. But it's a good sign."

Grandpa and Uncle Charlie both nodded, relief in their eyes. Mary said nothing, but she went to the cupboard and got out the coffee. She put the pot on to brew, and the aroma of it was soon wafting out deliciously around us.

We all settled in around the table with pleased looks on our faces. It was the first time in months that we'd shared afternoon coffee. There hadn't even been before-bed coffee for Grandpa and Uncle Charlie anymore. It was another of the things we had learned to do without. Coffee—weak coffee—

was reserved for breakfast, and each of us was allowed only one cup a day. Mary never touched it. She said that her nursing baby was better off without it, though Doc had said a cup of coffee wouldn't hurt young William. I figured Mary was just going without to save more for the rest of us.

It wasn't hard for me to go without—and I often did. Said I didn't feel like a cup, or it wouldn't sit quite right on my stomach, or something, and shared the cup with Grandpa and Uncle Charlie. Not a sacrifice for me. I could drink it or leave it. But Grandpa and Uncle Charlie were another matter. Especially that before-bed cup. They had done it all their lives as far back as I could remember.

So the coffee aroma that drifted to us was a celebration of sorts. And we all knew it. I guess that made it even more special.

Mary went even further. She sliced some bread and spread some of her carefully hoarded strawberry jam over it—thinly, I might point out. She set this on the table to go with the coffee.

Boy, what a feast! More than the coffee and jam was the promise. We'd had one rain—only a shower, really—but a rain. It meant that we'd probably be getting more, that things would soon be back to normal again. And what a relief that would be to us all.

But it didn't happen that way. A few more clouds rolled up, and we all hoped and prayed that they would bring us moisture. But the wind blew them right on by without so much as a sprinkle. Even the pasture land was beginning to look like barren ground. I knew I had too many cows feeding on it and that I should sell off a few more. But I just kept putting it off and putting it off, hoping and praying that rain would soon have things green again.

At last I remembered the good advice I'd received from Mr. Thomas, the farmer who years before had kindly showed me the proper way to farm. "A few good, healthy cattle are better than a bunch of skinny, sickly ones," he'd said, and I finally gave in and made arrangements to get half a dozen of them to town.

I didn't spend the money I got for them but tucked it away. Besides, it wasn't all that much anyway and wouldn't have made much difference in how we were living. The price of cattle had dropped something awful.

The hot, thirsty summer was a repeat of the previous one. As I walked about the farm trying to keep the barns and fences in order, my feet kicked up little puffs of dirt and sent them sifting up to stick to my overalls or drift away on the wind that was constantly blowing.

I'd never seen so much wind. The continual howling nearly got Mary down. She complained about few things—but the wind was one of them. I saw her unconsciously shudder when a gust rattled the windows or whipped grit against the panes.

All summer long she fought to save her garden. With our finances as they were, it was even more important that she have produce to can or store in the nearby root cellar. Day by day she carried water by the pail and dumped it on her plants, coaxing them, imploring them to bring her fruit.

Grandpa helped all he could, huffing and puffing under the heat of the sun and against the strength of the wind. Uncle Charlie was past the stage of being able to carry buckets, so he stationed himself beside William's cradle and watched over the sleeping baby in Mary's absence.

The garden did produce—but all of us knew that it wouldn't really be enough to see us through another winter with any kind of ease.

Toward the end of summer another calamity struck. The well that had served us faithfully for as many years as the farm had stood went dry. Grandpa himself had dug it and it had never failed before. I guess we'd always assumed that our water supply was unlimited. But now, no matter how hard I pumped, there was only a small trickle, and then we had to wait a few hours until we could produce a trickle again.

It was heartbreaking, especially for Mary. There was no way she could help her plants now. She left them to the elements, canning what she could as soon as it was ready.

I was thankful for the crick for the sake of the stock, but even the crick was lower than I'd ever seen it before.

There wasn't much to harvest that fall, but we went through the motions. I did manage to salvage a bit of grain that I hoarded away carefully for next spring's seed.

Surely next year would be different. We'd had dry spells before, but they'd never lasted for more than a year or two. We all set our jaws and readied ourselves for another slim winter.

William celebrated his first birthday. Or rather, we adults celebrated for him. He did seem to enjoy the occasion. We had a whole houseful over, almost like old times again. Nat and Lou and their family came along with Avery and Lilli. The house was alive and full of laughter and cheerful chatter, and William laughed and clapped and chattered right along with us.

No fuss was made, but each family brought simple food items with them. Lou had a big pot of rabbit stew and some pickled beets. Lilli brought deviled eggs and a crock of kraut. With the roast chicken Mary prepared in our kitchen, we had ourselves quite a feast. There was even a cake for the birthday boy—and some weak tea for the adults.

Sarah appointed herself William's guardian. She hardly let the rest get a chance to hold and cuddle him. But over her protests he did make the rounds. He was walking now, faltering, baby steps that made everyone squeal with delight and William beam over his own brilliance. He seemed to know just how smart he was and spent his time toddling back and forth between eager, outstretched hands.

It was a great day for all of us, but when it was over and a thoroughly exhausted William had been tucked into bed, a sense of dejection seemed to settle over the house. It was as though we had been released from our prison for one short afternoon and had then been rounded up and locked up again. The day had been a reminder of how things had been, and maybe each of us secretly feared it would never really be that way again.

We didn't speak of it, but we all knew it was there—a fear hanging right over us, seeming about to consume us, to hold us under until we ran out of air or to squeeze us into a corner until we stopped our struggling.

I didn't like the feeling. I wanted to break loose and breathe freely again. I wanted my wife to sew new dresses and cook from a well-stocked cupboard. I wanted my son to have those first little shoes for his growing feet, toy trucks and balls to play with. I wanted Grandpa and Uncle Charlie to be able to sit around the kitchen table and sip slowly from big cups of strong coffee.

For the first time in my adult life, I wanted to sit down and weep in frustration. And then I looked across the table to where Mary sat mending work socks. They had more darning than original wool, and I saw the frustration in her eyes. By the stubborn set to her chin I knew she was feeling the same way I was. It put some starch in my backbone.

"Why don't you leave that for tonight?" I suggested to her. "It's been a busy day."

I went to the stove and shook the coffeepot. There was just a tiny bit remaining. I poured in more water from the teakettle that sang near the back of the stove and set the pot on to boil.

"Bit left there yet," I said to Grandpa. "Why don't you and Uncle Charlie finish it up?"

Grandpa nodded without much enthusiasm. He was feeling it too.

I took the sock from Mary's hands, laid it aside and then led her up the stairs to our room.

We didn't talk much as we prepared for bed. As soon as we were both ready, I lifted our family Bible down from the shelf. We always read together before retiring. There was nothing new about that. What was different was the way I was feeling deep down inside.

"Would you read tonight?" I asked Mary.

She took the Bible from me and turned to the book of Psalms. Given a choice, Mary always turned to the Psalms. She began with a praise chapter—one that was meant to lift my spirits and bring me comfort. It should have done that for me. I had much to praise God for. But tonight—tonight the praise seemed all locked up within me. Mary hadn't read far before I was weeping.

I would never be able to explain why. Maybe I had just been carrying the hurts and the worries for too long, I don't know. Maybe I'd been trying to be too brave to protect the rest of my family. Anyway, it all poured out in rasping sobs that shook my whole body. Mary joined me and we held each other and cried together.

After the tempest had passed and we were in control again, we lay for hours and talked. Just talked, until long into the night. I don't know that we solved anything, but we lifted a big burden from each other. We shared our feelings and our fears. We joined, strength with strength, to weather whatever lay before us.

"We'll make it, Josh," Mary dared to promise.

"I still have the loan payment to make," I confided. "I only have a small portion of it saved, and I've no idea how I'll get the rest."

"We have more livestock."

"I hate to sell—"

"But we'll build the herd again. After the rains come—"

Always. Always that was our answer. Things would be better. We'd be back on our feet—after the spring rains came.

Chapter 22

Hope Upon Hope

I never wept over our situation again. Not that I viewed tears as weakness. Maybe I hurt so deeply that I knew tears would not ease the pain. Or maybe I came to a higher level of faith. For whatever reason, I never came near to tears again.

I sold off more of the livestock. There really wasn't much choice, but it pained me to see the herd I'd worked so hard to build less than half its former size. With the sale of the stock, plus what I'd managed to tuck aside and a bit of Mary's hard-won egg and cream money, we somehow managed to make another loan payment.

But that meant there was little money to tide us over the winter months. I took my rifle and hunted grouse and rabbit and managed to add a bit to the stew pot. Mary talked of butchering a few chickens, but she hesitated. We'd already used all the old hens and all but two of the roosters.

"It's sort of like killing the goose that laid the golden egg," Mary commented to me. "We need those eggs—both for ourselves and to sell in town."

I knew Mary was right, so we held off dipping into the flock further.

Then I thought about the piece of treed crick bottom on the Turley land, and I decided there might be a bit of money in cord wood. Mary clutched at the idea right away, her eyes shining.

"What a wonderful idea, Josh!" she exclaimed. "But I do hope the work won't be too hard on you."

"It's not the work that worries me," I admitted. "We'll need to find a buyer before it means any money."

"Oh, I'm sure we'll find somebody," she enthused. "Everyone needs firewood—even in hard times."

It turned out that we were able to sell it. All I could cut, the buyer at the lumberyard said. It seemed that he had some kind of connection with city folk and shipped the wood out by rail car.

But the earnings were a mere pittance. Took me two or three days of back-breaking labor to make enough to buy flour and sugar. Rumors were that the man from the lumberyard made himself a pretty good profit just to act as go-between. It bothered me some, but I felt I had little to say in the matter. I kept at it. At least it might see us through another winter.

I used Barney and Bess for the skidding, alternating them day by day. I didn't have the feed or the chop I normally would have been feeding my horses, so I liked to rest them as much as I could. Chester was a bit too light for the hard work or he would have done his share, too.

Somehow we managed. It was tough, but we all were able to keep body and soul together. I was thankful for that much.

The second winter of scanty snow came to an end. When the patches of dirty drifts melted, I was back on the land again.

It didn't take as long as usual to do the spring work. I didn't have enough seed grain to plant all of the fields. There was no use working up those that couldn't be planted. The soil would just erode even more.

Mary planted her garden too. She had carefully kept every possible seed so she wouldn't need to buy. She even exchanged some with neighborhood women. All together, she managed to get a reasonable garden in the ground. She knew better than to even start drawing water from the well. There simply wasn't enough there. She saved every bit of dishwater and wash water that was used, though, and carefully doled it out to her plants.

I had never seen anything like the dust storms that came that year. They rolled up from the west, raising hopes that maybe a rain cloud was on the way, and then blew in with nothing but flying dirt and empty promises. Dust lay over everything. Whole fields seemed to be airborne, swirling madly about us. Mary came to hate the dust even worse than the wind.

Along with the dust came the grasshoppers. There wasn't much for them to eat, but they seemed to flourish anyway. I knew even without walking through the fields that there would be *no* crop this year. I went back to cutting cord wood.

Near the end of August Uncle Charlie took sick. It was a Sunday morning, and Mary had our breakfast on the table and William all ready to go to church. Uncle Charlie still hadn't made his appearance. It wasn't like him. He lingered in bed now and then, having spent a restless night, but never on a Sunday morning.

We sat down to the table, our eyes on the stairway, thinking surely he'd be showing up at any minute.

Mary turned to me. "Do you think you should check, Josh?" she asked.

William pounded his spoon impatiently on the table and called in his babyish lisp, "Eat time. Eat time, Unc'a Sharie."

Grandpa forgot his worry long enough to have a good chuckle at William. Mary stopped the boy from banging his spoon, and I looked toward the stairs again.

I went on up then, and there was Uncle Charlie on the floor beside his bed. He must have been trying to get out of bed when he took a fall.

It scared me, I'll tell you. It frightened all of us. We abandoned our plans for church. Grandpa and I lifted Uncle Charlie back onto his bed, and I saddled Chester and headed out for Doc.

By the time we got back, Uncle Charlie was conscious and rational. He still wanted to go to church, but Doc said he had a pretty nasty bump on the head and was to stay in bed for a few days. Besides, it was already too late for church anyway.

After Doc had done all he could to make Uncle Charlie comfortable and left a bit of medicine for him, Doc and I walked down to the kitchen. Mary had poured a cup of morning coffee and set it at the table for him. She'd fed William, but the rest of us still had not had our breakfast. The familiar morning oatmeal had not improved with age, but we ate it anyway. It did fill the void.

Doc sat down for a neighborly visit. He told Mary of new babies in the community—even shared the secret of a few on the way, and told of people in town moving in and those who were moving out. He even shared bits and pieces of world news—things that we would have been getting out of the newspaper had we still been receiving one.

And then he turned his attention to William.

"Your boy sure looks healthy," he said to Mary, and Mary beamed.

"Come here, fella," Doc called to the toddler and William trotted over to be lifted up on Doc's knee.

"You ever see one of these?" Doc asked and dangled his stethoscope before William. I don't suppose there was a kid in our whole area who hadn't played with Doc's stethoscope at one time or another. And it had fascinated every one of us, too. William was no exception. He turned it around and around in his hand, then tried to stick the smooth, round end into his ear.

We all laughed.

"So you're going to be a doctor someday," commented Doc. "But you've got it backward. This is what goes in your ears. Here, hold still."

He assisted the little fella with the instrument, and William's eyes grew wide with wonder. I had a pretty good idea that he was hearing absolutely nothing, but the feeling of something holding his head from each side must have intrigued him. He sat perfectly still until Doc removed the ear pieces.

"Well, I'd best be running," Doc said at last. "Someone might be needing me."

He lifted William to the floor and reached for his hat. "Yes, sir," he said, his eyes still on William. "You're a nice, big boy for two years old. Almost two years old," he corrected himself. "Your mama has taken real good care of you."

I walked with Doc to get his team. It was an awkward moment for me. I hardly knew where or how to begin.

"Doc," I finally blurted, "in the past we've always paid you cash for your visits, but I'm afraid—"

Doc stopped me before I could even go on. "I know how things are right now, Josh," he returned confidentially. "We'll just put this here little visit on your account."

"But I don't have an account," I reminded him.

"You do now," said Doc, "and don't you go worrying none about it either. You can take care of it just as soon as you get another crop."

Doc came three more times to visit Uncle Charlie. On his last visit Mary had a little chat with him too. It seemed her suspicions were correct. She was expecting our second child.

I should have been happy—and I was. But this time I was worried too. How would we ever feed and clothe another child? William was already doing without things he should have had—and he was better off than most of the children in our area. Lou passed on to him many of the things Jonathan and Timothy had worn.

But in spite of morning sickness again, Mary was happy. It fell to Grandpa to entertain young William until Mary was able to be on her feet. I was still busy with cutting wood and unable to give much assistance in the house.

Uncle Charlie got steadily better, to our great relief. By

the time William celebrated his second birthday, Uncle Charlie was again able to join us at the table. By then Mary was feeling much better, too.

There wasn't any crop to harvest, so I just kept right on working in the woodlot. Now and then the lumberyard owner would pop by and have the wood loaded onto a truck and hauled to the railway yards. He'd pay me each time he made a pickup, and I tried hard to put some of it aside. But there wasn't much of it in the drawer when I went to count up the money. I'd needed to spend most of it for necessities throughout the summer and fall. I would have to sell stock again. Even with the sale, I wondered if it would be enough to meet the payment. My heart sank at the thought.

I was heading for my room to do some more figuring when Grandpa's voice stopped me.

I turned to look at him. He and Uncle Charlie were at the kitchen table. There was no coffee to drink, but maybe it was hard to break an old habit. Anyway, they still pulled up their chairs each evening and sat there—chatting, even playing an occasional game of checkers. But often they just sat, waiting for the time to go to bed.

Mary had already gone up to tuck William in for the night, and I knew it wouldn't be long until she would be waiting for our devotional time together.

"Got a minute?"

I nodded.

"Charlie and I think it's time we talk."

I didn't have any idea what was coming but I felt my stomach began to tighten.

"You got another payment to make," Grandpa said as I pulled out a chair and lowered myself onto it. It was a statement—not a question.

I nodded again.

There was silence for a minute. Uncle Charlie sucked in air, much as he used to suck in coffee.

"You got it figured?" went on Grandpa.

I lowered my head for a moment and then brought it up to face the two men. "No-o," I admitted. "No—not yet."

"In thet case," said Grandpa, shoving a lidded tin toward me, "we want ya to have this."

I looked from Grandpa to Uncle Charlie.

"If we'd 'a knowed what straights you was in, we'd 'a given it long ago. Feel bad we've been lettin' ya sweat it out alone," said Uncle Charlie, an unusually long speech for him.

"It's the Turley farm," I admitted. "It probably was a mistake to take on more land, especially with the drought."

"I figured it a smart move," Grandpa hurried to say. "One ya couldn't pass up, really. Just a shame thet we been prayin' fer rain ever since. But thet'll change. Just need time, thet's all. Just time."

I appreciated Grandpa's vote of confidence and Uncle Charlie's nod of agreement. Then Grandpa pushed the can farther toward me and this time I reached out for it.

I pulled it to me and pried off the lid.

I stared in disbelief. It was full of bills.

"It ain't much," Grandpa was saying, "but it might help some."

I knew then what I was looking at. It was the total life's savings of Grandpa and Uncle Charlie. I pushed the can back toward them, fighting hard to swallow.

"I can't—I can't take that," I finally was able to say.

"What'll ya do then?" asked Grandpa without hesitation.

"I—I—" I swallowed. "I still have some stock. I can sell—"

"We been thinkin' on thet," said Grandpa. "It don't seem like a good move. I mean—ya sell it all off an' then where are ya? Soon as the rains start up agin, ya got no herd to build on."

I knew he was right. I'd thought that all through myself and come to the same conclusion.

"We don't know when the rains—" I began, but Grandpa cut in.

"They'll come," he said simply. "Always do."

But when, I wanted to cry out. *When? After it's too late— after we've lost everything?*

I didn't say it. Instead, I looked first at Grandpa and then at Uncle Charlie.

"It might not be enough," Grandpa was saying. "We don't know how big those payments be. But take it. Make it do fer ya what ya can."

"But you've worked all your life to save this money," I persisted. "I can't just take it and—"

Uncle Charlie waved an arthritic hand as though to brush aside all my arguments. "Josh," he said, "you've been boardin' an' beddin' us fer several years now. Ain't either of us worth a lick a salt. But ya ain't hinted at thet. Neither has Mary. Now, iffen the farm goes—then what, Josh? This is our home too, an' I reckon as how we'd be hard put adjustin' to 'nother one."

" 'Zactly," agreed Grandpa.

"But—" I tried again.

"No 'buts,' Josh. Just take it on in an' make thet there payment, iffen it'll do thet, an' get thet monkey off all our backs."

I had no further arguments. I thanked the two men before me as sincerely as I could and tucked the tin under my arm. I had no idea how much money was in the can. It wouldn't be much, I knew. Grandpa and Uncle Charlie had never had the opportunity to stash away large sums. But maybe—just maybe it would be enough to keep us afloat. Maybe—just maybe—it would help us make it to another spring.

Chapter 23

Sustained Effort

There was enough in the tin can to make the loan payment—with some left over to help us through the winter. I went to town the next morning with the money tied securely in my coat pocket.

I was getting to hate trips to town and avoided them whenever possible. It seemed whenever I went there was news of another foreclosure and another area farmer forced off his land.

It wasn't as hard for those who had been there for years and were well established. Some had no payments due at the bank and could manage to sort of slide by even though money was tight. But for those who had just invested in land or stock or new machinery, the matter was quite different. It was almost impossible to stay afloat, given the economics of the times along with the drought.

It saddened me. I guess it also frightened me. The thought kept nagging at me that my turn might be next.

I didn't know what I'd ever do if I lost the farm. It wasn't just the fact that I loved it—had always loved it. I figured I had about as much of that farm soil running through my veins as I had red blood. I couldn't imagine myself anywhere but on that farm.

Grandpa had settled the farm. He and Uncle Charlie had

sweated and toiled and built it to what it had become. It belonged to us. To all of us. It belonged to my son some time down the road.

Farming was all I knew. I was not trained for anything else. I had no other home, no other possession, no other profession. If I lost the farm I would lose far more than a piece of property. I would lose my livelihood, my heritage, my family home, my very sense of personhood. I wouldn't fit any other place. I knew that without going through the experience.

And knowing all of that, and knowing also that Grandpa and Uncle Charlie shared my feelings, I took the gift of money they had given me and tried to buy the family a little more time. And I prayed that they were right. That the rains were soon due back again.

I felt better after I had made the payment. I didn't miss the surprised look on the banker's face when I drew out the small roll of bills, but he asked no questions and I volunteered no information. I was handed my receipt of payment and left the building.

I stopped long enough to buy a few groceries, among the parcels a pound of coffee for Grandpa and Uncle Charlie and some cheese for Mary. She had made several remarks over the last few days about how good cheese would taste. Then I bought a sack of grain to feed her chickens. It would do us all well if we could keep the hens laying.

I was about to head for home when I remembered to pick up the mail. There rarely was anything of importance, but I checked it out anyway. Later I wished I hadn't even gone to the post office.

Mr. Hiram Smith was ahead of me at the wicket. "Howdy, Josh," he hailed me and I returned his greeting.

"Another rough summer," he commented sociably and I agreed that it was.

"Hear more farmers are having a hard time."

I nodded to that too.

"Did you have any crop at all?" he asked.

"Not much," I admitted. "I turned the cows on it. Wasn't worth the time of trying to harvest it."

It was his turn to nod. "Too bad," he pondered. "Sure too bad. Farms're up for sale all over the place." He didn't even wait for a response from me. "Trouble is," he went on, "no buyers. Why, ya can't even give one away. Nobody's got money to buy. That's how it is. Too bad."

It was all the truth—but it was all old news by now. I was about to ask for my mail and move on.

"Ya hear 'bout Avery?" asked Mr. Smith.

I hadn't, and I stopped mid-stride. I wasn't sure I wanted to hear about Avery if it was going to be bad news—and from Mr. Smith's expression, it looked as if it would be. But Avery was my brother-in-law. If there was something wrong, I had to know.

"Lost his farm," said Mr. Smith, rather callously to my thinking. "Just gettin' started, too. An' him newly married an' all. Too bad." He shook his head one more time and moved toward the door, shuffling through advertising flyers as he did so.

I went all sick inside.

It was Mary that I thought of first. I knew how deeply the news would trouble her. *Poor Mary. And poor Lilli—and her expecting their first child, too,* I mourned.

Now the postmaster took up the tale of woe. "Sure too bad. Sure too bad," he repeated as he shook his head much as Mr. Smith had done. "Me, I can't even keep up with the comin' an' goin' anymore. Move in—move out. Jest like that. One after the other—"

"Where—where did Avery—?"

"Oh, he didn't move. Least not away from the area. He jest moved on home again with his folks. Same mailbox as always." The most important thing to the postmaster seemed to be keeping his mailboxes straight. I started to move away.

"Don'tcha want your mail?" he called after me, and I turned back. There was one letter addressed to Mrs. Joshua Jones and a few advertising pieces. I threw the flyers in the wastebasket as I walked past it, and stuck the letter for Mary in my pocket.

I couldn't get Avery and Lilli out of my mind as I headed the team for home. Most of all I dreaded telling the news to Mary. But I knew she had to be told.

I broke it to her as gently as I could and held her while she wept. Then we bundled up, left William in Grandpa and Uncle Charlie's care, and drove over to Avery's folks.

Just as I had been told in town, we heard directly from Avery that he had lost his farm. He was pretty down about it, but Lilli was keeping her chin up.

"We'll try again—later," she said confidently, "when the crops are growing again and the rains are back."

In the meantime she was sharing a house with five other people and her child would soon be number six.

"How are you?" Mary whispered to her.

"Fine. Fine," she insisted. "Just anxious to get it all over with. Only three more weeks now. That's not so long."

But the house was already crowded. Avery and Lilli had a very small bedroom off the kitchen. I couldn't help but wonder where they would squeeze in a small crib.

Times were tough. Really tough. But at least they had a roof over their heads.

In all the turmoil I had forgotten to give Mary her letter. I found it that night as I undressed for bed.

"Oh, I'm sorry," I apologized. "I forgot to give you this. I picked it up at the post office today."

I didn't add that I was more than a mite curious about the letter.

Mary tore the envelope open quickly and withdrew one formal looking page. She scanned it, then went back to read it more slowly. She looked pleased with the contents. I was relieved. I was afraid it might be more bad news.

"It's from the school-board chairman," she told me. "I wrote inquiring about boarding the teacher."

I was surprised. Mary had said nothing about it.

"He's happy to have him stay here," Mary continued. "The place where he's been boarding hasn't worked out well."

I knew that the present schoolteacher was a middle-aged, single man. He had been the butt of many community jokes, a rather strange, eccentric fellow.

I looked at Mary again.

"Are you sure you want to take him on?" I asked her.

"Can't you see?" said Mary. "This is a direct answer to my prayers. I asked God what I might do to ease our situation, and He brought this to my mind. So I wrote the letter and left it with God—and He has worked it out so that Mr. Butler is willing to stay here."

"But—" I began, but Mary wasn't finished.

"The money will help buy groceries for all of us, and I might even be able to help with the loan payment."

"But the work," I protested. "You have more than enough now, and with the new baby—"

Mary waved that argument aside too. "Grandpa helps in the kitchen and Uncle Charlie keeps William entertained. Mr. Butler will be gone most of the day and will be leavin' every weekend. Won't be much extra work at all."

She had it all figured. I couldn't help but chuckle.

"You're really somethin'," I said to Mary, gathering her into my arms. She just smiled and let the letter flutter to the floor.

Much to my dismay, Mr. Butler arrived with a spirited horse and a buggy. There had been no warning that I would be expected to stable a horse and provide feed. I couldn't even feed my own horses properly.

But even before I could raise the question Mr. Butler explained, "I've arranged for Lady Jane to be housed"—"housed," he said—"at the school barn. Todd Smith will be her groom."

I nodded, relieved. A *"groom," no less.*

"I needed the buggy to bring my things," he went on.

His "things" consisted of several trunks and suitcases and

a couple of carpet bags. I wondered how he would fit it all in the small bedroom off the kitchen and still leave himself walking room. I never did find out, for I never entered the room after Mr. Butler took possession, and he always kept his door tightly closed.

Even Mary didn't go in that room. Mr. Butler preferred to do his own "keeping." Once a week Mary laid out fresh linens and towels and Mr. Butler replaced them with the soiled ones. It was a good arrangement for Mary.

He was a strange-looking little man, all right. A large nose dominated his small face, and his chin was almost non-existent. Eyes, dark and piercing, hid behind thick, heavy-rimmed glasses. He was bald. At least I'm pretty sure he was, but he had this trick of combing his hair from deep down on the side and bringing it across the top to join the other side so you didn't really see the baldness. When he stepped out into the wind, he was very careful to pull his hat down securely until it almost included his ears. I couldn't help but wonder if he had nightmares about it suddenly blowing off, his hair flying straight up in the air, waving to all those who watched as his bald spot was exposed to the world.

He didn't have much to say to us grown-ups, but he took to William right away. With his love for children, I guess he made a good school teacher. Anyway, the time he spent in the kitchen with the rest of the family was whiled away with William and picture books. He would pull a chair near the warmth of the kitchen stove, lift William on his knee and spread out a book before them. They spent hours together, his quiet voice explaining to William the wonders of the Wall of China, the mysteries of the planet Mars, the secrets of the ancient Egyptians or the flight patterns of tiny humming-birds. I'd look across at Mary and suppress a chuckle, or at Grandpa or Uncle Charlie with a wink. William might be a sharp little fella, but what could a child of two possibly understand of all that?

Still, William went right back for more—every time he had the opportunity. And he sat there on that teacher's knee and drank in every word, his eyes wide with wonder, his chubby finger pointing at the pictures, his baby voice trying to repeat some of the difficult words.

When Mary would announce that it was William's bedtime, the teacher always looked rather disappointed, but he lifted William carefully down, closed his book and retired to his room.

We made it through another winter and I began to scan the skies looking for rain clouds. Though clouds did form from time to time, they just didn't seem to have much moisture in them. But I scraped together enough money to buy a bit of seed grain and planted a couple of my fields.

The birth of William had interrupted the harvest. Now the arrival of our second child brought me in from the planting to ride off for Doc.

Everything went fine, and before I could scarcely draw a breath, our second son joined the family. As soon as I had breathed a prayer of thankfulness that Mary and the baby were both fine, the reality of another doctor's bill took some of the pleasure from the occasion.

"I'll just add it to your account, Josh," Doc said quietly as I went with him later to get his buggy. We were getting ourselves quite a sizable account with Doc.

Our new boy was another beautiful baby. Plump and healthy with lusty lungs. William studied him in awe. Not until the new baby finally closed his eyes and his loud little mouth and went to sleep could we get William close enough to actually reach out a hand and touch him on the cheek. From then on he seemed quite pleased with his baby brother.

We named him Daniel Charles after Grandpa and Uncle Charlie, and the two men beamed as we announced the name.

We found a neighbor girl to take over the kitchen duties until Mary was able to be up and about, and somehow we managed. Baby Daniel settled into the family unit just fine, and I finished my bit of planting and went back to the woodlot again.

More of my fields drifted away as spring gave way to summer. I could only hope that some of the soil from many miles away might stop at my land. If the wind didn't work out some kind of exchange, I feared there would soon be no more topsoil to farm.

Poor Mary struggled with her garden. It was hard, discouraging work. Not much grew and the grasshoppers relished the bit that was there.

School ended and the teacher moved out. Mr. Butler promised before he left that he would be back again in the fall, a relief to all of us. We had learned to rely on that little bit of income.

William missed him. He kept asking for "Mr. Buttle and 'is books." Mary tried to explain, but of course the time frame of "months" is difficult for a child to understand.

One midsummer afternoon I went for a long walk across my dreary-looking fields. The stalks were stunted and scarce. I plucked a head of grain here and there, chaffing it between my hands. There was nothing much there. I could feel the burden on my shoulders heavier with each step. There was nothing to harvest—again.

I crouched down in the field and dug at the ground with a stick, flipping back dry, dusty soil. Down, down I dug looking for moisture that was not there. Nothing. Why hadn't the rains come? What had happened to our world? *Seed time and harvest. Seed time and harvest* kept running through my head. God had promised it. Had He failed to deliver on His promise?

For a moment I was swept with anger. I was tempted to shake my fist at the heavens. What had I done to deserve this? What had Mary done? We had tried to be faithful. We— But I stopped myself. I knew it had nothing to do with that. Then the many years of trusting, of leaning on my Lord drained the anger from me.

"I need you, God," I whispered. "More than ever, I need you."

It was with heavy steps that I returned to the farmyard. I couldn't shake from me the feeling of impending doom. I had fought for about as long as I could fight. I didn't have much strength left.

After supper was over and the dishes returned to the cupboard, everyone settled in around the kitchen as usual. I tried to busy myself with figures and plans, but my mind wouldn't concentrate. I finally laid it all aside and climbed the stairs to the room where my two sons slept.

What a picture they made. William clutched the teddy bear that Sarah had made for his Christmas gift the year before. His dark lashes fell across unblemished cheeks and the thick brown hair lay damp across his forehead.

Baby Daniel slept in almost the same pose as his older brother—arms atop his blankets, his head held slightly to the side. But there was no teddy bear. Danny clutched only the hem of the blanket Mary had made. Now and then he pursed his little lips and took a few sucks as though he was dreaming of nursing.

I stood there looking at them both and the insides of me went cold and empty. *They're countin' on me. They're countin' on their pa and I'm goin' to let them down. Both of them. Both of them—and Mary. And Grandpa and Uncle Charlie . . .*

I'd never experienced such pain. Deep, dark, knifing pain that brought no tears of relief.

I turned from my two sons and pulled the curtain back from the window so I could look out over the land I had loved and worked for so many years. There was no escaping it. We were facing the end.

I didn't even know Mary was there until she slipped her arms about my waist and laid her head against my upper back. A shudder went all through me.

She stood there for several minutes, just holding me, and then she spoke. Her voice was strong and even, though her words came to me in a soft whisper. "What is it, Josh? What's the matter?"

I had to get it out. Had to put it into words.

"We're gonna lose the farm," I said frankly, a cold harshness to my words.

Mary said nothing but I felt her arms tighten around me.

William stirred in his sleep and his hand pulled the teddy more closely against him.

"It's the payments, isn't it? If you hadn't bought Pa's farm—"

Of course it was the payments. I stirred from one foot to the other in my impatience.

"I just made the wrong move—the wrong decision. I thought it was right—at the time—"

"No, Josh," Mary hastened to interrupt, "it wasn't wrong. Not the decision to buy. It was a wise thing to do. The *timin'* was just wrong, that's all. And no one—no one could have foreseen the future. Could have known how things would go. No rain—"

Grandpa had said the same thing, and in my head I knew they were right. But my heart? I had prayed. Had asked God about the purchase.

"Sell it, Josh," continued Mary. "Sell it."

"Can't sell it," I said, my voice now baring the impatience that my shifting feet had shown. "There's no one to buy."

"Then let it go. Just let it go. I know you sorta bought it for me—and our sons. But we'd be better—There will be other farms over the years. Maybe even Pa's again. We can buy later for the boys."

"I—I can't let it go," I protested hoarsely.

"Did you promise Pa? He'd understand, Josh. He'd not hold you to it."

"No, I didn't promise your pa. He didn't ask for a promise."

"Then let it go. Let the bank have it."

I turned then and took Mary by the shoulders, looking deeply into her eyes. There was no light on in the room, but the moon spilled through the window making her face light with a silvery glow. I could even see the faint scar across her forehead.

"You don't understand," I stated, with a great effort to keep my voice even. "If they take your pa's farm, they take this one too."

I felt Mary's body tremble.

"I signed them this, Mary. I signed it over to the bank when I took the loan. If I don't pay—"

But I'd said enough. Mary understood. She pressed herself into my arms and began to weep softly.

Maybe her crying helped us both. At least it brought some tenderness, some compassion back into the coldness of my heart. I stood holding her, caressing her, letting her cry.

It didn't last long and then Mary straightened her shoulders and lifted her chin.

"We've come too far to give up now," she said. "There *has* to be a way." I shrugged helplessly. Mary wiped her nose and went right on. "We still have stock to sell. The teacher will be back. I don't need all of his money for groceries. You can take out more cord wood, we'll—"

"Mary, we—"

"We'll make it," she repeated. "God has seen us through this far—He won't let us down now."

For a moment I found myself wondering just what God had done on our behalf. The rains still had not come. We hadn't had a crop in three years. But Mary soon reminded me.

"Folks all about have been losing their farms, but we still have ours. We been meetin' those payments year by year— somehow. We are all still here, all healthy. We've always had food on the table an' shoes on our feet. He's seen us through all of this, an' He'll keep right on providin'.'"

I felt a wave of shame rush through me. God had been doing far more for my family than I'd been thanking Him for.

"We'll make that next payment," said Mary again, her

chin set firmly. She looked around the room. At me. At our two sons as they slept. "There's too much ridin' on it not to make it," she murmured in a half whisper; then I heard her simple, fervent prayer, "Help us, Lord, please help us."

We did make the payment. It was always a miracle to me. But we had to drain ourselves down to practically nothing to do it. We sold off almost all my good stock. I would have gladly sold the tractor and the Ford, but there were no buyers. What hurt the deepest was watching Chester go. We kept only the work horses because we simply could not get along without them. Chester brought a good price, even with the economy like it was. I could do nothing else but sell him. Mary cried and I think I died a bit when the man came and led him away.

With all of that, I was still short for the bank payment. And then a letter came in the mail from Pa Turley. When Mary opened it, money fell to the kitchen table.

"This ain't much," he wrote, "but I hope that it helps in some way."

"Did you—?"

"No," Mary shook her head. "Really. I didn't say—"

The letter went on.

"Hear what a tough time everyone is having so I thought I'd send each of my girls a bit."

Mary laughed and cried at the same time. We added the bills to our little pile. It just met the bank payment.

Chapter 24

Striving to Make It

There was nothing more we owned that we could sell as far as I could see. We'd already spent all of Grandpa and Uncle Charlie's meager savings. The woodlot on the Turleys' farm was quickly being depleted. With so few vegetables and fruits canned or stored in the cellar, Mary's task of putting food before her family was very difficult and certainly would take a much larger portion of the teacher's board money. In fact, I didn't think she'd be able to make it stretch to do even that.

We had our backs against the wall, that was for sure. I began to make some inquiries in town about some kind of employment. As I feared, I could find nothing.

Then our whole community was shaken with a tragedy. We nearly lost Doc. Guess there wouldn't have been anyone in the whole neighborhood whose loss would have affected us more—unless it would have been my uncle Nat. Both men had been leaned on a lot during our hard times and looked up to a good deal during the better times we had experienced.

It was a heart attack. Doc was rushed off by motor car to the small hospital in Riverside. Mrs. Doc went right along with him and stayed by his bed to wait out the illness.

Doc had likely delivered everybody in the area, thirty-five and under. He'd sewed up cuts, taken out appendixes, nursed us through mumps and all sort of things. We'd miss him being there for us. Fact was, we didn't know how we'd ever get along without him. We all prayed daily that his life would be spared, even if his full health was not restored.

In the days following the heart attack, I kept thinking on the account I had with him. I owed Doc a considerable amount of money, and I had no way in the world to pay it. I was fearful that Mrs. Doc—we always called her that for some reason—I was afraid that she might be needing the money with the hospital bills and all, and I knew that the right thing to do was go and see her about it as soon as I had the chance, even if I didn't have the money. I could at least promise small payments just as soon as I could scrape something together.

In a few weeks' time news came that Mrs. Doc was back at the house in town, Doc having improved a good deal. I decided I'd best get on in and see her.

It was tough—but I made the call. Mrs. Doc looked a bit surprised to see me; then she welcomed me in like a long-lost son. I guess she felt that way about all the "babies" Doc had brought into the world.

After a bit of chitchat about Doc and how he was doing, I got right to the point.

"I came about my account," I said.

She seemed a bit bewildered.

"I was afraid that you might be needin' payment with Doc in the hospital an' all," I explained further.

She shook her head emphatically. "Oh, Doc would never leave me in need," she stated. "He made sure that he had everything cared for in case anything should happen. He's a good man, Doc is," and the tears started to form in her eyes.

Relieved to hear that they were not in dire straits, I told her, "I'll look after the account as soon as I'm able. Things are a bit tight right now, but I hope to get a job and then I can send some money month by month."

"There's nothing to pay, Josh," she told me softly.

"But there must be. I owe him a fair bit of money—Uncle

Charlie, our baby. Just haven't been able to look after it yet."

Mrs. Doc went to a corner desk and withdrew a rather large ledger. "Come here," she said, and I went as bidden.

She leafed through the account book and I saw the names of our neighbors and friends listed there. They seemed to have fared better financially than the Joneses—I didn't spot a one of them who was owing Doc money. And then Mrs. Doc flipped another page and there was my name—Joshua Jones. Each entry was carefully made. Each sick call to our house and each of the deliveries, and the cost was clearly and carefully recorded in the column to the right. But it was the bottom of the page that made me gasp. There written beside the total was the distinct notation: "Paid in full."

"I—I don't understand," I stammered. "I didn't have money. Who—who—"

"Doc did," she said simply, the tears filling her eyes again. "The night of his attack. He must have known that something was wrong. He got up in the night. I found him here at his desk. Cancelled out every account in the ledger—every debt—Doc did."

"But—but—"

She closed the book softly and slipped it back into the desk drawer.

"He loves his people, Josh. His community. He never wanted to take—just to give. He likely would never have taken payment if he hadn't been looking out for me. I'm cared for now, and he doesn't need any more."

I couldn't speak. All I could do was embrace the elderly woman. Then I returned to the brisk, cool air of the autumn day. I had much to think about as I trudged the street, still inquiring about work.

I heard about a government work project that was hiring. Mary hated the thought of it, for it would take me miles away from home and the family. We talked about it until way into the night and finally decided that it was the only thing we could do. With most of the stock gone, there wasn't much choring; and with no feed to speak of, the few remaining farm animals mostly had to forage for themselves anyway. Even Mary's chickens had been turned loose to fend for themselves. There still was a cow to milk, but Grandpa insisted that he could manage that.

With great reluctance I packed a few things in a carpet bag and prepared to take my leave. I wouldn't be needed at home for the next spring's planting. There was no seed grain in the bins—nor any hope of getting the money to buy any. I would just simply work out until our world had returned to normal again. And who knew just when that might be?

It was heart-wrenching to have me leave. Mary wept as she stuffed worn and oft-mended socks into a corner of the bag.

"They'll never get you through another winter," she sniffed. "They're nothin' but patches now."

"Where ya goin', Papa?" William asked, but the lump in my throat was too big for me to be able to answer him. I pulled the young boy into my arms and buried my face against his hair. He thought it was some kind of a game and started messing up my hair and tugging on my ears, squealing with glee. I wondered just how long it would be before I heard the boyish voice again. The thought made my chest constrict and brought tears to my eyes.

I continued to wrestle with William until I had myself under control. It was hard enough for Mary. I was supposed to be her strength.

We did the rounds with hugs. I guess it was the hardest moment of my life. William cried when he couldn't go with me. As I looked at little Daniel sleeping peacefully in his cradle, I tried to picture how big he'd be by the time I returned. I would miss so much of his growing up.

"Don't forget to write," reminded Mary for the third or fourth time. "I've packed the paper and envelopes in the side pocket there."

I nodded. I'd write. That would be all I'd have of home.

"Don't worry about things here," repeated Grandpa. "We'll manage just fine."

Oh, God, I groaned inwardly, *why does it have to be this way?*

Mary stepped out onto the cold back veranda for one final goodbye. She clutched her sweater tightly around her and turned to me with tears streaming down her cheeks.

"Don't worry, Josh," she whispered encouragingly in spite of the tears. "We'll manage—somehow."

I held her for a long time, trying to shield her from the cold, from the pain of parting and the heavy task of assuming all the responsibilities that I should be there to shoulder. *Why? Why?* I kept wondering, but the wind that whipped across the yard and tore at the weather-worn shutters had no answer.

"You'd best get in. You're freezing," I said to Mary, and I kissed her one last time and stumbled my way down the steps to the wagon. Grandpa was waiting to drive me to town to catch the local train.

I'd never realized how far it was to town before—nor how quickly our farm faded from view as we topped hill after hill.

The work camp was filled with men like myself. Desperate men—trying hard to make it through another winter in the only way that seemed open to them. Decent men—forwarding every penny they could spare back home to wives and family.

We talked about home in the evenings, after the work of another chilling, grueling day that numbed our bodies and tortured our muscles. We lay on our hard bunks and told one another stories about our wives, our children. It was the only pleasure we had. Except for the times when we allowed ourselves to use one more of our carefully rationed pages—one more envelope—one more stamp—so we could write a letter home. We lingered over those letters, savoring every word, pouring our love and longing into each sentence.

No one ever bothered a man who was writing. A hush fell

over the bunkhouse and each man took to his bunk in respect for the one who held the hallowed position at the single, crude desk. Writing home was a sacred rite. It was as close to the family as we could get.

Mail day was even more special. We each hoarded every speck of privacy as we pored over our letter. And then we did a strange thing—we went over and over every tiny item of news it held with everyone in the bunkhouse.

The work was difficult. I'd considered myself used to hard work, but this new thing—this swinging of a pick into hard-as-granite soil as we chopped to make way for a new canal across the arid, frozen prairie—was something quite new for me.

Many gave up and went home. Their backs simply could not endure the strain. It was never a problem for the job foreman when men quit. He had a long waiting list of men who yearned for a chance to put their bodies to the test and earn precious money for their families.

We had four days off for Christmas. Most of us walked the fifteen miles to town that night after putting in a full day's shift. We wanted to catch the train in the morning.

When the train pulled in to my familiar station, I stopped in town just long enough to buy a small trinket for each family member before I hoisted my bag and hurried home.

You should have heard the commotion. They hadn't known I was coming. We hugged and cried and hugged some more and everyone tried to talk at once, knowing full well that the time would pass too quickly for us to get everything said.

I couldn't believe how the boys had grown. I kept saying it to Mary over and over and she'd just smile.

We had a simple Christmas together with Lou's family. In spite of bare cupboard shelves, Lou and Mary managed to put together a tasty meal. The children didn't seem to miss the turkey and trimmings. They had fun just being together. That night Mary stayed up into the wee hours of the morning trying to darn my socks again. She patched my overalls and sewed buttons back on my coat, but there didn't seem to be much she could do about my worn-out mittens. The pick had been awfully hard on them.

"Josh," she said, "there's just no way to fix them."

I nodded. "They're fine," I assured her.

But the following morning when I joined the family at the breakfast table there was a new pair of mittens. She must have stayed up again most of the night in order to knit them. They were the same color as her chore sweater, which I noticed was no longer hanging on the peg by the door where she always kept it. I tried to swallow away the lump that grew large in my throat.

I left again right after breakfast. It was no easier than the first time. I had no idea when I'd be home again.

I guess it was my Bible and the time I was able to spend reading it and praying that got me through that long winter. Several other men in the bunkhouse turned to worn Bibles too. We talked about the things we were learning. It helped us to sorta put other things into proper perspective.

I told them about Willie one night. About how much he had loved God and how much I had loved him and how we had named our first son after him and all. They listened quietly.

"It's funny," I admitted. "He always went by 'Willie' even though his name was William. We named our boy in honor of him, and I think of Willie most every time I look at my son—and yet—yet—I've never been able to call him Willie. Never. Don't know why. Guess it still just hurts too much."

Heads nodded. I'd never been able to share that with anyone before. I guess I figured they wouldn't understand. But these men—there was a strange friendship between those of us who shared the simple, crude bunkhouse. Maybe because we were all so vulnerable. Maybe we had nothing to hide. We all knew just where the other one was coming from. None of us had reason or cause to boast. We were sorta laid bare, so to speak, before one another. And we needed one another.

I told them about Camellia too. Though I didn't bother to try to explain what Camellia had meant to me at one time. I just told them about Camellia and Willie and how she had gone out to Africa even after Willie had died there.

They were rightly impressed with Camellia.

And then I told them about the letter I'd had to write to the Mission Society, how it had been one of the hardest things I'd ever done in my life. How I'd told the Mission Society I just didn't have the money to support Camellia for the present and that just as soon as the rains came and I had another crop, I'd take up the support again.

A nice letter came back from them saying they understood and had managed to piece together Camellia's support from some other sources; but that hadn't taken the sting out of it for me.

"It's sure tough right now," mused a fella, Eb Penner. "Not just fer us, but fer the churches. I hear as how some missionaries have even been brought home. Jest no money."

"Hard fer the preachers, too," continued Paul Will. "Our parson hardly gits enough to git 'em by—an' he has 'im a family of seven. Grabs any job he can to make a dollar or two, an' so do his younguns—but ain't no work fer anybody."

"I stopped goin' to church," came from the corner bunk where Tom reclined, rubbing his hands as though he could work off some callouses. " 'Tweren't no comfort there, far as I could tell. Ever' Sunday, there was just more bad news of someone losin' their place or bein' outta food or some such. We was all asked to pray. I got tired of prayin'. Nothin' ever come of it anyway. Seemed I should be doin' more fer those in need than jest sayin' a prayer or two—an' I had nothin'— nothin' left to give."

No one in the room expressed shock. We'd all fought the same thoughts, the same feelings at one time or another.

"I kept on goin' anyway," admitted Eb. "I mighta felt a little helpless in the midst of my sufferin' brethren—but I'd a been downright lost without 'em."

"You see the collection plate?" Paul said. "Pittance. I don't know how any preacher's family can git by. Sure, a chicken here, a jug a milk there, but still I can't figure it. Tithe of nothin' is still nothin'."

The man was right of course. We'd always given our tithe. Even Mary's egg money was carefully counted and a tenth laid aside. But even at that we only dropped a few cents in on Sunday, and ofttimes there was nothing at all. We wondered, too, how Nat and Lou ever managed, but they made no complaints. God provided, Lou always said with a smile, but their clothes were threadbare and their table scantily served. It had been hard, all right, on those serving the churches.

"Well, one of these days it'll all get turned around again," said someone on a brighter note, and the conversation went in another direction. We all had great plans about what we'd do just as soon as the dry spell was over. For many it meant starting from the bottom again. They had already lost all they had. Businesses, farms, belongings. But still, to a man, we clung to that seemingly illusionary promise of the future.

I wrapped old rags around my hands to try to keep Mary's new mittens from developing holes. I wasn't worried about my bare hands on the cold pick handle. It was just that I couldn't stand the thought of ruining her gift to me—the mittens her love had kept her up all night to provide for me. The rags worked after a fashion, and then the weather finally began to warm up, and I tucked the mittens away and went barehanded. The frost left the ground, making the pick work a bit easier.

Being a farmer at heart, the melting of the ice and the warmth coming up from the soil sent my blood to racing. It was hard for me to keep my eyes off the skies. If only—if only the rains would come.

But even if they do, I reminded myself, *I'll still need to stay with my pick and shovel.* I had not been able to save even a few pennies. I sent all that I made back to Mary and the family so they could get by.

Chapter 25

Another Spring, Another Promise

That night I wrote another letter to Mary. I seemed to get more and more lonesome with each passing day. Would the ache in my heart never ease? I had thought that it would get easier with time. It hadn't. Not at all.

After I'd written my letter, I lay on my bunk for a long time just thinking. Then I took my Bible and began to leaf through it, looking for some kind of comfort in its pages. I read a number of Mary's Psalms and they helped, but I was still aching with the intensity of my loneliness.

I need my family, I kept saying over and over to myself. *I need Mary.*

But I was caught in a box. If I went home to Mary I would surely lose the farm. Even if I wasn't able to save anything for the bank loan, my being here away from my family would sow "good faith," I reasoned. Yet I wondered how much longer I could hold on here. If only—if only God would provide some way for me to make those payments—to hold the land. If only—if only the rains would come so the land could produce again.

I started praying. "God," I admitted, "I'm at the end of myself. There's nothin' that Josh Jones can do to provide for a future—any future for Mary, for my sons. I can hardly provide for the present. I don't know which way to turn, Lord.

I just don't know how we can go on like this. I need them. They need me. But to lose the farm. What would we do then? Where would we go? We have nothin', Lord. Nothin'."

The Bible slipped from my fingers and rested on the bunk beside me. I picked it up and held it to my chest for a moment, thinking and praying silently, then I shifted it back to read again. My eyes fell to the page that had opened before me. At some time in my growing years I must have read the passage, for it was underlined as though it had impressed me. I read it again now.

> Although the fig tree shall not blossom,
> neither shall fruit be in the vine;
> the labour of the olive shall fail,
> and the fields shall yield no meat;
> the flock shall be cut off from the fold,
> and there shall be no herd in the stalls.
> Yet I will rejoice in the Lord,
> I will joy in the God of my salvation.
> The Lord God is my strength.

I reread the passage again and again until the tears that filled my eyes prevented me from reading it further.

It was all coming clear to me. The welfare of my family didn't depend on my strength. If so, they would be utterly destitute. I had been totally inadequate. But even more astounding, it didn't depend upon my fields either, or the herds that I had so carefully built. It was God all the time—just like Mary had tried to tell me. It was God who had cared for my family—had met their needs. We didn't need anyone or anything else.

" 'I will rejoice in the Lord—the Lord God is my strength,' " I kept repeating over and over. Oh, what a freedom! I could finally let go. I could shift my heavy load onto another's shoulders. Somehow—somehow God would work it out. Somehow He would see us through. Maybe we *wouldn't* keep the farm—but if not—well, He'd help us to manage without it. Somehow!

By now soft snoring reached to me from the other bunks and I knew the men around me were getting much-needed rest. Yet I continued to inwardly pray and praise until late into the night. When I rose the next morning, it was with new strength.

When I picked up my pick and shovel and fell into line, the task had not changed—but my attitude had. God was in charge now—I would simply wait for Him. But for now—for now I was on the payroll of the government. They expected a full day's work. All through the morning the sound of rhythmic blows sounded on the gravelly banks around me. The work continued on the irrigation canal gradually worming its way across the barren and desolate prairie land. By this time in the season, the sun had climbed higher in the sky and beat on our backs with intensity, making us sweat heavily with each swing of the pick or scoop of the shovel. Men complained of the heat as ferociously as they had complained about the cold.

"Wish it would rain," grumbled a voice to my right. "Sure would be a relief from this dust." I wasn't the only one who often lifted his eyes to the sky, but still no clouds formed.

I lifted my pick again to let it strike the ground with a dull thud. My back ached, my shoulders ached, my arms ached. I was about to swing again when a voice stopped me. Someone was calling my name.

"Jones," I heard again. "You're wanted."

I hoisted my pick and shovel and followed the beckoning hand. One never dared leave tools behind. You were useless on the job without them, and there simply was no money to replace them should they disappear.

"The phone!" shouted the messenger. "Over in the foreman's shack."

I flipped my pick and shovel over my shoulder and started at a jog for the building, my insides churning. Who would be phoning me and what possible message could they have?

With a trembling hand I picked up the receiver. There was a crackling in my ear.

"Hello!" I hollered into the mouthpiece.

"He—lo," came back a broken response. It was Grandpa. My whole body froze. Something must be terribly wrong. He wouldn't squander money on a telephone call unless it was extremely important.

"That you, Boy?"

"It's—it's me. Josh," I managed.

"Hang on!" yelled Grandpa.

I was about mad with anxiety. Why would he call me and then say "hang on"? Then another voice came on the line.

"Josh?" It was Mary. I felt great relief. At least Mary was all right.

"Josh?" she said again.

"Mary! Mary, what's—"

"It's raining, Josh." Silence. "It's raining."

I looked out at the clear, hot afternoon sky. There wasn't a cloud in sight. No—wait! Way to the northwest I could see clouds against the distant horizon.

"It settled in right over us. It's been raining for three days now. I waited to call until I was sure it wasn't just a shower. I—" But then Mary began to weep.

There was a bit of a pause and next thing Grandpa was on the line again. "Rainin', Boy," he informed me. "Third day. Just comin' down like ya haven't seed in years." He chuckled. "Clouds still hangin' over us. We near got drowned comin' into town."

"Sun's still shining here," I managed to reply. I was trembling now, still hardly able to believe the report.

"Maybe it'll move yer way after it's finished with us," Grandpa chortled.

Then he spoke words that I will never forget. "Come home, Boy," he said.

"Come home?"

I heard him swallow. "We already got some crop in."

"Crop?"

"Yep."

"Who?"

"Mary an' me. Some of it's showin' already. This rain will really bring it."

"How'd you—? Where'd you get the seed?" I floundered.

"Bought it."

"Bought it *how*? Where'd you get the money?" I asked, unable to grasp what Grandpa was saying.

"Mary gathered it—somehow—she's been savin' pennies. Little bit each month from what you've sent. I don't know how she did it, but she managed to git herself quite a little pile."

"But surely that wasn't enough to—" I could imagine the small bit of seed those few dollars would buy.

"Well," confessed Grandpa, "she—she also sold the silver tea service."

"What? Where?"

"Some lady—out-of-towner. Seemed to want it real bad. Took a mighty fancy to it. Paid a good price, Mary said."

I was too stunned to speak. I knew how much that tea set had meant to Mary. For a moment I just stood there, thoughts whirling round and round as I tried to take in everything Grandpa was telling me. The silver tea set—gone. Mary saving, planting. A crop already in the ground and growing. It was all too much—too much for me.

The realization of the cost of the call finally got me talking again. "Is she still there? Mary?" I asked.

"Yep," and I heard Grandpa hand her the phone.

"Mary?"

"Yes." Her voice was no more than a whisper.

"Mary, I'm coming home."

There was only a little sob, caught somewhere in Mary's throat.

"I'm leavin'—I'm leavin' right now."

"Oh, Josh," sobbed Mary.

"Mary—I love you."

I hung up the receiver then and turned to the foreman at

the desk. "I'm leavin'," I informed him. "I'm going to pack up my gear and will be right back to pick up my pay. Someone else can have my spot on the crew."

He nodded. It was done 'most every week. An exchange made.

I ran all the way to the bunkhouse. I was going home! *I'm goin' home!* I exulted. *Back to my wife—my Mary. Back to my family. Back to my farm.* We hadn't lost it. The rains had come. Sure, things were tough. Sure, we had a ways to go in order to rebuild, but we still had our home—our land. We were going to have another chance. God was giving us another chance for seedtime—and harvest!

Epilogue

Though the years following the drought were difficult for the Jones family, Josh eventually became known as the best and most prosperous farmer in the area. But with the increase in crop production and the rebuilding of his herds, Josh never did flaunt or waste his wealth. Besides Camellia in Africa, he eventually shared in the support of nine other missionaries.

To the family were born six children. William and Daniel were joined by Andrew, Violet, Irene and Walter. Andrew was the one to farm the Turley home place. And like his father and mother before him, he too became actively supportive of missionaries, among whom were three members of his own family. William went to Sierra Leone, Violet to Japan, while Daniel pastored a small mission church among the Canadian Indians. Irene married Phillip Moresby, the son of the doctor who came to take Doc's place. Phillip too trained as a physician and joined his father in the family practice. Walter, Josh and Mary's youngest, eventually was lost in the Korean war.

All five of the remaining Jones children married. To Josh and Mary were born twenty-three grandchildren, and they saw the arrival of seventeen great-grandchildren to bless their old age.

Grandpa lived to be ninety-six, but Uncle Charlie left behind his arthritis-ridden body at the age of seventy-four.

The family has scattered now. With the passing of time and the mobility of our age, they no longer cluster about the home farm. Where do they live? Well—here and there. Perhaps—just perhaps—you share your neighborhood with some of them.

CHRISTIAN HERALD
People Making a Difference

Christian Herald is a family of dedicated, Christ-centered ministries that reaches out to deprived children in need, and to homeless men who are lost in alcoholism and drug addiction. Christian Herald also offers the finest in family and evangelical literature through its book club and publishes a popular, dynamic magazine for today's Christians.

Our Ministries

Christian Herald Children. The door of God's grace opens wide to give impoverished youngsters a breath of fresh air, away from the evils of the streets. Every summer, hundreds of youngsters are welcomed at the Christian Herald Mont Lawn Camp located in the Poconos at Bushkill, Pennsylvania. Year-round assistance is also provided, including teen programs, tutoring in reading and writing, family counseling, career guidance and college scholarship programs.

The Bowery Mission. Located in New York City, the Bowery Mission offers hope and Gospel strength to the downtrodden and homeless. Here, the men of Skid Row are fed, clothed, ministered to. Many voluntarily enter a 6-month discipleship program of spiritual guidance, nutrition therapy and Bible study.

Our Father's House. Our Father's House is a discipleship program located in a rural setting in Lancaster County, Pennsylvania, which enables addicts to take the last steps on the road to a useful Christian life.

Paradise Lake Retreat Center. During the spring, fall and winter months, our children's camp at Bushkill, Pennsylvania, becomes a lovely retreat for religious gatherings of up to 200. Excellent accommodations include an on-site chapel, heated cabins, large meeting areas, recreational facilities, and delicious country-style meals. Write to: Paradise Lake Retreat Center, Box 252, Bushkill, PA 18234, or call: (717) 588-6067.

Christian Herald Magazine is contemporary—a dynamic publication that addresses the vital concerns of today's Christian. Each issue contains a sharing of true personal stories written by people who have found in Christ the strength to make a difference in the world around them.

Family Bookshelf provides a wide selection of wholesome, inspirational reading and Christian literature written by best-selling authors. All books are recommended by an Advisory Board of distinguished writers and editors.

* * *

Christian Herald ministries, founded in 1878, are supported by the voluntary contributions of individuals and by legacies and bequests. Contributions are tax deductible. Checks should be made out to: Christian Herald Children, Bowery Mission, or Christian Herald Association.

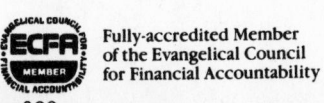 Fully-accredited Member of the Evangelical Council for Financial Accountability

Administrative Office:
40 Overlook Drive
Chappaqua, New York 10514
Telephone: (914) 769-9000